BLACK

BLACK

J. A. FAULKERSON

BLACK
The Bear on Our Backs

BOOK ONE

J. A. Faulkerson

BLACK
The Bear on Our Backs

BOOK ONE

by
J. A. Faulkerson

ISBN: 979-8-9910333-1-2
First Printing

Published by
J. A. Faulkerson Books
Culturally Coded Content
culturallycodedcontent@gmail.com
www.jafaulkerson.com

BLACK
Building a Legacy of Activism Community & Kinship

Dedication

Dedicated to our Black African and Black American ancestors,
who endured beatings, and personal tragedy and heartbreak,
so that we,
their Black contemporaries,
can take hold of the inalienable rights and privileges
enshrined in the United States' Constitution.

CHAPTER ONE

Jason Black cleared his throat as he delivered the closing remarks to his oral presentation. Judging from his white classmates disinterested facial expressions, he could tell they weren't feeling him. Many of them seemed to be visibly disgusted by what he was subjecting them to. But the same could not be said about the handful of black and brown classmates seated at desks near the middle of the room.

Jason had titled his term paper, and the PowerPoint slides being projected on the screen behind him, *The Politics of Race*. He had no doubt that the title alone made even the most progressive white person in the room uncomfortable. But after spending a little more than three years taking classes at the University of Tennessee, in the colleges of Business and Arts and Humanities, he felt obligated to turn up the heat in the final semester of his third year. Most of his peers would graduate that following semester, in the Spring, but he would be graduating early, in the Fall, in December. The year was 2015, the fifth week of the Fall semester.

Jason had come to UT on a full athletic scholarship. During his days in North Carolina, at Wake Forest High School, he made a name for himself by becoming one of the fastest 100-meter sprinters in the nation with a time of 10.18. A number of schools - the University of North Carolina, North Carolina State, the University of Florida and the University of Alabama, to name only a few - wanted him to bring his talents to their institutions, but Jason chose the University of Tennessee. While the UT football team had a tradition of producing great wide receivers who would go on to play professionally in the National Football League, it also had another longstanding tradition of producing great sprinters, the most prominent being Simon Gathers. Gathers was the gold medalist at the 1984 Olympic Games, winning with a time of 10.13 seconds.

The person who seemed to be the most interested in Jason's presentation was Dr. Benjamin Whitaker. The slight redness on Dr. Whitaker's pale face let Jason know that even he was taken aback by some of the things Jason was saying. But as a tenured Professor with the Department of Political Science, Dr. Whitaker had heard much worse rebukes of the white majority, especially from overly opinionated black students like Jason. While Jason didn't pride himself in knowing all things black history, he knew enough to know that white people had much more to do to right their wrongs against their black American siblings.

"Race has always been used as a wedge issue in elections," Jason said to Dr. Whitaker and his classmates from the front of the room. "Democrats have used it. Republicans have used it. Even Independents have used it. And with President Nelson Dupont, America's first, black president, completing his second term next year, I fear it's going to be used even more once Dupont has vacated the presidency, this time by Republicans.

"We already see this happening in the lead up to the 2016 presidential election. Malcolm Stillwell, the New York real estate mogul and wannabe politician, has demanded that President Dupont share his birth certificate with the American public. Stillwell is telling everyone who will listen that Dupont is not an American citizen because his father is a French national. Dupont countered Stillwell's argument by saying that he was born in Hawaii and spent his childhood in Hawaii with his white mother and later his white grandparents after his mother died. So, it should be apparently clear to you and me what's going on here. The Republican Party is painting President Dupont as an illegitimate leader just to sow doubt in the minds of the white electorate. These statements about President Dupont fall in line with efforts to make black men the face of American criminality."

Jason would go on to talk about how Stillwell's birtherism claim was nothing more than a test, a test to see if the white electorate would be more susceptible to manipulation by the Republican Party in the upcoming presidential election. It was. Therefore, Jason theorized that members of the Republican Party would go out of their way to appeal to the white electorates' fears and resentments about the effect of Dupont's Affordable Care Act and defense of Social Security. The Affordable Care Act, or DupontCare, expanded health care coverage to over thirty million more American citizens. Social Security guarantees payments to American citizens who paid into the system during their employment. Jason concluded his remarks by saying this position will also allow members of the Republican Party to denigrate Dupont Administration-era policies that call for recompense and reparations to black Americans.

"Questions?"

Madison Wilson, a blond haired, blue-eyed white girl seated on the front row, was the first to raise her hand. Jason acknowledged her with a head nod.

"I was talking with my parents the other night," Madison began, "and my father said Malcolm Stillwell is what this country needs, because he's not a career politician. He pointed out that some of these elected leaders, specifically Hillary Rosen Clifton, President Dupont's current VP, have been serving in public office for over twenty years or more. So, my question to you is how do you feel about term limits? Do you think they would help take race out of our politics?"

All eyes shifted from Madison back to Jason.

"I do, think they would help," he replied. "But not in the here, the now. White male patriarchy helped establish our nation, and this same white male patriarchy is going to do everything it can to ensure it retains its power, influence and control over the masses, prevent a woman from becoming president.

"Do I have a problem with Hillary Rosen Clifton serving in public office for, what, almost forty years? Of course, I do. But what has she accomplished in those forty years? Plenty, if you ask me. She worked closely with President Dupont to pass the Affordable Care Act, and she was instrumental in drawing more attention to the need for responsible federal gun control legislation. I didn't like when she referred to young, inner-city black males as super predators in the years leading up to her support of the 1994 Crime Bill. But if you recall, the very next year, she acknowledged her mistake and openly agreed with her most outspoken critics that the bill made it easier for police officers to target black and brown citizens. She even came forward in the months leading up to the 2008 presidential election to apologize to people that look like me. She also became one of the biggest advocates for workforce reforms around sexual harassment against women. So, in my mind, her actions have always been speaking louder than her words."

Jason searched the room for other raised hands. Seeing none, he returned to his seat to mixed applause from his classmates. This did not surprise him. The audience was mostly white. There were only five persons of color in the room, with all but three being foreign nationals, from countries like Spain and France. But Jason also knew that he and his three classmates of color would be voting in the 2016 Presidential Election. He would undoubtedly be voting for Hillary Rosen Clifton, but he could tell a majority of his white classmates would be voting for Stillwell, because, like Madison pointed out, he wasn't an establishment candidate. This truth saddened Jason because he knew a majority of the legislators in the Democratic Party governed to serve all of the people while their Republican Party counterparts a select few.

Madison was the next presenter, and it would have served Jason well to track what she was saying. But he had a difficult time focusing on her. This Political Science class, an elective titled *Political Philosophy*, was the last course he had to take in order to satisfy his graduation requirements. The course description piqued his interest, as it stated that registrants would conduct research that enables them to create philosophical solutions to real problems. What he had just presented was nothing more than the framework for his final paper. He elected to focus on race and racism, resulting from the role both played in disrupting his family's prosperity. It is what claimed his father's life when he was six years old. With Jerome Black not being around to nurture his older brother Jeremiah and him, Jason's mother Cynthia struggled to make ends meet as an English teacher at Wake Forest's Heritage Middle School. Her love for Jerome Black ran deep, evidenced by her opting to be both mother and father to Jeremiah and Jason, vowing to never bring another man around to supplant what Jerome Black had sown into her sons.

Both Jason and his older brother Jeremiah worshipped their father. Even at five years of age, Jason knew Jerome Black commanded respect from those around him. As an attorney with the Raleigh, North Carolina branch of the National Association for the Advancement of Colored People, or NAACP, Jerome Black was the first in line to represent black and brown victims of white prejudice, racism and discrimination.

Jason recalled those first times when he and his brother would accompany their father to his office, mostly during the summer months, and he would play with his action figures and trucks on the carpeted floor. Jerome Black would be sitting behind his oak desk reviewing case law while a then eight-year-old Jeremiah sat on the windowsill reading books that their father had preselected for him - *The Miseducation of the Negro* by Carter G. Woodson, *Why We Can't Wait* by Dr. Martin Luther King, Jr., and *Native Son* by Richard Wright, to name only a few. Then came the day when the boys were with him at the office, and Jerome Black caught not one but both of his boys reading seminal texts written by black authors. Jason remembered his father smiling and winking at him as he peeped at the title of the first "big person" book Jason had selected to read by himself, *"The Souls of Black Folk* by W. E. B. Dubois. Jason would later graduate to *The Autobiography of Malcolm X* by Alex Haley as told by Malcolm X.

Jason was told that his father died because he was in the wrong place at the wrong time. While visiting the East Raleigh home of a potential client, he exited his pickup truck only to be met with the sound of gunfire and a rain of bullets being shot in his direction from across the street. The single gunshot to the front left side of his head led to his immediate death. However, the autopsy also revealed gunshot wounds to the backs of his left torso and left thigh.

After Madison's presentation ended, Dr. Whitaker dismissed the class. Jason had already packed up his belongings, so he was one of the first to get up and exit the room. As he and his classmates filed out of the classroom to mill around in the building's lobby, Jason watched as a few of them formed groups, seemingly to discuss what they had just heard from the day's presenters. He was surprised that none of them approached him to debate the most controversial elements of his presentation. Jason surmised that their avoidance of him was due to discomfort, their fear of saying the wrong thing only to be perceived as racists, bigots even. Jason lowered his head and shoulders, his book bag dangling by one strap off the left side of his back, to exit the building for the short walk back to his off-campus Shelbourne Towers apartment.

"What up, White?" Jason greeted Greg White as he walked through the door of their Shelbourne Towers apartment.

"What up, Black?" White replied. White was Jason's roommate, as well as a fellow sprinter on the school's track and field team. As the door slammed shut behind Jason, he glanced up briefly while his fingers continued to work the controller to his PlayStation 4 game system. "How'd it go?"

Jason didn't offer an immediate response, as he tossed his book bag onto the carpeted living room floor, next to the recliner. He then made his way to the kitchen to snatch a Gatorade from the fridge. He returned to the living room, bottle in hand, and dropped to the recliner.

"As well as could be expected, I guess," Jason replied, screwing the cap off the Gatorade bottle. "Some people just don't get it."

White, who was dressed in black, compression shorts and a black t-shirt with a Power T on the front, hit the pause button and laid his controller on the coffee table. He then threw his legs up on the sofa and peered over at Jason with clasped hands between his inner thighs.

"That's some pretty heavy shit, man," he said. "And it's a lot for people to take in without the proper context. Doesn't mean what you're saying is wrong. Them being uncomfortable about what you're saying just shows how right you are."

Jason took a swig from the Gatorade bottle. "You different, White. Always have been. I appreciate that."

"We white folks done did some foul shit, bro'. And some of us keep piling it on, just so we can feel good about ourselves and hold on to whatever power we think we have. But you know. My pops, my mom, didn't raise me to be like that. We were all about developing relationships with people no matter what their color. Besides, even this white boy is getting tired of white people's shit."

"Guess who I got the most push back from."

"Madison."

"Yeah, man. She made a comment about Malcolm Stillwell not being an establishment candidate. I didn't disagree with what she said, but can you see that idiot becoming president?"

"I can."

"Really?"

"Really. He may not be the sharpest tool in the toolbox, but he knows how to play to crowds. People - well, white people really - are going to eat him up. He's the opposite of President Dupont. He's white like them, me. And with his slogan being 'Make America Great Again', he's forcing them to reflect on how things were seemingly great for them before Dupont became our first, black president. His power play is textbook, bro'. Vote for me to make America, make America...white again."

"You voting for him?"

"Nah, bruh. I'd be voting for Dupont if he could do a third term. Clifton is getting my vote."

"Mine too."

Jason pulled at the lever on the side of the recliner, causing it to fall back. "This right here, you and me, gives me hope, White" Jason proclaimed as he peered up at the stained ceiling. "We been roomies for, what, two years now. You my boy. But all these white people coming out of the wood works to condemn that new *1619* New York Times magazine series is some wild shit, man. *1619: The Year Black Lives Should Have Mattered.* Nicole Sinclair-Lewis ain't playing."

"Have you read it?"

"No. I haven't. But I plan to. No time now."

"I was at the library the other day, just scanning the magazines on the bookshelf. Saw one, *Newsweek*, *Time* maybe. Didn't read it, but it had the leaders of that 1776 Patriot Movement on it, Garrison Hawkins and Jonathan Blaylock. Had Stillwell's silhouette hovering in the background behind them. Shit freaked me out. They're putting Stillwell out there like he's some Great White Hope."

"And making an even bolder statement about the country's founding," Jason added, "about it being founded in 1776, and not in 1619 like Sinclair-Lewis is saying. They also letting us know it was founded as a white nation." Jason returned the recliner to its upright position to sit on its front edge. "We have to do better. All the gains, the progress, black folks made during the 50s and 60's, and it now feels like it's all about to be taken from us."

"If you think that, you done lost sight of who you are."

"What do you mean?"

"Dude, you're one of the fastest men on the planet. Your platform gets bigger and bigger each time you step on that track and drop a fast time. And if you win gold next year in Rio, you're gonna get paid. But you're also going to have more influence. People are going to want to hear what you have to say because of who you will be, an Olympic gold medalist, an Olympic champion."

Jason paused briefly to ponder White's words. "Wouldn't it be something if we could get more black athletes, and their white allies, together to create something that rids the world of all this racially motivated hate?"

"It would. But you first have to convince those same black athletes, white allies like me, that their efforts won't be in vain. Hell, bro', the government hasn't even apologized. Probably never will. If they did, they would open themselves up to liability."

"True that." Jason reared forward to snatch the docked PlayStation controller from the charging station. "Enough of that. Put Madden in so I can whoop that ass."

Later that day, Jason found himself stretching with White and the other sprinters and hurdlers on the Tom Black Track infield, near the steeplechase pit. As he sat there, he looked up to see the new girl, Patricia "Trish" Newman, jogging toward the entrance of the stadium with the other female middle-distance runners. Seeing her caused him to fondly reflect on their first lengthy encounter three weeks earlier on the basement level of the University of Tennessee Bookstore.

Trish had been by herself, but as Jason watched her movements from the other side of the bookstore, he could see the frustration on her flawless, pecan-brown face. He would learn later that her frustration came from not being able to find a copy of the textbook she needed for one of her Marketing classes.

"If they don't have it here," Jason had said, "maybe they're holding a few copies at the library. But you need to get over there fast. I'm sure there are others thinking the same thing."

Trish, who was a third-year transfer student from Villanova, had smiled at that. "Thank you, uh..."

"Jason. Jason Black."

Jason had accompanied Trish to the John Hopkins Library, and sure enough, they were able to secure a copy of Trish's required textbook. In fact, it was the last remaining copy from a batch of ten. Trish placed her hand on his forearm and thanked him for his help. Jason just nodded before watching her turn to walk away.

The jovial demeanors and playfulness on his teammates' faces were reminiscent of the hopefulness all athletes feel at the beginning of a new season. Three months earlier - June 11 through June 14, 2015, to be exact - the men's team had competed against the nation's best to bring home another NCAA outdoor track and field championship trophy for the school. And because they had only lost seven seniors to graduation, both coaches and athletes were confident their title defense would be a successful one.

Jason dropped to the grass, his eyes still locked on Trish as she and her female teammates entered the stadium from the sidewalk. Trish ran toward the middle of the pack. Jason had long observed that she wasn't all bones like most of the team's other female middle-distance runners. Baby had back...and a modest-sized rack. But what impressed Jason the most was how down to Earth she was.

As the daughter of Tribe Records Founder and CEO Cornelius Newman, her family's wealth entitled her to a hint of haughtiness. But based on the way she interacted with the people around her, he almost felt compelled to ignore the fact that she was a member of Black America's upper crust.

White, who sat on the infield grass with Jason, performed a hamstring stretch with his right leg extended, left leg bent under him. He snuck a glance at Jason and couldn't help but follow the trajectory of his gaze.

"Dude," White exclaimed. "Let it go. Her boyfriend is Tommy Rollins, starting pitcher for the Atlanta Braves. She's not gonna drop him to be with your broke ass."

"Bruh," Jason replied. "It's not even about that. I just can't help myself. The girl is fine."

White switched up his legs, now extending his left leg and leaning into it.

"I agree. But you're going to have a better chance with her roommate Angelica. She's feeling you, man. Saw her looking at you the other day in the caf."

Hurdler Don "Rev" Porter interjected, "Steer clear of Trish, J. I met her father when he dropped her off. Mug had to be six four. Probably weighs two hundred forty-five pounds. He'd break you. Like a twig. But all of you mugs are foul. Need to come to church with me on Sunday. Fall in love with Jesus."

Most of the guys within earshot of Rev laughed at that. Some of them would show up at Abounding Grace Community Church on Sundays, but not Jason and White. While they were considered good men with big hearts to the people who knew them, for reason known to them only, they seemingly had lost all hope in religion and the religious.

Jason stood, twisted his body, flapped his arms. White and a few of the others followed his lead. Hurdler Kenny Thompson was the first to trot toward the stadium exit. Everyone else sprung to their feet and fell in behind him.

White skipped once, twice, to loosen up any lingering tightness in his legs, quicken his pace. "I feel you, though. Her brother Mitch did run by you at Nationals like you were standing still. Still can't believe the mug dropped a nine six on you."

Jason winced at the mere thought of Mitch Newman's historic performance. It all went down on the track straightaway in Eugene, Oregon's Hayward Track and Field Stadium.

The sprinters had settled into their starting blocks. Mitch, a fourth-year student representing the University of Florida Gators, was in lane two, Jason, a second-year student representing the University of Tennessee Volunteers, lane four. It had been standing room only for the meet's marque event, the men's 100-meter dash.

As Jason knelt upright in his blocks, he could see White standing in the bleachers, along the front rail, a stopwatch in his right hand, inches from his face. White had run a 10.19 in the preliminary round, but this time wasn't fast enough to advance him to the quarterfinals.

White had known it was going to be a fast one, especially after watching Jason drop his personal best by eleven tenths of a second in the quarterfinals, to 9.90. It was Jason's first sub-10 hundred.

Jason had stared down the green, plasticine track at the wind gauge and motion detectors positioned at the finish line. The large digital Seiko monitor would display the winning time and wind speed, which was measured in meters per second. A flock of white-shirted volunteers fluttered near the finish line.

Jason placed his hands on the track, shoulder width apart. Thereafter, the starter's voice could be heard over the stadium loudspeakers telling the 100-meter finalists to get set.

BANG!

Jason had wasted little time sprinting into the lead, but Mitch was nearly even with him. With forty meters to go, Mitch had pulled even with him before taking the lead for good around the sixty-meter mark. The rest of the field flashed across the finish line behind them. While Jason had broken the previous world record of 9.79 with a 9.77, Mitch crossed the finish line first with an even faster time, 9.68.

Jason and White trailed the pack as they moved further away from the stadium. Jason looked over at White and said, "I may have a little something-something for him this year."

White smirked. "I hope so. The brother thumped his chest as he was crossing the finish line. If he had run through the tape, his time probably would have been much faster, like in the nine five range. They're going to consider him the favorite next year."

White's words stung Jason, not because of their bluntness but because of their truthfulness.

He playfully barreled into White's right shoulder and fell away.

"Believe, mug. All I need you to do is believe."

CHAPTER TWO

Light rain pelted the windshield of Roscoe Baker's F-150 pickup truck. He just sat on the driver's side, peering in the distance at the dilapidated apartment building. Patrolling the Fort Sanders neighborhood had never been on his to-do list. It frustrated him that Crestridge Apartments had once been a safe haven for UT and Knoxville College students who desired respite from the hustle and bustle of their respective campuses. Now it was a hotspot for drug peddlers and their victims, black teenagers who supposedly had ties to the Blood and Crip street gangs. But at 63 years of age, and as a 25-year veteran of the Knoxville Police Department, it was the only respectable job Baker could get that paid a livable wage.

As the wipers took intermittent swipes at the downpour co-alescing on his windshield, he got a clearer view of the five, teenage black boys sitting on the stairs in one of the complex's breezeways. He winced as one of the boys took a hit off a lit joint.

A KPD squad car rolled by on the deserted street to his left. Baker cursed the officers for allowing these teenaged thugs to rule the neighborhoods surrounding the UT campus. But Baker had always been a man of action, not words. Therefore, it wasn't long before he exited his truck - pistol strapped to his torso un-derneath a black windbreaker - and boldly sauntered over to the boys.

"A little late, don't you think?" Baker declared in a deep, au-thoritative voice. "Curfew was thirty minutes ago."

The biggest boy in the bunch stood up.

"Not for us, old man."

One of his partners in crime added, "That's right. So, get lost or get hurt."

Baker's left hand grazed the windbreaker's right flap, at the zipper. Big Boy shrunk away when he caught sight of Baker's pistol. The other boys staggered to their feet. The lit joint seemingly dropped out of nowhere to land on the pavement a few feet from where Baker was standing.

Baker continued, "I'll be bringing the hurt, young man, espe-cially if you don't leave this place. There are good people trying to sleep around here."

Big Boy and his friends hastily stumbled to the far side of the breezeway, scattering into the darkness like a herd of startled roaches.

When all of the boys were gone, Baker stomped the lit joint under the sole of his booted right foot. He then sauntered back to his pickup truck.

Andy Holt Apartments is a co-ed facility on the outskirts of the UT campus. If you're an Andy Holt resident, the attendants there would usually acknowledge you in the lobby with nothing more than a head nod before allowing you to get where you needed to be. But Willie Moore, a skinny Caucasian third-year student, would always go out of his way to greet Trish at the lobby door.

"Thank you, Willie," Trish said as her roommate and teammate Angelica Mason and she passed him to enter the lobby, book bags hanging loosely by their straps on their backs. Willie smiled at them as he held the door open.

"My pleasure, Trish," he replied. "Angelica. Y'all have a nice evening. Hear?"

Angelica chimed, "We will, Willie. You do the same." They then snickered as they stepped onto the elevator.

But when they reached their third-floor dorm room, their conversation had nothing to do with Willie Moore. Trish sat in one of the chairs around the kitchen island. Angelica retrieved her canister of ice-cold water from the refrigerator, and then drank some of it, her free hand resting on the island counter.

"What about Jason?" Trish asked, pushing the right strap of her covered bra further up her shoulder. "What's his story?"

Angelica's gaze snapped to Trish.

"Why you want to know about him? You thinking about dropping Tommy?"

"No, girl. My daddy would have a fit if I did that. Just curious. He strikes me as shy, that's all."

"He's one of the smartest boys I know. One of those deep thinkers."

Angelica sat up a little straighter, clasping her hands together. She continued, "He is cute, though."

Trish returned the favor with a snappy gaze of her own.

"What?" Angelica feigned surprise.

"You, Angelica. You like him, don't you?"

Angelica retreated to the living room, where she snatched the remote from the coffee table to turn on the television. Wheel of Fortune host Pat Ramirez was congratulating the day's winner.

"I do. Before you got here, we dated, last Spring. One of his homegirls – April – told me that she saw him kissing some chick at one of the malls there in Raleigh. I confronted him about it, and he didn't deny that it happened. He then told me he couldn't do it no more, that steady relationships aren't for him."

"You gave it up, didn't you?"

"I did."

"Was it good?"

"Hell, yeah. And it was big. But after we called it quits, I got to thinking about the four weeks we were together, the conversations we used to have. We talked about our hopes, our dreams, politics even. He told me about his father, how losing him was his motivation for doing well in school. He may not admit it out loud, but we had a connection. He wasn't just out to hit it and forget it." Angelica pounded the left side of her chest with her fist. "Something here tells me that we're destined to be together, as husband and wife. He just has to get his hormones under control."

"But why would you want him back? Especially after he done cheated on you."

"Because of the way I felt when we were together. It just felt so right."

A grunt-chuckle from Trish, then, "Good luck with that, girl. Tommy proposed to me over the summer. We're engaged to be married, but I told him we needed to hold off until after I graduate."

"Why hold off? You love him?"

"I do. But I have to get myself right first. I'm not going to be one of those wives who just sit on their asses all day. I have goals too.

Angelica changed the subject. "What's it like down in Atlanta?"

"Love the winters, deplore the summers. Too hot and humid. But we spent a lot of time at Sojourner Vista, hiking up in the mountains, basking in the sun along the Gulf Coast. Even recorded a single for my father. He loved it. Driving down next month to add a few more tracks to what I hope will be my debut album."

Angelica's gaze moved from Trish's eyes to the florescent green sports bra covering her ample breasts, black tights her lean legs.

"Why are you putting yourself through all this, girl? I came here because of Coach Sinclair. Heard she was a great sprint and long jump coach. But your parents got money. You could probably live off that trust fund they got saved up for you."

"Yeah. I know. But I've been running the eight and the fifteen since junior high. Nothing's going to stop me now. Not with an Olympic berth on the line. Besides, I want to make my own way."

Angelica twirled and released her comforter's loose stings around her index finger. "I envy you."

"Why?"

"Because life comes so easy for people like you." She kicked her sandals to the floor, and then sat in the recliner. "You live in big houses. Attend private schools. Take Caribbean vacations on a whim."

Trish stood and walked over to the living room window. She pulled at the drawstring to open the blinds. Night had fallen on the plaza below, but steady streams of UT students either played basketball or volleyball under the streetlights on the outdoor courts between the aquatic center and track stadium, or just sat conversing on concrete benches.

Angelica continued, "Remember what I told you about my mama, how she used to have all them men up in the house?"

"Yeah, girl."

"Well, that was only half the story. One of those men got me pregnant. Had just turned fifteen. Tried to hide it from my mama, but she eventually found out. Took me down to the clinic herself to get an abortion. That same night, she killed the man. Stabbed him in the chest with a butcher knife, while he was sleeping."

"Where is she now?"

"Where do you think? She locked up. I was a 'Ward of the State' for a few years. Made my rounds to a few foster homes, group homes. My father didn't want anything to do with me, us, and Mama and her sister were never close. Hell, Aunt Helen could barely take care of herself."

"Is that why you're majoring in social work? To help women who have gone through the same kind of stuff?"

"I guess so. The counselor I had back then made sure I didn't blame myself for what that bastard did to me. My mother forcing me to have that abortion. My new counselor, though, is teaching me how to love again."

Trish leaned against the concrete wall and took another sip from her covered cup. Standing there, she considered Angelica's words, concluding that they were in direct contrast to the extra things she did most weekends to pay her bills.

Angelica was only receiving a partial scholarship, a scant cry from what she needed to pay her tuition, room and board. But when she learned from another girl that Angelica worked weekends as a waitress at the Cherokee Country Club, she gasped. But it all made sense to her now. Angelica was using her beauty and charm to garner the funds she needed to get through college. The country club option was better than the alternative, taking her clothes off for cash at *The Mouse's Ear.*

Angelica asked, "Hey. Remember that event I told you about, the one for local, state and national members of the Problem-Solving Caucus?"

"Yeah."

"Well, they're looking for entertainers - singers, comedians, bands - to lighten the mood. Pays good money."

"How much we talking?"

"About three thousand dollars, for the evening. Interested?'

"I don't have to wear the bowtie and slacks, do I?"

"Nah, girl. All you have to do is look gorgeous in a sequin dress and sing a few Anita Baker and Toni Braxton songs."

Trish smiled. "Sure. Why not?"

CHAPTER THREE

Jason sat upright on his bed, the light from his nightstand lamp reflecting off the sling blade knife that he repeatedly slung open and closed in his left hand. In his other hand was the most recent letter he had received from Jeremiah, his older brother. Jeremiah was a Marine who had spent the last two years fighting Al-Qaeda terrorists in Afghanistan. Jason was relieved that his brother's tour of duty would be coming to an end soon. President Dupont had asserted during one of his 2012 debates with former Massachusetts governor and business tycoon Mitchell Richardson that he had every intention of withdrawing all American troops from the region no later than December 2014.

Three pictures of Jeremiah partying with some of the Afghan women lay on the bed to Jason's right. Jason studied a fourth one of Jeremiah dipping and French-kissing one of the Afghan women, as his colleagues seemed to be cheering him on in the background.

Jason tossed the picture aside. Still playing with the sling blade - open, close, open close - he silently read his brother's letter:

"What's up, little bro'?" Jeremiah wrote. *"I pray Coach High-smith is treating you right over there in Knoxville. Wish I could be there with you, but duty calls. Just keep me in your prayers as I continue to fight this senseless war."*

Jason got up from his bed - sling blade in one hand, letter in the other - and walked over to the desk and chair in the corner of the room. He then spun the swivel chair around and sat.

"Still can't believe I grew the balls to finally enlist. But I'm here now. A proud Marine. When I first got here, I thought being fired upon by Taliban soldiers would be par for the course. But that hasn't been the case at all. Yeah. We have to keep our guard up. But the natives want a change. They want to be free. And the women? Bruh', they are fine, as you can see from the pictures I sent you. May have to kick the sisters to the curb."

Jason grunted and smiled.

"Well, I better sign off. 'bout to go on a raid up in the mountains in a few hours. Just wanted you to know I'm thinking about you, Mama. Looking forward to seeing y'all in about six months, and for good next December. Run fast this year. Your bruh-man, Jerry."

Jason placed the letter on his desk. He then reflected on the last time his brother gave him advice on the fine art of sprinting. That was four years ago, in the summer of 2007, on their old high school track in Wake Forest, North Carolina.

Jeremiah had settled into his starting blocks while Jason stood a few feet to his left. He then exploded from the blocks, raced down the track, slowing his roll at the forty-meter mark.

"See how my lead arm swung up with more force during the drive phase?" Jeremiah had asked his younger brother as he limped back to the starting line. Jason watched as his brother breathed in harder than usual, his clenched hands above his head. "That's how you get a jump on everyone else."

He kicked Jason's blocks in the third lane before positioning himself behind them.

"Your turn," he said. He waved his brother into the starting blocks.

Jason bent over at the waist to stretch his hamstrings before squatting and placing his feet on the starting block pads. He rocked slightly before becoming completely still.

"Set!" Jeremiah spat. He discreetly wiped away the spittle on his lip and chin. "Go!"

Jason pushed away from his blocks and asphalt track with a tremendous amount of force, his lead arm and leg in perfect sync. A wide-eyed expression appeared on Jeremiah's face as he watched his brother sprint down the track, at a much-faster clip.

Jeremiah cupped his mouth with both hands. "Good stuff, Jase," he shouted down the track. "Good stuff."

After completing an interval workout, the brothers threw their gear into the back seat of Jeremiah's Mustang convertible and headed home. When they pulled up to the curb in front of their single-family home, they spotted their mother, Cynthia Black, sitting on the front porch chatting with Saudia Jacobs, the elderly woman that Cynthia had allowed to stay in her home two years ago following the death of her best friend and Ms. Ja-cobs' daughter, Claudia Jacobs. Claudia Jacobs had died from breast cancer. Both women sat in identical rocking chairs. Ms.

Jacob's legs were covered by the wool blanket that she had been knitting for her two-year-old granddaughter.

"Speak of the devil," their mother Cynthia exclaimed.

"And his apprentice," Ms. Jacobs added, chuckling.

Cynthia then pointed to the glass screen door to her right. "Food's in there on the table. Just stick it in the microwave."

Jeremiah leaned in and kissed his mother on the cheek. As he pulled away, she looked up at him with pursed lips. Jason waved but wasted little time retreating inside.

"Gotta get the boy straight, Ma," Jeremiah exclaimed. "'fore I get out of here."

"But y'all pulling some late hours, Jerry," Cynthia exclaimed. "What time is it?" She peered down at her watch for the answer. "Seven o'clock. You told me you'd be home by six." She sighed out of frustration. "How'd everything go?"

Jeremiah placed his duffle bag on the concrete stairs. He then leaned against the iron cast left pillar that supported the awning.

"He's pissed," Jeremiah replied. "Doesn't want me to leave. Told him I'd stay in touch. Write him at least once a month while I'm over there."

"Not buying it, huh?" Ms. Jacobs interjected, not taking her eyes off her knitting.

"No, ma'am. He wants me to be here to see him win state. But the Marines aren't gonna give me time off to see him run. Told him that he just needs to get one of his teammates to record it so he can send it to me."

"Not the same. You know how he is, baby. Always trying to impress you."

"And he really did his thing today. His start is getting better. I think he's going to do it this year. Hate to say it, but he may break my school and state 100-meter records."

White stood over the stove browning hamburger meat. Lasagna noodles boiled in a pot to his right. He flinched when Jason entered the kitchen from the bedroom, dressed in a grey UT hoodie with orange lettering and matching sweatpants.

"Smelling good up in here, bruh'," Jason exclaimed. "What's for dinner?"

"Lasagna," White replied.

"For us? Or one of your Carson Newman freaks?"

"Us, bro'. Gotta eat, don't we?"

Jason chuckled as he passed through the kitchen to the living room. White watched him closely as he bent over to stretch his hamstrings. But then Jason farted from his bent-over position, causing White to cup his hand over his nose while trying to suppress his laughter.

White's reaction caused Jason to let out a loud yelp of his own. But their attention shifted to the television when they heard the news anchor mention Olympian Calvin Louis.

"There is growing concern in the world of sports. About a new performance-enhancing vitamin..."

A yellow and black pill appeared on the screen.

"...known as the Yellow Jacket. Scientists say this vitamin can't be detected during random drugs screenings. And they fear its widespread use could put the legitimacy of athletic performance in jeopardy."

White removed the skillet from the fire, turned the burner off. He joined Jason in the living room, causing Jason to momentarily glimpse over at him. White used his hand to cup his nose, a clear indication that the smell of Jason's passed gas was still making its rounds through their two-bedroom apartment.

The news anchor continued, "WRAL correspondent Keith Reynolds caught up with eight-time Olympic gold medalist Calvin Louis, to get his take on this latest development."

"As you know," Louis began, "I was pretty vocal about steroid use leading up to the '88 Games. Everyone knew Ken was juicing; we just couldn't prove it." Louis took a swipe at his nose. "But I was relieved when they busted him. As athletes, we want assurances that everyone is abiding by the same rules, playing on a level playing field."

"And what are your thoughts about this new Yellow Jacket vitamin," Reynolds asked.

"Really don't have any. I just know anyone who uses banned substances - be it the Yellow Jacket or H-G-H - cheapens their victory. They didn't win. The drug won. And as far as I'm concerned, they're nothing more than cheats. End of story."

Jason reached for the doorknob.

"I'm out."

CHAPTER FOUR

Jason trotted down Cumberland Avenue, hoodie covering his head, oversized *Bose* headphones his ears. He could hear himself humming the lyrics to rapper MC Maximus' *I'm Losing My Mind* as he headed down Cumberland Avenue toward downtown Knoxville.

When he reached the corner of Cumberland and Twenty-First, he jogged in place, patiently waiting for the crosswalk light to change from red to green.

"Nigger!" The idiotic cry of a white dude seated on the passenger side of a speeding Chevy Silverado pickup truck. All Jason could do was shrug and keep it moving. It wasn't the first time he had been called something other than his name. It wouldn't be his last.

The light turned green, and the countdown began for him to cross. Jason's long strides took him across Cumberland Avenue, to 20th Street and away from the comforts and protections of the UT campus.

Baker exited the BP Gas Station through the sliding, glass door. He held a bottle of chocolate milk in one hand, a box of glazed *Krispy Kreme* donuts in the other. As Baker walked over to his truck, Jason's sudden appearance from the side of the building startled him.

"Punk," Baker muttered under his breath as Jason strode past him and across the parking lot.

Upon reaching his truck, Baker placed the donut box on top of the covered bed of his truck. He used his free hand to open the driver-side door. With the door open, he placed the milk bottle in the console cup holder. But like most Americans, he couldn't resist the allure of a hot, glazed *Krispy Kreme* donut. So, before placing the donut box on the passenger-side seat, he pulled one from the box and pushed half of it into his mouth, savoring its sweetness.

Jason circled around a light post for the return trip back to Shelbourne Towers. As he made his way up Forest Avenue, he spotted an older, white woman, in her early 50s perhaps, getting out of her parked SUV. She opened the back passenger-side door to pull out two bags of groceries. When she saw Jason approaching on the sidewalk, she abruptly slammed the SUV door, and then dashed to the front door of her townhome. Fumbling with her keys on the porch, she almost dropped them. She calmed herself right before Jason reached the walkway leading to her front porch, opening and stepping through the door and into her abode.

But Jason couldn't resist making light of the situation. He slowed to a trot near the woman's parked SUV. Feeling the heat of the woman's glare, he spun on his heels to run backwards. A wide grin appeared on his face, a clear indication that he found the woman's antics humorous. He playfully waved at the woman before facing forward again to resume his trek back to the towers.

Jason rounded a corner for the final leg of his run. As he quickened his pace, a black, F-150 pickup truck did a U-turn on the other side of the street and rolled towards him. Jason slowed to a trot when he saw the truck cross the center line on the two-way street. He stopped completely when the truck's driver brought it to a screeching halt in front of him.

Baker got out of his truck, and then walked over to Jason with his hands in his pockets.

"Whatcha doing out here, boy?"

"Minding my business. You?"

Hands still in his pockets, Baker stopped several feet away from Jason.

"Got a complaint about someone harassing residents a few blocks down. You him?"

Jason walked over to and through Baker, his left shoulder grazing Baker's right. It was then that Baker reached over to grab and pull at Jason's hoodie. Baker's pistol had been drawn and was pointed at the ground.

Jason elbow-slapped Baker's hand away.

"What's up with you, dude? I ain't got nothing to do with that."

But Jason's eyes widened when they caught sight of Baker's pistol being pointed at him. Because the right side of his body was angled away from Baker, he immediately dipped his right hand into his pocket to grab hold of his sling blade. And with a slow and silent flick of his wrist, he exposed the blade.

"Turn around," Baker ordered. "On your knees. I know it was you."

Jason turned his back to Baker, his grip tightening around the sling blade's handle.

"But it wasn't me, dude. Really. I run track for UT. I'm not lying. Call my coach."

Baker slowly inched closer. As he stood over and behind Jason, he once again placed his hand on Jason's hoodie. Tightening his grip, he pulled at it, forcibly guiding Jason to the pavement. The

Whispering near Jason's right ear, Baker said, "Gonna be one less nigger..."

But before Baker could finish his sentence, Jason spun toward Baker's rear, simultaneously plunging the blade deep into Baker's rib cage. Roscoe Baker let out a blood-curdling howl as the pistol fell from his hand to the ground. The clap of a single gunshot rang out as the pistol bounced from the pavement to the grass, causing Jason to search for cover that wasn't there.

Utter shock is the best way to describe Jason's reaction as he watched Baker back away from him, writhing in pain. His jacket was visibly wet with his own blood. Baker's pistol now lay a few feet away from him, in the grass.

Baker looked up at Jason, the knife protruding from his rib cage.

"They're gonna lock you up, boy. Throw away the key. All you had to do was cooperate." Then, the most damning statement. "Gonna believe me, not you. I was the one standing my ground."

At first, Jason slowly backed away from Baker. The nerve of this man. He was the one who had been forced to defend himself. But as area residents, mostly Whites, exited their modest-sized homes in response to hearing gunfire, the full weight of what he had just done dawned on him. He had stabbed a white man under the cover of streetlights in the conservative South.

Seemingly overwhelmed by the repercussions of his actions, and the consequences that were sure to follow, Jason turned, glanced back at Baker one last time before sprinting into the night.

CHAPTER FIVE

The average year-round temperature in Southern California is 70 degrees. And the honeys, and hunks, are always out, their fit bodies exposed for all to see. Yes, you may run into celebrities who just so happen to be out on the town for fun, relaxation and libation. But the only people sweating them are members of the paparazzi, who live, and die, to capture individuals like Holly Madison saying or doing something...newsworthy?

Mitch Newman could have cared less about keeping up with Holly Madison. Like everyone else, he knew she had a hit television show with the same name on the *E* television network. But as he squatted, his back against the concrete wall underneath the University of California Los Angeles' (UCLA) Drake Stadium bleachers, he had a decision to make.

In one hand, he held a half-empty water bottle. In the other were two yellow and black pills, what some experts referred to as Yellow Jackets. Like everyone else, he had heard Olympic great Calvin Louis complain about their use, about how any type of performance-enhancing drug use cheapens one's victory. But damn, he ran a 9.68 last year at nationals, taking first place and setting new American and World records in the 100-meter dash. He knew if he stopped taking it, he would no longer be great. He would be normal, average even. And that would raise suspicion about him from the brethren, lead to further drug testing and a lifetime ban from the sport.

Mitch stood, took a sip from his water bottle. His gaze shifted from the Yellow Jacket pills to the trash barrel to his right. And then he thought about his father, how he stood in the stands with a stoic expression on his face while others danced and hollered, gleefully dishing out high fives after seeing Mitch cross the finish line first. The Florida Gators men's team did not win the team trophy that day – that honor went to the University of Tennessee Volunteers – but by taking first place in an individual event, he had hoped that his father's full admiration and respect would follow.

Mitch stood and took another sip from the water bottle. He then tossed the Yellow Jackets into the trash barrel. Duffle bag hanging from his shoulder strap, Mitch trotted through the breezeway to the outer edge of the track. A swarm of shirtless, UCLA distance runners raced by, causing Mitch to pause briefly to allow them to pass before crossing over to the infield. He spotted his coach, Franklin Moses, clowning around with Assistant Coach Jacob Wilson just left of center field. Coach Moses looked up when he saw Mitch approaching.

"What's up with you, Newman?" Coach Moses asked, looking down at his wristwatch. Mitch winced. "You're thirty minutes late. D-Mo and 'em already out on their warm-up run."

"Got stuck in traffic," Mitch replied, wincing. "Won't happen again."

Coach Wilson interjected, "L-A rush hour ain't like the A-T-L, Mitch. You gotta give yourself at least an hour from where you're coming from."

"I overslept."

Mitch threw his duffle bag to the infield grass.

"You might as well hang with us," Coach Moses added. "They probably heading back up Charles Young by now." He spread his arms then crossed them. "What's this I hear about Trish transferring to U-T? Had some pretty fast times at Villanova."

Mitch started stretching. "Yep. Did it to be closer to Pops. About to take her singing career to the next level."

"He thinking about bringing her on at Tribe?"

"Something like that."

Coach Wilson shook his head. "If it were me, those spikes would be in the closet."

"Not Trish. She's too damn good at what she does. Girl still holds the Georgia state record in the girls' four hundred. Fifty-one point nine seconds. But she prefers the eight and the fifteen."

"Think we'll see her accepting any Grammys anytime soon," Coach Moses asked.

"Wouldn't bet against it. She sang the national anthem up at Turner Field last year, at one of Tommy's home games. People talking about her being as big as Beyonce'."

Coach Moses studied Mitch as the shirtless, male distance runners raced by them on the track.

"We're glad you're here, Mitch. Usain and his crew run a tight ship over there in Gainesville. I know it was tough leaving them."

Usain Tyson was the Head Coach of the University of Florida Track and Field Team.

Coach Moses continued. "You still taking your vitamins?"

Mitch reluctantly peered up at Moses, with a stern expression on his face.

"Yeah," he lied. "Wouldn't be here if I wasn't. Not after all you guys did for me last year."

D-Mo and 'em – about five other athletes, mostly sprinters and hurdlers – appeared at the stadium entrance. Some were bent over, while most of the others stood tall with their hands clenched behind and above their heads, catching their breath. Coach Wilson directed a frown at Mitch, a knowing glance at Coach Moses, before dismissing himself to greet the group.

Coach Moses dropped to the infield to draw closer to their star athlete.

"Look, Mitch, we appreciate you coming all this way to train with us. But if you're still having problems with the way we do things 'round here, I'll let you out of your contract, no strings attached."

Coach Moses straightened his legs, his gaze remaining fixed on Mitch.

"If it'll make a difference, you can stop taking your vitamins. No one here is holding a gun to your head."

Coach Moses stood. Mitch followed his lead.

"That nine point six eight was only the beginning, bruh. You're going to run much faster in the months leading up to the Rio Games. With the way you ran last year, I wouldn't be surprised if you posted another nine six at the Trials, a nine five at the Games." He placed his hand on Mitch's shoulder. "My hope, though, is you'll stick with the program. If you do, you're going to be a very rich man. You get me?"

Mitch nodded his head in the affirmative, but it wasn't easy. The only other person who at least suspected that he was a fraud was Cornelius Newman, his father.

His father was no fool. He had been a sprinter at Kent State University. But all Mitch could think about at that moment was the stern expression on Cornelius Newman's face when he skipped over to the fence surrounding the track to accept slaps to his back from his family and friends. The only one not smiling was his father. He stood in the background, his arms crossed. Mitch knew his father suspected what he already knew.

"You're juicing, aren't you?" Mr. Newman had asked while they stood on the ninth-floor balcony of Eugene Oregon's Hyatt Regency Hotel hours after his historic sprint. The rest of the family, which included his mother, Carmelita Newman, two sisters, Trish and Rayvyn, and about a dozen other family members, were inside, in the living room and dining area, still buzzing about Mitch solidifying his spot as the world's fastest man.

"Don't lie to me, boy," he had continued under his breath as his jaw tightened. "I need you to tell me the truth. Now."

A long pause, as Mitch had thought carefully about his response. He even looked away briefly because the fire coming from his father's eyes was so intense.

"No," Mitch had lied again, peering over at his father with a straight face. "The time was fast, faster than I expected, but I blame it on the genes."

Mr. Newman had then leaned on the railing that wrapped around the oversized balcony. Mitch had shifted his weight from his left leg to his right, nervously awaiting his father's response.

"Compliment received," Mr. Newman had replied, "but I know you're lying. Just don't know why. You're better than this, boy."

"I'm not lying," Mitch had said. "Just ran the race of my life."

"But you dropped more than a tenth off your personal best, son," Mr. Newman had said, placing emphasis on his retort with a slap to the top rail. "That's not possible unless you're juicing. Remember, I ran fast times back in the day. Maybe not as fast as what you're running, but they were considered fast during my era."

"I'm not juicing," Mitch had repeated. "I've been tested repeatedly, and no performance-enhancing drugs have been found in my system. Just working Coach Moses' program like every-one else, that's all. Why can't you just be happy for me?"

Another long pause, as Mr. Newman looked away to consider Mitch's denial. He then looked up and said, with tears in his eyes, "I can't, and I won't. Secrets like this, when they are re-vealed, will destroy you. Yeah, you're riding high on the wave now, but when the world learns that you are nothing but a damn fraud, you're not going to like how you feel." He had then drawn closer to Mitch, glaring down at him with a scowl on his face. "And because you lied...lied to my fucking face, don't come crawling back to Daddy when they out your lying ass."

And with that, Mr. Newman had turned on his heels to go back inside the hotel suite. Mitch had turned away, shaken to the core by his father's outright dismissal. He now stood alone, both literally and figuratively. His relationship with his father would never be the same.

"Fuck him," Mitch had whispered under his breath. "I'm my own man now. World's fastest."

Trish swayed as an upbeat melody emanated from the speak-ers. She was in the bowels of the UT University Center, re-hearsing one of her songs. Her fellow musicians, a strange assortment of friends she had made since transferring to the school, sat in the background, one on the guitar, the other two piano and drums.

Trish acknowledged Keisha Daniels' thumbs up with a head nod. Keisha and Reggie Clark sat on the other side of the Plex-iglas, over the audio control board. Both Keisha and Reggie bobbed their heads as Trish's singing and the band's playing in-tensified. When the singing and music stopped, Keisha stood, and joined Trish and the band in the sound booth.

"That sounded great, girl," Keisha said. "But we need more. What's up?"

Trish grabbed her half-empty water bottle from the podium shelf, removed the cap, and sipped.

"Tommy," Trish replied, licking the moisture from her lips.

"What's he up to now?"

Sensing that the conversation would last longer than five minutes, Trish's band mates excused themselves. Fifteen-minute break before they moved to the next set.

Trish continued. "He's not coming up this weekend. Got a double header at Turner. I wanted y'all to meet him."

"Can't be mad at a man for doing his job, Trish."

"I'm not. You don't know Tommy, though. We been through Hell and high water together. Done lost count of the number of times he's cheated on me. Now that he's playing Major League ball, I'm afraid of losing him."

"If you did, he was never yours in the first place."

Trish nodded in agreement and shrugged her shoulders.

"Sometimes I wonder if coming here was the best thing for our relationship. I mean, he always said he wasn't into long-distance relationships."

"But you wanted to test him?"

"Yeah, girl."

"I would have done the same thing, 'specially if I had caught him cheating on me." Keisha claimed one of the empty stools and sat. "What would you do if you found out he was still messing around on you?"

"Drop him, like a bad habit."

Keisha pursed her lips. "Would it really be that easy?"

"No. The man treats me like a queen when we're together. But I'd have to do something. Let him know how trifling he is."

"If it were me, I'd hurt him real bad...if you know what I mean."

Trish chuckled. "Ouch!"

CHAPTER SIX

As Mitch peered out at the Pacific Ocean from one of the benches lining the Santa Monica Pier, he kicked himself for not coming right out and telling Coach Moses that he was no longer taking his vitamins. But how could he? Especially after what happened to Nevel Grimes five years earlier.

He had just completed his Saturday evening run. Sitting there, he thought about Beatrice Carter, Nevel's girlfriend, and how she had been so adamant about Nevel's death not being an accident. It occurred three days before the start of the 2007 outdoor track and field season, in what has come to be known as the Diamond League Championship Series. With a personal best 100-meter time of 9.84, Nevel was well on his way to dominating the sprints that year.

Beatrice had told Mitch that Coach Moses had pleaded with Nevel to remain committed to the program, painting a vision of him standing on the podium at the 2008 Beijing Olympics with no less than three gold medals dangling from his neck. This vision undoubtedly appealed to Nevel, but he knew these victories would be even sweeter if they resulted from his diligence in the weight room and on the track.

When it came to simulated demonstrations of speed, Nevel hung tough in practice with those teammates that remained dedicated to the program. That's not to say he was beating these teammates, only that he didn't lose much ground by not taking the Yellow Jacket. But Moses expected his athletes to post times that made spectators take second and third looks at their stopwatches. Because Nevel was no longer inclined to take his medicine like everyone else, Beatrice suspected Coach Moses was guilty of foul play.

Mitch stood, twisted his body to the left and then right, and then turned to make his way back to his parked car. As he waded through the hordes of natives and tourists, along the wooden pier, a brilliant, orange-yellow sun set behind him. It was then that he thought about his father. Mitch knew he would one day have to come clean with him. But he also knew this confession would have to wait until after he qualified for, and won, the 2016 Rio Games' 100-meter dash title. He knew he could do it without the Yellow Jacket vitamin, but he also knew Coach Moses would never be satisfied with times that were slower than his new world record.

"Hey, stranger."

Mitch turned to see his girl Yasmin Ortiz walking toward him through a swarm of students, professors and administrators, textbook up to her chest. Mitch was sitting on one of the many leather sofas situated around the UCLA Student Center lobby. Before she arrived, he had been skimming through a copy of the July 2015 *Track & Field News*.

Yasmin had graduated in December 2014 with her Bachelor of Arts degree in Film, Television and Digital Media. Her goal was to direct and produce blockbuster films. But because she knew how hard it was for a bi-racial woman (her father is Latino, her mother African American), or women of color for that matter, to join the ranks of Hollywood's premier directors and producers, she decided to supplement her undergraduate education by enrolling in the school's Master of Business Administration (MBA) program. She knew success as a new filmmaker would rest with her ability to employ sound business principles and practices.

The two had met for the first time a month earlier, in November, after a Jay-Q and Bianca concert in the upscale *L.A. Live* entertainment district. Mitch was sitting in a booth in the P. F. Chang restaurant with Calvin Walker and Kevin Moore, two fellow sprinters with the Team Elite Track & Field Club. The first thing Mitch saw as he looked up from his glass was Yasmin and one of her girlfriends. They were rounding the bend, behind a petite, Filipino waitress. Yasmin's toned, black stocking-covered legs protruded from underneath her black leather, hip-hugging mini-skirt. As the two girlfriends passed him, she gave him a wink and a nod. Mitch could feel his heartbeat quicken from the weight of Yasmin's lingering gaze and toothy smile. Calvin and Kevin's eyes were locked on her girlfriend's rack.

"Look at you, Newman," Kevin Moore had exclaimed from the other side of the table. "Been here three weeks and already getting looks from the ladies."

Calvin, who had been sitting next to Kevin in the aisle, leaned to his right, seemingly to see where the waitress was about to seat them. "Ain't that the chick from that show *Playa' Delight*?" He was referring to Yasmin's girlfriend. "Monica Sinclair?"

Kevin could only see her backside from his vantage point. The ornate, wooden wall that extended about three feet above them blocked his view. "Can't see her from here," he replied. "But if it is, baby-girl is stacked like a deck of cards."

Mitch turned to peek over his shoulder. He had caught sight of Yasmin as she sat. As her legs parted for that initial scoot onto the padded bench, Mitch's eyes smiled as her cherry-colored panties blinked at him. She looked up and somewhat discreetly blew him a kiss.

Kevin had said, chuckling, "You should go over and get her autograph, CW. Add it to your collection."

"You just hating, Kev, 'cause I got Shavon Berry's autograph, and a pic. Should have went with me, bro'. Plenty of freaks at the San Diego Comic-Con." He sipped at his Daiquiri. "And believe you, me, I got plenty of trim that week."

The two men had been so preoccupied with their own banter that they failed to notice that Mitch had slipped away. When they looked up, they found themselves staring at an empty bench. Calvin leaned to his right. Kevin stood to tower over his friend, leaning in the same direction. They then watched as Mitch sauntered over to the ladies' table to stand, his hands being repositioned from his front pockets to the back. He must have said something funny because it evoked an immediate chuckle from the ladies. They then invited him to sit down. As Mitch slid onto the bench next to Monica, directly across from Yasmin, he turned to wink at Calvin and Kevin.

"Daaaaaaaamn," Calvin had exclaimed under his breath.

Yasmin sat on Mitch's lap, her arms wrapped around his neck, wet kisses being applied to his lips. Mitch fought to wiggle his tongue into her mouth, but Yasmin abruptly pulled away.

"Why you looking so serious over here?" she asked, seductively raking her tongue over her damp lips.

"I did it," Mitch replied. "I stopped taking those pills."

A slight hesitation. "And that's a good thing?"

"Yeah. It is..."

"...but you're worried. Worried that you're going to come up short. That your times won't be as fast."

Mitch shrugged his shoulders. "Right. If I don't run as fast as I did in Oregon, officials down at the IAAF are going to get suspicious. And when they start questioning me, I'll have to come clean. If I don't, I could receive a lifetime ban."

Yasmin transitioned to the love seat to the right of Mitch. "Explain to me again why you just won't build on what you already started. You said it yourself; it's undetectable. No chance of getting caught. Why run against the grain?"

Mitch rolled his magazine up and leaned forward in the chair. His brow tightened as he looked over at her. "Isn't it obvious, Yaz? At next year's Olympics, I want it to be about me, not the vitamin."

"But if you stop taking it, your times will be much slower. Right?

"Probably. But I have a lot to do with that. Just means I have to train harder. More intervals on the track. More reps in the weight room. If I can hold on to my form, it's a mute issue. But if I don't, the IAAF will bury me."

"It's more than that, though." The back of Yasmin's neck now rested in the palm of her bent arm. "Isn't it?"

"I guess so." Mitch flopped back in the chair. "I never should have agreed to come here to train. Should have kept my ass in Gainesville. But that nine six. Hard to say no after becoming the fastest man on the planet."

"If you hadn't come here, to California, to train, we would have never met. I would probably be miserable with some other man. But you, you made me feel special from jump. Still can't believe you fell for me, and not Monica. Her good looks. Her big boobs."

Mitch propped his leg up on the coffee table as he burst out laughing. When his laughter subsided, Yasmin reached over and grabbed his hand.

She continued, "I know your father didn't fully appreciate what you did on the track that day. Fuck him. You said it yourself. You're the fastest man on the planet. You want to be crowned Olympic Champion, in the one and the two. I want to direct a blockbuster film and win a few Oscars. The way I see it, you and I are all that matters.   She flashed him one of her trademark toothy smiles. "Come on, baby. Lean on me, if you're not strong."

"Hah!" Mitch belted. "Corny."

Mitch was the first to stand. Yasmin stood and slid up the length of Mitch's extended arm until her head rested on his burly chest.

"What we doing for dinner tonight," Mitch jokingly asked.

Yasmin looked up at him, a sly smile on her face. "Whatever you're cooking."

"In-and-Out Burger it is."

Coaches Moses and Wilson sat next to each other in the front seat of Coach Moses' BMW sedan. The sedan was parked in a lot adjacent to UCLA's track and field stadium. The day's practice had ended more than an hour ago, and night had fallen over the City of Angels, but Coach Wilson had told his boss, friend and mentor that he knew for a fact that Mitch Newman posed a real and imminent threat to their speed and strength factory.

"I already have blood on my hands, dude," Coach Wilson gruffly exclaimed. "I ain't doing it no more."

Coach Moses looked over at his friend and colleague, studying him. He could tell Coach Wilson was starting to lose it, whatever "it" was. But there was nothing he could do short of taking him out. Of course, if he did that, he would be the operation's sole proprietor. Heck, he had blood on his hands too.

A few days after establishing a new world record in the women's javelin, Hazel Beacham became frantic about being found out. Like countless times before, her blood screen had come back negative. Again, the ingredients that fueled the Yellow Jacket vitamin were undetectable. But Hazel didn't just break the world record, she shattered it. Much to Moses' chagrin, she developed a conscience after the full weight of what she had just done hit her. Consequently, the decision was made to eliminate her before she had a chance to blow the whistle.

Hazel was not obese like most of the world's other female javelin throwers. Her nickname within track and field circles was Wonder Woman. She was whiter than white with black hair, stood six feet, three inches tall, and possessed the face and body of a moderately overweight supermodel. She was also strong as an ox, bench-pressing three hundred pounds, squatting over five.

"Look, nigga'," Coach Moses began, "if you want out, get to stepping. I can do this all by myself or get someone else up in this joint. Things are finally starting to simmer down after we put Nevel down. I don't need the IAAF, or the FBI, poking around again, not when our athletes are poised to solidify Team Elite in the history books." He reached up and gripped the steering wheel. "There's money out there, Jake. Millions of dollars. For them. For us. That's why they're vetted. Find their strengths, weaknesses. Make sure they're just as greedy as our black asses."

"I get that, bro'," Coach Wilson replied with a hint of remorse. "And don't get me wrong. I'm still game. But Newman is connected, man. His father is the CEO of a major music label. If we have to take him out, that's going to present some major complications for us."

Silence hung in the air between them. Then, "What month is it? August? If he doesn't break ten seconds by the end of March, we'll get someone to take him out, before the Olympic Trials in June. But I'm like you, bro'. Don't want to be the one doing the killing. That shit weighs heavy on you."

"But I sleep better most nights knowing you're the only person who knows my secret."

"True that. Feeling's mutual. And our supplier has just as much to protect as we do. Paying him good money. I'll reach out to him later today, see if that operative of his is doing her job."

"I like that tune." A smirk appeared on Coach Wilson's face. "Did you really screw her before you smothered her with the pillow?"

"Yeah, man. Off and on. For three hours straight. In her apartment. Had to see what she was working with. Had to wrap my jimmy, though."

"Was it good?"

"For me it was. Just wish I had taken a dip weeks before she decided to bounce on us. You know her strong ass would have broken me down. Nothing worse that sticking it to a honey who's too drugged up to love you back."

"You one crazy son-of-a-bitch." Coach Wilson reached for the door and slithered out. "Will I see you at church tomorrow?" he asked as he collected his duffle bag and water bottle from the truck floor. He draped the duffle bag's shoulder strap over his neck and allowed the water bottle to dangle from his right hand.

"Yes, sir. Gotta get my praise on."

Coach Wilson chuckled. He then extended his balled-up fist to his friend and mentor. Their fists collided in midair, simultaneously opening soon after to signify twin explosions. Coach Wilson then shut the passenger-side door. Coach Moses grinned as he watched his partner in crime turn right to walk over to his parked SUV.

CHAPTER SEVEN

A strong, gust of wind slammed into Jason face as he made his way down the dark alley in downtown Lenoir City, which was about 30 miles west of the UT campus. A few more weeks of summer were expected, but based on the unusually cool nights, Jason could tell Upper East Tennessee would be receiving its fair share of snow this winter.

Twenty-four hours had passed since his encounter with Roscoe Baker. Twenty-four hours that saw him successfully steering clear of police squad cars and the officers they carried. After the encounter, he knew he couldn't return to the comforts of his two-bedroom Shelbourne Towers apartment. That's the first place they would have looked. And his mother's home in Wake Forest was out of the question. For starters, it would have taken him seven hours to get there by car. And he didn't have any money. His wallet had been left up in his apartment. However, he did have his cell phone. Never left home without it. But if he couldn't find a charging cord, it would be nothing more than a paperweight.

After walking all night, and on and off for most of the day, he had made it down to the Lenoir City exit, off Interstate 75. He had turned his hoodie inside out to hide the Tennessee track and field lettering on its front. Unfortunately for him, he couldn't change the color of his skin. As he moved further west of Knoxville, he knew his skin color would be more of a liability than an asset. While cities like Lenoir City, Athens and Chattanooga had black populations, the fact still remained that their numbers were low. Jason knew the white folks in that part of the state would shoot first, ask questions later, especially if they recognized him as the black man who stabbed the white Fort Sanders security guard.

Through chattering teeth, Jason swallowed hard as he slowly made his way up a steady incline. Multiple cars passed but he didn't pay them any mind. But a wide grin appeared on his face when his eyes caught sight of McDonald's golden arches.

White had been cooking lasagna before Jason had stepped out of the apartment to take his evening jog. Jason knew it would taste good. White knew his way around the kitchen. But the churning in Jason's stomach was becoming more intense. If he didn't get something to eat soon, he would be hard pressed to complete another mile.

Jason spotted a disheveled and bearded white man – probably in his early-to-mid-thirties – fumbling with the red lid that covered one of the McDonald's trashcans. The man wore a green, camouflage jacket over a maroon hoodie with the letters D B on the front and faded jeans. Jason assumed he had been in the military, Amy perhaps. He watched as the man removed the lid and laid it to the ground. He then leaned over to pull white paper bags and hamburger boxes from the barrel inside. The man bit into a half-eaten Big Mac that he had removed from one of the paper bags, even as he caught sight of Jason approaching from his right. When Jason stood a few feet away from him, the man looked up, smiled, and then offered Jason a bite. Jason waved him off as he headed toward the restaurant entrance.

Once inside, Jason immediately made his way toward the restroom. A black, teenage girl sat at a booth with two white teenage girls and a white teenage boy. Jason made brief eye contact with the black girl, causing her beaming smile to turn into a frown. Her changed demeanor did not go unnoticed by her white friends. However, Jason was more preoccupied with the picked over meals on the table in front of them.

A half-eaten Quarter Pounder with cheese.

Two chicken nuggets in a box container.

A Filet of Fish sandwich with tartar sauce on its edges.

Enough fries to feed a family of four.

"You know him?" Jason heard one of the white girls whisper after Jason had walked past their table.

"No."

Jason had to pass an elderly, white couple before pushing his way into the men's restroom. He paused in the doorway as he got a whiff of someone's recently flushed dunk. But his eyes lit up when he spotted a white McDonald's cup with a plastic straw protruding from it resting on the left side of the urinal closest to him.

The cup was filled with orange soda and ice. Jason removed the lid to smell it. Concluding that nothing fowl had been done to it, he took a sip even as he used the urinal to relieve himself.

The elderly couple was still in the corner doting over each other when Jason exited the restroom. He loosely held the white cup in his right hand. The teenagers were lined up in front of one of the indoor trashcans, on their way to the parking lot. Jason placed the white cup on the table that they had just relinquished and sat. The trashcan was positioned right where he needed it to be, out of the sight of the store manager and his workers.

A few minutes later, the elderly woman got up and wobbled to the women's restroom. With her husband's back to him, Jason wasted no time walking over to the trashcan. He reached in and pulled out the cartons and bags that the teenagers had just tossed into it. A hasty exit followed.

Grainger Park was but a stone's throw away from the McDonalds. That's where Jason escaped to as the sun continued to set on the horizon. Once there, he sat on top of a picnic table that was about twenty feet from the paved trail. He ate the cold fries first, pulling each of them from the bag and then savoring them as he chewed and swallowed. After all of the fries were gone, he got to work on the Quarter Pounder with cheese followed by the Chicken McNuggets and Filet of Fish sandwich. The remainder of the orange soda, and the ice cubes that kept it cold, completed his meal.

"You him, ain't you?"

Jason craned his head to his right. With nightfall approaching, the lone streetlight randomly flickered on and off. There, sitting under an Oakwood tree, was the trashcan diver that he had encountered moments earlier. The man's hoodie now covered his head.

"What do you mean?" Jason replied, feigning ignorance.

"You that boy who stabbed that man."

"Don't know what you talking about. I know it's hard to believe, but all black people don't look alike."

"That may be true, but the person pictured on that student ID that they been showing all morning on the television sure looks a lot like you."

Jason felt himself grinding his teeth. "Say it is me. You 'bout to turn me in?"

"Nah. How's that gonna help me? But if you keep goin' into restaurants like you're doin', one of these self-righteous motherfuckers might."

Jason threw the wrappers and containers into the McDonald's bag, as well as the now-empty cup. After throwing his trash into one of the nearby barrels, he joined the man under the tree.

"What's your story, dude? Why you out here in this heat, rummaging through trashcans?"

The man seemed to chuckle at Jason's questions. "Old lady kicked me out, about three months ago. Called me a liar and a cheat."

"Are you?"

The man smirked. "Did two tours in Iraq, one in Afghanistan. Hard to be a one-woman man after not getting any loving."

"But why the streets? Don't you have family around here, people who will let you crash at their place?"

"Nope. Just me, myself and I. Hitchhiked my way down from Gate City. Virginia. My old lady didn't like the fact that I was drinking and smoking Crack. Lost the job her father lined up for me down at Eastman. Headed to New Orleans to live with my cousin. His ass is 'bout bad as me, but I know he won't judge me for my bad decisions."

Jason winced at the thought of two addicts living under one roof. He almost felt sorry for the men. He had completed three tours in George W. Slush's Iraq War. In an alternate universe, the man would have been considered a hero. But now that he had taken up civilian life, there was no one out there to catch him when he hit rock bottom.

"What's your name?" Jason asked.

"Dawkins," the man replied, reaching across his body to extend his hand to Jason. "Charlie Dawkins."

Then, while shaking Charlie's outstretched hand, "Jason. Jason Black."

Charlie pulled his knees to his chest. "You'se a big boy, but you don't look like no killer. What happened between you and that security guard?"

Jason drew his bent legs closer as he fought to come up with a reasonable response. He then reached between his legs to pick at the blades of grass.

"I don't know, Charlie. Seems like he just came out of nowhere, to harass me. All I was doing was getting my jog on. But then he pulled his gun on me, told me there was going to be one less nigger tonight. Had no choice really. He was going to kill me."

"I hate that. They be pulling that kind of shit up in Gate City. Racist cops mostly. Think they God's gift to humanity. But they wouldn't have survived a day in Iraq, or Afghanistan. Hell, I probably would have taken them out myself for being so stupid."

"You lose someone over there?"

"Yeah. My boy Malcolm. He got caught up in some friendly fire during a midnight raid on an Al-Qaeda compound up in the mountains. His being black didn't bother me. But it did bother some of those other bastards. Investigation cleared them of any wrongdoing."

"I have a brother serving over there. Name's Jeremiah. He a Marine."

"He must be a bad ass. We Army grunts have nothing but respect for them boys."

Jason smiled at that. But then he saw a beam of light being shone in their direction. He looked over to see Charlie shielding his eyes, as the light rested on him, and him alone. Charlie used his un-illuminated right hand to signal to Jason that it was time for him to go. Jason crawled behind the tree, stumbled toward the bottom of the hill, and, for the second night in a row, found himself sprinting into the night. But he stopped in his tracks as a second officer standing near the bottom of the hill captured him in a beam of light.

"Where do you think you're going?" the second officer asked with his gun pointed at Jason.

Jason immediately raised his hands over his head, but not for long. The far corner of the park was a sea of darkness, so, after stepping to his left and then to his right, he dove into it. As he ferociously pumped his arms, and allowed his long, loping strides to carry him further from the light in a zig-zag pattern, he prayed the officer wasn't one to shoot unarmed suspects in the back. But when he heard three quick shots ring out, he knew this officer had already assumed that he was armed and dangerous simply because he was black.

Thelma St. James had chosen Spelman College over other Historically Black colleges and universities because of her mother. Hilda St. James had attended the all-girls school but dropped out when she was four months pregnant with Thelma. Thelma had wanted to make her mother proud by fulfilling her mother's unfulfilled dream. But Hilda had encouraged her daughter to do it for herself, not for her.

Thelma hadn't been back to Memphis since 1986, the day she gave her mother a long, hearty hug, and then got into her Uncle Otis' car for the six-hour drive to Atlanta. The night before, Thelma and her mother had sat in the back yard talking. Hilda told her daughter to never return to Memphis, at least not until after she had walked across a stage to accept her degree. And during nightly telephone conversations, she encouraged her to steer clear of the "niggas" who just wanted to "hit it and forget it" rather than put a ring on it. Thelma had responded kindly, boldly predicting that she would graduate in three years.

Graduating early had been important to Thelma. She had something to prove. During her first three years of high school, she was more follower than leader. She hung with a group of neighborhood girls that called themselves the Hood Rats. Red was their favorite color for good reason. They were aligned with the Oakville Gangsters, or Ogs, a group of young and old, black thugs that terrorized residents of Southeast Memphis' Oakville area, and self-identified with the Compton, California Bloods.

Many of Oakville's wannabe thugs lived right beside Thelma and her mother, in the Walter Simmons Estates housing development. As a young child, Thelma grew up idolizing these cats. Many of them would roll through the neighborhood in nice cars with spinning rims. Their necks adorned with gold chains, their fingers and wrists expensive jewelry. So, when one of her freshmen classmates, Michelle "Eminem" Mason, told her how the Hood Rats were raking in dough by serving as mules for the Ogs, Thelma wanted in. A mule in this sense is someone who smuggles and hides drugs for OG-affiliated gangsters.

Hilda never knew how connected and involved Thelma was with the Ogs. She also didn't know that, at 15 years of age,

Thelma once had had consensual, unprotected sex with no fewer than ten teenage boys, all OG members, during an all-night orgy and drinking party at BMW dealership owner Brian "B-Smooth" Sampson's ten thousand square foot mansion. Fortunately for her, her mother had taken her down to the clinic a few months prior to get her on the pill. Therefore, the only complication she had from her initiation rite was a yeast infection that was treated immediately and cured. But by letting these boys have their way with her, she opened herself up to these same boys approaching her again for second and third helpings.

Thelma hid and smuggled drugs for her OG brothers for most of her sophomore year (1983-84), a portion of that following summer. She took a job working the cash register at the neighborhood Kroger so her mother wouldn't become overly suspicious of her whereabouts, but, more importantly, how she was earning her money. Having a part-time job became the alibi she needed to discreetly transport cocaine bricks to the next person in the supply chain. The product would ultimately wind up in the hands of the Ogs' number one client group – white Anglo-Saxon Protestant males. But you would have never known this by the way the Shelby County Police Department patrolled the predominantly black Southeast Memphis area.

But her service as an OG mule came to a screeching halt midway through the summer of 1984. The Shelby County Police Department had conducted a targeted sting operation that led to B-Smooth's arrest, as well as several members of his OG drug peddling operation. Fortunately for Thelma, none of the Hood Rats were ever implicated. While the Ogs were driven by their love of money and power, they would die before rolling over on the young women who helped funnel product into the Memphis market. For Thelma, this was a relieving sign. However, it was Hilda St. James who gave Thelma the impetus she needed to exchange her evil ways for more noble causes.

"What's this?" Hilda asked. She held a rolled-up bundle of one hundred dollars bills in her left hand. "You dealing?"

Thelma had been busy completing a homework assignment at the kitchen table. But when she saw her mother holding her cash, she leapt from the chair, snatching the bundle from her mother.

"Why you messing with my stuff, Ma?" she angrily exclaimed. "That's money I saved up from work."

Hilda squinted as the corners of her mouth tightened. "You lying. Gotta be over two thousand dollars in that roll. I know Kroger ain't paying you that good." She sat in one of the side chairs. "Besides, I found it under your mattress when I was changing your sheets. Should be in the bank collecting interest. What's going on, girl?"

After a moment of careful consideration, Thelma spent the next hour and a half telling her mother everything. When she had nothing more to confess, she anxiously awaited what she thought would be an explosive response from her mother.

But Hilda didn't offer one. Instead, she reached across the table and took her daughter's hands into her own. "Thank you."

"For what, Ma?"

"For telling me the truth. Just know it would have broken my heart if you had been caught up in all that mess." She then breathed in deeply. "I still remember that sixth grade paper you wrote, the one you wrote about Wilma Rudolph. It was so good. And I thought you were so smart. Told me then that you were going to college. Not to run track like Wilma, but to become a lawyer. But all that talk ended when you started hanging with that girl. Michelle. You still want to go to college, don't you?"

Thelma shrugged her shoulders before nervously tapping her pencil on the legal pad. "I guess so. But Spelman ain't gonna take me now, Ma. I got a two-point three GPA. I need at least a two five to even be considered."

"Get to work then," Hilda replied, standing. "Become the person God created you to be."

Right then and there, Thelma committed herself to bringing her grades up. D's and F's were replaced with B's and C's, with two or three A's sprinkled in for good measure. Consequently, she graduated from Memphis' Sheffield High School with the two-point five grade point average she needed to be considered for enrollment at most American colleges and universities.

Thelma chose Spelman College in Atlanta over Tennessee State University in Nashville. Her first three months on campus saw her reflecting on her previous associations with the Hood Rats and Oakville Gangsters, how God had shielded her from incrimination. Because she became overly concerned about the dynamics that prevented the vast majority of black Americans from obtaining a semblance of this country's prosperity, she decided to pursue her undergraduate degree in Sociology with a minor in African American Studies. She was once part of the problem. Now, she wanted to be one of the ones devising solutions to these problems.

Even though Thelma did graduate in three years as her class's salutatorian, she knew going to an HBCU had been a risky move. Risky because most employers didn't think an HBCU degree was worth the paper it was printed on. So, when she had a chance meeting with Harvard University Law Professor Reshonda Gates in 1990 – a Spelman graduate herself – at a child abuse prevention conference in Nashville, Tennessee, she had no idea her fortunes were about to change. Professor Gates was one of the nation's most revered legal scholars. More importantly, she was black. When she was a lawyer with the U. S. Department of Justice's Civil Rights Division, and not a Harvard Law School professor, she investigated claims of work-related prejudice, racism and discrimination.

But it was her ties to former United States Supreme Court Justice Thurgood Marshall and Law Professor Derrick Bell that impressed her the most.

Marshall was the chief lawyer in the *Brown vs. Board of Education of Topeka, Kansas* case, where the judges ruled that segregation in public schools is unconstitutional. Bell, on the other hand, won similar civil rights cases, mostly in the Southeastern United States, but obtained prominence for the development of Critical Race Theory. CRT posited that racism is so deeply rooted in the makeup of American society that it has been able to reassert itself after each successive wave of reform aimed at eliminating it. Therefore, many of the progressive lawyers of the day used it to dismantle systemic racism.

As they continued to chat that evening at the bar on the basement level of the Doubletree Hotel, Professor Gates told Thelma about her ties to Justice Marshall, how she clerked for him when he was on the Supreme Court, how she considered him a mentor even. She said he motivated her to excel in school, major in Pre-Law, pass the bar, and then secure employment with the DOJ.

Professor Gates had taken a sip from her martini glass. "How do you want to be remembered?" she had asked. "What do you want engraved on your tombstone?"

Thelma had taken more than a minute to ponder this question. "I don't know," she replied. "I always saw myself just being a social anthropologist, someone who studied the issues that keep black people from progressing. Devise solutions for them. But after I graduated, with a four point oh mind you, the only job I could find was with the Knox County Department of Social Services. Love my job, but I feel as if my skills are under-utilized."

"How so?"

Thelma's left arm fell from the cushioned bar as she spun her barstool toward Professor Gates. "Just don't feel like I'm making much of a difference. Yes, I'm completing CPS investigations that send mean-spirited parents to jail, but I always envisioned myself doing more. Hell, I was born in 1968, on March 20, fifteen days before Dr. King was assassinated. I didn't fully understand the significance of this date when I was in high school. I was too busy running, with the wrong crowd. But I did at Spelman. My black professors there reminded us that we are the Black Diaspora's Talented Tenth, and we are obligated to use our skill sets to force America to do right by its black citizens."

Professor Gates had smirked before tucking one of her misplaced braids behind her ear. "And those professors were right. We all share that obligation. The question you must answer for yourself is how do you get there? More importantly, though, you need to know what you want your contribution to be. Will it be blatant, in your face, or subtle, more behind the scenes?"

The white, clean-cut bartender had interrupted their conversation, placing another martini on the bar in front of Professor Gates. He used his eyes to measure Thelma's desire for another gin and tonic. Thelma had shaken her head no. He had given her a thumbs-up as he turned to check on the other patrons seated around the oval-shaped bar.

"You should apply to Harvard, our law school. I don't know what it is, but I'm getting a positive vibe from you. The way you carry yourself, present yourself to others and me. It's a very charismatic vibe. You would make a great defense attorney."

Thelma had mulled over that last sentence. At the time, she didn't know what that meant, but it became much clearer once she started pursuing her law degree at Harvard under Professor Gates' tutelage and mentorship. By the time she graduated from Harvard with her Juris Doctorate degree in 1995, and ultimately passed the Massachusetts state bar examination, she knew she was wholly committed to defending the rights of black Americans who had been wrongfully accused of crimes.

But it was Thelma's apprenticeship with the Thurgood Marshall Law Group's School for Racial and Economic Justice, while she pursued her jurisprudence degree, that solidified this commitment.

As an apprentice, Thelma had to attend several workshops, seminars and retreats that were mostly held throughout the year on the campuses of historically black colleges and universities like Howard University, Morehouse College, Spelman College, Tuskegee University, Jackson State University and Morgan State University. Many of the sessions were facilitated by MLG's three founding principals – Professor Gates, Morehouse's Kelvin Cochran and Columbia's Malcolm King – but other black law professors and black SREJ graduates also served on the faculty, freely sharing their informed insights.

The most intimate exchanges between SREJ faculty and students occurred between meetings, at the Great Smokey Mountain retreats. Thelma had learned that MLG's principals purchased land near the foothills of the Chimney Top mountains, and then proceeded to develop and operate the black owned and operated Sojourner Vista Mountain Resort and Conference Center. The resort was open to the public throughout the calendar year, but one week in the months of February, June and November were literally designated as Blackout weeks, as they were used as set asides for SREJ workshops, seminars and conferences. The luxurious rooms, about 150 units, would be occupied by a predominantly black assortment of lawyers, intellectuals, and students (as well as their diverse group of allies) for the purpose of researching and discussing the underpinnings of systemic racism while simultaneously developing practical strategies for its eradication. Thelma used the time they had between sessions to network with faculty members and her fellow SREJ cohort. Developing authentic relationships with other like-minded individuals was what the MLG principals wanted, and Thelma wasn't one to disappoint.

But she grimaced hard after reading the *Knoxville News-Sentinels'* front page story. Fort Sanders security guard Roscoe Baker was reportedly stabbed with a sling blade knife during an altercation with UT sprinter Jason Black. Baker was in critical condition at Fort Sanders Medical Center after being taken there by ambulance. Black had yet to be apprehended by the police.

Thelma read the story while seated behind her desk in her law practice's Downtown Knoxville office, which overlooked the Tennessee River to the left, Neyland Stadium to the right. Even as she read the story, Thelma knew Tennessee's *Stand Your Ground* legislation would come into play by the case's white victim.

A sinking feeling consumed Thelma. The recently passed legislation benefited more Whites than Blacks. Consequently, if she happened to be the lawyer representing Jason, she would have a difficult time convincing what would undoubtedly be a majority-white jury that Baker was the aggressor. However, she had high hopes that this sentiment would change once she had a chance to hear Jason's side of the story.

But she wondered if even that would be enough. She recounted the cases of recent black victims who weren't allowed to tell their sides of the story – Eric Garner in New York, John Crawford III, Tanisha Anderson and Tamir Rice in Ohio, Michael Brown, Jr. in Missouri, and Walter Scott in South Carolina. All of these black victims were unarmed during their fatal shootings. Jason Black was armed with a sling blade knife. Consequently, it would come down to who the sitting jury determined was within his legal right to stand his ground.

Thelma knew Jason's case would be a heavy lift for the Marshall Law Group, but win or lose, it was also one that could best inform the American public about the improprieties within the criminal justice system. In most, if not all, of the cases, all of the defendants were protected by qualified immunity, which protects law enforcement officers, as well as other government employees, from being sued for violating a person's constitutional rights, unless those rights were "clearly established. The Tamir Rice case was the lone exception, as the acquitted murderer was a security guard like Baker. But because Jason was still alive to testify against him, the sitting jury's racism and prejudice would be on full display, especially if its racial/ethnic makeup did not reflect Knox County's racial/ethnic makeup, and they didn't exonerate Jason Black of the levied charges.

But what troubled Thelma the most is she knew the kid, or at least his father, Jerome Black. As she studied the black and white newspaper headshot of Jason dressed in his UT singlet, she couldn't get over the fact that he was the spitting image of his father.

Thelma knew Jerome Black to be one of the National Association for the Advancement of Colored People's most respected and revered defense attorneys. And when he was among the living, he served as an SREJ faculty member, offering strategies that lawyers use when representing black and brown defendants. So, when she and members of her SREJ class were told seventeen years ago, in 1998, that he had been shot dead in East Raleigh, they questioned the validity of the police reports.

These suspicious reports said Jerome Black was caught between the crossfire of two rival black gangs, the Bloods and the Crips. While facsimiles of these gangs existed in Raleigh, North Carolina, their members were not prone to displaying this level of violence. Even back then, Thelma knew something more nefarious was afoot. However, because of her young age, she was

25 at the time, she was not in a position to conduct an independent investigation of the matter. She had hoped that one of the MLG founders would look into it. But how could they? They were too busy prosecuting cases against rogue police officers and defending wrongfully convicted black and brown defendants.

Swallowing hard, Thelma folded and placed the newspaper on her desk before turning her chair slightly to the right to peer out at the boats floating along the Tennessee River.

CHAPTER EIGHT

Trish shut the trunk to her Volvo sedan as Angelica claimed her spot in the passenger's seat. She could tell Angelica appreciated the invitation to accompany her on her weekend trip to Atlanta. Sister-girl couldn't stop smiling. Angelica had told Trish two days before their scheduled trip that she was looking forward to meeting her parents, as well as Trish's 16-year-old sister Rayvyn. It would have been even sweeter if Mitch had flown in from California. When she met him at the 2015 nationals, before she even knew who Trish Newman was, she couldn't take her eyes off of him. Every member of Trish's family was a mix of light-skinned beauties and cuties.

"Gotta beat this rush-hour traffic," Trish exclaimed as she steered the sedan onto Andy Holt Boulevard. "Mama gets to worrying when I drive at night. She's looking forward to finally meeting you. Hates that she didn't get a chance to come up with Daddy, meet you then."

"Labor Day weekend, girl," Angelica replied. "Ain't nothing going on around here."

"Thought you may want to work some extra shifts or something, earn a few extra bucks."

"I wish. You can believe what you want to believe, but Labor Day weekend is one of our slowest weekends of the year."

Trish pulled the sedan onto Papermill Drive, steering it onto Interstate 40 for the four-and-a-half-hour drive to Atlanta. Angelica didn't get much sleep. She arrived back at their Andy Holt apartment around four a.m. Consequently, all Angelica had time to do was close her eyes for about an hour before waking up at five thirty to throw a few outfits into a small suitcase, apply soap and water to her underarms and coochie, throw on a blouse and a pair of Capris, and claim her seat.

Trish had told her the night before that she wanted to be on the road before six to avoid the holiday rush out of Knoxville. But as Trish's grip tightened around the steering wheel, she had the sinking feeling that Angelica wasn't being completely honest with her. Something else was up, and she would use this trip to pry the truth out of her.

"Did you hear about Jason?" Trish asked, briefly taking her eyes off the road to glance over at Angelica. Angelica leaned her head and body against the passenger-side door, a clear indication that her intent was to get a few more hours of sleep.

"No. What happened?"

"White says he's on the run. Jason called him. Said some white security guard pulled a gun on him. Threatened to kill him. Jason stabbed him with that knife of his. The one he's always playing with on the plaza."

"Jason wouldn't just stab someone for no reason. It had to be in self-defense."

"You would hope. All they kept saying on the news last night is he's wanted for questioning."

"But you and I both know what that means."

They said it together. "Guilty."

Then, Angelica asked, "Why do they do that?"

"What?"

"Charge and convict our black men before hearing their side of the story."

"Don't know, girl. I just hope they give him a chance to turn himself in. No need to turn him into another Oscar Grant."

Oscar Grant III was a young, black male who was shot once in the back in 2009 by a white San Francisco Bay Area Rapid Transit police officer in Oakland's Fruitvale subway station. Grant was reportedly unarmed. After this incident, black Americans across the nation were in an uproar, asserting that the white police officer executed Oscar not for being belligerent but for being black. After the shooting, peaceful and violent demonstrations ensued. However, the Bay Area judicial system was slow to indict the BART officer, who claims his intention was to taser Grant, not shoot him dead.

It was late morning when Jason stepped up on the curb and walked up the hill toward the Interstate 77 truck stop. As he straddled the edge of the asphalt road, an eighteen-wheeler slowly rolled along beside him, to his left. The male driver steered the truck further left, toward the diesel gas pumps situated toward the rear of the platform. The drivers of other cars and trucks either approached or abandoned the other pumps that surrounded the tiny building that housed a Subway restaurant and mini mart. As the bubbling sensation in his stomach intensified, Jason found himself reminiscing about those times in grade school when he and his friends would get the truckers to honk their horns with nothing more than simple hand gestures.

"Give me fifty on pump number three," Jason heard a bearded, black man say to the white woman working the cash register as he stepped into the mini mart. Other customers stood in line behind him, patiently waiting to pay the piper for their purchased goods. But as Jason made his way toward the back of the mini mart, toward the refrigerated drinks, his biggest concern was not being noticed by the white woman working the register, or the overweight security guard standing to her left, near the entry door.

Jason's sweatshirt had been tied around his waist for more than an hour. The Southern heat and humidity caused sweat to boil up from his pores to drench his tagless t-shirt. Jason knew the stench from his body was unbearable to the people that had exited the mini mart as he had entered. As he walked down the aisle, he made a note to wash up in the bathroom at his next stop.

Jason scanned the refrigerated drinks. To the left were the beers, the right juices. In the middle were the Gatorades and sodas.

Jason reached inside for a Gatorade. He then made a beeline to the restroom in the back of the mini mart. Once inside, he twisted the cap off and drank all of it with big gulps. In less than a minute, he found himself wiping his wet mouth with the back of his hand.

But when he exited the restroom, the same security guard that had been standing by the door was waiting on him.

"Sir," the security guard began, his thumbs resting along the top edges of his black belt. "You can pay for your drink at the counter over there."

Jason's eyes shifted from the security guard to the exiting doors to his right and back again. The inner tube of flesh around the security guard's waist eased concerns about him being taken by force. But Jason also knew a full-blown confrontation would tip off local law enforcement.

Jason's eyes darted to the white woman at the cash register. A smirk on her face, she waved him to her, even as she rung up the lone customer in line. The security guard swooped in be-hind Jason as he walked to the counter down the middle aisle.

A double chime rang as someone entered the mini mart from Jason's left.

"J?" the mini-mart's newest patron exclaimed.

Jason turned toward the voice. He then found himself smil-ing at the sight of Angelica walking toward him, red purse dan-gling from a strap across her bosom and shoulder.

"What's going on, girl?" Jason replied, extending his arms to-ward Angelica for the ensuing embrace. He had made a point not to utter her name. With the cameras rolling, he didn't want to make it easier for the authorities to identify his ready-made accomplice.

Jason continued, "I was just about to pay for a drink, but I just remembered, I left my wallet in the car. Think you can help a brother out?"

The lone patron brushed past them to exit.

"Sure," Angelica replied, nervously sliding her hand along the purse strap. "No problem. Just let me get what I came in here for."

Minutes later, the woman working the cash register watched as Angelica phished a twenty-dollar bill from her purse and placed it on the counter. With assurances that payment would be made, the security guard returned to his post. Jason could tell the woman on the cash register still had her apprehensions. But these apprehensions didn't stop her from swiping the bill up, pulling Angelica's change from the register drawer, and then slapping it on the counter.

"Thank you," Angelica said, collecting her bagged purchases.

Head held low, Jason bit into a Snickers candy bar and then followed Angelica past the security guard and out the exit door.

Trish sat in the driver's seat scrolling through email messages on her smart phone when Angelica tapped the passenger side window, bidding Trish to unlock the doors. After opening the passenger side door, Angelica reached in to tilt her seat forward. Trish's eyes widened when Jason appeared outside the opened door.

"Hey, Trish," he exclaimed. "How you been?"

Trish fixed a nervous gaze on Angelica, as if to say we can't be seen with this fool. But then her attention shifted back to Jason. Relenting, she replied, "Fine. You?"

"Tired. Hungry."

"Where you headed?"

"Anywhere but here. Could sure use a ride."

"Did you do it? Did you stab that white man?"

"Yep. Self-defense."

Her lips turned up at that. "Get in."

CHAPTER NINE

Coach Moses scurried toward the stone-brick entrance to Dr. Carson Meeks' elaborate mansion of stone, mortar and wood. As he ducked under the ornate stone archway, he took one final look at the full moon, and then stepped up on the concrete landing. While he always felt comfortable when he visited this part of Santa Barbara, California, he also knew his dark complexion made him an easy mark for the local patrol cops.

He did his best to stay within the required speed limit. He didn't want to give them cause for pulling him over. But multiple trips to Santa Barbara had made him more vigilant, more purposeful. Dr. Meeks' associates at Gerimetric Pharmaceuticals developed and supplied the goods he needed to keep his speed and strength factory in business.

Dr. Meeks and three of his Stanford Medical School class-mates had concocted the Yellow Jacket formula in the garage of a house they were renting in Arlington, Massachusetts. At the time, they had no idea how their magic pill would be used to enhance athletic performance. Initially, their mission was right-eous. All they wanted to do was create a vitamin that helped elderly patients enhance their mental sharpness and physical prowess. Never in their wildest dreams did they think the then unnamed drug could be used to turn gifted athletes into lower case gods.

The door swung open, and Coach Moses found himself star-ing into the eyes of Dr. Meeks' longtime maid, Rosalina Hernandez.

"Hello, Mr. Moses," she greeted with a wry smile as Coach Moses walked past her to enter the house. "Great seeing you again, sir. How is your wife, and little Franklin?"

"I wouldn't know. Nakema left me about two months ago. Moved back to Arlington, Texas. Took the boy with her. To be closer to her parents.

"So sorry to hear that." She extended her arm toward the far hallway as she shut the door behind Coach Moses. "He's up-stairs, in his study." Then, while walking away, "Have a good day."

"Thank you, Rosalina. You do the same."

Coach Moses had visited Dr. Meeks' sprawling estate over a hundred times during the ten years they had been in business together. His first visit there had been somewhat upbeat. Dr. Meeks had instructed his Italian butler Renaldo to give Coach Moses a tour of the mansion and the grounds surrounding it before escorting him to the guest room for the first of many two-night stays there. Coach Moses had been told over the telephone by the man known only as The Broker that Dr. Meeks was the chiropractor to the stars, but even that didn't prepare him for the level of prosperity that Dr. Meeks' side business afforded him.

Dr. Meeks was seated behind a mahogany desk, leaning forward, typing notes into his MacBook Pro, when Moses appeared in the doorway. His bi-focal glasses rested near the tip of his nose as he looked up.

"Moses, my friend," Dr. Meeks greeted, sitting upright. "Come in. Have a seat."

Coach Moses was already headed to the seating area to the right of Dr. Meeks' desk. That's where most of their previous conversations had occurred. However, this time Coach Moses sat on the love seat, the one running parallel to the right wall. He knew Dr. Meeks preferred sitting in the chair closest to his desk. He wasn't the type of person to have his back facing the door, even in his own house.

Still typing, Dr. Meeks asked, "How was the drive up from LA?"

"Longer than usual," Coach Moses replied. "But I managed."

Dr. Meeks head snapped to Coach Moses as he removed his fingers from the keyboard. He could sense that Coach Moses was not in the best of moods.

"So, the athlete you were so excited about is trying to develop a conscience, huh?"

"That, sir, would be an understatement."

"Tell me again what you saw in him. I thought his dream was to be an Olympic sprint champion."

"It is. But like the others, he wants to do it on his own terms, without his Flintstone vitamins. But you and I both know how that story ends. We all end up losing."

"And you fear this will be the straw that breaks the camel's back?"

"Yes, sir. I do. Still recovering from the last IAAF investigation. I should have seen this coming, though. Boy was fickle, skittish even, when we were trying to get him through that first batch."

Dr. Meeks stood, walked over to the bookcase on the far side of the room. He tilted one of the books forward, causing the multi-level bookcase to slide away to expose the walk-in closet behind it.

"Human behavior is hard to predict, my friend," he began before disappearing into the unlit closet. Coach Moses watched as the light inside flickered on then off. Seconds later, Dr. Meeks reappeared, carrying a medium-sized box. "But we know that every man can be bought, especially if the price is right."

Dr. Meeks placed the box on the coffee table, and then sat in the recliner across from Coach Moses. "You misread him. We all make mistakes. But like you told me before, he's driven by his desire to please his father. That is his Achilles heel, the weapon you can use against him."

Coach Moses' brow tightened. "So, you think that will motivate him to work the program?"

"Maybe. Maybe not. But I just read a blurb in *Fast Company,* that Cornelius Newman's record label was almost on the verge of collapse before that guilty verdict.

Dr. Meeks was referring to the trial of Tribe's chart-topping rap artist Xavier Charles, the X Man. Charles reportedly was cheating on his wife with a woman named Adele Evans. This news broke his wife's heart, and the fact that they had twin girls complicated things. However, when his wife was found dead from a single gunshot wound to the head in their suburban Atlanta home, Xavier Charles became the prime suspect in her murder. The X Man trial was major news. He was pronounced guilty, receiving a life sentence for murder, even though no fingerprints were found on the murder weapon.

Dr. Meeks continued, "Mitch knows what kind of pressure his father was under during the X Man Trial. He doesn't want to say or do anything to add more stress to Cornelius' already stress-ful life." Dr. Meeks patted the side of the box, which was filled with 100 16-ounce bottles of the Yellow Jacket vitamin. "Invite him to dinner. Have a heart-to-heart with him. After that, ask him...ask him how his father would feel if he learned about his...his little secret."

"She there yet?" Mitch spoke into the telephone's receiver from the edge of the waterbed. He lay on his side on the bed in the bedroom of his two-bedroom condominium apartment. The sound of the shower running could be heard from the bathroom to his left.

"No, she's not," replied the voice of his mother, Carmelita Newman. "She called about an hour ago, before they left Knoxville, then about fifteen minutes ago, saying something came up. Not going to get here until the morning."

Mitch still cared about Trish, even though their relationship had become tenuous in the months leading up to his high school graduation.

Trish had told her big brother that Perry Greg had raped her. Mitch didn't want to believe her. Even though Perry was one grade behind him, one year ahead of Trish, he had been one of his best friends since elementary school.

Trish and Perry had just left a late night showing of Terri Tyler's 2010 film *Why Did I Marry You?* They had been dating for three months, and Trish had yet to give Perry any. But that night, Perry wasn't buying Trish's claim that she was saving herself for marriage. Her kisses before, during, and after the movie were too passionate, intended to create a rise in his loins. He just knew she wanted him. So, after the movie, when he walked over to the soda fountain to refresh their drinks, he added something special - a Mickey - to hers. As the night wore on, her weakened mind and body made it virtually impossible for her to resist his advances.

Mitch did get up in Perry's grill after learning more about Trish's sickness a few days after their date. Mitch suspected that Perry had been up to no good. If he wasn't, why would he break up with his sister two days after the alleged rape occurred? They had been virtually inseparable since Trish's freshman year. It warmed Trish's heart to see her brother standing up for her. But she wanted him to do more than just stand up for her. She wanted Mitch to do something she couldn't do, which was pound Perry's face into a bloody pulp.

But he didn't.

And because he didn't, Trish allowed him to fly to Gainesville, Florida, to begin his new life as a student-athlete at the University of Florida, knowing she resented him.

"Well, when you see her, tell her I said hello." Mitch swallowed hard. "How's he doing?"

"Good. Just feels betrayed. He put his company's reputation on the line for that boy, only to find out he was lying the whole time."

"That's just how Pops is, Ma. Always giving people the benefit of the doubt. He home?"

The sound of dripping water stopped. Mitch looked up to see Yasmin stepping out of the stand-up shower, and onto the small area rug outside of it, to dab her face, neck and breasts with a towel. When she sensed Mitch staring at her from the bedroom, she turned to her right, sticking her tongue out at him.

"Why you asking questions you already know the answer to, boy?" his mother replied with a chuckle.

"Oh, yeah. We are talking about Pops." Mitch smiled as he soaked in his mother's chuckles, and Yasmin's toned, naked body.

"How you adjusting to that California weather?"

"As well as can be expected. Was a hundred and three degrees the other day."

"What's your indoor schedule look like?"

"Millrose Games at Madison Square Garden. Eastman Relays at East Tennessee State. Thinking about renting a car and driving down that weekend. From Johnson City, it's only a five-and half-hour drive."

"Now, you know that's too many hours on the road. Just take one of them crop dusters out of the McGhee-Tyson Airport? Be here in a little over an hour. Would give you more time to spend with your family."

Mitch could hear the desperation in his mother's voice. She craved the company of anyone with a mouth. With Trish just up the road in Knoxville, and he an American Airlines flight away in Los Angeles, he knew most of his father's time was being spent in the studio, or connecting with new talent in places like New York, Chicago, DC and Miami. Mitch knew his father was paying scant attention their marital relationship.

Earlier in the year, Cornelius Newman had even flown over to Los Angeles to wine and dine Latoya Lawson and a slate of other promising singers competing on the hit NBC television show *American Popstar*. The plan was for the two of them to get together, but too many meetings with prominent singers and music executives made it necessary for them to put it off until next time. But with Coach Moses pressuring him to take his vitamins, the less time he spent with his father the better. His father already suspected that he was juicing. He didn't have the nerve to look his father in the eyes knowing his fast times were equivalent to desert mirages.

"It would have been great to see you and your sister here together. Y'all need to talk. She only has one brother, you one sister. Need to let bygones be bygones."

"I wish it were that easy, Ma. I really do. I should have done more. I knew Perry was no good, but I gave him a pass. Yeah. He used to be my boy, and, at the time, I wanted to keep it that way."

"Saw his mother the other day at the mall. She asked about you."

"What'd you tell her?"

"That you over in California training...to become an Olympic sprint champion."

"Did you ask about Perry?"

"No. Didn't want to add salt to her wounds. But you do know the boy's in prison, don't you?"

"No. I didn't. I was jabbing my finger in his face the last time I saw him. What'd he do?"

"Dealing drugs. Paper said he was part of some Georgia Tech drug ring."

Mitch shook his head at that, as Yasmin sashayed naked across the room, seductively bending over at the waist to pull a pair of red lace panties from the dresser drawer.

"Hey, I gotta go. Tell Trish I asked about her. Okay?"

Yasmin licked her lips, her eyes now locked on her prey. She pushed her panties away from her puckering privates and down her long legs. A once reserved smile possessed Mitch's face as he watched her exit the bedroom.

"Should I tell your little sister that you love her too?" his mother asked.

Yasmin returned holding a glass of water in one hand, two Yellow Jacket vitamins in the other. Her exposed breasts heaved up and down as she plopped onto Mitch's lap, inches from Mitch's face. She then straddled his thighs while motioning for him to open up. Mouth open, Mitch used his free hand to squeeze Yasmin's toned buttocks.

Yasmin pushed the capsules into his mouth and then held the glass up to Mitch's lips for him to drink.

Mitch allowed the water and capsules to swirl in his mouth before swallowing hard.

"Yeah," he replied. "Tell her...tell her I love her."

Carmelita Newman placed the plate of steaming, buttered pancakes in the center of the dining room table, alongside the smoked sausages, eggs, orange juice and milk. She had hoped that Trish would come downstairs to at least set the table, but she didn't. She surmised that her daughter was probably worn out from the four and a half-hour drive down from Knoxville. This brunch would allow them to catch up. But as she turned away from the table and made her way back to the kitchen, she was greeted by an approaching Trish, Angelica...and Jason.

"Morning, Ma," Trish greeted, trying her best not to laugh at the wide-eyed expression on her mother's face. But Mrs. Newman ignored her.

"This the boy they looking for, isn't it?

"Yes. It is."

Jason extended his hand to her. "Good morning, Mrs. Newman." Mrs. Newman loosely gripped Jason's extended hand. "You probably don't remember, but we met once before, at last month's nationals."

Trish interjected. "He the guy that finished second."

"I remember him," Mrs. Newman exclaimed, her hands going to her hips. "Recognized his name when I heard it on the news. But he running from the law, for stabbing a man, Patricia. Your father don't need this right now."

Angelica moved from behind Trish to step in front of her. "Hi." She offered her hand. "I'm Angelica. Trish's roommate." Mrs. Newman shook Angelica's hand and released it, her gaze momentarily leaving Jason to let Angelica know she wasn't being dismissive of her.

"I should have known you was up to no good when you said you were checking into a hotel. Who checks into a hotel three hours from home? Your daddy's not going to like this, not after all the stress he went through trying to defend Xavier."

An awkward pause, causing Trish to shift her weight from her left foot to the right. Both Jason and Angelica nervously awaited Mrs. Newman's response, verdict really. Trish felt relieved when her mother extended her arm toward the dining room.

"You all go on in there and get you something to eat. Cornelius' flight arrives tomorrow, around noon. We'll discuss this more when he gets home." Then, as Angelica walked past her, behind Jason, she added with a tap to Angelica's shoulder, "Don't mind me, child. Trish done told me all about you. Thank you for being such a good friend and roommate to my baby."

"Maaaaa!" Trish howled.

"Well, you are. Always will be. Don't care how old you are."

"But Rayvyn is younger than me." She turned toward the long hallway. "Where is she anyway?"

"Work. Child has her orientation this morning. Just got a job down at the Buckhead Mall, at the Gap."

"Good for her. But with her looks, she should be thinking about becoming a fashion model."

"What's your major, Jason?" Mrs. Newman asked.

Jason laid his fork back on his porcelain plate and his head slowly tilted up.

"Business," Jason replied, "with a minor in Political Science."

Angelica interjected, "He's probably going to be one of those talking heads on MSNBC, Mrs. Newman. Explaining how...how someone like Malcolm Stillwell can run for public office."

Jason let out a muffled chuckle. Long before his altercation with Baker, Angelica and he had shared their hopes and dreams about their respective futures. During an encounter with her at Circle Park, which was in front of the building that housed the College of Communications, and the financial aid and Bursar's offices, he uttered his "first" comment with an air of cockiness. After that, Angelica was through, blushing, looking up at him with a silly grin on her face, ultimately allowing him, for the first time later that day, to have his way with her in the bedroom of his Shelbourne Towers apartment.

"Well, yeah. That's true. And I will. I'm in my last year, last semester really. But my focus is on getting ready for trials, the Rio Games."

Jason watched as Mrs. Newman grimaced. "Not going to happen, chile'. Not with the law breathing down your back."

"Yes, ma'am. I know. That's why I'm ready to turn myself in. Answer for what I did."

A stern expression on Mrs. Newman's face followed. "Right or wrong, you gotta stop running. It's only gonna make things worse for you. Believe me. You don't need that, not when you got all these hopes, these dreams." She paused to use her fork and knife to cut off a piece of pancake and insert it in her mouth. Then, as she chewed, she continued, "They say they want to serve and protect, but when it comes to black men like you, they often shoot first, ask questions later. But if you're innocent like you say you are, the truth will come out."

"I hear you, and I respect what you're saying. But the thought of spending one second in jail makes me cringe." Jason wiped his mouth with his linen napkin before placing his elbows on the table and leaning in. "Have you heard anything, about how he's doing? They didn't say anything about his condition last night on any of the local stations up in Chattanooga. Hope he's alright."

"Last I heard," Mrs. Newman replied, "his condition is stable. Which is good, but that doesn't mean he's out of the woods yet. They say you just missed hitting a major artery. He lost a lot of blood. What were you thinking, chile'?"

Leaning back in his chair, Jason looked down and away. The heat emanating from the three women's eyes was intense, as they awaited his response, Mrs. Newman with her arms crossed. And as he sat there, trying to come up with one, he shuddered as images from that horrific night flooded his brain.

"Living," he replied. "That's all. I just wanted to live."

Jason exited the Newman's pool house holding a steaming mug of coffee. As he walked barefoot toward the gazebo, wearing one of Mitch's old Florida Gator t-shirts (a blue one) and orange shorts, the sun could clearly be seen rising on the eastern horizon. Jason maneuvered up the five steps to the left of the gazebo to sit on one of the cushioned, circular benches lining the railing. He drew the coffee mug to his lips and sipped.

Today would be a good day.

"You up early."

It was Trish, walking toward him from the pool deck. She was dressed in a pair of black boxing shorts (with the word Pink written in pink on the back) and a white sports bra. Jason's tongue swiped at his lips at the sight of Trish's nipples pressing through the bra's fabric.

Jason sat up straight, placing the porcelain mug on the square top of the end table to his right. Trish claimed a seat on the bench a few feet down from him.

"Had a hard time sleeping."

"Scared?"

"That would be an understatement. Terrified is more like it."

"Why? You're here, not there. And you're free. That's what you want, isn't it?"

"No doubt." But then, through quivering lips, "What I really want is for all of this to be over. It's like I'm living a nightmare. And I wasn't the one in the wrong."

Trish moved closer, first placing her left hand on his thigh while draping her right arm across his broad shoulders. Her heart skipped a beat as the expression on Jason's face let her know that his pain was real, that it ran deep. Moving closer still, she used her left hand to caress his face. When he didn't pull away, she leaned in to apply multiple kisses to his cheek before doing the same to his pouty lips.

Their mouths opened freely, their tongues entering, exiting, the other's mouth, somewhat subdued at first, but escalating as their animal instincts started to take over. Soon, Trish found herself French-kissing Jason while straddling his lap. Even before she started grinding her pelvis against his crotch, the bulge in Jason's shorts let her know he was ready for what she was more than willing to give him. So, when she reached between her legs to push her boxers and panties aside, and Jason simultaneously lowered the front of his shorts, his fully erect penis slid effortlessly into her vagina.

The thickness and length of it surprised Trish at first, causing her to let out a muffled yelp when he entered her. After that, each downward thrust caused her vaginal lips to swell around it, and she grunted each time the crown bumped against the bottom.

Two and a half minutes later, the grimace on Jason's face let Trish know the once imminent explosion was upon them. That's when the downward rocking of her pelvis became steadier, more forceful, more deliberate even. And even though she was directing Jason's thrusts toward her G spot, she knew he would go limp long before she could get hers. And she was alright with that. This was her gift to him, a moment of pleasure to ease his pain before the full brunt of his personal storm bore down on him.

Jason's eyes opened. A stream of sweat rolled across his cheek onto the tip of his nose. His right hand swiped at his boxers, the other the sweat on his brow. He rolled over until he was lying on his right side. Through the pool house's horizontal blinds, he could see the window to Trish's upstairs bedroom.

His dream had felt so real.

CHAPTER TEN

Daddy's home," Trish exclaimed, getting up from the sofa. All of the girls – Trish, Angelica and Rayvyn – had been sitting around the wooden coffee table on the carpeted living room floor playing Spades. Jason had been dealt in as well, being teamed up with Rayvyn, who sat across from him on the floor with a knowing grin on her face. But he preferred handling his business from the sofa.

It was well past two. Cornelius Newman's flight had been delayed. He was scheduled to land at Atlanta's Hartsfield International Airport at 10:45 a.m. But due to inclement weather approaching from the west, his flight didn't leave Chicago until 11:50 a.m.

Trish was the first to stand and then walk toward the spiral staircase leading to the downstair foyer. She glanced over at Jason long enough to note the changes in his facial expression and body language.

Chuckling, Rayvyn placed her cards face down on the table. "Don't sweat it, dude," Rayvyn reassured him. "Daddy's a big, ole' softy. Yeah, he's a hard man to please sometime, but if you explain things the way you explained them to us, he'll come around. Besides, Mama done told him about you being here. Probably done told Mitch as well. The fact you're still here is a sign they're all right with it."

"What's up, Old Man?" Trish greeted her father during her descent down the stairwell. Mr. Newman had been standing in the foyer, responding to a text on his smart phone. When he saw his daughter approaching from on high, the glum expression on his face melted away, being replaced with a more gleeful one.

Mr. Newman slipped his phone back into the leather briefcase's side pocket. "You, baby girl," he replied, dropping his briefcase onto the hardwood flooring. He then hugged Trish, even as she wrapped her arms around his torso. He applied a kiss to the top of her head before breaking free to draw back and look her over.

"Glad to see they're feeding you well up there in Big Orange Country." He then reached over to squeeze her left triceps muscle, which Trish flexed in an attempt to impress him. "Damn, girl," he exclaimed, squeezing. "They done got you lifting weights too."

During this exchange, Rayvyn bounced down the spiral staircase followed by Angelica and a sheepish Jason.

"She still ain't got nothing on me, though," Rayvyn proclaimed, walking over to greet their father. Mr. Newman pulled his youngest child to him, applied a kiss to the top of her head. But as he peered up, over the top of Rayvyn's head, he spotted Jason standing above him, along the stairwell railing.

Trish, who now stood to her father's right, introduced Angelica first. Mr. Newman shook Angelica's hand, a smile on his face the whole time, but one could tell he was still preoccupied with Jason, who had finally summoned enough courage to walk all the way down the stairs. "And this is Jason," Trish said.

"Glad to see you again, sir," Jason said as he shook the older man's hand.

Mrs. Newman entered the foyer before her husband could say what he wanted to say. The two made eye contact, and Jason knew volumes were being spoken between them without a word being uttered.

"It's good seeing you too, Jason," Mr. Newman replied, hands at his sides. "I do need to know what you done got yourself into, though. You and Mitch have a date with destiny. America's best bets for medals next year. You don't need this kind of drama right now. Not with the Jamaicans lighting it up.

Mr. Newman was right. While Mitch and he finished the 2014-2015 outdoor season with two of the world's top five 100-meter dash times, the Jamaicans had three sprinters under 9.90. Again, Mitch was the world's top sprinter at 9.68, making him the favorite for gold at the 2016 Rio Summer Olympic Games, but Jamaican Nigel Grimes was only a half step back at 9.70. But more about that later.

"No doubt. I've heard what they been saying about me on the news. None of it is true. I'm innocent. Just stood my ground. Defending myself. Didn't do nothing wrong."

Mr. Newman waved his hand a few inches from Jason's face. "Slow your roll, son. We'll talk. Just give me a minute."

With that, he collected his briefcase and retreated to the upstairs master bedroom with his wife in tow.

"I told you," Trish tried to reassure him. Rayvyn seconded this motion by slapping Jason on his buttocks before racing off to her room.

Jason sighed, relieved that he had stared into the eyes of a lion and survived. His banishment to the streets had been delayed, if only for another day or two. But he couldn't shake the regret that he was feeling. The Newmans represented the kind of black family he only became familiar with from watching reruns of *The Hugh Crosby Show*. He now found himself questioning his decision to get into Trish's car, for he knew his very presence would place her and her family at great risk.

But a false narrative was being floated about him, one that cast him as a black fugitive who was armed and dangerous. The fact that his chosen weapon had been a sling blade knife, not a firearm, was being omitted during the telling of his story. This way, when the cops rolled up on him, they would be free to shoot first, ask questions later. And if they were lucky, the judge would give them a pass for just doing their job in a lawful manner.

Jason opened the screen door from the pool deck to step inside the enclosed patio. Dressed in one of Mitch's old Florida Gator sweatshirts and black Under Armor sweatpants, he wiped the sweat from his brow as the late summer heat beamed down on him. Mr. Newman was seated at the glass-topped table, already eating the meal that his wife had prepared for them.

"The plates are over there on the bar," Mr. Newman exclaimed. "Go ahead and get you something to eat."

Jason did as he was told and then joined Mr. Newman at the table. At its center, in separate Pyrex dishes, were smothered pork chops, a sweet potato casserole, corn on the cob, greens, and yeast rolls. Jason had high hopes this would not be his last supper.

"They say you're innocent," Mr. Newman began, "that you were defending yourself. That's what they say. But why should I believe them?"

"Because I'm not like that," Jason replied. "I'm not a liar."

Jason used his knife to shave off a piece of his pork chop, which was smothered in white gravy.

Mr. Newman continued. "I trust my daughter's judgment. She can read a person like a book. Has a natural gift for discernment. Been that way since grade school. If she says you're innocent, then that's it. You're innocent. I just want to know why you headed this way, and not North Carolina. They recruited you out of Wake Forest, didn't they?"

"Yes, sir. They did. But I knew it wasn't safe going home."

"You have people down this way?"

"No. I don't."

"You should call your folks then," Mr. Newman exclaimed, tilting his head toward the cordless phone sitting upright in its cradle on the bar counter. "They need to know you're okay."

Jason laid his fork and knife on the table next to his plate and then pushed away from the table, preparing to stand. But he remained seated, leaning forward with his elbows on his thighs, seemingly considering all the scenarios that would write themselves just from him making this one call.

"I can't, sir. That's what the cops want me to do. And I can't take that risk."

"What are you going to do then? Waste a whole year because you don't have the courage to face up to your problems? I know your father didn't raise you to be like that."

Jason's jaw tightened.

"You knew my father."

"I did. Jerome was well known in the black legal circles back in the day. Senior attorney with the NAACP. Only met him once, during one of our Sojourner Vista Black-Out weeks. That was two weeks after those monsters 'reportedly' shot up his car."

Jason peered over at Mr. Newman with a confused expression on his face.

"Reportedly. You make it sound as if the report about him getting caught in the crossfire of two rival gangs isn't true."

"Forensic evidence doesn't lie, and there was plenty of it. But there had to be two shooters, one positioned behind him, the other in front of him. The fatal shot, the one to your father's heart, came from his front."

"Why wasn't any of this shared on the news when it happened?"

"Because someone higher than these shooters wanted to bury the truth. Remember, Jerome was the Benjamin Chubb of his day, and he was about to represent Sally Mae Foster, a black woman whose black son was brutally beaten and murdered during a routine traffic stop. One of the responding officers, Otis Rosenbaum, is the son of Herman Rosenbaum, the City of Knoxville's mayor at the time."

Jason allowed this new information to settle in his mind. He had read news reports about members of white militia groups being implicated in the murders of high-profile black and brown people. These militia group members were also recruited to drive through black inner-city neighborhoods in old cars, wearing blackface, to perform drive-by shootings of black citizens. When the news media reported on the latter, the common refrain was it is further evidence that black-on-black crime is getting out of hand.

"What is this Sojourner Vista," Jason asked.

"Sojourner Vista is a resort up in Sevierville, about thirty miles east of Knoxville. black-owned and operated. They put on trainings up there for black lawyers, their allies, benefactors. I'm an ally and benefactor. And if I'm not mistaken, your father was a one of their trainers. I was an up-and-coming businessman. Captivated by what MLG represents."

"And what is that, sir? What does this MLG represent?"

"A coordinated effort to legally secure remedies and reparations for members of the Black Diaspora."

Jason felt the fingers of his right hand tap the table once, twice, thrice. He then stood and walked across the room to the phone. Mr. Newman proceeded to finish off his meal as Jason inputted the first three digits of his mother's number.

"I can't do it, sir," Jason exclaimed, pressing the phone's end call button. "I can't have them tracing the call back to this number?"

"That's not important right now," Mr. Newman replied, rolling his eyes as he chewed. "Your mother needs to know you're alright."

"You all didn't do anything wrong, though."

"Really doesn't matter, does it? Besides, that's not your problem, it's ours. You're the one on the run. For how long? A week. But the man you stabbed. He's going to live, son. But you. You won't truly live again until you're able to put all this mess behind you."

Jason rubbed the back of the cordless phone against his leg. He then returned it to its cradle and reclaimed his seat at the table.

"I don't get you. Why aren't you worried, about what they may do to you for letting me stay here?"

"Because, like I said earlier, you and Mitch have a date with destiny." Mr. Newman pushed his empty plate to the center of the table and then leaned back in his chair, his right hand rubbing his full belly. "I also know what they'll do if they catch sight of your black behind on these streets. You're right where you need to be."

Jason used a napkin to wipe his eyes and mouth. "Trish told me on the way down that you got your bachelor's degree from Morehouse. Were you there during that mass shooting in '91?"

"I was. I was completing my fourth year. Broke my leg trying to take cover. Ended any chance I had of qualifying and competing in the '92 Summer Olympic Games in Barcelona."

"What was it like back then?"

"A lot worse than it is now. Did everything they could to keep us down – beatings at the hands of the police, trumped up charges to have reasonable cause to lock us up. But we never stopped marching. Wanted our children to be treated as equals, be the fulfillment of Dr. King's dream."

Jason crossed his legs at the knees. "This man – the security guard that I stabbed – had a gun. Held it up to my head. Whispered in my ear. Said there was going to be one less nigger that night. Why are they like that, sir? Why do they hate us for being...for being black?"

"That hate is real, son. But their fear of us is much worse. They fear what we will do if we ever manage to amass power, influence, control. But I worked hard for what I have. Turned a ten-thousand-dollar bank loan into a multi-million-dollar record label. But I'm not about to use my wealth to exact revenge on white folks. I'm going to steer the course, use it to produce and direct vocalists, rappers, people who just want to entertain, enlighten and educate, use their creativity to bring enlightenment and healing to the world."

Jason paused momentarily, allowing Mr. Newman's words to sink in. It was at this moment that he envied Trish, her brother Mitch and sister Rayvyn. Their father did something most black men only dream about. He received his college degree knowing that he wanted to start and operate a successful business enterprise. And the fact that it was still thriving was a testament to his commitment to excellence. More importantly, though, his children had inherited this same commitment, not ever wanting to fall short of their personal goals. With Cornelius Newman at the helm, they had developed the championship mindsets that would serve them well in the present and the future.

Jason worshiped the ground his brother Jeremiah walked on, but during times such as these, he wondered what their lives would have been like if Jerome Black had been around to teach them how to be men.

"Not gonna lie," Jason said. "I'm scared. Scared of what they may do to me. Will what I have to say even matter? And if it doesn't, will they lock me up, ruin my chance to compete at the Rio Games?"

"As long as you're here, we'll never know, will we?" Mr. Newman replied. "But know this: You are innocent until proven guilty. You're going to receive a fair trial, son. You can bank on that. But the thing every black man in America worries about is staying alive long enough to have his day in court."

"You think your boy Mitch is going to bring home the gold next year?" Jason slid to the front edge of his seat. "That 9.68 he ran against me back in April was pretty amazing."

"You weren't too shabby yourself, brother. Anytime you break ten seconds, you're rolling. But you did even better. You broke nine eight."

Jason had to smile at that.

"Heard he's out in California training at UCLA, with Franklin Moses. Coach Moses was one of my idols. Former world record holder. Winner of three world championship titles back in the late eighties. If I break nine eight again next year, I'm thinking about moving out there. Have him train me."

Mr. Newman cringed at that. "Franklin and I go way back. Was like a brother from another mother when we ran together at Morehouse. Called me a few days after Mitch's first sub-10 race. Said Mitch was a physical specimen. Could see him running nine seven, nine six even. I couldn't argue with the brother. Not after all he's accomplished."

"Does that make you angry? His accomplishments. 'Cause you always gave him a run for his money, before you broke your leg in that car crash."

Mr. Newman shrugged and chuckled.

"Not going to lie. It used to get to me, in the beginning. Had a difficult time seeing how God was using the injury to bless me." He stood, walked over to one of the pool house's plate glass windows. The sun could clearly be seen setting on the horizon. Jason remained seated, sneaking glimpses at Mr. Newman's back as he finished off his meal.

"What I told Mitch then," Mr. Newman continued, "and what I will tell you now, is sport is nothing more than a means to an end. It paid for the bachelor's degree I received from Morehouse in Business Administration. But after I earned my MBA from Harvard, smart decisions, and a bevy of divine connections, put me in a position to run my own business."

Mr. Newman turned slightly to look back at Jason. Season-ending injuries to his hamstring and groin aligned Jason's thoughts with Mr. Newman's true sentiments. Mr. Newman returned to the table; his arms crossed then hung before he sat back down. "I would have given anything," he finally confessed, settling back in his chair, "to race that brother again in '92, in Barcelona. I wish my boy well in his pursuit of gold, but the life you lead off the track is more important than the life you lead on it."

"You know I'm going to give him a run for his money."

"I know," Mr. Newman replied. A wide grin followed by a chuckle. "Wouldn't have it any other way." He then leaned back in his chair, his clasped hands coming to rest on his full belly. "But this problem of yours isn't just going to go away. You have to confront it head on. You ready to do that? You ready to bring an end to this pause and hit play again?"

Jason's left foot channeled his nervousness, tapping repeatedly on the carpeted floor. "I don't know." He shifted, scratched the back of his neck, before leaning forward in his chair. "I guess. I just want it all to be over. At this rate, I'm going to miss indoor."

"You dying inside, right?"

Jason shrugged before nodding in the affirmative.

"I know the feeling. But mine came from not being able to train because of injury. You got the fuzz breathing down your back, trying to figure out where you at. How about I arrange a meeting with my friend Kelvin Cochran? He's an attorney friend of mine, with that law group I was telling you about. Out of Memphis. He should be able to broker a deal with the authorities up there in Knoxville. May even agree to represent you himself, or hand you off to one of his firm's other defense attorneys."

Jason spotted Trish and Angelica standing on the back patio with someone, a tall, light-skinned brother with a tight fade. Mr. Newman glanced to his right to see what had captured Jason's attention.

"Look who's here," he exclaimed, standing with a wide grin on his face. "Tommy Rollins." Then, with body leaning out the pool house door, he shouted, "What up, Mr. October? Think you can pay this old man a visit?"

Jason then watched as Tommy stepped off the patio to weave through a maze of pool deck chairs. Trish and Angelica were in tow, but after stepping off the patio deck, they veered right to sit together on the edge of the swimming pool, where they submerged their freshly polished feet into the still water.

The two men greeted each other outside the pool house with a handclasp, hug, slaps to backs. As soon as they separated, Tommy glanced over at Jason through the screen of the pool house door. Jason rocked back on his heels once, twice, before making his way outside.

"This him?" Tommy asked the rhetorical.

"Yeah, man," Mr. Newman replied.

Tommy offered his hand to Jason. Jason shook it, but you could tell he was bracing himself for the judgment that was sure to come. But Tommy just nodded his respect while allowing Mr. Newman to usher him inside the pool house. He then urged Jason to join them.

"They out to get you, bruh," Tommy exclaimed as they sat at the table. "Saw his son on the tube the other night with his father's attorney. Some older white guy named Mason Chase. We were in Baltimore playing the Orioles. Chase made a point to say his client was 'standing his ground.' Even used the excuse that white police cops often use. Said he 'feared for his life.'"

Mr. Newman interjected, "Well, at least we know what his defense will be. Terrible law. Just gave trigger-happy white men a license to shoot first, ask questions later." He sighed. "The truth is going to come out, Jason. We just have to get you lawyered up."

"You thinking the Marshall Group?" Tommy asked while chewing his mashed potatoes.

"Yeah."

The corners of Jason's mouth tightened. "When can I meet him? The head guy. Kelvin Cochran."

"It depends," Mr. Newman replied. "They're still recovering from losing Xavier's case. But they may be able to fit you in. If they can't, I'm sure they know someone who will."

"I'm good with that," Jason said. "I guess."

"Damn, nigga'," Tommy interjected. "Loosen the hell up. Cochran's the man. Brother has ties to Civil Rights icon Thurgood Marshall. Worked as his page the last two, three years of his time on the Supreme Court. The brother has stories to tell, I'm sure. But right after Marshall passed, in ninety-three, he realized more had to be done to protect black people's constitutional rights."

"That's when he established the Marshall Law Group in ninety-five," Mr. Newman added. "Was seeing too many black brothers, sisters, shot dead in the streets by the police, or arrested for crimes they didn't commit."

Tommy chimed back in. "Black lawyers and representatives from the major civil rights groups banded together to protect our constitutional rights. They vowed to use the courts to make Dr. King's dream a reality."

Jason could feel his body relent as he sensed that these brothers had his back. They were going to do whatever they could to help him receive a fair trial. But in the back of his mind, he worried. He worried, again, that his mere presence here, in the Newman's home, would place them at risk of being charged for harboring a known fugitive.

Jason asked, "Who they gonna believe, though? Him or me?"

"You let Cochran's attorneys worry about that," Mr. Newman replied. "Believe me. They're going to turn it into a media circus, but that's what you, we, need. If they're able to put what happened to you in the public square, it may force a debate about police brutality. That's what this Baker guy was about to do to you. Brutalize you. As far as I'm concerned, you reacted the way you did to protect yourself."

"Happened to me last week," Tommy said. "Driving home after practice, and this white cop pulls me over. I was sporting an Atlanta Braves baseball cap, but he didn't recognize me. As far as he was concerned, I was just another black man who he thought had no business being in that neighborhood. When a second squad car arrived, pulling to a stop across the street with two cops in it, he ordered me out the car. I told him I wasn't getting out of the car because I didn't do anything wrong. Do you know the mug reached in and tried to pull me out through the window? Claimed I was resisting arrest. But it was all for show. The three other cops standing behind him were his witnesses. I eventually got out. They roughed me up. Fortunately, one of them did recognize me. If not for that, the night probably would have ended differently, with them arresting me on some trumped-up charges."

"That's the kind of shit that makes me mad," Jason vented. "They always profiling us, as if black people don't have money. Can't be rich, famous, powerful. But we're making a way out of no way every freaking day."

Mr. Newman stood, preparing to return to the big house. "And that's why you have to make it back to Knoxville alive, not in a body bag. I'll give Cochran a call once I get back to the house, set something up for tomorrow morning. That alright with you?"

"Yeah. I mean, yes, sir."

"Great." Mr. Newman waved toward the cordless phone. "Now, go on over there and call your mother. She probably pulling her hair out thinking about you. You're alive. Well. She deserves to know that."

Mr. Newman collected Jason's dirty plate and fork, stacked them on top of his own, and then gave Tommy a look that let him know he was responsible for carrying his own. As he watched the two men exit the pool house, Jason could feel his heart sink. He knew his being a fugitive was breaking his mother's heart. Three years earlier, in 2012, in the moments before he boarded that Greyhound bus for the five-hour ride from Wake Forest to Knoxville, she beamed with pride. He, and Jeremiah, were fighting hard to carve out better lives for themselves. Leading mediocre lives would not be an option for them, only excellence. And while it saddened her to see him, her youngest child, leave her nest, she let it be known that she looked forward to the days when he would return to this same nest to tell her all about his exploits on and off the track.

Jason snatched the phone from its cradle and dialed his mother's number.

"Hello." His mother's gruff voice boomed from the earpiece.

"Hey, Ma," Jason exclaimed. "It's Jason."

A long pause on the other end, as his mother's sniffles let Jason know that tears of joy were being shed.

"You alright?" his mother asked once she regained her composure.

"Yeah. I'm good."

"Where you at?"

"Can't say. Just know I'm well." A slight pause, as Jason reflected upon his mother's many sacrifices. Single-parent mother being forced to raise two boys following his father's fatal shooting death.

"Love you, Ma," he continued. He wiped at the tear that was about to drip from his right eye. "And don't you worry. Everything is gonna be alright."

And with that, he ended the call before the cops monitoring it could pinpoint his exact location. Mr. Newman had told him earlier that their number came up private but warned that the cops had bugging devices that could cut right through that. It was a sure bet they knew he was lying low in the 404-area code.

Jason's attention shifted to the sun setting on the distant horizon, framed nicely by the pool house's plate glass window. As he marveled at the sight of it, he couldn't help but recall lyrics from rapper Ice Trey's song *Good Day*, He knew if all this hype around Kelvin Cochran were true, tomorrow would be the beginning of better days. And his dream of qualifying for and competing in the 2016 Rio Summer Olympic Games would remain alive.

The Tara Club was founded in 1940 following the 1939 release of the film *Gone with the Wind,* which was based on author Margaret Mitchell's 1936 novel by the same name. In the film, Tara was the name of the fictitious plantation in the state of Georgia and was notably located five miles outside Jonesborough in Clayton County, on the east side of the Flint River about 20 miles south of Atlanta. The club was established by Tobias Ingram, whose great, great grandfather Roosevelt Ingram actually owned the Dorsett Shoals Plantation, located a little over 25 miles west of Atlanta. Unbeknownst to many, the club was created to be a safe haven for white elites who were obsessed with the idea that the South, the Confederacy really, would rise again.

Tobias Ingram firmly believed the stories that his parents and grandparents had told him about how the enslaved black people that picked cotton on the Dorsett Shoals Plantation were treated. Sure, they weren't compensated financially for their labor, but they did receive at least 2-3 meals a day and free lodging. He had also been told that the enslaved, black people were able to freely share their grievances with the foremen overseeing their work, and the white foremen would respond kindly. Tobias had been told that these same foremen didn't have to whip their enslaved, black laborers; all they had to do was make them feel comfortable in the tiny, dilapidated shacks they called home.

Tobias had the privilege of reading Roosevelt Ingram's personal journal. In it, Roosevelt wrote about how angry he was when then-President Abraham Lincoln issued the Emancipation Proclamation that freed enslaved, black laborers on January 1, 1863, and the Civil War ended on April 9, 1865 with Confederate soldiers being defeated by Union soldiers. In his heart of hearts, Roosevelt confessed that the country had reached the point of no return, and that the enslaved could never be enslaved again.

But what inspired young Tobias the most was his great, great grandfather's challenge to members of the white race. Roosevelt Ingram asserted that the United States of America was founded by white people for white people in 1776. Because the founding fathers were white, he wrote about how imperative it is for white people to maintain a high degree of supremacy over black people primarily, but nonwhites as well. To accomplish this goal, Roosevelt Ingram suggested that white people assume total and complete control of the United States' corporate sector so black people and nonwhites would have to come to white people to secure jobs that paid livable wages.

Malcolm Stillwell walked around the Tara Club's rustic, meeting chamber amid its polished oak walls. An oversized, circular antique table that seated twelve was positioned in the center of the room. Standing there in his suit and tie with a short glass of whiskey in his right hand, Stillwell admired the painting of Tobias Ingram perched high on the far wall, directly behind the Club President's chair, the head of the table. There were other paintings on the walls as well, mostly of Confederate War generals like Robert E. Lee and Stonewall Jackson. Stillwell found himself having to nod every now and then at the handful of white colleagues that passed in front of him or milled around in other parts of the spacious room. With him vying for the Republican Party's presidential nomination in the Fall of 2015, he knew the anticipation in the room was for him, what he would say about the current state of the new Confederacy.

In 2014, members had elected him president of the Confederate States of America. And by rule, any CSA member elected to high office within the CSA must secure significant leadership positions within the Union government based in Washington, DC., or in state houses all across America. Their aim was to infiltrate Union-controlled legislative, judicial and executive governmental branches on the local, state and national levels with CSA operatives. By taking these necessary steps, the hope was the Confederate States of America could strategically restore and maintain White Rule across all segments of American society.

Hans Gobler, Chair of the Republican National Committee, nodded at Stillwell after sipping from his short glass. Stillwell walked over to the circular table to stand behind the chair at the head of the table, the portrait of Tobias Ingram looming large behind him. The twelve, white men in the room joined Stillwell, first standing behind their assigned chairs. Three of these men were considered elder members of the CSA's innermost circle because of their seniority.

The twelve men standing around the table placed their right hands over their hearts. "I pledge allegiance," they proclaimed in one voice, all peering up at the Confederate flag prominently hanging from the ceiling high above the center of the table, "to the flag of the Confederate States of America, and to the Republic for which it stands, one Nation, under God, indivisible, with liberty and justice for all."

The three eldest members were the first to sit down. Stillwell, Gobler and the seven others followed suit.

"Good evening, brothers," Gobler greeted.

"Good evening," members of the CSA's Inner Circle replied in unison.

"We're here today to give our blessings to our brother Malcolm Stillwell, who, in a few short months, will be vying for the Republican Party's nomination for the U. S. Presidency. I believe he is an excellent choice, as he has openly demonstrated allegiance to the Confederate States of America's core ideas – that this country, the United States of America, was founded in 1776 by white leaders to be a white nation for white citizens, that white, Anglo-Saxon Protestant men are endowed by the Creator to subdue and subordinate its land, its women and its savages, and that states should have the right to chart their own destiny, craft, execute and legislate their own rules for how they will conduct their affairs."

Stillwell's head was downcast during Gobler's opening remarks. But he could sense the three elders studying his every move from the other side of the table. These elders included

95-year-old Lance Chamberlin, 93-year-old Bruce Delaney and Eunice Baker's 91-year-old father Broderick Turnbull.

When Stillwell looked up and across the room, his eyes met those of Lance Chamberlin, who sat directly across the table from him, between Delaney and Turnbull. The portrait of Tobias Ingram's great, great grandfather Roosevelt Ingram, with matching Rebel flags to the left and right of it, loomed large behind them. The wrinkles in Chamberlin's face could not hide his displeasure and disdain for Stillwell. Chamberlin had long questioned Stillwell's fitness for the CSA president's role, and he had reservations about him being elevated to the Union presidency. Chamberlin thought Stillwell was too self-centered, only caring about himself and his fortunes. He balked to the other elders when he heard Stillwell talk about women liking when celebrities like him grab them by their pussies, and even suggested that if his 39-year-old daughter Elena Stillwell wasn't his daughter, he would date her.

Elder Chamberlin was the first to speak.

"It shouldn't surprise you that your most recent remarks disturbed me," he exclaimed. "What you do with women, behind closed doors, is no one else's business. But it became public because you were speaking to a reporter, one who was recording every word that came out of your mouth."

Elder Turnbull interjected, asking, "But is that a bad thing? He's now the top contender for the Republican nomination, leading in most polls by more than forty percentage points. I, for one, am happy with that. Makes me feel more hopeful that he will win the nomination."

"I agree," Elder Delaney said. "If he is elevated to the Presidency, he will force the media to focus more of its attention on what he does and says, not on what our Confederate operatives are doing to craft bills and enact legislation that is in line with the CSA's core principles."

"And I'm all for that. Believe me, brothers. But our people, our operatives, have to also project a certain level of decency, command respect from others. The public should not question their adherence to Christian values, selflessness over selfishness." Chamberlin paused to collect his next thought. "The man sitting before us now has spent his entire life stepping on others to be the most despised man on the planet."

Stillwell sat upright to place his elbows on the table. "Can I speak now?"

"Yes," Elder Chamberlin replied. "You many speak."

"I have been a member of this order for more than half my life," Stillwell continued. "I'm seventy-six now, so that's over thirty-seven years. In that time, I created a business, the Stillwell Organization, that offers services, products, that the public wants. We have rental properties in Manhattan, casinos in Vegas and Atlantic City. All of this was accomplished because of my vision, under my leadership."

Stillwell took a few beats to scan the room. The multiple head nods motivated him to press on.

"And let's not forget the support I leveraged from the Russians, the Saudis, and the neo-Nazis in Germany. Their private dollars are being deposited into our coffers daily without being detected by the IRS. Our confederacy is not a registered business entity. Know this, brothers: our white international allies want us to succeed. Not so they can bring America under their control. No. They support us because they believe in the core CSA principles that Hans shared with us earlier. They too want White Rule to be expanded to every corner of the world."

With that, Elder Chamberlin relented, allowing Elder Delaney to take the lead.

"Where will you take us now, President Stillwell?" Delaney asked, trying to be funny in a supportive kind of way. A few chuckles could be heard around the room, but most of the men stared at Stillwell with stern expressions on their faces.

"Our covert operations to make the niggers look bad, think less of themselves, must continue."

"I agree," a middle-aged Inner Circle member to Stillwell's left exclaimed. Stillwell knew him as Paul Davidson, CEO of Horizon Wireless, a cable, internet and cell phone service provider. Besides Stillwell, Davidson was also one of the Inner Circles' most vital members, as his technologies helped CSA operatives conduct surveillance of their staunchest opponents. "But some of these ops are starting to go sideways. Five of our law enforcement operatives were arrested, tried and convicted late last year up in Baltimore for those drive-by shootings. The Union loyalists in the Baltimore police department now know that some of their officers, our White Knights, are shooting black people in black neighborhoods wearing black-faced masks."

"But you must admit the operation has been successful," Kevin Bakke, CEO of the Bakke Media Group, interjected from Stillwell's right. "Especially when you look at things from a global perspective. We have them believing these shootings are being carried out by black thugs, gangbangers. We have to keep the pressure on. More and more of them are starting to believe they're their own worst enemy. It also makes it easier for our white legislative operatives to criticize liberal Democrats for their soft stance on black-on-black crime."

Stillwell allowed his hands to fall flat on the table. "I have concerns about this Jason Black case. I fear a not guilty verdict against him could jeopardize our efforts to expand Stand Your Ground laws in other states. I predict that his lawyer, this Thelma St. James, is going to counter Mason's lawsuit with one of her own, undoubtedly putting forth his own Stand Your Ground defense."

"That law was first implemented in 2005, in Florida," Bakke exclaimed, "If he prevails, more niggers will be able to use it in their defense against our targeted acts of police brutality, murders by white Confederate operatives even."

Michael Wilkins, CEO of Wilkins Construction, added, "More than anything, it will make more white people sympathetic to their fight for equal rights, equal protections." Wilkins slowly tilted his head toward Elder Chamberlin. "How should we respond, sir?"

Elder Chamberlin's gaze shifted from Wilkins to Stillwell. "I believe Malcolm here knows what needs to be done."

"I'm afraid I don't sir," Stillwell replied, removing his arms from the table to sit up straight. "What would you have me do?"

"Win," Elder Chamberlin said, a sly grin fully evident on his wrinkled face. "The fate of our Confederacy is on you."

CHAPTER ELEVEN

Thelma steered her BMW sedan alongside the brick-encased mailbox, then reached inside through the driver side window to retrieve her mail. Flipping through it, she realized that most of it was junk mail – a coupon for 50 percent off at Kohls, a postcard encouraging residents to elect Tiffany Cain to the Knox County school board. Thelma placed the stack atop the dashboard and then settled back into the driver's seat to steer the sedan down the long driveway and into her now-gaping garage.

She heard a faint beep as soon as she stepped from the garage into the foyer. Messages were waiting to be listened to, but they would have to wait. Sister-girl was tired, evidenced by the way she slowly lumbered up the spiral staircase and into the master bedroom. But that's what happens when you stay up late watching The Tonight Show with Jason Lennox, knowing you have to wake up at six the next morning to arrive on time for an eight thirty meeting. Once she reached her bedroom, though, she disrobed, throwing her skirt, blouse, panties and bra askew on the carpeted floor. Standing under the shower head, she allowed the spewing water to roll down the length of her naked body, washing away the suds, a day's worth of funk.

Earlier in the day, she had spoken with Timothy Murray, her bi-racial cousin. As one of the Marshall Law Group's contracted investigators, there was no doubt she was going to ask him to assist with the Jason Black case. He had spent 20 years with the Knoxville Police Department, first as a uniformed officer, later as a detective. And he still had contacts there, so he was the first to tell her about Jason's suspected location. Thelma knew what protocols the department would follow once he had been located, but she also knew justice for black men was handled much differently south of the Mason-Dixon Line.

"Can you assure me that he's going to be apprehended without incident?" she had asked Timothy, cell phone pressed firmly against her cheek. "It's Baker's word against his, you know?"

"Yeah," Timothy had replied. "I know. Just hope someone gave your boy the talk. If he resists, there's no doubt they're going to ship him back up here in a body bag."

"Let's just hope it doesn't come to that. He's innocent until proved guilty, right?"

"Right."

Thelma couldn't help but reflect on another telephone conversation, the one she had two days earlier with Cynthia Black. Thelma was scheduled to speak with Cynthia, in Wake Forest, North Carolina, the following Saturday. If Jason was apprehended and returned to Knoxville before this meeting, she would be able to let Cynthia know that her son had been taken into custody without incident. But past experiences with the KPD made her question whether being in custody was a guarantee that he would be safe. Roscoe Baker was a retired police officer. He undoubtedly had friends working as guards down at the county jail. Many of them were probably licking their chops in anticipation of getting a few body blows and kicks in for their recovering mentor, friend.

Thelma shut off the water then collected the drying towel from the rail. She used the towel to dab at her face and neck before using it to wipe between her legs and at all parts south. Towel wrapped around waist, she exited the bathroom with a bottle of scented lotion in hand and walked over to her king-sized bed to sit. She squirted a silver dollar-sized glob of lotion into her hand, rubbing it onto her toned legs, telling herself that Timothy was a good man, even though their mothers – cousins – had been at odds with each other for years. Over the white man that Yolanda, Timothy's mother, would ultimately marry. Jacob Murray had been intimate with both of them, and it infuriated Nicole that he only married Yolanda because she became pregnant with Timothy.

Timothy was six months younger than Thelma, and if Timothy and his parents had continued their residency in Memphis, the two of them would have been in the same grade and probably would have attended and graduated from the same school. But Jacob Murray knew remaining in Memphis would be foolish. So, he accepted a Social Work professorship at Penn State University, and once he was settled, he flew Yolanda and

18-month-old Timothy to State College, Pennsylvania. They married at the county courthouse, with Jacob promising to renew their vows a year later on one of the Caribbean Islands.

Thelma was proud of her cousin. He was a handsome man, his pale skin allowing him to pass for White. And even though their parents' relationship needed a face-lift, and they knew the reasons why, they did everything they could to develop a bond that could never be broken. Since they were both the only children in their respective households, Timothy would come to epitomize Thelma's brother from another mother.

She offered Timothy counsel during his high school years after being teased by the white boys at his school after they learned his mother was black. Racism was still alive and well back in the mid- to late 80's, and even though Timothy was passing, the white boys in the know called him a "white nigger" to his face.

Thelma sized up Timothy's white girlfriend and soon-to-be wife Susan and shared her conclusions with him when they returned to Memphis from college to attend the Saint James family reunion.

She told Timothy that he better get his shit together when she learned from a mutual acquaintance that he had been cheating on Susan with some of his fellow, black officers and courthouse clerks. Thelma was told he did it to reclaim a semblance of his blackness. This news troubled Thelma immensely, because her hopefulness about her own future nuptials grew from seeing them together, happy. Even though much of her time had been devoted to being a Knoxville-based lawyer with MLG's Knoxville branch, she still made a point to give Timothy and Susan the time and space they needed to strengthen their marital bond.

"All you're doing is contributing to the problem," Thelma had explained. "You need to come clean, Tim. Let her know you're not perfect, that you have made mistakes. Only then can y'all begin to heal. These other women can't give you what she has already given you. Heck, she and them boys need you more than you need them hoes down at the department."

Over time, Thelma's consistent bluntness eventually wore Timothy down. He confessed his transgressions to his wife, and she forgave him. Of course, he had to sleep on the couch for a few weeks, but he didn't mind. He was the one who screwed things up. If that was the penance he had to pay to keep his family together, so be it. But Timothy also started viewing Thelma in a different light. He let Thelma know that he respected her now more than ever before. She had indeed become his closest cousin.

But Thelma's mental walk down memory lane ended when she heard her cell phone vibrating on the nightstand.

"Thelma," Kelvin Cochran's voice boomed through the speaker.

Thelma looked across the room at the round clock perched on her bedroom wall. It registered ten o'clock p.m. "It's late. Started to let it go to voice mail, but I saw your name come up. I hate Caller ID."

"Glad to hear I mean that much to you," Cochran laughed.

"What's up?"

"What do you know about what's going on with Jerome's son Jason?"

"Only what has been publicly shared."

Slight pause as Cochran gathered his thoughts.

"We have him," Cochran continued, "and he's safe. He's laying low until we can devise a plan for his extradition up to Knoxville." Cochran breathed in heavily, mostly through his nose. "Wanted to know if you'd be interested in representing him."

Thelma didn't want to come across as over-zealous, so she allowed a beat to pass before responding. "The thought had crossed my mind. Probably will be one of the biggest cases this area has ever seen. What took you so long to reach out to me?"

"I had to do some research. Jerome is the boy's father."

"Do you think him being Jerome's son will be considered a good thing?"

"No. I don't. Probably a liability. One of those cold cases that raise more questions than answers. The last thing they said about Jerome after he was murdered was he had illicit substances in his system. But even if that were true, it doesn't excuse the fact that no arrests have been made after all these years. The killer is still out there."

The next day, Thelma found herself staring at Roscoe Baker and his attorney, Mason Chase, from across a conference table. As she tapped one of her expensive pens against the legal pad on the table, she grew increasingly irritated by Chase's smug retorts. It was obvious he had no respect for her. Thelma attributed these sentiments to her being a female. Her being black seemed to complicate things even more. Timothy, who was seated to Thelma's right, snapped her out of it by bumping his knee against her knee under the table.

Thelma could tell Baker's wounds had yet to fully heal six weeks after they had been sustained. Every time Baker scooted back in his chair, he winced in pain while placing his left hand on his injured rib cage. Baker's two adult children, Roscoe Jr. and Rosalind, sat in the chairs against the wall behind them, listening intently. But Thelma could tell they were just itching to join the conversation in their father's defense.

"If he's down in Atlanta," Baker began, "why's it taking you so long to ship his ass back up here?"

"We understand your concern, Mr. Baker," Timothy replied, "and your frustration. But Atlanta's a big city. A lot of places for him to hide. The fact he has no known relatives in the area complicates things even more."

Chase interjected. "Stop with the smoke, Detective Murray. I was playing this game long before you were in your mother's womb. You all know where he is; you just haven't received the warrant permitting you to drag him back up this way."

"And I'm sure you're aware, Mr. Chase," Thelma replied, "that justice is a bit slow in the Deep South."

"I am aware of that, Ms. James."

"St. James," Thelma corrected him.

"My apologies."

Thelma continued, "We invited you here so we could hear your side of the story. You allege that you were investigating a complaint made by a Miss, Miss Sandra Talbot. She reportedly called 9-1-1 to let them know, and I quote, a black man was running around the Fort Sanders area scaring people, unquote. Did you know Jason Black is a world-class sprinter? That he was on the final leg of his weekly midnight run when all this went down?"

"No," Baker replied. "But I was watching the news up there in the hospital. I saw the feature that WBIR did on him. Seems like a good kid. Fast. Just don't know why he stabbed me."

"Did you say anything to him?" Timothy asked. "Something that may have frightened him?"

Chase softly slapped the table in front of Baker before Baker could answer. "My client was not the instigator, Detective Murray. Ask anybody who lives there, in the Fort Sanders area, and they will tell you how much they admire and appreciate Mr. Baker for his protection, his dedicated service to the residents who live there."

Baker added, "I love my job. I want to keep my job. I would never do anything that would cause me to lose it."

"But the fact still remains that Mr. Black stabbed you," Thelma said. "Usually, when someone lashes out like that, they're trying to defend themselves. Was your firearm out, or was it holstered, Mr. Baker?"

Chase waved Baker off, letting him know he wasn't obligated to answer Thelma's question. He didn't.

Thelma chuckled inside before curtly remarking, "Should I take that as a yes, Mr. Baker? That you had it out?"

Chase's agitation was visible to everyone in the room. Thelma surmised that he had already had the first of many candid conversations with his client, the kind that lets the latter know he had his back merely because they both were members of the same Good Ole' Boy Network. It didn't matter that Baker had been in the wrong by pulling his firearm out on what he knew at the time to be an unarmed, black man. All that mattered is they live to see another day by spreading the type of propaganda that makes Jason look bad. And the message they wanted the public to hear loud and clear was that Fort Sanders Security Guard Roscoe Baker was "standing his ground" when a "young thug" plunged the blade of a sling blade knife into his rib cage. Upon hearing these two words, certain members of their targeted base would plug their ears when Jason, a law-abiding citizen, tried to tell his side of the story. In short, they wouldn't give him the benefit of the doubt, for his black skin trumped any positive actions he may have taken during the altercation.

A few hours later, she and Timothy were sipping lattes at a nearby Starbucks. It was becoming increasingly clear to Thelma that Roscoe Baker had been both instigator and escalator. She told her cousin that the photos of Baker's wound suggested that Jason had stabbed him from below, not above, suggesting that

Jason may have been knocked to the ground. But she would be hard pressed to prove this point, resulting from the amount of time that had elapsed since the altercation first occurred. Jason's bumps and bruises had healed, as had Baker's.

"Someone had to see all of this go down," Thelma said. "Did you all interview residents in the area?"

"We did," Timothy replied, "but everyone we have spoken with say they came out when Baker was bleeding out on the ground. One person did say she saw a young, black man running away. But nothing more than that."

Thelma crossed her arms at that. To her, it was hard to believe no one witnessed the altercation from beginning to end, videotaped it even. In 2015, every cell phone owner had the ability to record newsworthy events. But as Thelma sat there, she thought about all the unarmed, black men who had been shot since the 2009 shooting of Oscar Grant III by a Bay Area Rapid Transit police officer. It was because of him that Americans of all hues now used cell phone video recording devices to hold police officers accountable. Even the first, black president, Nelson Dupont, encouraged the nation's police departments to require members of their forces to wear body cameras. Such actions protected these brave men and women in blue from being falsely accused of criminal behavior, because video evidence did not lie.

But what pleased Thelma even more were the chants coming from the black community. "Black Folk Matter." When she first heard it, she marveled at its simplicity. Isn't it obvious? Black folk matter too. But apparently it wasn't, resulting from the amount of pushback BFM activists had received from unenlightened members of the white community.

These unenlightened Whites countered BFM with chants of "All Folk Matter!" and "Blue Lives Matter!" They were under the impression that BFM activists were saying black folk are more important than white ones. But that was not what they were saying at all. For them, black folk matter because they haven't mattered for so long.

Four hundred years of slavery.

Fifty years of Jim Crow legislation, relegating black Americans to second-class citizenship.

Ongoing incidences of brutality at the hands of bad cops, who allowed their fears and resentments about black people to lead them down slippery slopes of thought and feeling to become operationalized as misbehavior.

Members of the black American-led Black Folks Matter movement respected and adored the good cops, the ones who faithfully and honorably fulfilled their oaths to serve and protect them. These good cops worked hard to befriend law-abiding citizens and did not think black people were more prone to criminality than white people. They judged people on what they did; not on what they looked like. And that made a world of difference. With this mindset, the good cops were still able to apprehend and lock up the bad guys, maintain law and order in American neighborhoods.

Thelma knew the Jason Black case would bring discussions about the current state of black Americans into the national spotlight. It would also solicit an uproar from the White American community. Many White Americans were becoming increasingly frustrated with black Americans incessant demands for social and economic justice. They contended that slavery ended 146 years ago, on December 18, 1865. The playing field was now level, so these same black Americans no longer had an excuse for living mediocre lives. That much was true. But to gain a semblance of parity with White Americans, they had to work twice as hard to succeed in integrated schools, even "act White" when seeking employment. This was the dance White America wanted them to perform now, even though members of their group allowed racial bias to cloud their judgment. BFM activists were having none of it.

For Thelma, the Black Folk Matter Movement was nothing more than a continuation of the Civil Rights Movement of the 1950s and '60s. Because she was born in 1965, she and countless other black Americans born before the April 4, 1968 assassination of Dr. Martin Luther King, Jr. were the beneficiaries of the bus boycotts, the sit-ins, and the marches. But what made this current version different from its predecessor were its leaders and their followers. Both could not be readily identified because the Black Folk Matter Movement seemingly sprung from the grassroots, in response to how bad cops and an unjust criminal justice system were treating black and brown men. Many in the BFM movement surmised that the criminal justice system was strategically being used by a racist segment of the white populace to keep black people in their place. More importantly, though, they knew beyond a shadow of a doubt that its implementation was helping them recapture a black labor force that had been lost to them after the Civil War.

Thelma reached into her briefcase to pull out her copy of *USA Today*. The headline read, "NRA's Fight to Protect Citizens' Right to Stand Their Ground."

"Did you read this?" Thelma asked as she unfolded the newspaper and laid it on the table. Timothy leaned in to get a closer look.

He chuckled. "Yeah. I read it. Shocked the hell out of me. During times like these, Lampley usually doesn't have much to say."

"He's only speaking out now because he knows Baker was wielding a gun, Black a knife. Probably making a play for guns being the preferred weapon of choice."

"But what difference does it make? It's going to come down to who went on defense first. Right?"

"Right." Thelma folded the paper, allowing her thumb to rest inside the fold as she held onto it. "I just wonder what the fallout will be. You and I are on the same page. We both believe in the Second Amendment, that people should have the right to bear arms. But after what happened back in 2007, when that Asian kid shot all those students at Virginia Tech, you would have thought the NRA would be leading efforts to reform our gun laws. How many did he kill? Twenty-five? Thirty?"

"Thirty-two. Wounded seventeen."

"How are your brothers in blue reacting to all this? They think civilians like me should have a right to stand our ground?"

"Most of them support that right, but they also know having more heat on the street only complicates things – for them, not for the people packing it. Most civilians are packing for selfish reasons. What we do is selfless. We put our lives on the line for them."

Thelma allowed her cousin's words to marinate for a few ticks. He was right. But in her seven years as a prosecuting attorney, nine as a defense, she knew a small minority of these officers joined the force with ulterior motives. All of them had taken an oath to uphold the United States Constitution, the Rule of Law. They were even required to take it one step further, vowing to serve and protect the people who were kind to them, as well as the people who wanted to do them harm.

But Thelma knew the police unions had a tremendous amount of influence over these officers. The first person that Roscoe Baker contacted from the hospital after he was well enough to speak was his union rep, Harrison Stane. Stane was more of a publicity hound than prosecuting attorney, resulting from the fact that, in recent months, he could often be seen on the big three networks – CBS, ABC and NBC, as well as CNN - touting Baker's virtues. Judging from what Stane said during these interviews, his goal was to get ahead of the story, place reasonable doubt in the minds of potential jurors.

Thelma had learned from reading Baker's KPD personnel file and supplemental police reports that Stane's relationship with Baker had become more than a working one in 1988, when he led the team of defense attorneys that exonerated Baker of all charges related to an excessive use of force charge. Responding to a domestic violence incident between a black man and his white girlfriend, Baker reportedly perceived the black man as an imminent threat because he kept making snide remarks to the responding officers, and more than once brushed up against Baker's shoulder, to him, a blatant act of defiance. Moreover, the black man reportedly disregarded Baker's multiple requests to calm down. But the brother didn't want any part of that. He was feeling too good, floating sky high from the crack cocaine that he and his white girlfriend had been smoking before the uniformed officers arrived. It wasn't until the black man reached into his pocket to retrieve the identification that the responding officers had been asking for that Baker got rough with him. Thelma surmised that "the reach" provided the cover Baker needed to justify throwing the black man to the ground to straddle his body and repeatedly strike him across the face with his balled-up fists.

"I want to nail the son of a bitch," Thelma exclaimed. "Forensics don't lie. Black was on his knees. Probably held at gunpoint. That's why Chase didn't allow him to answer the question."

"How soon can we get to Black?" Timothy asked. "Did they provide a timeline for when they were bringing him in?"

"No. They didn't. Matter of fact, the local authorities don't even know yet."

"Well, who told you?"

"That's on a need-to-know basis, and right now, you don't need to know. Just know, I was asked if I wanted the case. Was on the fence at first, but as you can see, I said yes. Going to get back to me early next week on when he wants to turn himself in."

Timothy swiped up his wrappings and threw them into the white paper bag on the table between them. He then reached over to scoop up Thelma's as well.

"You still flying over to Wake Forest this weekend to visit his mother?"

"Yeah. Need to know what makes this kid tick."

That Saturday, Thelma found herself swerving a rented 2015 Honda Accord up to the curb in front of Cynthia Black's single-family home. It was early morning, so most of the residents were up, taking sips from mugs containing their morning coffee, which is what Thelma had wanted. The less attention she drew to herself, the better. She had called Cynthia the moment she stepped off the plane and was walking through the Raleigh-Durham International Airport with her carry-on luggage in tow, impeccably dressed in a pants suit, but no heels, just Nike Air Jordain sneakers.

As they talked on the phone, Cynthia told Thelma for the umpteenth time how appreciative she was that the Marshall Law Group had agreed to take her son's case. Thelma wasn't mad at her; that's what happens when the firm named after the late U. S. Supreme Court Justice Thurgood Marshall expresses a willingness to fight for defendants' right to equal protection under the law.

As Thelma turned the car off and removed the keys from the ignition, she noticed that the door to Cynthia's home was already open. Cynthia stood in the doorway, watching Thelma get out of her car and walk toward the front door, carrying a credenza folder. She greeted Thelma with a smile on the front porch, even hugging her briefly before showing her inside.

"Have you spoken to your son?" Thelma asked from the kitchen table as Cynthia prepared a plate for her near the stove. Thelma held a pen in her right hand, prepared to write important details on her tabled legal pad.

"I have," Cynthia said, placing a plate filled with grits, pork bacon and buttered toast on the table in front of Thelma. "But he wouldn't tell me where he's at. Just told me that he's safe."

"Glad to hear that." Thelma grabbed her fork and shoveled some of the grits into her mouth. Just like Mama's, she thought as she swirled the grits around in her mouth with her tongue before swallowing. "Have you ever known him to be violent?"

"Never." Cynthia said, claiming a seat to Thelma's left. "He made good grades in school and was a star athlete – played football, ran track. Jeremiah – that's his older brother – thought he should have stuck with football. Believes he could have made a lot more money as an NFL running back. I told the boy to follow his passion, not the money, and he did. Now, he's the number two sprinter in the world."

"You think he has a shot to bring home gold next year?"

"I do, but he's going to be hard pressed by that Newman boy. That second-place finish at last year's national meet devastated him. But I told him to just keep working hard. Now that the Newman boy is graduated, he's hoping to win his first NCAA title this year. But that probably won't happen."

"Why?"

"Because I know him. Gets worked up about things that don't matter. Probably a nervous wreck right now. Wish they would just leave my baby alone."

Thelma broke off a piece of the pork bacon and inserted it into her mouth. "That's why I'm here," she said, chewing. "We want them to leave him alone. We know where he is now. The

Marshall Law Group has been hired to represent him. We're scheduled to fly down to Atlanta within the next two, three, days to extradite him back to Tennessee."

Cynthia's cell phone was inches away from her clasped hands, in the center of the table. She grabbed it and said, "It's been hard. Hearing your child's voice on the phone, but not having a number to call him back on."

Thelma reached for Cynthia's phone. "Can I?" she asked. "Can I plug in my number so you can call me the next time he calls you?"

Cynthia unlocked her phone by plugging in her four-digit code and handed it to Thelma. Thelma accessed Cynthia's contacts, and then proceeded to use the phone's virtual keyboard to enter her name and number.

"Our goal is to get Jason back on the track," Thelma said, handing Cynthia's phone back to her. "But we must first get him over this legal hurdle. After that, we will all look forward to seeing him vie for Olympic gold."

Cynthia smiled at that as she fought back the tears.

CHAPTER TWELVE

Jason sat silently in the center of the back seat as Trish steered her car into an empty parking space underneath Tribe Records' downtown Atlanta headquarters. Because it was a Sunday, many of the parking spaces were empty, except for the two closest to the elevator. The row of cars parked there belonged to the sound engineers and musicians that would mix their acoustics with Trish's vocals. Angelica sat next to Trish in the passenger seat, turning around slightly every now and then to see how Jason was faring.

Trish and Angelica agreed the night before that it would do Jason good to get out of the house, experience a slice of normalcy before turning himself in. Even before they arrived, Trish had planned on visiting Tribe Records so Trish could record at least two additional tracks for her debut album. Jamal Jenkins, or JJ, the lead sound engineer for her project, initially expressed reservations about having Jason on site, but he changed his tune when Trish told him that no one would see him because he would be walking directly from the car to the elevator to the studio.

When the tenth-floor elevator swished open, Jason was overwhelmed by the lobby's African-themed fixtures. It was midday, so the sunlight shining down on them from the skylight reflected nicely off the marble-covered walls and greeter's desk. A collage of Tribe Record's most notable artists was featured prominently on the far wall, behind the greeter's desk. Of course, no one was there to greet them, as support staff didn't work on weekends, but Jason could only imagine how busy the place was during the weekdays. During the drive over, Trish had told Jason that the Atlanta headquarters alone had over one hundred employees assigned to several different departments, including legal, A & R, promotion, artist development, marketing, publicity, and new media, to name only a few. The same was true for the company's Los Angeles, Chicago, and New York offices. Trish told Jason that her father decided to headquarter the record label in Atlanta because of its predominantly black population, and the black musicians, actors, directors, and producers living there had declared in both word and deed that they wanted to make Atlanta the central hub for black creative expression.

Jason's eyes widened even more when he stepped into the spacious sitting area that was surrounded by two separate recording studios, one on the right, the other on the left. Toward the back of the room was a full kitchen with a stove, refrigerator and microwave, and a dining room table that seated ten. L-shaped sofas and love seats were positioned throughout the room, ensuring that seating was available for both musicians and their guests.

When Trish, Angelica and he entered, a seated JJ was the first to get up from one of the L-shaped sofas to greet Trish. The four male band members and one male and two female background singers either stood as well or walked over from the kitchen to get acquainted with their visitors. JJ's embrace of Trish was a little long, causing Jason to think that their relationship was indeed a special one. He knew she was engaged to that major league baseball player, Tommy Rollins, but he could tell her love for music extended to those individuals who helped her create her art.

Once JJ released her, Trish proceeded to hug and kiss the band members and background singers. Both Jason and Angelica just stood back watching it all, feeling uneasy but finding comfort in each other.

"Let me introduce you to my friends," Trish exclaimed when the pleasantries ended. She extended her arm toward Angelica. "This is my girl, Angelica. She runs the two and the four."

JJ shook Angelica's hand. "Nice to meet you," JJ said.

"And this here is..."

"...Jason Black," one of the band members, the bearded one, interjected.

One of the background singers added, "They been talking about him a lot lately on the local stations. Especially after that Stillwell dude started talking about him."

JJ took Jason's hand into his own and proceeded to shake it vigorously. "Glad you could join us, bro'," he said. "But your girl here is twenty minutes late. We need to stop with all these introductions and get to work. I ain't trying to be here all day."

Chuckles of agreement reverberated around the room, accompanied by the sight of a few nodding heads. Seconds later, Trish playfully scooted over to the refrigerator to retrieve a bottle of water, and then returned to file into Studio One behind the background singers and band members.

JJ pointed a television remote at one of the four LCD monitors attached to the wall. All four of them came to life. "You all make yourselves comfortable while we go in here and put in this work."

"We need to talk," Angelica said, "about us." She and Jason were now seated in separate seats along the elbow of one of the L-shaped sofas. JJ's directions to Trish blared through the wall speakers, but only served as background noise. "That night, you told me that you weren't looking to get in a steady relationship with anyone, with me. Why? Is something wrong with me?"

"No, girl," Jason replied. "Look at you. You fine. I just don't need any distractions right now. Need to focus on running fast times, that's all."

But even as Jason uttered these words, he couldn't stop himself from staring up at the monitor, at Trish. Angelica cleared her thought to snap his attention back to her.

"But did it mean anything to you? You were pushing up on me hard before I let you kiss me, let you touch me, touch me down there. Those talks we had before any of that happened, about your hopes and my hopes, your dreams and my dreams. Didn't think I had it in me. Being that open, with you. It felt good, so right."

Jason leaned forward and started fingering the Berber carpet.

"No doubt. That night, I saw so much of you in me, me in you. Wild that we both want to help people. You're working to become a therapist; I want to own and operate my own business. In what? I don't know. All I know is I want to create jobs for people that look like you and me."

Angelica reached over and placed her right hand on Jason's left. "And you will." She patted Jason's hand then reeled it back in. "Just don't forget about us little people when you blow up. Whatever you decide on doing is going to be great."

"Appreciate that. And when I get down, depressed, I would love to have you as my therapist."

Jason was the first to see Tommy Rollin enter the room holding a bouquet of flowers.

"Glad to see they got you out the house," Tommy exclaimed as he dapped Jason up. He then peered up and across the room to see Trish on the monitors singing into a hanging microphone, her ears covered with headphones. "How long they been at it."

"About fifteen minutes," Angelica replied. "We got here a little late."

"She's starting to sound better than I remember. She's definitely a star in the making. She may take home a Grammy right out the box."

Angelica nodded in agreement. Jason pursed his lips while leaning forward on the sofa's front edge. Angelica glanced over at Jason, immediately sensing how Tommy's presence brought about a change in his demeanor.

"You like her, don't you?" Angelica asked Jason after Tommy stepped away from them to slip into the control booth.

"What's not to like?" Jason replied. "But she's taken."

"And I'm not."

"But you told me yourself that you're alright being friends, friends with benefits."

"That's what I thought I wanted. But not now. I know now that I deserve more. I'm feeling you, J."

Jason took note of the way Angelica looked at him as she licked her lips. The fact that he instinctively licked his lips let him, and her, know that they really did feel the same way about each other.

Jason placed his hand on Angelica's knee. "Don't think I don't appreciate you, for standing by me while I'm going through all this bullshit. But I'm a nervous wreck right now. I wasn't looking for trouble. It found me. So, what I'm really saying is I'm not someone you want to be with right now."

Angelica placed her hand on top of Jason's. "I appreciate you telling me that. But don't get it twisted; I'm always going to be here for you."

"Even for a booty call."

"No!" Angelica loudly blurted while slapping Jason's hand off her knee, smiling. Chuckles from them both before the exchange of a long, loving stare. "I'm your friend, J. Always will be. But I can't pretend to know what you're going through. I get it, though. You have to do the internal work right now. Find peace in the midst of your personal storm."

Jason slapped his thighs and then stood. "Enough of this mushy stuff." He extended his hand to Angelica. Angelica gripped it to allow him to pull her up from the couch. "Let's go on up in here and listen to this girl sang."

Angelica smiled as Jason led her by hand to the door leading into the Studio One control booth.

"You really said that?" Tommy exclaimed loudly from the head of the table. "And you titled it *The Politics of Race?*"

Rows of dirty dinner plates were scattered on the table as Jason, Trish, Angelica, Tommy, and the band members and vocalists sat around it. Standing near the far wall, under the television monitors, and behind the metal containers keeping the food warm, were three members of Tribe Record's kitchen staff cleaning up their mess.

All eyes turned to Jason. "I did. But I ran it by my boy White first. Boy grew up in Henderson, North Carolina. He's white like them. He told me the shit I was saying made him feel uncomfortable, but he also said it wasn't about him, white people even. It's about us black people being treated as equals."

"White sounds like a good brother," Tommy replied. "If I did that, talked about race around my white teammates, someone would complain to the manager, or the owner, and they wouldn't waste any time shutting that shit down."

"Why are you so fascinated with politics, J?" Angelica asked. "The first time I met you, we were eating ribs and wings on The Strip, at Smokey's. You started ranting about Nelson Dupont, how people don't fully understand his true historical significance. Who the hell talks about Nelson Dupont when they're picking rib meat from their teeth?"

Jason leaned back in his chair, trying unsuccessfully not to laugh at the image Angelica had just dropped into his mind. "Probably shouldn't have gone there, especially since you were the one picking rib meat out your teeth." Everyone burst out laughing at that. "But seriously, I blame it on my father. Jerome Black. Always made him smile when he saw my big brother and me reading, books by black authors, the ones writing about social change and empowerment."

"Was?" Tommy said. "He died?"

"Yeah. When I was a kid. Cops said he was in the wrong place at the wrong time. Got caught in some gang warfare-type shit." He peered over at Trish, who sat close to Tommy, her head on his burly chest. "But like I explained to Trish and Angelica, he may have been targeted. At least that's what Mr. Newman led me to believe."

The bearded band member shook his head. "Something similar happened to my old man," he said, "when we lived in LA, in Compton. He wasn't an attorney; he was a trash man. But he was there, loving my mother, using the little bit of money he made to provide for his kids. White cop shot him in the back of his head while he was working. Said he thought my old man fit the description of some man who robbed one of the local banks earlier in the week."

A few ticks went by as everyone in the room processed what was being shared. The common theme here was the deaths of black men at the hands of white hitmen and police officers.

Jason broke the silence. "Wouldn't it be something if Bronson James did more than just dribble a basketball?" he asked. Bronson James was one of the most dominant power forwards in the National Basketball League, playing for the Cleveland Cavaliers. "Lord knows he has everyone's attention."

"Why put all that pressure on Bronson, though?" Tommy quipped. "The man has a family to feed. He don't need no controversy right now. Not when he's raking in all that dough."

"But shouldn't winning the struggle mean more than raking in the dough?" Trish asked. "James has been in the game since '03. I think he has made enough money to take care of his family."

"Would you do it, bro?" Jason asked. "Would you raise your fist like Tommie Carlos and John Smith did in '68, at the Mexico City Olympics, to protest voter suppression and police brutality?"

Tommy shifted uncomfortably in his chair, looking down and away. When he lifted his head, Trish was staring at him dead in his eye, patiently waiting, like everyone else, for his response.

Tommy replied, "Not by myself. I would need the support of my teammates. They would never say it out loud, but we black players know these white owners don't like when we bring up sensitive subjects like racism. It's all about the Benjamins, bro'. They pay us the big bucks to keep our mouths shut."

"You ever consider that that's why we're losing," Jason continued, "allowing them to suppress our votes, brutalize and shoot us dead in the streets? All these black men with all that influence, not just on black people like you and me, but on everyone, Whites included. Great seeing all these Black Folk Matter shirts on the courts and in the fields, but if attitudes are to be changed, they must be the ones initiating the conversation with their fan base."

"Are you willing to do the same, dude?" Tommy blurted back. "The last article I read about you said you're one of the fastest brothers on the planet. You willing to put your track career on the line for a bunch of ungrateful Negroes who are unwilling to help themselves?"

Trish interjected, saying, "That's the white man talking, Tommy. You know better than to talk like that, paint all black people with the same brush. Too many of us marching in the streets to call them ungrateful."

"Well, I just want the brother to answer my question." Tommy then stood to hover over the seated Jason. "What's it going to be, dude? Yes or no?"

Jason stood. As he walked over to the dessert table, he replied, "Definitely going to be a yes for me. Really don't have a choice, do I? Not when I'm facing an attempted murder charge, and Stillwell trying to turn me into his personal shill. But this struggle, for equal rights, equal protections, has always been about power, influence, and control. If influence is the only tool I have in my toolbox, I can't be afraid to use it to improve outcomes for myself, people who look like me, all of us."

"But at what cost, bro'? That's all I'm saying. Once these white motherfuckers start labeling you, calling you an angry, black man, there's no bouncing back from that."

"No doubt. But maybe that's what we should stop doing, wearing our emotions on our sleeves. Maybe we should find new ways to showcase our excellence, wear that on our sleeves instead. That has nothing to do with black supremacy or black power. It's about showcasing how we as a collective overcame all these obstacles to thrive despite living among people who hate and despise us."

"Just talking about it won't be enough, though," Angelica said. "J, remember when we were talking on campus before things got sour, and you told me about the Greenwood District in Oklahoma? Black Wall Street? You told me the black people there established their own businesses and were intentional about allowing their black dollars to circulate in their community two or three times before they were spent in neighboring white communities. We have to get back to that. Create black spaces where black people can grow, learn, build, and thrive, together."

Angelica's response evoked light applause and muffled chuckles from everyone in the room. Both Jason and Tommy chuckled the loudest because they knew Angelica had unknowingly charted a path to the kinds of actions that needed to be taken.

Angelica fixed her gaze on Jason.

Jason licked his lips as he winked at a smiling Angelica.

The next morning, Carmelita Newman stood on the porch, watching, a warm cup of coffee in her hand, as Trish and Angelica loaded up Trish's car for the return trip to Knoxville. That weekend, Jason did win her over. "He's a charming young man," she told her husband as they lay beside each other in bed, the wall-mounted television in front of them providing background noise. She now considered him to be a "nice boy," someone who could make her laugh when she really wanted to cry. But he wasn't her child; he belonged to someone else. Why should she care?

Now that Rayvyn and she were being left alone with him, she made it her mission to find an answer to this question. She knew Trish's return to Knoxville would have her preoccupied with her studies, and getting her mind, her body, prepped for another long track and field season. And her husband continued to accumulate more Frequent Flyer Miles than he needed, as his travels that month alone had taken him to business meetings in Los Angeles, Las Vegas, Nashville and New York. If she didn't care what happened to this boy, she knew she at least had to know why.

When Jason was nowhere to be seen on the Newman family radar, she treasured those moments when she could sit alone in the family study reading her bible. The books – mostly classic, others contemporary – made her feel as if she were in a library, an independent bookstore even. But she was home, in the castle that her husband had built for the kids and her through his unwavering pursuit of his passion. She tried, but she could not shake the sinking feeling in her stomach that told her that this boy, this Jason Black, didn't belong.

And that's when it hit her. All of those sermons at Victory Fellowship Church, all of those mission trips to Africa and Haiti, had been building up to this moment, a moment predicated on this young man's salvation. She closed her bible, stood, and walked out of the room, through the house, and out the patio door.

Standing on the patio, on a Friday night, she could see the light from the television flickering through the lone window on the near side of the pool house.

Good.

He was awake.

She knocked on the pool house door.

A shirtless Jason opened the door.

"Hey, Mrs. Newman," Jason exclaimed, smiling.

Mrs. Newman looked away, causing Jason to chuckle a little under his breath before retreating back into the pool house. The door closed slightly but not all the way. When it opened, Jason had covered himself with another one of Mitch's old Florida Gator t-shirts.

"Mind if I come in?" Mrs. Newman asked, squeezing the leather bible that she held in her right hand tighter.

Jason tapped the door, causing it to open wider. "It's your home, not mine. Come on in."

Before she made her way into the pool house, Mrs. Newman had preconceptions about what she would see, smell, once she stepped inside. That first weekend, Trish and Angelica had whispered to her more than once behind Jason's back, referring to him as a "real ladies' man," often seen at The Last Lap and school parties whispering sweet nothings into co-eds' ears. Mrs. Newman knew the type. The same description used to be applied to her husband, back in the day, when he was running with the Morehouse College Omegas. But to her surprise, Jason was keeping the pool house clean, even taking the initiative to place a new insert into the Air Wick air freshener plugged into the electrical outlet on the far wall.

Carmelita Newman sat in the cushioned chair that was part of a set.

"Tomorrow's the day," she seemed to announce rather than exclaim.

"Yep," Jason replied as he snatched the remote from the coffee table to mute the television.

"Any reservations."

Jason shrugged. He had plenty. It had been a little over four weeks since he bolted from the crime scene, and more than three quarters of that time had been spent with the Newmans. But now his day of reckoning was less than twenty-four hours away, less than twelve really. Mr. Newmans' Marshall Law Group friend had assured him that he would receive a fair trial. He was quick to add, however, that he would probably have to spend a night in a Knoxville jail cell due to the Tennessee authorities receiving a same-day notification of his surrender. They argued that if they had notified them any earlier, he would have been arrested, arraigned before the Magistrate, and released with a future court date summons.

"I wanted to come down here," Mrs. Newman continued, "offer you some words of encouragement." She slid her index finger across the top edge of her bible, where the ribbon dipped between the pages, and opened it to a pre-selected passage. Her eyes then went from the passage to Jason and then back to the passage. The look on Jason's face let her know that he had apprehensions about the biblical truths she was about to share with him.

"Did you grow up in the church?" Mrs. Newman asked.

"Yes, ma'am. I did. Ma made us sit on the front row, my brother and I, when we were younger. Got baptized too when I was about eleven or twelve."

"What happened after that? Trish seems to think you and your friend Greg are doing the devil's work."

Jason chuckled at that.

"Funny she would say that. Must be keeping her own Last Lap outings on the down low."

Carmelita Newman's head dropped at that, frantically flipping through the pages of her bible. The wrinkles in her neck were few and far between, which was saying a lot for a woman her age. More importantly, though, she was still working her petite yet fit body. One glance at her slim thighs, firm yet thick backside and ample bosom had Jason thinking about the possibility of Trish and him being together, as lovers. If Trish could cause heads to turn like her sixty-something-year-old mother, he would consider himself a lucky man. Unfortunately for him, he wasn't her man. Tommy Rollins was.

Mrs. Newman leaned back in her chair while looking up from her bible to gaze over at him.

"What you're going through is nothing more than a test," Mrs. Newman exclaimed. "Samson was tested, and he failed. So did King David when he slept with Bathsheba and had her husband killed. Even Thomas doubted that Jesus, the Messiah, had risen after being entombed for three days. But what is so amazing about their stories is how God continued to use them, even after they messed up."

"You saying I messed up, for defending myself?"

"No. I'm not. I just don't want to see you squander this opportunity. This opportunity to shine light on the historical mistreatment of black men and boys, black women and girls."

"You mean be a spokesperson for all that is wrong with the American criminal justice system? I don't want no part of that, ma'am. I just want my life to be normal again."

"Normal? Please! It's us against them, and they're going to try and make you the poster boy for why Stand Your Ground should be the law of the land. To them, you're nothing but a thug, a black one at that. That's why you have to stand strong. That's why you have to be strong."

Mrs. Newman crossed her legs at the ankles.

"You scared. I know. But you shouldn't worry."

"But I can't, stop worrying I mean. Never been handcuffed. Locked up."

"Not a good place to be. But that's out of your control. You control what you say, your testimony. Finally get a chance to tell your side of the story. Just tell the truth." She closed her bible and then held it high enough for Jason to see. "This book, this Holy Bible, lets us know what happens when we tell the truth. It sets us free."

Mrs. Newman then reached under the coffee table to retrieve what appeared to be a dusty box containing a leather-bound bible.

"Take it." Jason's hand seemed to linger in the space between them before he accepted her gift. "It's yours. Just promise me you'll read it, starting with the Book of John, in the New Testament." She leaned back in her chair. "I used to tell the girls that they had to be like Jesus. I'm telling you the same. They're going to free you, child. That's what I'm feeling in my gut. Mitch won't be the only one in that 100-meter final if you just allow God to work in and through you."

Mrs. Newman stood, and Jason followed suit, filing in behind her as she made her way toward the pool house door.

"Thank you," he said. "I will. Tonight. Before I go to bed."

Mrs. Newman shook her head and smiled. Jason's tightened jawline let her know he was lying. She then stepped out of the pool house and onto the lighted pathway surrounding the swimming pool.

"Be well, child," she exclaimed as she walked away. "The time for you to let your light shine is now."

Later that day, Thelma steered her rental car into the roundabout in front of the entry door to the Newman mansion. She had come to Atlanta to spend a few days with Jason before Kelvin Cochran flew down from Memphis the following day so the three of them could fly up to Knoxville together.

As she disembarked from the vehicle, Thelma thought back to her video call with Jason the week prior. Kelvin Cochran was on that call as well, doing the initial introduction before signing off to allow Jason to talk freely with his new attorney. Mr. Newman sat beside Jason, chiming in every now and then to offer words of support and encouragement. When it was time for him to speak, Jason vociferously reiterated his innocence, letting Thelma know that his intent was not to end Roscoe Baker's life; he just cared about himself, his desire to live to see another day. Thelma assured Jason that others would see it the way he saw it. "That's why I'm stepping up to the plate to defend you."

Moving forward, Thelma stressed the importance of showing the judge and the jury that he was the one being harassed, that he was the one standing his ground. But during that same call, she became the bearer of bad news, as she let Jason know that the nine-member University of Tennessee Board of Trustees had suspended him from all university-related activities until further notice by a vote of 7-5 for violation of the student conduct code. This news rocked Jason to the core, and at one point, he removed himself from the room, retreating to the bathroom.

While there, he stood in front of the mirror staring into the eyes of his reflection, allowing the full weight of this news to wash over him. He would not be allowed to resume his participation in the one class that would allow him to obtain his bachelor's degree in December in business administration. And he would not be closing out his collegiate track and field career as a UT sprinter with Southeastern Conference and NCAA championship wins in the indoor 60-meter and outdoor 100-meter dashes. Although he made the final in both races during the 2014-2015 seasons, Mitch Newman, representing the University of Florida Gators at the time, had won both titles.

Thelma was greeted at the entry door by a black maid and butler. The butler descended down the concrete and brick stairs to retrieve Thelma's overnight bag from the rental. The maid greeted Thelma, asking her about her flight down from Tennessee, as they both stood in front of the gaping door waiting on the butler to rejoin them. Once he did, with Thelma's overnight bag dangling from his right hand, the maid closed the door behind them and led Thelma deeper into the expansive mansion. The butler broke off near the stairwell to the right to take Thelma's overnight bag up to her guest room.

"Thelma," Mr. Newman greeted when he saw Thelma standing in the door leading into the study. Jason, who had been sitting on a sofa with a stoic expression on his face, stood, extended his hand to shake Thelma's hand as she entered the room, and then sat back down. Mr. Newman walked from behind his desk to direct her to the sofa across from the one Jason was sitting on. "How was the flight down?"

"Turbulent," Thelma replied, "but I made it."

A different maid entered the room holding a tray with three glasses filled with iced sweet tea. She then walked in front of the three, allowing each of them to take one from the tray, before exiting the room.

"Kelvin is flying down from Memphis on Thursday," Thelma announced. Jason smiled as he recognized her type, a no-nonsense, let's get down to business kind of gal. Thoughts about her work ethic had flooded his mind during his video call with her, but this truth became more prominent now that she was sitting in front of him.

Soon, Mr. Newman encouraged Jason and Thelma to take their conversation out back, on the patio deck. They followed through with his admonition, and once they were on the patio deck, the clear, blue sky and white clouds hung above them as if they had been painted.

"You say you knew my father," Jason said. They were now seated on one of the wooden benches aligned with the patio railing. "That you were saddened by his loss. Can we talk about it? Him?"

"Sure," Thelma replied before swallowing hard. "Jerome was one of us, part of our Racial and Economic Justice Network. Always challenging us to do more than what we were doing."

"What do you mean?"

"Your father grew up in Jackson, Mississippi, right? During the late fifties and sixties. White people went out of their way to silence black voices, make black people feel like they didn't matter, that they weren't citizens. Hell, they even convinced them that they couldn't vote. He once told me the more black people tried to keep to themselves, build out their predominately black communities, the more the white people there tried to infringe upon their civil liberties."

"Yeah. He used to take us there during the summers, to visit with family. Not much has changed. Black poverty on one side, white affluence on the other. Had no choice but to think the worst about white people."

"It's not just there. Same thing occurs up and around Knoxville, and even in places like Charlotte and Memphis. They always find a way to take what they want, mostly by raising taxes. They call it urban renewal, but once they're done renewing these places, black residents can't afford to live there anymore."

"Is that why he was in East Raleigh that day?"

"That's what I heard. He was scheduled to meet with 80-year-old Rosalyn Turner, a retired elementary school teacher. She and her husband had purchased their downtown home in 1984 when the rates were low. After Mr. Turner died, she was living off two pensions, hers and the one Mr. Turner received from the local newspaper, the News & Observer. He was a truck driver. Your father had gone over there to help her develop a plan for keeping her property."

"Is what they said about the increased gang activity true? Were the Bloods and Crips beefing with each other?"

Thelma scrunched up her lips. "Chile', please. That's something the Raleigh Police Department made up to hide what was really going on."

"What do you mean?"

"Crimes like home invasions and carjackings were taking place, shootouts even, and young black men, many of them teenagers, were being arrested. When you turned on the local news, they went out of their way to flash their black faces on the screen. Many of us thought this was a calculated move on the part of the RPD and the local news media. Back then, we felt they were trying to convince the public that East Raleigh was a crime-ridden area that needed to be cleaned up. And our guts told us that these crimes were being committed by the very people they had hired to serve and protect the residents there."

"That explains why they haven't identified a suspect after all these years. That was like seventeen years ago."

"It was." Thelma turned slightly to square up with Jason. "How were things with your mother, brother and you after that?"

Jason's head dropped as he turned to his right, offering Thelma nothing more than his shoulder. "It was hard. I still get emotional when I think back to seeing him lying in that casket. Eyes closed. Not moving. I wanted to believe he was just sleeping, taking a nap. Even thought I could wake him up just by shaking him. But Mama just kept telling us that he's gone to be with the Lord."

"I know the NAACP came through for you all."

"Yeah. Volunteers with the chapter and our church, Now Faith, moved us into our new home. Too many memories of our father in the old one. Mama didn't have to work. She was receiving Daddy's Army pension. But she kept on working, as an English teacher at Heritage Middle School. Staying busy helped her shoulder the loss."

"And based on what I've been reading in the papers, you used the loss as motivation as well. Right?"

Jason shrugged at Thelma's reference to his exploits on the track. He then looked up and out at the trees and foliage on the other side of the concrete fence that surrounded the back-yard to the Newman's lot. Swirling winds caused the leaves to flutter.

"Why'd they say he had drugs in his system?"

"I don't know, Jason. Seemed highly suspicious to us as well. Mr. Cochran reviewed the autopsy report. He shared that it is possible that the Medical Examiner doctored it up to make it look like Jerome contributed to his own demise. But we really don't know and may never know."

Jason shrugged his shoulders at that and then leaned forward to stare down at the deck's wooden planks. When he peered back up at Thelma, a look of desperation covered his face. "I'm one class shy of graduating college," he proclaimed. "My brother Jeremiah didn't go to college, he decided to join the military, the Marines. So, I'm going to be the first child in the family to earn a degree. Was looking forward to it, hearing Jeremiah and her shouting my name up in the bleachers when they heard my name, saw me walking across the stage in my cap and gown. Me graduating means more than competing for an Olympic gold medal. It's what he would have wanted, me grad-uating from college."

"We will walk and chew gum at the same time," Thelma replied. "You will be reinstated, and you will be allowed to grad-uate in December."

Jason pursed his lips at that, bowing his head downward to say a silent prayer. Looking up again, he said, "Thank you, again, for agreeing to take on my case."

"None needed. I'm honored, really. Your father will al-ways be remembered as a good man. Serving as your defense attorney is me paying off a debt I owe to him."

Two days later, Jason found himself dispensing hugs as he prepared to join Mr. Newman, Kelvin Cochran, and Thelma St.

James in the back of a stretch limousine for the short ride to Atlanta's Hartsfield International Airport. Mr. Cochran thought it best to fly him to Knoxville on a Sunday to decrease the level of scrutiny he would receive from the media. Thelma had explained during a sit down in the family study that Roscoe Baker's team seemed to be all in on their Stand My Ground defense. Jason's legal team would have to counter their arguments with indisputable proof that Jason was the victim, the one who had been standing his ground.

Jason's clenched hands sank deeper between the crack of his thighs as the limo rounded the rotary and made its way down the paved pathway, away from the Newman mansion. They were seated in the limo's spacious back compartment, with Mr. Newman to his right, Kelvin Cochran and Thelma on the seat facing them.

"What are they saying up there?" Mr. Newman asked. "In Knoxville? Probably done nailed him to the cross. Right?"

"Close," Thelma replied. "They're portraying Baker as the local hero, someone who was just doing his job. But if Jason's account is drastically different, all that's about to change."

"How do you see it playing out?" Jason asked.

Mr. Cochran and Mr. Newman exchanged knowing glances, leaving the door open for Thelma to break it down.

The limo resonated from the vibrations of an airplane flying overhead. All eyes darted to the windows on either the left or the right. Jason and Mr. Newman had the best vantage point because they were seated in the back. Outside, the traffic control tower loomed large over the buildings that housed the boarding gates. The expressions on Mr. Newman and Jason's faces let them know their short ride to the airport was coming to an end.

Thelma continued, "We're going to have a nonstop flight to Knoxville's McGhee-Tyson Airport. After that, we disembark from the plane, enter the terminal, and officers with the Knoxville Police Department will take you into custody."

"Are they going to lock me up," Jason asked with a shaky voice. Thelma could hear the nervousness in his voice, but in these kinds of cases, she had no choice but to be a straight shooter.

"Unfortunately, yes," Thelma replied. "But only for a few hours, until I've had time to file a motion for you to be released on bail. That motion has already been drafted. Just need to file it with the court."

"Do we know how much that will be?" Mr. Newman asked. Jason turned to his right. Mr. Newman repositioned himself in his seat, winking slyly at the young sprinter. "Can't have this brother caged up for too long."

Jason's jaw tightened as the limo rolled under, through and past one of the many bridges holding up the passenger tram. He would forever be indebted to the Newmans for taking him into their home, but he knew that the financing of his defense would be costly. What if the jury and the judge ruled that he was indeed guilty of the charges levied against him? How would he be able to look Mr. Newman in the eyes? Hell, how would he be able to look his own mother and brother in the eyes?

The limo came to rest near the curb, and Mr. Cochran was the first to get out. Thelma followed, being pulled from the vehicle by her hand by Mr. Cochran. Once she was out, Mr. Newman exited, followed by Jason.

Standing several feet from the Gate B terminal entrance, Mr. Newman placed his hand on Jason's shoulder. Thelma and Mr. Cochran now waited patiently on the other side of the sliding, glass doors.

"I don't want you worrying about anything, young buck," he explained. "We got you covered. Just promise me one thing."

"What's that?" Jason replied, as the limo driver rolled his recently purchased luggage to him.

"Promise me you'll be there, in the Olympic 100-meter final next year."

All Jason could do was smile. He didn't know Mr. Newman that well. He had only been living with his family for five weeks. And Mr. Newman was rarely there, as he spent most of his time flying back and forth to New York and L. A., and destinations in between. Jason often wondered how Mr. Newman's wife could remain devoted to him with a schedule like that. She had needs as well – spiritual and emotional but especially physical. And she wasn't an Old Maid either, holding her own with her younger daughters in the looks department. At this moment, he felt sad for her, because his situation was nothing but one more reason for Mr. Newman to neglect her.

Jason eventually replied, "I'll be there. Just don't get mad at me for crossing the finish line first."

Mr. Newman grimaced as he patted Jason on the back. The mere mention of his son's name was cringe worthy. His son was a cheat, and he knew it. But he also knew a vitamin-free opponent had to defeat Mitch, humble him, before he would be able to regain his sense and sensibilities.

Mr. Newman extended his arm, waving Jason to Mr. Cochran and Thelma. Jason made his way toward the sliding, glass doors, pulling at the handle of the rolling suitcase Mr. Newman had purchased for him. But as he reached the door, he stopped and turned.

"Thank you," he said. "For all you have done, and are doing, for me. Don't know how I'll ever repay you."

"No repayment is necessary, young buck," Mr. Newman said. "Your mother, your father, raised you right. Just be the man they hoped you'd be."

On the plane now, seated and flying at an elevation of thirty thousand feet, Jason couldn't shake Mr. Newman's last words – "Just be the man they hoped you'd be." Jeremiah had said something similar before he had to report to Fort Bragg, North Carolina for boot camp. At the time, Jason was battling anxiety and depression, making failing grades in most of his classes, and getting sent to the principal's office for insubordination on more than one occasion. His teachers didn't care that he was the star running back on the Wake Forest Cougars football team. They didn't even care that he clocked 10.5 in the 100-meter dash his freshman year. Grades mattered. It had been up to Jason to get with their program.

While laying low with the Newmans, Jason had made multiple calls to his mother. Each time, she let it be known that she was happy to hear his voice, thanking him for letting her know that he was okay. She told him what the reporters had been saying about him, alleging that he had attacked a white security guard. Jason told her that was a "bold-faced lie," and then recounted for her what really happened.

"I didn't want to die," he cried.

Hours earlier, she had told Jason over the phone that she would be there, in Knoxville, to greet him. Her sister, Betty, lived in the small town of Morristown, Tennessee, and Hilda indicated she would be driving over to stay with her before reporting to the Sojourner Vista Resort and Conference Center for an extended stay. She said she would be there with him at the resort until the matter was resolved. Jason asked about Jeremiah, wanting to know if he knew, had heard. Hilda answered in the affirmative to both questions.

"After I told him you were on the run, he lost it," she explained. "He was concerned for your safety mostly. He was relieved when I told him that you had called, elated upon hearing you were surrendering."

Jason, seated in the window seat, next to Mr. Cochran, pushed the window shade down. Seconds later, his eyes closed, and he fell into a deep sleep.

CHAPTER THIRTEEN

"Thought you had the nigga' under your spell, girl," Coach Wilson exclaimed, "but it looks like he's 'bout to step on us."

The corners of Yasmin's mouth tightened as she peered over at Coach Wilson through squinted eyes. Coach Moses snickered on the other side of the table. They were sitting in a corner booth, at a San Diego *Applebee's*, far removed from Los Angeles' bright lights. Coach Moses knew his friend and colleague had already been skating on thin ice with Yasmin for quite some time. So, rather than add more wood to the fire, he kept his mouth shut, not wanting to get caught up in the imminent shit storm.

"There you go again," Yasmin replied under her breath. "Trying to tell me how to do my job." She moved her leg from under the table. Then, with all the calm she could muster, she added, "How about you stay in your lane, and I stay in mine."

"Chill, you two," Coach Moses interjected. "We ain't got time for all that."

"Of course," Coach Wilson replied.

"Besides. He's back to taking his vitamins. Daily. That's all that matters. Right?"

Coach Moses watched Coach Wilson shift uncomfortably in his chair. Coach Wilson's eyes flashed from Yasmin's covered breasts to her skinny jean-encased hips and thighs, then to the floor. The smirk on Yasmin's face let Coach Moses know that she suspected what he already knew.

"You definitely doing something right," Moses said. "Old boy is even getting to practice on time, raring to test the limits of his speed. Couldn't say that a few weeks ago."

"Just make sure you honor your end of the deal. Five thousand every month during the operation. A quarter mil by the time he's standing on the podium with the gold medal draped around his neck."

"I don't renege on my deals, sweetheart. As long as no one suspects anything, a lot of people are going to make a lot of money off Mitch Newman." A slight pause, as Coach Moses motioned to their waitress for another round of beers. After the waitress acknowledged him, he continued, "How do you feel about him? Experience has shown me that good sex makes people lose their minds. You not about to lose your mind, are you, sweetheart?"

Yasmin swung her leg back under the table and slid to the middle of the padded bench. "No. I'm not. He's a good man and all, but I'm not about to fall head-over-heels in love with him."

Yasmin's hands went to her lap, where she clasped them together, right when the waitress arrived holding a tray with two bottled Budweisers and a martini. The waitress winked at Yasmin as she placed Coach Moses' Budweiser on the table first followed by Coach Wilson's Budweiser and Yasmin's martini.

"Will there be anything else?" the waitress asked, her gaze rising from Yasmin's cleavage to her made-up face.

"No," Coach Moses replied. "That'll be all, for now."

The waitress reluctantly turned on her heels, but when she did, she was immediately flagged down by two white guys in suits seated at an adjacent table.

"We're depending on you to suppress that conscience of his," Coach Moses continued. "Appeal to his vanity."

"Doing my best. But he keeps bringing up his father, the strain in their relationship. Like I told you before, he believes his father knows."

"But has he told him anything?" Coach Wilson asked.

"No. He hasn't. He just misses him. They haven't spoken to each other since he set the world record."

Coach Moses and Coach Wilson exchanged knowing glances.

Coach Moses said, "We're depending on you to let us know immediately if loses his focus again, mentions anything to his father. Nigga' knew what he was getting into when he signed on. The less Cornelius knows the better."

"What does he say to you when he says he wants to stop taking his vitamins?" Coach Wilson asked.

"He believes he could have broken the record without them. Says all he has to do is train harder."

"Wouldn't be enough," Coach Wilson replied, leaning back while crossing his arms. "Those vitamins are the key to him running fast times. That's why he must stay the course. Remember, his success is our success."

Yasmin nodded her head with pursed lips. She understood what was at stake, but she also regretted seeing Mitch so unhappy. She never knew her father. And even though her relationship with Mitch had an expiration date, she couldn't help imagining Cornelius Newman becoming the father figure she never had simply through her faux relationship with his son.

Yasmin remembered the first time she met Cornelius Newman in person, during a ski trip to the Mt. Snow Ski Resort in Vermont. She and Mitch had only been dating for a little over six months, and during that time Mitch would always tell her that his parents would love her. She had never been a fan of snow - she preferred lying on a Caribbean beach in a two-piece bikini reading a good book. But being up there with Mitch's father, mother and sisters allowed her to see another side of Mitch.

Rayvyn had been the most outspoken, spilling the tea about how a teenage Mitch would spend a lot of his time in the bathroom, supposedly taking "a crap." Mitch would give her the angry eye in an attempt to shush her. He didn't want Yasmin knowing that he was in the bathroom jacking off. At 14 years of age, with thick glasses and pimples covering his caramel-colored face, none of the girls at his school would give him the time of day. They knew he came from money, and he had already been named the second string running back on the varsity football team, but they considered him ugly because of these features. All this changed after his mother took him to get soft contact lenses and a few dermatology consults. Once his facial acne cleared up, the girls started viewing him in a more positive light. And many of them started vying for his attention. He wasted very little time obliging them, albeit sexually.

Yasmin could tell that Trish viewed her relationship with Mitch as suspect. While sitting in front of the fireplace one evening, Trish told her how much she disliked Mitch's last girlfriend, her classmate Nadine Watts, a white girl. She had shared that Mitch was infatuated with Nadine because of her pretty face, big tits and tight ass. And because she allowed Mitch to hit it on the regular, Mitch was quick to shower her with gifts. But Trish had known early on that Nadine was more into the perks that come with being with one of the Newman kids than Mitch himself. So, when she confronted Nadine about her trifling ways in the school parking lot, Nadine got so upset with Trish that she swung at her, missing. Trish had retaliated, slapping the right side of Nadine's face. For the next three days, Nadine walked around the school with Trish's handprint there. Mitch would eventually drop her like a bad habit after finally being able to see what his sister saw.

"Is that you?" Trish had asked. "Are you with my brother for all the wrong reasons?"

"No," Yasmin had lied. "I don't even know what the wrong reasons are."

"I know you done looked my father up on the Internet. And you know that Tribe Records is a subsidiary of the Newman Multimedia Group. You in this because of what this could do to your film making career, aren't you?"

"No. I'm not."

Mitch's eyes slowly flickered open as the wheels of the 747 touched Panama City's Tocumen International Airport landing strip. Yasmin peered over at him, smiling, from the window seat. They were seated in First Class.

"Welcome back, sleepy head," Yasmin said. "Didn't take much to knock you out."

Mitch chuckled, and replied, "Like a baby in a bassinet."

"Well, I hope you don't sleep your way through this trip," Johnny, Yasmin's older brother, exclaimed from the aisle seat to their left. "It's Panama, dude. Tyrone is depending on us to make this weekend unforgettable."

Tyrone Campbell was one of Yasmin and Johnny's childhood friends, and this trip had been planned by Tyrone's wife Helena several months in advance to celebrate Tyrone's 30th birthday. Mitch had never met Tyrone; he was just falling in line with what Yasmin had planned for them. But he looked forward to getting to know Tyrone, who he had learned was a rising Executive in Training, or EIT, at Amazon, and Helena, an English professor at Penn State University.

During his previous conversations with Johnny, Johnny had told him that Tyrone is an avid golfer. Johnny recounted for Mitch excursions that he had gone on with Tyrone that had him golfing on some of the finest golf courses in the land – Pinehurst in North Carolina, Augusta National in Georgia, and Oakmont in Pennsylvania. As a teen, and even as a young adult, Mitch had golfed on these courses and more with his father. However, his travels with Cornelius Newman had never taken him to Panama. So, he looked forward to spending three days golfing at the Buenaventura Golf & Beach Resort in Rio Hato, the next two relaxing poolside at the JW Marriott in Punta Colón, and gambling during the evening hours at the Ocean Sun Casino

"You all can golf all you want," Yasmin said. "That's what we're here for. Just don't have my baby hurting himself out there. Remember, he's a world-class sprinter, okay? Going for gold at next year's Summer Olympic Games." She patted Mitch's left hand with her right. "And if unforgettable has anything to do with knocking boots with one of these Panamanian bitches, you niggas' better think twice."

Johnny's girlfriend Tonya leaned forward in her seat, as if to say, "Tell it, girl!"

"They got all this." Yasmin cupped her breasts, "But they still desire that." Yasmin eyed the Panamanian beauty seated in front of them, who stood up right at that exact moment for a restroom break. Seeing that the front restroom was occupied, the Panamanian beauty turned on her heels and proceeded to walk in their direction.

Tonya slumped back in her chair, conceding the point to Yasmin. Unbeknownst to them, Mitch and Johnny were simultaneously receiving a passing wink from the Panamanian beauty as she walked down the center aisle on her way to the rear restroom. Because they were seated in aisle seats, both did double takes, their bodies twisted in their seats just so they could see what the Panamanian beauty was working with from behind.

"Damn!" they seemed to say as they looked at each other with wide-eyed expressions. Seconds later, they burst out laughing, even sharing a fist bump.

Yasmin and Tonya just rolled their eyes and shook their heads.

Helena had contracted with Elite Panamanian Tours, or EPT, to handle shuttle transports from Tocumen International Airport, and the itinerary for the first three days of their Panamanian adventure. The plan was for all the couples to meet up at Panama City's La Rana Dorada Restaurant for appetizers, and even a light lunch if they so desired, before they boarded a stretch limousine for the three-hour drive from Panama City to Rio Hato. When they arrived at the restaurant, Tyrone was the first to get up from the table to greet Johnny first with a brotherly embrace and pounds to the back and Yasmin second with an embrace and kiss to her cheek. Helena, Marvin, and Marvin's wife Millicent immediately followed Tyrone's lead, offering more hugs and kisses to the new arrivals. Their EPT tour guide Harris, a bearded white man from Chicago, was seated by himself at a table next to Helena, cleaning the meat off his last Buffalo wing, stopping intermittently to lick the sauce off his fingers. When he caught sight of Mitch and Yasmin entering the restaurant, Harris wiped his face and hands clean with a napkin in anticipation of shaking hands after Helena introduced him to the group.

"Glad you all could make it," Helena said when everyone was seated. Mitch watched as Yasmin patted Tyrone's elbow, reassuring him that his happiness was their number one concern. "What you are about to experience would not have been possible without Yasmin and Millicent, my partners in crime. But now that we're all here, I'd like to turn the floor over to our tour guide, Harris."

Harris stood. "Hey, guys," he said, somewhat nervously at first, with a hand wave. "Welcome to Panama. We have a very busy four days planned for you. I know Helena has already sent you the itinerary, so I'm going to leave that one alone. But we have a limo waiting outside, a few blocks down the road, to get you over to the Buenaventura Beach and Golf Resort." He looked over at Tyrone. "Wish I could be out there with you guys, Tyrone. Beautiful course. But steer clear of those sand traps."

Tyrone chuckled at that, with Mitch and the others joining in.

Mitch and Yasmin's luxury suite at the Buenaventura Golf and Beach Resort was an open floor plan, with a king-sized bed taking up most of the space in the room. A desk and chair lined the left wall, along with a cabinet for the miniature bar and refrigerator. But what Mitch looked forward to the most was watching Yasmin remove her robe through the interior shutter blinds to get into the oversized jacuzzi bathtub.

They had arrived in their stretch limousine around ten, so night had already fallen on the resort. As Yasmin and Mitch stepped onto the suite's patio deck, they could see and hear other guests talking and laughing near the tranquil stream below. Palm trees swayed as winds from the Pacific Ocean made their leaves flutter. And the only evident light came from the occupied bungalows. Sensing that Yasmin, who was dressed in a form-fitting, yellow sun dress, was entranced by it all, Mitch pulled his smart phone from his pocket and snapped away, capturing her beauty, her innocence.

"Why do you keep doing that?" Yasmin asked.

"Because you're fine," Mitch replied. "Can't let moments like this pass us by, not when we're in paradise."

"Stop." She turned toward the sounds of the Pacific to their left. She grabbed his hand and pulled him to her, resting her head on his burly chest. "Just enjoy."

But their ears soon caught the sound of Tonya moaning in the adjacent room. An even louder shriek from Tonya caused Yasmin to stand up straight with widened eyes.

"Sounds like somebody couldn't wait," she said.

Yasmin then turned and leaned back on the deck railing. She removed and tossed her sun dress in what seemed like one motion. Standing there now, in nothing but her lace bra and matching panties, she extended her arms and spread her legs, an invitation to Mitch.

"You mind helping me with the rest?'

Hours later, an exhausted Mitch lay next to Yasmin atop layers of disheveled sheets and a comforter.

"You know I have that thing in Tennessee in October," Mitch said. "Have me on some panel talking about student-athletes getting paid. The leaves will be changing then. Real treat if you've never seen it."

"You know I can't go. I have class."

"Your loss then. Staying at the Sojourner Vista Mountain Resort. It's black owned and operated, considered the Great Smokey Mountain's lap of luxury."

Mitch paused briefly to collect his thoughts. Yasmin lifted her head off his chest to gaze up at him.

"What's wrong?" she asked.

"My pops is going to be there," Mitch replied. "So, I think I'm going to fly down to Atlanta a few days before, tell him everything."

Yasmin studied Mitch's furrowed brow. But she also heard Moses' voice, telling her to let him know when Mitch begins to take his eyes off the prize. But how could she? How could she betray the trust of a man who just wanted things to be right with his father?

"You should," Yasmin lied. "He's your father. He should know. But if you tell others, everything you worked for is going to be lost. You know that, don't you? How will you respond when the media comes after you?"

"Not talking about telling the world, just my pops. I know how USA Track and Field and the IAAF operate. I would receive a lifetime ban from the sport. All I want to do is tell him that I'm no longer taking it. Just pray he understands."

Yasmin turned her back to Mitch. "You still plan on going back to Florida to train with Coach Tyson?"

"Yeah. He knows me, my body. Gotta return to my roots, bae. Without the drugs. My times were fast before the Yellow Jacket, and they will continue to be fast once it's out of my system."

Mitch touched Yasmin's shoulder, bidding her to face him. She relented, facing him but looking past him.

"What's up?" Mitch asked.

Yasmin closed her eyes. "They're going to come after you if you start posting slower times." Her eyes opened as she breathed in deeply. "I don't know why you don't accept the fact that shady isn't always bad. You should stick with Coach Moses' plan. Make that money."

Mitch scooted to the edge of the bed to sit upright. "But I know Pops. He's going to demand a change in plan. I have no problem telling him that I'm done with it. You shouldn't either."

A brief pause, as Yasmin considered Mitch's words. Seconds later, she slid from under the covers, retreating to the bathroom and shutting the door behind her.

Alone again, Mitch used both hands to massage the tightness in his temple. He then wiped his watering eyes. It was at that moment that he felt the distance widen between Yasmin and him, and this truth caused his sadness to reach a new low.

CHAPTER FOURTEEN

The look on the Knoxville Police Department deputies' faces let Jason know he was public enemy number one. As soon as he and his legal team exited the McGee-Tyson International Airport terminal and entered the baggage claim area, they were greeted by a single row of five deputies, with all but one of them being white, and a mix of local, national and international news reporters. The crowd also included hordes of disinterested passengers, who undoubtedly were only there to retrieve their luggage.

The stern expression on the deputies' faces and open postures indicated they were licking their chops to snap the handcuffs on Jason's wrists. But they would have to wait. Thelma St. James was intent on setting the record straight, all for the purpose of ensuring Jason received a fair trial. So, as Jason positioned himself beside her, to the left of the podium, he breathed in deeply before exhaling as Thelma placed her leather portfolio binder on the podium and tapped the microphone to make sure it would pick up what she had to say. Jason had been allowed to surrender. And unlike Trayvon Martin, Eric Garner, Michael Brown and so many other black men before him, he would be able to gain an audience with an impartial judge and jury before telling his side of the story.

For much of the walk from the airport terminal to its baggage claim area, Jason hung his head, not trying to make eye contact with anyone. When he lifted it briefly to peer out at the faces of the seated and standing onlookers, he knew they knew who he was and what he had done to that security guard, who also just happened to be a retired Knoxville police officer. But it was the furrowed brows of the white men that troubled him the most. He surmised that many of them, most really, viewed Roscoe Baker as a saint, someone who could do no wrong. And now that he was back in Tennessee, a red state in the year 2015, he knew that many of these white men would be standing outside the courthouse venue in the coming days, chanting, "Blue Lives Matter" or "All Lives Matter," all for the purpose of suppressing what he, a black man, had to say, and counter the "Black Folk Matter" chant that boomed like thunder claps from the mouths of black activists protesting police brutality and demanding criminal justice reform.

But Jason's countenance improved when he peered out into the faces of the black and brown onlookers, both male and female. Several of them saluted him with balled up Black Power fists raised high in the air for all to see. It was a struggle for Jason not to return the gesture, but he knew, without anyone having to tell him, that this type of gesture from him would be misinterpreted by members of the mostly white audience. Moreover, it would force the polarized American populace to retreat even more to their respective racial/ethnic camps, the same way it did during the 1995 O. J. Simpkins Trial. In this scenario, you either viewed the issue from a white perspective or a black one.

Jason embraced the support he received from members of the Black American Diaspora, but he wanted his message to appeal to a broader array of rationally minded individuals. Truth be told, he wanted to embrace those white individuals in the crowd, and across the nation, that he fondly referred to as his white siblings in the struggle. For they were the ones who would make the difference, resulting from the fact that they are committed to creating a more perfect union, not just making

America white, uh, great, again. More importantly, Jason knew his white siblings in the struggle harbored a special kind of love for black neighbors like him, not a special kind of hatred.

"If I can have your attention," Thelma's voice boomed from the stand-alone speakers behind her.

A hush fell over the crowd.

"My name is Thelma St. James of the Thurgood Marshall Law Group's Knoxville branch, and I am the Lead Attorney for Jason Wayne Black. By now, many of you have heard that a deal was brokered with Georgia's Fulton County Police Department for Mr. Black's extradition back to Knoxville to answer to assault and battery and attempted murder charges filed by lawyers representing Triple A Security's Roscoe Hubert Baker.

"I will not be answering any questions from this podium today, but we wanted to let the public know that Mr. Black is about to be taken to the Magistrate for his arraignment and booking. But let me be clear: Here in the United States of America, and the state of Tennessee, our criminal justice system says a person is innocent until proven guilty. Mr. Black is innocent of the charges against him. We do not dispute the fact that Mr. Black did engage in a physical altercation with Mr. Baker, but we note that Mr. Black was defending himself, or doing what most people do when they're defending themselves: standing his ground. Our aim is to prove this in a court of law.

"I would also like to address comments that the Republican nominee for President, Mr. Malcolm Stillwell, made the other day about Mr. Black on the Fox News Channel. Rather than give my client the benefit of the doubt, he made a calculated decision to disparage Mr. Black, using terms like 'Super Predator' and 'Thug' to describe him. I assure you; Jason Wayne Black is not a super predator or a thug; he is a law-abiding citizen. And come next year, he will represent this great country, the United States of America, at the 2016 Summer Olympic Games in Rio de Janeiro, Brazil. Why? Because he is one of the fastest men on the planet at one-hundred and two-hundred meters. So, my message to the Republican presidential nominee: Leave the legal commentary to legal professionals like me. Thank you."

With that, Thelma waved Jason to the black deputy who awaited him with handcuffs in hand. Jason extended his arms to him, and the deputy snapped the handcuffs onto his wrists. After that, the lead deputy led Jason out of the airport as two other deputies took positions on Jason's right and left flank. Once outside in the open air, Jason used the moment to close his eyes and pray to Carmelita Newman's God, in hopes that all would be worked out in his favor.

From his favorite recliner, Roscoe Baker used the remote to switch from the local ABC affiliate back to the Fox News Channel. His teenage granddaughters Candice and Deloris sat on the carpeted floor, while his son, the girls' father, Roscoe, Jr., or just Junior, stood behind him. Baker's wife Eunice sat in the matching recliner across the room, busying herself with her quilt knitting. On the screen in front of them, Baker's attorneys responded to Thelma St. James' Stillwell rebuke.

"The Republican Presidential nominee, Mr. Malcolm Stilwell, is not on trial here," Mason Chase, Baker's lead attorney, began. "Jason Black is. For stabbing my client, Roscoe Hubert Baker, with a sling blade knife. I recently learned from Mr. Baker's surgeon that the blade just missed severing a major artery, by one to two millimeters, mind you. If this artery had been severed, my client would have bled to death." Chase paused for dramatic effect. "Folks, don't let Thelma St. James inject politics into this case. The evidence clearly shows that Jason Wayne Black was the instigator during this altercation. My client, Mr. Baker, is the only one who sustained a life-threatening injury, and Jason Black walked away without a scratch on him."

Junior placed his hands on his father's shoulders and squeezed. His giddiness at what they were witnessing even made Baker a little jubilant, but that was to be expected from his one and only son. Junior always had dreams of being a self-made man, rise to the same level of prominence as Malcolm Stillwell even. But it was clear from his reaction that the best he could do was take pride in his father's name being mentioned in connection with something the real estate investor turned politician said.

"Calm down, boy," Baker shrugged, causing Junior to release him. "Not like we won the lottery. But the police union has my back. That blackie doesn't stand a chance."

The girls looked up at their grandfather from the floor. Eunice just smirked as she continued her knitting. She had seen this movie before – Baker pushing his weight around like he was the city's enforcer – and she didn't like it. Yes, representatives from the Knoxville Police Union would rush to defend his good name, but the public scrutiny of her and their family just didn't feel right. She agreed that black people returning from the North to Southern cities like Knoxville brought their problems with them, but she also recognized that in the United States of America, they had a right to live wherever they damn well pleased.

Eunice was hopeful that Malcolm Stillwell and Republican legislators would institute legislation that kept more of the blacks in poverty so it would be easier to contain them. She knew her white family couldn't be contained; thanks to Baker's security guard salary, but mostly to his monthly KPD pension payments, as well as the monthly pension payments she received from her former employer, Federal Freight & Logistics. She worked for FFL for 27 years, with 10 being spent as the Southeastern division's Regional Manager.

Baker pointed and said, "Deloris, go pour me a glass of Mamaw's lemonade." Deloris hopped up from the floor and darted toward the kitchen. He then looked over at his wife. "I can see those wheels in your head turning," he said, somewhat sarcastically. "What you got to say about all this?"

Eunice replied, "What I always tell you: You should have been minding your own damn business. But you never do. Always thinking you must be the one maintaining order in the neighborhood. Now, you're going up against someone who has the will, and the means, to fight back."

"What do you mean?" Baker asked, accepting the tall glass of lemonade from Deloris. "He's a nigger. Just like all the others."

Eunice peered over at Candice and Deloris, determining that what she was about to say would be more than their young minds could handle. "Girls, I need to speak with your Paw and PaPaw alone. Please go to the basement."

The girls got up and exited the room.

"But this one is not like the others, sweetheart," Eunice said as her hands fell to her lap. "He is college educated. The college-educated ones don't hold back. They know their rights. They're more enlightened. Much different than the uneducated ones."

Junior interjected. "But the Union has his back, Maw. That must count for something, right?"

Eunice released her knitting tongs to wipe the perspiration from her brow with a handkerchief. "I wish it were that easy, son. I really do. But it's not; not in this case. Right now, the Group probably has investigators collecting as much information as they can on the boy. But that St. James bitch did something that many people probably didn't even notice."

"What's that?" Baker and Junior asked, almost in unison.

"She called him an Olympic hopeful. Calling him that is going to solidify support mainly from liberal and progressive Democrats, and possibly some moderate Republicans who feel it is their patriotic duty to support…"

"But I'm backed by the Blue," Baker interrupted gruffly, "our Confederacy. There are more of us than them."

Eunice pursed her lips with a roll of her eyes. "Stop thinking that. The talking heads on Fox News are going to serve the Confederacy's purpose by telling their faithful viewers that the country is not getting browner, blacker, but they're lying. It's true. We Whites are an endangered species, about to become the majority minority, and there is nothing we can do to change that. Yes, your white brothers in Blue are shooting as many of them as they can dead in the streets, even when they're unarmed. They also give fellow confederates assurances that they won't receive the same kind of treatment. But this new tidal wave of racial and ethnic diversity is going to expose the Confederacy's unspoken pact with white police officers, and when that happens, there's nothing we can do to put the genie back in the bottle."

Both Baker and Junior peered over at Eunice, nodding their heads to signal they understood the full implications of this sea change. Junior peered over and down at his mother with admiration. Deep down, Baker envied her, but he also respected her willingness to never dumb things down.

When Eunice spoke, she injected truth into all her statements. He also knew that her employment with FFL ushered her acceptance into the good graces of the Confederate States of America, a network of white Anglo-Saxon Protestant males that included the likes of Malcolm Stillwell. The CSA's number one objective was to keep persons of color out of corporate boardrooms, not allow them to participate in the crafting of decisions that preserved white people's privilege.

"So," Baker continued, "the play is to use my high-profile case to sow more discord, division, right?"

"Right," Eunice replied with a wink. "That's what the CSA has always done, especially during the fifties and sixties. Can't have another Martin Luther Coon rising up to lead them to the Promised Land. We must keep them in a perpetual search for another black messiah, prevent them from discovering the power within. That's why we must get Stillwell elected as a Republican. His acceptance by conservative Republican voters will allow the CSA to have more control over the party's platform, which will guarantee the preservation of Confederate Rule."

"Will they allow me to be seen with Stillwell?" Baker asked.

Eunice pursed her lips. "Of course. But did you really have to ask? The CSA is playing chess not checkers, sweetie. Like it or not, you are the bishop that they will be using to propel Stillwell to the Oval Office."

A seated Cynthia Black placed her left hand on the plexiglass wall as she held the telephone receiver to her ear. Jason, dressed in an orange jumpsuit, stared back at her, the telephone receiver pressed against the left side of his face and ear, on the other side of the dividing wall. It pained Cynthia to see her youngest son behind bars. She and Jerome had raised their boys to be upstanding members of the community.

"How's Aunt Betty," Jason asked.

"She good," Cynthia replied. "She out there, in the lobby waiting. They only allow one visitor to come back at a time. She'll be back here to see you when I'm done."

Jason thought back to the last time he saw Aunt Betty, more than four years ago during his high school graduation party in Wake Forest. Her daughter, his cousin Melody, was there as well, as usual saying he had a "big block head" like the Peanuts character Charlie Brown. Melody was two years older than him, and at the time, she was attending Howard University in Washington, DC, majoring in Print-Journalism with a minor in African American Studies, and she was gearing up to take her first semester of classes in her major. Her goal was to become an Investigative Journalist like the *New York Times'* Nicole Sinclair-Lewis, author of *1619: The Year Black Lives Should Have Mattered*.

Melody was Aunt Betty's only child. Aunt Betty had raised Melody without receiving any emotional and financial support from Melody's father. At the time, Jason thought to himself, What's up with these brothers? But the answer to this question never came easy, if at all. Jason knew even back in the day that much of the support Aunt Betty had been receiving through the years came from his mother, the monthly funds that Cynthia was receiving from her teacher's salary and her husband's NAACP pension.

"I'm sorry, Ma," Jason cried, a lone tear gliding down his right cheek. "This one is on me."

"You don't have to apologize to me, boy. Just be strong. Always know that there is light on the other side."

"I'm trying, but it's hard."

"I know, baby. But they don't see it that way. As far as they're concerned, you're another black man who was trying to cause trouble in a white neighborhood. You know how they do, especially down here in the South. All the times they stopped and frisked you and your friends when you all were in high school, and then acting all nice after they learned who you were. It don't change when you go off to college, get an education, a good job. To them, you will always be black, another nigger."

"I just wish someone would talk to me like I'm a first grader, make it all make sense. I'm always grinding, trying to be a better person, striving to be the best at what I do, for my school, my country, and this is the treatment I get. Why isn't he in here with me? Why does he get to walk free? It's not right, Ma. It's not fair."

Cynthia wiped the wetness in her eyes. She could sense Jason's anxiety rising. She knew his heart was racing a mile a minute. So, she did the only thing she could do at that moment: She placed her right hand back on the plexiglass dividing wall. With a slight nod of her head, she bid Jason to place his right hand on the other side of the wall with hers. He did, allowing it to rest there as they continued to talk.

"I need you to know that we're here for you, boy, that we believe in you, what you say that man did to you. I also need you to know that you're in good hands. This Thelma St. James is good people, paid me a visit when you were in Atlanta. Just follow her lead. Allow what's going to happen to happen."

"I will." Jason removed his hand from the wall and sat upright in his chair. "They're taking me to this place, Sojourner Vista. Are you going to be there?"

"That's where we just came from. Drove down from Morristown last night and checked in. So, yes, we'll be there when you get out."

"What's it like?"

Cynthia smiled. "Typical resort, up in the mountains. Indoor and outdoor pools. Jacuzzis. Indoor track. Fitness and business center. Game room. They have us in one of the single-family cabins above the main building. Two bedrooms with queen-sized beds, two with king-sized beds, with a living room, dining room and kitchen. You're going to love it."

"Ms. St. James told me it's black-owned."

"Yeah. All I saw when we stepped into the lobby were well-dressed black and brown people checking people in and directing people to where they needed to go from behind the concierge's desk. Ms. St. James also said something about some racial and social justice conference being held there in a few weeks. Whomever owns the place is making sure their black ownership is on full display."

"Don't know how I should feel about that."

"If it were me, I'd feel great about that. Means black people have your back."

"I guess you're right."

Hearing that Jason Black had turned himself in made Roscoe Baker feel uneasy. He and his wife had been a part of the 1776 Patriot Movement since its 2008 inception, when Nelson Dupont, the United States' first, black president, was elected. He agreed with the organization's founding principle - that white people founded the good ole' U. S. of A. as a white nation in 1776, and, consequently, they are the main group entitled to its rights, privileges and freedoms. It didn't matter to them that the land that their British ancestors settled on was already occupied by Native Americans, who in their eyes were savages. It also didn't matter that their British ancestors essentially just came in and told them that this land is our land now. Baker, and others like him, believed in Charles Darwin's Survival of the Fittest maxim. The fact that their white ancestors had the ingenuity and technology to subdue the land that would later become the 50 states known as the United States of America showed that these same white ancestors were stronger than all the rest.

But Baker also had reservations about seeing Jason again, in person, in a courtroom. The boy had stabbed him, and deep down he knew their physical altercation would never have happened if Jason had not been confronted by him on the street. Startling a white woman wasn't a big deal. He also found it hard not to admit that Jason had a right to defend himself if he thought his life was in jeopardy. Hell, he was holding a gun to Jason's head. Granted, Baker had only pulled his gun out to scare Jason; he had no intention of pulling the trigger. Had he known that Jason was carrying a sling blade knife, he wouldn't have brandished his gun at all. He would have just talked with him, given him a warning.

Baker told all of this to his wife. Eunice just stared back at him with an emotionless expression on her pale face. Baker had seen this expression many times before, when she caught him doing stupid things and making idiotic comments. But this time, things were different, and she was quick to tell him why they were different. "Your incompetence will force the Confederacy to come to your defense. And while we will never shirk our responsibility to one of our own, it's way too early for Mr. Stillwell to reveal where he stands in relation to the CSA's founding principle, or on the question of you having the right to stand your ground as a law enforcement officer. Our focus must be on casting a cloud over these series of New Times articles about 1619 being the year black folks should have mattered, and convincing white parents that Critical Race Theory is being taught to their white children in public K-12 schools."

The series that Eunice was referencing, **1619: The Year Black Folks Should Have Mattered**, is a long-form journalism endeavor developed in August 2014 by Nicole Sinclair-Lewis, writers from *The New York Times*, and *The New York Times Magazine*, which aims to re-frame the country's history by placing the consequences of slavery and the contributions of black Americans at the very center of the United States' national narrative. The content of the book initially ran as a series of articles in both the newspaper and the magazine, and in early 2015, came out in book form.

Prior to the publication of the first article that Sinclair-Lewis' wrote for the series, college professors with ties to the Confederate States of America's faux 1776 Patriot Movement came together to craft a response to what they viewed as a big lie.

When their week-long discussions had ended, they came out with their own book, **1776: The Founding Fathers' Vision for America**, and recruited white neo-conservative writers, journalists and laypersons to inundate publications and social media platforms like Twitter and Facebook with posts that debunked the assertion that black Americans should be at the center of the United States' national narrative. The leaders of the 1776 Patriot Movement also felt they had the white American electorates' blessing, as the Democratic Party suffered major losses during the 2014 midterm elections. While the Democratic Party still controlled the United States presidency, the CSA co-opted Republican Party controlled the House of Representatives and the Senate. They also maintained a six to three majority on the U. S. Supreme Court.

Critical Race Theory, or CRT, had nothing to do with black Americans being at the center of the United States' narrative. Even the leaders of the 1776 Patriot Movement knew that Critical Race Theory was only being taught on college campuses, to graduate students in law schools. But because black Americans were seemingly gaining more prominence in American society yet were routinely being subjected to police brutality at the hands of mostly white police officers, they hatched schemes that cast CRT as the proverbial boogey man.

These 1776 Patriot leaders felt white students were being put in positions were they had to feel uncomfortable about something (slavery and Jim Crow legislation) that they had nothing to do with. It never dawned on them that black Americans remained in a perpetual state of discomfort because of the legacy of slavery and Jim Crow legislation. However, with less than 10 percent of the black American electorate classifying themselves as conservatives, members of the Republican Party, as well as 1776 Patriot Movement leaders, pressured Republican legislators in the House of Representatives and Senate to make this claim out loud, and rain verbal diatribes down on public K-12 superintendents who allowed their teachers to use the 1619 series and other diversity, equity and inclusion materials to teach students about prejudice, racism and discrimination. But little did they know that their efforts would run counter to enlightened black Americans' ongoing struggle to make schools more diverse, equitable and inclusive. They also failed to acknowledge that their efforts made it more difficult for black Americans and other Americans of color to accuse prejudiced white Americans of making racist remarks, committing racist acts.

To say Baker was, and continued to be, a reluctant participant in the 1776 Patriot Movement would be an understatement. As a police officer, he had many run-ins with members of Knoxville's local Ku Klux Klan chapter, and these run-ins prompted many heated discussions with his first partner, a black man named Bobby Ford, in the police headquarters' break room. The year was 1985, and Baker had only been with the KPD six months. Bobby, on the other hand, was fast approaching his 10th year in the force. Bobby would often share stories about his duty assignments as a United States Marine Officer in the Korean War (1966-1969) and the Ugandan coup d'état (1971) with Baker, and Baker would commend him often for his service. Baker gained a tremendous amount of respect for Bobby, especially when he noticed how Bobby would restrain himself when they were present when other officers, the white ones mostly, were arresting black suspects. Bobby and he would watch as these other officers beat these black suspects into submission before letting them know why they were being pulled over or why they were knocking on their doors. One time when they were alone, Baker asked Bobby how the treatment of these black suspects made him feel.

"Not much I can do about it," Bobby replied. "These mutha-fuckas gonna do what they do. But at the end of the day, it's no skin off my back. Just want to put in my time without no drama, and then add this second pension to my first."

But Bobby's words didn't match up with his actions. While Baker never saw Bobby mistreat any of the department's appre-hended, black suspects, or confront his colleagues about their role in this mistreatment, he saw how Bobby served and pro-tected his black community both in and out of uniform.

Most of the crimes that Knoxville Police officers had to re-spond to occurred in East Knoxville, the black part of town. Bobby opted to live in East Knoxville with his wife Mariam and their fraternal twins Michael and Lisa. Bobby also volunteered as a coach throughout the year with the East Knoxville Parks and Recreation Department and the Amateur Athletic Union, or AAU, mostly to coach his son's basketball teams. Baker saw a man who was committed to helping all children, regardless of their race/ethnicity, discover both their athletic and scholas-tic gifts. So, when he agreed one year to help Bobby coach his then 13-year-old son Michael's AAU youth basketball team, he was amazed that Bobby made all of his players participate in a two-hour study hall before practice, on Tuesdays and Thurs-days, with adult tutors that he had recruited from the commu-nity himself. When Baker asked Bobby why he did what he did, Bobby replied, "Because it's all about outcomes. If we adults give them the time and attention they need, help them keep their priorities straight, they will grow up to become productive members of society, the leaders we need them to be."

The more information Baker received about Jason Black, the more he realized how far he had deviated from Bobby Ford's lessons. He now knew that Jason was a sprinter on the Univer-sity of Tennessee Track and Field Team. But Jason wasn't your average sprinter; he had the second fastest time in the world.

He was now fully aware that in 2016, Jason would be vying for a gold medal, representing the USA, at the Rio Summer Olympic Games. The fact that Jason had achieved this amount of success let Baker know that Jason was one of the fortunate few black American males to overcome difficult circumstances and was well on his way to becoming the productive citizen that Bobby had dedicated his life to helping build firmer foundations for success.

"I should drop the charges," Baker said to his wife. He was standing over the kitchen island, making himself a peanut butter sandwich. Eunice sat at the kitchen table sipping the fresh cup of coffee that Baker had prepared for her.

Eunice swallowed hard. "Drop the charges? It's a little too late for that, don't you think? Mr. Chase is already preparing his case against the boy."

"But it just doesn't feel right. He's an athlete at UT, sweetie. A track athlete. Never seen the boy run. Hell, I've never felt the need to go to one of the track meets they hold over there every year. But we're UT graduates ourselves. We're season ticket holders to the school's football and basketball games. Would we have filed suit against Willie Sloan if he had stabbed me?"

The mere mention of Willie Sloan's name caused Eunice to shift in her seat. Sloan, a black man, was a standout wide receiver on the Tennessee football team from 1979-1982. After graduating from Tennessee, Sloan was drafted by the Chicago Bears in the 1982 National Football League draft. Sloan would go on to set single-season and all-time receiving records during his tenure with the Bears and is best known as the Chicago Bears player who caught two passes for touchdowns in Super Bowl XX. In that game, the Bears defeated the New England Patriots 46-10.

"That's just it. He's not Willie Sloan. He's not even worthy of being mentioned in the same breath as Willie. So, dropping the charges is out of the question. Mr. Chase has already discussed your case with Mr. Stillwell. And Mr. Stillwell wants to use the issues surrounding your case to win the presidency. Once he wins in November, I have been given assurances that we will be well compensated for our efforts."

CHAPTER FIFTEEN

"He turned himself in yesterday," Tyrone said, while he, Mitch, Johnny and Marvin ate their breakfast on the Buenaventura Golf and Beach Resort's expansive rear patio deck. "And they're really going after your father, dude. Saying he should be jailed for harboring a fugitive. They even have Stillwell sounding off against him."

Mitch shrugged. He recognized that by allowing Jason into his world, his father was essentially telling the world that he believes in Jason's innocence. But this acknowledgment of Cornelius Newman's sentiments caused him to squirm in his seat. Would he summon the same resources for him once he told him about his cheating ways? Probably not. Mr. Newman's good name would be on the line, and his good name meant everything to him.

"Stillwell is an opportunist," Mitch replied. "He's going to milk this for all its worth, in hopes that people who share his beliefs on this one issue will vote for him in November."

"But won't that affect your father?" Marvin asked. "His business? That don't worry you?"

"Not in the least," Mitch said. "Sounding off against racist mofos like Stillwell has been par for the course for my pops."

Johnny interjected. "You see the lawyer who's representing him. St. James. Thelma. Chic is fine."

The foursome chuckled at that. Johnny is always thinking with the head between his legs, not the one on his shoulders.

"She's good people too. Black is in good hands."

"He gave you a run for your money at last year's nationals," Johnny said. "Pushed you to that world record. You got anything more in the tank?"

"You'll just have to wait and see, nigga'," Mitch blurted out. "Just recently returned to the lab. But I know he's going to be training just as hard as me."

"Did you all see that front page story this morning. They're rioting in Baltimore after that boy Freddie Gray died in police custody. Read that things have been peaceful for the most part, but buildings are still being burned to the ground. The Republicans think Dupont should do more. You know that's going to be a major talking point leading up to the election."

"No doubt," Mitch replied. "But what more can President Dupont do? These people in these streets are exercising their constitutional right to protest, protest police brutality. Hell, look what these cops did in Chicago. Shot that boy Laquan McDonald sixteen times in the back. That shit ain't right. Boy wasn't even armed, just high as a kite."

"That's just it, though," Tyrone said. "All they look for is the smallest crack in a black man's armor and then they pounce. Sometimes fatally, other times they just do it for show by beating brothers down."

"Starting to get old," Mitch said, "tired. And our so-called civil rights leaders are more reactive than proactive."

"But we shouldn't hate brothers like Cal Sharper," Marvin said. "I watch his show *Politics Black & White* every Sunday on

MSNBC. He's up there right now marching in the streets with the protesters. Has anyone here ever done that? Marched in the streets? I know I haven't. Don't think I could."

"But why," Mitch asked.

"Because them seeing me marching in the streets would get my ass fired. I'm a senior executive with my company. The crackers there just want to protect their bottom line, their profits, both individually and corporately. If they saw my black ass out there, they would go out of their way to come up with some trumped up reason to fire me."

Johnny interjected, "That's some real shit, bro', and I feel you. Yasmin and I grew up in Puerto Rico, which you all know is a US territory." Johnny paused to allow his last statement to sink in. Mitch pursed his lips while shaking his head. Marvin had an incredulous expression on his face. "Puerto Ricans have been pushing for statehood for years, if not decades, but no one seems to be listening. Same thing is happening in Washington, DC. This is why so many of us marched in the streets. We wanted to be heard. But these conservative Republicans are tone deaf, bro'. They don't care. Not about to add more black and brown voters to the mix."

Mitch leaned back in his chair. He was amazed at how astute these brothers were politically. Hell, he was amazed that he had so much to say about current issues, politics even. He attributed his change in mindset to the impending end of the Nelson Dupont presidency. It had been great seeing a black man leading the country, if not the world. But the emergence of Malcolm Stillwell as the leading candidate in 2016 for the GOP nomination was an eye opener. It brought white supremacy into clearer focus. It let you know that seeing President Dupont's black face in the oval office for two presidential terms didn't sit well with at least forty percent of white Americans. This forty percent was now intent on convincing a portion of the remaining sixty percent that Nelson Dupont and members of the Black American Diaspora have been, and were, scheming to deprive them of the privileges that they had inherited from their white ancestors' enslavement and oppression of black Americans.

Mitch proclaimed, "We black and brown people have to focus on ourselves more. That's what they did back in the 50s and 60s. That's how they got shit done."

"Easier said than done, Mitch," Johnny replied. "They done figured out different ways to enslave us. After Trayvon Martin got shot back in 2012, athletes in the NBA and NFL spoke out against what happened, the not guilty verdict against that white security guard. That's when the Black Folk Matter Movement was formed. To me, black athletes wield a lot of power, bros'. But like you said before, we react, we don't pro-react. If we did more of the latter, hit white people where it really matters, in their pockets, we probably would see some real change. But black athletes don't do that because they don't want to get cut from their teams for being seen as distractions. All these mofos want black athletes to do, at least the ones in the NBA, is shut up and dribble."

He's right, Mitch thought. But what Johnny was saying wasn't news to him. His father had preached this same message to him long before he became a highly recruited high school football player, a world-class sprinter. And while he now had a platform to speak from as the world's fastest man, the pressure of keeping the cap on his secret was too much to bear.

Even though Coach Moses and Coach Wilson shared his beliefs about black uplift and excellence, he knew they had too much power over him. The same was true of his Team Elite teammates. Any one of them would fight to be the first in line to keep the club's secrets from being exposed. In other words, they would collectively pounce at the opportunity to denounce what Mitch would say about them, all to protect the club's reputation for producing track and field champions.

"When you win gold next year," Johnny exclaimed, "you should do what John Smith and Tommie Carlos did back in '68. Do the Black Power Salute while wearing a black glove on your right hand during the playing of the national anthem."

Mitch chuckled. That would definitely get their attention, he thought. But he also knew this one gesture would cause white investors to look the other way. While many of them prided themselves in being supportive of black Americans' struggle for civil rights, most, if not all, of them succumbed to the will of white American consumers. They knew that any talk of or demonstrations in support of past and present wrongs against black people would ruffle white American's feathers, make them feel uncomfortable. Mitch and others knew the key to making money in America in 2015 was bowing down to the throne of white power, influence and control. He also knew a Smith/Carlos-type demonstration would be fodder for Malcolm Stillwell, who would use it as Exhibit A in the white conservative campaign to show how ungrateful black Americans have been after receiving legislative recompense for his white ancestors' past abuses. This lie about black Americans' ungratefulness begets another one, one that falsely claims that black Americans aren't doing enough to help themselves.

"Gotta win it first," Mitch replied. He stood, followed by Johnny and the rest. "Let get on out here and at least try to make par on these eighteen holes."

Mitch stood over the teed-up golf ball, tightly gripping his left-hand driver. The group was on the seventh hole, a Par 3 at a little over 150 yards at the Buenaventura Golf and Beach Resort course, so his goal was to drive the ball into the fairway to avoid the bunkers to the green's left and right edges, and then use his pitching wedge to get his ball up on the green.

Johnny had been the first to tee off. His club hit the ball squarely, and it obtained the height all golfers seek when driving off the tee, but it had landed in the left bunker, less than ten feet from the green. After Mitch, Marvin would try to get his ball on the green in one shot, followed by Tyrone.

Smack. Mitch's club hit the ball squarely and sailed in the direction of the flag. When his fluorescent orange ball landed on the green, less than five feet from the hole, Tyrone announced, "Shot of the day." A smiling Mitch accepted a high five from Tyrone and then Marvin as he returned to the golf cart that he was sharing with Johnny. From the cart's driver's seat, Johnny extended his fist to collide with Mitch's in midair.

"Awesome shot, bro'," Johnny exclaimed as Mitch flopped into the seat beside him. "That one would make Bear Woods envious."

"Looks like being the world's fastest man transcends to golf as well," Johnny announced as they watched Marvin tee up his shot.

Mitch chuckled. Johnny wasn't present when he broke the 100-meter world record, but he knew he had watched it plenty of times on YouTube. Whenever Johnny would visit Yasmin and him in California, he would make a point to accompany Yasmin to Drake Stadium to watch him train from the stands. He appreciated the gesture. But deep down, he held high hopes that Yasmin had kept his secret sacred, even from her brother. If things ever went sideways with Yasmin, he wanted to have peace of mind that Johnny couldn't be called as a witness to testify to what she had told him.

"You and Yasmin been kicking it for a minute now," Johnny proclaimed.

"Coming up on a year," Mitch replied.

"What are your intentions, with my sister. You thinking about putting a ring on it?"

Mitch turned to get a quick glance at Johnny before facing forward again to watch Marvin tee off. "We never talk about it. So focused on our goals, bro'. She's in grad school, and me, well, you know. Maybe we'll start having that discussion sometime next year, after the Games. But she's only in the first year of a two-year program. Probably won't happen until after she graduates."

"Do you love her?"

A noticeable pause as Mitch pondered Johnny's question. "Yes," he replied. "I do." A grunt from Johnny confirmed for him that Johnny was drawing inferences from his delayed response. But he also knew professing his love for Yasmin to her brother was a lie, for he had doubts that she even loved him. Even though he told her that he wanted to stop taking the Yellow Jacket vitamin, she was the main person fueling his dependency on the vitamin. Consequently, the reality of the situation was starting to settle in. Yasmin Ortiz liked Mitch Newman, but she loved the idea of being associated with the World's Fastest Man, and the perks that came with it even more.

"I do," Mitch eventually lied. "I really do."

Thunder and lightning on the 17th hole caused the quartet to pause their play. To avoid the rain, they sought shelter under one of the restroom structures situated across the eighteen-hole golf course. Marvin pulled four beers from the cooler attached to the back of his cart, walking over to offer them to his mates.

Tyrone placed his on the table while studying the score card. "And the top dawg on the leaderboard is Tyrone Campbell," he announced, doing his best to sound like the late Howard Cossell of ABC Sports, "followed by Mitch Newman."

Johnny, who was seated to Tyrone's right, held his right hand high, inches from Tyrone's face, then slowly opened and closed it. "Ain't no shame to my game," he replied. "Just out here to support the stroking of your big-ass ego."

All four of them laughed, with Tyrone laughing the loudest. Tyrone then shifted his attention to Mitch. "You only down two strokes, Mitch. But that world-class speed ain't gonna help you today. Whatcha got, whatcha got?"

"Oh, don't worry, bruh. Plenty of gas in this tank. You better hope I don't eagle this next hole. If I do, you're going down on 18."

Tyrone's wide grin slowly melted away as he became more serious. "What does that feel like, being known as the world's fastest man, I mean?"

"Feels good," Mitch replied, "but I don't pay too much attention to the noise. When I step on the track, I just want to run my own race. It's always me against the clock, not the people lining up to my left and right."

"How much faster do you think you can go?" Marvin asked. "You ran a nine six eight, and you were rolling. Any nine fives or nine flats in your future?"

Mitch shrugged as he felt the urge to squirm in his seat. The question made him feel uneasy. He knew the answer to Marvin's question was yes, but deep down he knew this could only happen if he followed Coach Moses' advice and continued to take his vitamins. Never one to disappoint, he said, "Yeah. It's possible."

"And you think you'll be the one to do it?" Johnny interjected.

"No doubt," Mitch replied with confidence. "I'm a fighter, bruh. No one is gonna dethrone the King of Speed without a fight."

"You think Black will be in that race?" Tyrone asked.

"Hard to say. But my pops has skin in his game. He should be alright."

During this exchange, Marvin sat across from Mitch, scrolling through the news feed on his smart phone. The tightness around Marvin's lips let Mitch know that he was disturbed by what he was reading.

"These crackers are out of their damn minds," Marvin exclaimed as he slowly swiped through an article.

"What they saying?" Tyrone asked.

"That this motherfucking security guard was defenseless after Black knocked his gun out of his hands. What kind of sense does that make? Black was the one jogging on the street. Prick probably walked up on him with his gun drawn. He wasn't even a threat."

Johnny interjected, "That's how they do. They either drawing or firing first and then asking questions."

Marvin placed his smart phone on the table. "Brother don't deserve this kind of heat. That jerk Stillwell is already aligning his candidacy with this case. Using catch phrases like Back the Blue and Blue Folk Matter. Why do they feel the need to do that, in cases that involve black people? Don't our lives matter too?"

"Hell, yeah, they do," Tyrone said, emphatically. "But none of that shit matters to them. They're in it to score cheap political points at Jason Black's expense. They're willing to say and do anything to sow division, discord and disorder."

"It's deeper than that," Mitch offered before chugging at his beer. "They're winning over voters before we can even cast our votes early or on election day. Hell, they, the Republican Party, used to be about less government regulation and lower taxes. But if you do the research, you'll see they're the ones misappropriating taxpayer dollars, not the Democrats."

Tyrone carefully considered Mitch's words. During the 2012 presidential election, he had voted for former Massachusetts governor Mitchell Robbins, the Republican nominee, in hopes that the businessman would get the American economy roaring again. To him, electing Nelson Dupont to a second term would have been a mistake, resulting from the fact that he viewed Dupont as a divider not a uniter. While the idea of keeping the first, black president in office was appealing to most black folks, he also knew the white U. S. electorate feared and resented losses of privilege, influence and power.

"I've done the research," Mitch said, "and you're right, they do spend more than the Dems. But their spending is hidden in tax breaks for the rich, funded by higher taxes on middle- and working-class Americans. Shit is foul, but elections have consequences."

Mitch shifted his attention from the group to their surroundings. The rain had stopped, and the sun was emerging from behind the dark clouds. He stood up, extended his arms, and continued, saying, "These political campaigns are nothing more than dog and pony shows. For Republicans, even negative press is good press. That's why Stillwell and other prominent Republicans can afford to hitch their wagons to the white security guard and rain fire on the black sprinter. Not right, but they think if they beat that drum loud enough, repeat the same lies, they will attract their kind of people, turn voters into lifelong loyalists."

Tyrone joined Mitch on the edge of the structure's concrete slab, as Marvin and Johnny tossed their beer bottles in a nearby trash barrel. "You all know I'm a high school principal, in Southlake, Texas."

"Yeah," Johnny replied. "A damn good one."

Tyrone continued, "The right-wingers are on a crusade, bruhs. Trying to take over local school boards and city governments across the state. Austin is the only Democratic strong-hold in Texas, but Republicans are waging an assault there as well. But Tennessee has always been red. Going to be hard for Jason Black to get a fair hearing there, especially with Stillwell attaching his fortunes to his demise."

"So, you think that's why he jumped at the chance to make a statement?" Mitch asked. "You think Hillary Rosen Clifton will come out to support Jason?"

"Probably," Tyrone replied. "But when she does, the pundits are going to say she's no different than Stillwell. Going to call her a Democratic opportunist."

"Sounds like we can't win for losing," Marvin added.

"We really can't," Tyrone continued. "School board meetings are designed to give parents a voice. Not a lot of black people living in Southlake, so a lot of our black parents don't do a lot of talking. They just grin and bear it, mostly when white parents rail against the efforts Carroll is making in the area of diversity, equity and inclusion. They're not trying to rock the boat. We need them. But that all changed when some idiot hung a noose in our star receiver's locker. After that, it was like the light bulb just came on for our black, Southlake parents. They appeared before the board in droves, telling stories about how their chil-dren were being mistreated by white students in the district, as well as by some of their white teachers.

"I felt the pressure too when I tried to fire one of those racist motherfuckers. The local teachers' union came to the lit-tle prick's defense, telling me that firing him would be too ex-treme. The union president told me the teacher's use of the n-word during his history lesson was nothing but a slip of the tongue, like what these kids hear in their rap videos. Said he shouldn't lose his job because of it. I disagreed. Now, my head is on a swivel because I know they're coming after me. But the hardest pill to swallow is seeing this dude in my all-staff

meeting with a smug expression on his face. Can't fire his ass.
Shit would splash back on me. Crazy. Wanted to rip that mug's
heart out."

"Damn, bro'," Johnny exclaimed. "That's foul."

"Yeah," Mitch added. "Not right."

Tyrone surveyed each of their faces. He was emotionally
moved by their sincerity. "But I say all that to say this: They're
about to make Jason Black the face of American criminality.
Mark my word. Their play is all about confusing the American
electorate, sow discord and division within the black community, which votes for Democrats more than ninety percent of the
time."

"But how does Black fit into all that?" Johnny asked as he
flopped into the golf cart's driver's seat. "It was self-defense.
Case closed, right?"

Tyrone continued. "Wish it were that simple, bro', but it's
not. This brother is about to get called everything but the name
his mother gave him. They're also going to use that Stand Your
Ground law to prove that security guard was in the right, that
he was just doing his job when he confronted Black. Probably
give him natural immunity from prosecution for all those years
he was a police officer."

Marvin's eyes widened as he claimed a seat next to Mitch.
"Would be great if other elite athletes came to Black's defense.
Take this case to the court of public opinion. That's where the
black community's power lies. In the hands of black athletes."
He glanced side-eyed at Mitch. "He needs someone like you,
bro', the world's fastest man, to call a spade a spade, rally some
of these other elite athletes to stand beside him."

Mitch shrugged at Marvin's call to action as he steered their
golf cart onto the paved pathway and towards the 18th hole.

CHAPTER SIXTEEN

It was a 70-degree day in Atlanta's North Buckhead community. For Cornelius Newman, that always meant getting up early to clock five miles on the road. But the more he thought about jogging down the paved roads of his upper-middle class neighborhood, the more his body told him that now was not the time.

Mr. Newman lived for days like this – when he had the house all to himself. His wife had told him the night before that she and Rayvyn would be getting up early the next morning to get their hair done. But as he lay there, in his bed, on his back, he knew his six-pack abs would only return by him putting in work.

A full month had passed since Jason drove off with the Marshall Law Group's entourage. He wished them well in their fight to help Jason get his life back. But his thoughts were also on Mitch. After all he had gone through with Xavier Charles, followed by his providing a safe haven for Jason, he knew he would one day have to offer a similar defense to his lying son.

Seeing Mitch cross the finish line with a slim lead at the previous year's nationals was something he had been dreaming about since Mitch first became interested in track and field. He recalled how he knew early on that Mitch was destined for athletic greatness. When he coached him at eight years old in the I-9 Sports Youth Flag Football League, he did everything he could to not show favoritism toward his son. He knew the other parents, the white ones mainly, would have a fit if he did. But after the first two games, and two lopsided defeats, he changed course, making Mitch his featured running back. He ensured his starting quarterback fed his other running backs and receivers. But he also knew when and in what situations to instruct him to either hand the football to Mitch or throw it to him. Ninety percent of the time, when the ball was in Mitch's hands, he would score long touchdowns, casting the white parents into a joyful frenzy. Winning brought everyone together.

Mitch's star continued to rise during his tenure at North Atlanta High School. After Mitch rushed for over a thousand yards as a freshman, his coach made him a starter on the varsity team. Mitch didn't disappoint his coaches. He rushed for over fifteen hundred yards his junior year, over two thousand his senior year. His exploits on the field garnered the attention of coaches at all of the Southeastern Conference schools – University of Georgia, University of Tennessee and University of Florida, to name only a few. Atlantic Coast Conference and Big Ten schools came calling as well. He ultimately opted to take his talents to the University of Florida in Gainesville so he could run track during the football off season.

After prying himself out of bed and scooting to the bathroom in nothing but his boxers, Mr. Newman studied himself in the framed, embroidered mirror. Sixty-five never looked so good. He then wet a washcloth and proceeded to wipe his face with it before changing into his running gear. As he sat on the recliner in the bedroom's sitting area to put on his running shoes, he abruptly stopped, slumping forward, shoes untied.

A feeling of despair was beginning to set in. He long considered his wife his best friend, but he knew he wasn't giving her his best, especially as he had worked with the Marshall Law Group attorneys to exonerate Xavier Charles. Throughout that entire ordeal, he worked long hours with Tribe Records' public relations director to stay in front of any damaging stories that the media could derive from the situation. However, that meant spending long hours strategizing in his Atlanta office, and even more on flights to Los Angeles, Chicago, Boston, Nashville and New York to vet new recording artists.

As he sat there, with his shoes untied, he realized that he longed to be in the company of his wife and kids. And in the final analysis, he also realized that his lack of attention to family matters may have been the reason Mitch thought it was okay to lie to his face about taking a banned substance.

Three miles into his five-mile run, Cornelius Newman's phone vibrated. He flipped open the pocket of his Freetrain Vest to survey the text message on his phone. "What's going on, old man?" the message from Mitch read. "At the house now but would love to meet for coffee. Meet me at Starbucks when you're done with your run."

Thirty minutes later, a sweaty Cornelius Newman stepped into the downtown Buckhead Starbucks. Surveying the room, he spotted Mitch sitting in a booth adjacent to the plate glass window. A bottled water and cup of coffee were positioned on the opposite side of the table, indicating that Mitch had taken the liberty to order for him.

Mr. Newman flopped into the seat next to Mitch. "Hey, son," he said, an emotionless expression on his face.

"Hey, Pops," Mitch replied, rising to stand before faltering under his father's steely glare. "How you been?"

"Good. You?"

"Great."

"What brings you to town?"

"Headed up to Sojourner Vista for the Racial Justice Conference. They have me speaking on a panel, about student-athletes getting paid."

"Should they?"

"Hell, yeah," Mitch replied with emphasis. "Have to get paid when the getting is good."

"That should be an interesting conversation. Patricia called me the other day to get my thoughts."

"What'd you tell her?"

"That they should. The coaches and college administrators, which are mostly white, shouldn't be the only one's getting paid. And the price of a four-year scholarship still doesn't come close to the time student-athletes put into becoming great athletes."

"Took the words right out of my mouth." Mitch chuckled. Mr. Newman reluctantly cracked a smile. Mitch looked up at his father then away. "Hey," he uttered, blinking nervously. But before he could continue, Mr. Newman raised his hand to shush him.

"Why now?" he said. "Been over six months."

"And I regret every second. But I'm here now, wanting to make things right."

"Well, say your piece. 'Cause I sure as hell said mine."

Mitch swallowed hard. "They had me doing some foul shit over there in Cali, Pops."

"Had?" Mr. Newman replied. "You not with Team Elite anymore?"

"No. I'm not. Plan on running unattached moving forward. Hoping to return to Gainesville, hook back up with Coach Usain."

"They had you on the Yellow Jacket, didn't they?"

"Yeah."

"How long you been drug free?"

"About two weeks."

"Feel any different."

"Not really. But I won't really know until I get back on the track. Running Millrose in February to work on my start. After that, I'll open outdoor at the Prefontaine Classic before returning to Eugene for Trials."

Mitch's countenance dropped as he mulled over what he was about to say next. Looking up, he continued, "What would you have done if you were me?"

Mr. Newman drew his hand to his chin as he looked past Mitch at the activity on the other side of the window.

"The right thing," he replied. "I would have done the right thing."

"But the right thing is the hardest thing."

"But it still has to be done? If you don't, everything you accomplish on that track is going to be a lie."

"Right."

"Look, son, we all make mistakes. Some mistakes just receive more attention than others. You're an elite athlete. The World's Fastest Man. When people get word of your next race. it's going to draw attention. But we both know your times aren't going to be fast, not without the Yellow Jacket. It's good that you're training clean now." Then, "Who else knows, besides Moses and his coaching staff?"

"My girl Yasmin. She knows."

"You all tight?"

"I guess so. At least we were. We haven't talked much since I told her that I was done with the Yellow Jacket, Team Elite. She just up and left my ass in Panama. Moved out. Not returning any of my calls."

"Well, it really comes down to what you think is best. You do need to tell the world what you did wrong. The 100-meter dash record is sacred, son. Think Jesse Owens in 1936, Harrison Dillard in 1948, Bob Hayes in 1964, Jim Hines in 1968. When you tell the world what you did is up to you. Just know, moving forward, you have to put in the work to run legitimate times."

"So, do you think I should come clean after the Rio Games or before?"

"I'm not going to make that decision for you. What matters right now, in this moment, is you came clean with me. But I also see that you want to do things the right way. My prodigal son has returned."

Mitch locked eyes with his father and smiled. He then reached across the table, and with their hands clasped, they rose together to embrace over it.

"Love you, Pops."

"Love you too, son. Welcome back."

Carmelita Newman was all smiles as she watched from the porch as Mitch and her husband exited Mitch's rented BMW and then proceeded to walk toward the front porch. Mitch trailed behind his father. As he drew closer, Mitch couldn't contain his smile, especially after his mother stepped off the porch to embrace him. She held him for what seemed like an eternity. Eventually, Mitch was able to pull back and say, "I love what you did to your hair."

Rayvyn watched this family reunion from the gaping front doorway. "About time you brought your lame ass home," she exclaimed.

"Language, young lady," Cornelius Newman interjected, affectionately tapping her on the head in passing. Mrs. Newman turned to glare over at her.

Mitch opened his arms wide as an invitation to his baby sister. Rayvyn accepted, embracing him tightly. Mitch kissed the top of her braided head. "Missed you, kid."

"Missed you too, big bro'," Rayvyn replied as she released him.

After placing his luggage in his bedroom, Mitch joined his family in one of the mansion's many sitting rooms. He confessed his wrongdoing to his mother and sister, apologizing for not representing the Christian values that informed the way they were supposed to lead their lives. He admittedly had become a heathen, someone who disregarded the rules of fair play, and this saddened him.

"Well, it's not the end of the world," Mrs. Newman consoled. "Just know we love and appreciate you. That will never change."

Rayvyn interjected, "But you still have a big head."

They all chuckled at that.

Later that night, as Mr. and Mrs. Newman prepared to settle in for the night, Mrs. Newman asked from her side of the bed, "This is a hard pill for you to swallow, isn't it?"

"Yeah," Mr. Newman replied.

"Why? He's a grown man, prone to make mistakes. He finally came to his senses and told us, though. That is what you wanted, right?"

"It is. But when he testifies before USA Track and Field and the IAAF, he's going to be suspended, maybe even receive a lifetime ban from the sport."

"But he always knew what the consequences would be."

"He did."

"So, what's the problem?"

Mr. Newman paused momentarily before offering a response. He then replied, "Seeing him set that world record was like a dream come true, Bae. Even at an early age, I knew he was special. Thought his training with Moses would push him over the top. That's why I applauded his wanting to go out to California to train with him. I guess I'm just pissed at myself for giving him bad advice."

"But you didn't know, Cornelius. No one did. You have to let it go. Forgive yourself. If you don't, the guilt is going to eat you up from the inside out. When that happens, it affects everyone around you, us."

Mr. Newman peered up and over at his wife from his side of the bed. "Our family is already receiving heat for harboring a fugitive. You ready for the heat that we're going to receive for being the parents of a cheater?"

"After all we went through with Xavier, I consider this par for the course. Besides, this is his problem, not ours. If it comes down to him never running track again, so be it. But he will always be our son, and the good Lord above is going to pull him, us, through."

"I think you missed your calling."

"What do you mean?"

"I think we need to have a chat with Pastor Joplin. You need to be preaching from the pulpit."

"Please," Mrs. Newman replied through pursed lips. "Good advice, that's all. Anyone who hears it has a choice: Take it or leave it."

Like most of the other people in the Panama group, Johnny was concerned about Yasmin's sudden and unannounced departure. It was unlike her to just up and leave, especially during a time when the stakes of the Mitch Newman con job were at an all-time high. Moses was depending on both of them to ensure Mitch remained on the Yellow Jacket vitamin until after the Rio Games.

Johnny had never been one to shy away from a con. They were guaranteed a minimum of 200,000 dollars, to be split equally between them, if Mitch won Olympic gold, and even more if he broke his own world record. Yasmin leaving him alone in Panama for one full day with Mitch and the others had made him feel uncomfortable. He did ask Mitch the question, what happened? Mitch stuttered up a storm before finally admitting to Johnny that Yasmin left because they didn't see eye to eye about something. Because he was in the know, Johnny immediately knew what this something involved.

Johnny had attempted to reach Yasmin by phone after it became obvious to him that she was no longer in Panama, but she didn't respond to any of his calls or texts. However, he noted the text message that she had sent to him on the day of her departure, the one in which she wrote that she would be waiting for him at his Rancho Cucamonga home. Johnny fabricated an excuse for dropping Tonya off at her place, but Tonya had told him that was fine because she had something else to do. He and Tonya had agreed to reconnect with each other later in the week.

"What the hell were you thinking?" Johnny exclaimed when Yasmin opened the front door to his home before he could knock or press the doorbell. Yasmin stepped aside to allow Johnny to lift his wheeled suitcase over the doorway lip and walk past her. "You know Moses is going to be pissed."

Yasmin pushed the front door shut and locked it. She then followed Johnny down the long hallway leading to the open dining room, kitchen and living room areas. "I know," she replied. "But what else was I supposed to do."

"Well, for starters, you could have come to me first before leaving. We done invested too much time in this con to give up now."

Yasmin walked to the living room to sit in the recliner. She drew her legs under her. "All he wants to do is do things by the book, Johnny. He feels he can run fast times without the Yellow Jacket."

"Well, Moses is saying that's not possible, at least not this early. As soon as he stops taking it, he's going to become weaker and slower. And when he crosses the finish line last in future races, people are going to become suspicious, start speculating about what we know, what Moses knows. And that guaranteed money that Moses promised to pay us is going to go out the window." Johnny dropped to the love seat to lean forward with his hands clasped. "There's more to it, right?"

Yasmin locked eyes with Johnny for two, three, ticks before diverting her gaze elsewhere.

"You starting to have feelings for him, aren't you?" Johnny pressed.

"I am," Yasmin replied. "He's s a good man. But that's not all. I'm pregnant."

Johnny's jaw dropped.

"Does he know?"

"No, he doesn't. He's been blowing my phone up with calls and texts. But I haven't responded. I'm not going to respond."

"How far along are you?"

"Took the test once I arrived back home. It's on the counter in the guest bathroom."

"You're not thinking about having it, are you?"

"No. I'm going to get rid of it. But I was starting to have some real feelings for him. In another life, he would have been the perfect husband for me, the perfect father to our children."

"Fuck that," Johnny shouted as he bounded to his feet. Then, while slowly pacing within the small space between the living and dining room areas, he said, "Maybe you should have it. Would make him think twice about weaning himself off his vitamins. I can't do this by myself. You know that. Don't you want to get paid?"

"I do, but not like this, Johnny. I'm starting to see things the way he sees them. Didn't at first because I only viewed him as another mark. But the more our relationship grew, the more respect I had for him, how he wants his shit to be legit."

Johnny slapped the palms of his hands on the kitchen island and left them there as he leaned forward to ponder his sister's assessment. He had no arguments about Mitch being a good man, but he could only think about the amount of money that would be lost by ending the con now.

"You want to tell Moses," Johnny asked, "or is that something you want me to do."

"I can do it," Yasmin replied, extending her legs and allowing them to drop to the carpeted floor. "He should have seen this coming."

"How could he, Yaz? How could I? You recruited me, remember? Said old boy had to at least meet one of your family members to make it believable. Never thought you would turn soft on me. Just know he's not going to be happy."

"What's the worst he can do to me?"

Still learning forward, his palms on the kitchen island, Johnny turned his head slightly to stare directly into Yasmin's eyes.

"Shoot you, me, in the heads and dump our dead bodies in a ditch," he finally replied. "All to keep his secrets secret."

Yasmin winced at this thought as she leaned forward to consider her next move, her face cupped in the palms of her sweaty hands.

Trish placed her left hand on her stomach in an attempt to tame the butterflies that were swirling there. Her big night had arrived, again, courtesy of Angelica, and she wanted to impress the racially diverse audience of Democrats and Republicans that had converged that evening on Knoxville's Cherokee Country Club. As she peered out at the audience from backstage – the men dressed in tailor-made suits with red or blue ties, the women red or blue evening gowns – she had heard that Tennessee's white governor, Colton Kensington, and members of his mostly white and Republican-controlled Tennessee state legislature would be in attendance, as well as members of the Malcolm Stillwell presidential campaign. She also read in the paper that the chairs for the Democratic National Committee, Patrick Ahern, a black man, and Republican National Committee, Hans Gobler, a white one, would be present as well. The event had been billed as an evening of libations and entertainment for members of the Tennessee General Assembly's Common Ground Caucus.

From what Trish gleamed from her reading the article that had been published in the *Knoxville News-Sentinel* the day before the event, the Common Ground Caucus was created by Democratic State Senator Julian Banks, a black man representing Memphis' 29th District, and Republican Representative Donovan Gobler, a white man, and Hans Gobler's son, representing Nashville's 5th District. Both of these men were in their late 20s, and according to the article, they created the Common Ground Caucus so Tennessee state legislators from both sides of the political spectrum could come together once every quarter to reach areas of agreement on the host of issues that came before them. Unbeknownst to many, Hans Gobler had his son on a short leash, advising him often about reaching agreement on those issues that enriched Republicans but steering clear of gun control legislation talks. Donovan knew full well why his father offered this advice. While he represented approximately 710,000 5th District residents, like his father, he dually pledged his allegiance to the Confederate States of America.

When she and Angelica had arrived at the club a full hour before the event's start time, they had been greeted at the door by the club's Director of Special Events, Megan Sinclair. The first thing Trish noted about Sinclair was her height. Sinclair was about three inches taller than she was – five feet, 10 inches to her five feet, seven inches. Trish would learn later that Sinclair once was a shooting guard on the Texas Longhorn women's basketball team.

"We appreciate you being here," Sinclair had told Trish upon releasing her hand. "Angelica has told us so much about you."

"I hope it was all good," Trish had said, peering over at Angelica and then back at Sinclair.

"Oh, it was. I was sold after listening to your demo CD. Had my staff listen to it too. They all agree. You could be as good, or better, than Whitney Houston. Told Julian and Donovan that booking you would be a treat."

But even as Trish had soaked in the positive rays that Sinclair was sending her way, she still winced when she spotted Patrick Ahern and Hans Gobler entering the building together, surrounded by their protective details, to greet other corporate and political elites in the lobby. Trish and Angelica had watched as Sinclair dismissed them briefly to advance on the two men and their entourages. The bodyguard closest to Sinclair had extended his arm to block Sinclair's advance but relented when Gobler provided the gesture that allowed her to pass.

Like so many other Americans, Trish had no love for modern-day Republicans, more specifically Malcolm Stillwell. She knew Stillwell had not been scheduled to make an appearance, but the fact that Republican voters had nominated him for a presidential run was telling. She had heard Stillwell talk about women liking it when someone like him, a celebrity, grabbed them by their pussies. And she didn't appreciate it when he drew an equivalence between war-mongering white nationalists and peaceful Black Folks Matter counter protesters who converged on Philadelphia, Pennsylvania in July 2014 for the Founded 1776 Rally. Because many of the white nationalists brandished pistols, shotguns and assault rifles, the rally was deemed unlawful. And the night before the rally, the white nationalists marched across the University of Pennsylvania campus carrying burning torches and proclaiming, "You will not replace us." The "you" that they were referring to were black Americans, other persons of color, Jews, Muslims, gays and lesbians, and any Whites that supported these group's individual and collective grievances.

"Conservative Republicans buy black albums too," Trish had recalled telling Angelica before they left their dorm room. "So let me go over here and make this money."

"Look, girl." Angelica said as she noticed Sinclair waving at them. "She wants you to come over."

"You coming with me, aren't you?" Trish had asked while slowly walking toward Sinclair and the two political operatives.

"Nah, girl. Did you forget? I'm the help. They want to meet you, not me."

Trish had glanced back to see Angelica disappear through the swinging door leading to the country club's kitchen. She then found herself flashing a toothy smile as Sinclair introduced her, and she had reached out to shake Ahern's and then Gobler's hands. But her toothy smile had dissolved into a smirk as she sensed Gobler undressing her with his roaming eyes. And undressing her wasn't hard to do, as the only piece of clothing that she had on under her spirited red, white and blue sequin dress were silk panties from Victoria's Secret and the blue fishnet hosiery that covered them. She was also conscious of her movements. Any sudden move would have caused either one of her bra-less breasts to pop out.

"You're a beauty," Gobler complimented.

"Thank you, sir," Trish replied.

"We look forward to hearing you sing," Ahern interjected.

"Thank you," Trish repeated. "I feel honored being here."

With that, Sinclair had waved a male usher over to lead the two men and their protective details into the spacious ballroom. As he walked away, Ahern looked back at Trish and said, "Tell your father Ahern said hello." Trish had nodded back at him, even as she recalled the special fraternal connection that Ahern had with her father. She had remembered meeting him three years ago at a social justice forum held at Nashville's Tennessee State University, a historically black college and university, or HBCU. She had learned then that Ahern graduated from Kent State five years after her father. But because they are members of the same fraternity – Alpha Phi Alpha Fraternity, Incorporated – she knew they were more than brothers; they were family.

"I will," Trish had replied as Ahern made a modified fist with his right hand, one that saw him insert his thumb between his index and middle fingers, and pound it twice on his chest, over his heart. Trish returned the gesture. They both knew the gesture to mean one for solidarity, achievement, prosperity and excellence within the Black Diaspora worldwide.

Trish had then stepped away, returning to the comforts of the country club dressing room that Sinclair's staff had prepared for her. A feeling of relief rushed over her as she dropped to the love seat and removed her high heel shoes. Sitting there, her legs crossed at the knees, Ahern's gesture had continued to play in her mind. Truth be told, it had caught her off guard because it had been a while since anyone had flashed it at her in public. But she also knew Ahern had flashed it to let her know she had this, and he would applaud her performance if no one else did.

But she also found herself reflecting on those times when her father took Mitch, Rayvyn and her with him to the Sojourner Vista Resort and Conference Center during their early childhood and adolescence to be introduced to the stealth movement – one dedicated to promoting black solidarity and empowerment within the Black Diaspora – that was first birthed in the aftermath of Supreme Court Justice Thurgood Marshall's 1954 legal victory in *Brown vs. the Board of Education of Topeka, Kansas*. While Cornelius Newman wasn't even born when this stealth movement began, he became one of its biggest supporters in the 1980's and '90s, steadily underwriting its agents' efforts at the dawn of the new century as Tribe Records achieved prominence within the entertainment industry both domestically and internationally.

Forty-five minutes later, Trish found herself standing on stage in front of a packed house with her band mates, four members of the University of Tennessee's Pride of the Southland Band. There was Reginald Avery on drums, Yusef Blanton on piano, and Roosevelt Freeman on guitar. And to her right were the three background singers, Pauletta Goins, Garrison Hines and Danella Simmons. The male musicians were dressed in blue suits with red and white pin stripes, the vocalist solid ensembles, with Pauletta wearing a red gown, Danella a white one, Garrison a blue suit.

As Trish belted out a medley of popular songs from artists like Whitney Houston, Anita Bateman and Toni Saxton, Angelica smiled up at her from among the sea of attendees seated at tables covered with a mix of red, white and blue linen coverings. She watched as Angelica walked around her assigned tables near the back center of the ballroom to fill attendees' glasses with sweet tea or ice water. But she also felt the butterflies in her stomach fluttering away as she saw a number of the black attendees snapping their fingers or rhythmically moving side to side from their seats. A number of them opted to stand and dance. During her performance of Houston's "I Wanna Dance with Somebody", she and Reginald shared knowing chuckles, as a number of the white attendees struggled to sync their movements with the black ones.

Garrison felt honored when Trish asked him days earlier to end their night with a rendition of Lee Green's "American Pride". He stepped forward to claim the solo spot, Trish backwards to stand beside Pauletta and Danella.

The musicians played the soft prelude to Green's hit song, an anthem during times such as these, as Garrison slowly paced from one side of the stage to the other, the microphone pressed firmly against his chest. But before he could complete the first stanza of lyrics, three older, white attendees – one female and two male – stood from the center of each of the three sections of tables, holding up handmade signs that read, "White Power", "White Folks Matter" and "AMERICA: Est. 1776 by Whites". They then proceeded to repeatedly chant in unison, "You will not replace us!"

Two suited white security guards wasted no time leaping in front of the stage, causing Trish and her band mates to scramble to the back. From their vantage point, they watched as the other members of the country club's security team, as well as the Secret Service, snatched the signs away from the protesters and then roughly escorted each of them through the doors on the other side of the ballroom. Once the room was clear of protesters, Donovan Gobler stepped onto the stage to snatch a microphone from its stand. Julian Banks joined him, standing to Donovan's left as Donovan prepared to speak.

"Our sincere apologies for that outburst," Donovan exclaimed into a microphone while motioning Trish and Garrison to join him at the front of the stage.

They did.

"That wasn't part of the program."

Donovan then paused to gather his thoughts. "This year marks the two hundred and fortieth anniversary of our country's founding. And we all know our ancestors experienced many lows mixed in with highs. We the people have struggled to maintain a democracy for all of us rather than a select few. But we're here, citizens – red, yellow, black and white – looking past our differences in hopes of creating a more perfect union. My hope is you all will leave this place more committed to overcoming your differences, operate together from this place we know as common ground. Let's be problem-solvers, not troublemakers."

Donovan Gobler then extended his right arm to draw Trish and Garrison closer. Trish smiled back at him before peering out into the audience to see a vast majority of its members shaking hands or sharing warm embraces. However, she quickly noted that Cotton Kensington, Hans Gobler and a number of the other conservative Republicans weren't moved by Donovan Gobler's words. Many of them were already retreating to the back of the ballroom to exit the building.

Trish knew from news reports on the major television networks that Stillwell had resurrected an old trope from the Richard Nixon administration – Make America Great Again. This MAGA trope was considered a racist dog whistle to white Americans then, and Trish knew many black Americans considered it a racist trope now, for it appeals to white people's fears about non-whites making America less great through their constant aspersions on white privilege, their resentment of non-whites wanting them to feel ashamed of their whiteness.

Trish then peered over to her left to see Patrick Ahern peering up at her. Two pounds with his modified right fist to the left side of his chest followed by a head nod. Trish returned the gesture, nodding even, and then watched Ahern exit the ballroom with his security detail in tow.

"They're everywhere," Trish exclaimed as she and Angelica exited the country club to walk to her car, now dressed in sweats and sneakers. But when she tilted her head up, she noticed a slightly porcine, black woman standing on one of the concrete islands near it, covered in a buttoned trench coat. As they drew closer, Trish realized it was her cousin Stacy Abraham.

"I know you didn't drive all the way up from Atlanta to support little ole' me," Trish said as she and Angelica drew closer to her.

Stacy just smiled back at Trish before draping her arms around her and pulling her close. "They wouldn't let me in," Stacy replied. "But if they had, you know I would have been the one making the most noise."

Smiling, Trish allowed her arm to rest around Stacy's waist as she introduced her to Angelica. Stacy reached over and shook Angelica's hand. But then the expression on her face became more somber.

"What is it," Trish asked.

"Looks like that voter suppression problem we have down in Georgia is bigger than we thought."

"They're gonna be asking us for our driver's licenses. If you don't have one, you'll have to apply for a special voter ID."

The three of them had taken their conversation to Stacy's Embassy Suites' guest room, where they all sat on either sofas or love seats in the spacious living room. Stacy explained immediately after they sat down that she drove up from Atlanta to Knoxville for an exclusive interview with Patrick Ahern. "He told me that the gerrymandering that is going on in Georgia, primarily in Fulton County, is by design. Said their goal is to break it up into three voting districts in hopes that two of these districts will be called for Republican candidates."

"Does he think they'll be successful?"

"He does. Buckhead City is about three quarters white. Not a coincidence that the white population has been growing there. Homes are affordable but not too many black people can pay the high property taxes. If they break the county into three districts, they only need to win two to turn the county red."

Angelica just sat there, somewhat amazed at these women's knowledge of Georgia politics. On the drive over to Stacy's hotel, Trish told her that Stacy was a political reporter with *The*

Atlantic. She also learned that Stacy's mother Yolanda was Cornelius Newman's older sister.

"But there's something even more sinister going on, cousin," Stacy continued. "There are rumors that the Confederacy never died, that it just took on a different form, aligning itself with the Republican Party. My realtor sources are even telling me the conservative-minded white people moving into Buckhead City are using loopholes in the homestead exemption. This exemption allows homeowners to reduce the amount of annual property taxes they owe on their legal residences. Heard many of these white homeowners receive monthly subsidies from a private investment firm called Heritage Capital to pay their annual property taxes, reduce the prices they pay for their homes."

"And because it's private and not public, it can be selective in who it gives these subsidies to."

"Exactly."

"That ain't right," Angelica exclaimed, exasperated.

"Doesn't have to be," Stacy replied. "Only has to be legal."

"Do the black realtors have a plan?" Trish asked.

"Talking about taking them to court," Stacy replied. "But they know their position is weak. Too many other white-owned and operated investment firms out there are doing the same thing. The best they can do is compete with them by creating their own."

"Why are they so slow to do it then?" Angelica asked.

Stacy replied, "Because affluent Blacks are reluctant to invest in their own people. But a lot of this reluctance comes from not knowing what the problem is or going after white dollars. Remember, white people, at least the racist ones, have convinced the larger society that black people have been lazy since they stopped working for free. These days, they're quick to ridicule black people for not improving conditions in our inner cities. They keep focusing on the dilapidated housing, the rampant drug use, the black-on-black crime. But they never talk about how corporations are complicit in the republican Party's effort to create a voting block that keeps their candidates in power. That's what's going on in Fulton County. Their aim is to rob black citizens of their electoral power through gerrymandering."

Trish said, "I heard the rent is much higher in these areas as well. Also by design?"

"No doubt," Stacy replied. "Doesn't keep black and brown people from moving there. That's where the good manufacturing jobs are. But wage earners living in these households have to pool their money just to make rent every month. Not right, but that's their reality. Others just continue to live in the inner city, but they have to endure long commutes, either by car or train, just to get to and from their low-wage jobs. They're being hit with expenses that rural whites don't have to pay."

Angelica shifted in her chair, placing her right elbow on the table. As she listened to this exchange, she couldn't stop thinking about her native Charlotte, North Carolina, where white investors from other states were buying up black residents' downtown, single-family homes and then demolishing them to build luxury apartments and condominiums, with a few contemporary single-family homes sprinkled in on the outskirts. The new property owners would then charge exorbitant prices that only mid- to upper-middle class Whites could afford. Consequently, if your household income did not exceed $100,000, you would be hard pressed to pay your annual property taxes.

Stacy reared forward in her chair. "If Malcolm Stillwell wins the Republican Party nomination, and then goes on to win the presidency, I fear he and other Republican legislators are going to make life harder for black and other nonwhite Americans."

"Why do you think that?" Trish asked.

"Isn't it obvious, girl?" Stacy stood and then proceeded to make a pass in front of the wall-mounted television. "We black people have been the only racial/ethnic group seeking reparations for what they did to our ancestors, how they made their lives living hells. If the rumors are true, the members of this Confederacy are the ones leading efforts to suppress our voices, our votes. Hell, impede our ability to be excellent. And if they continue to afford more privileges to white people, like what we're seeing in Fulton County, we're going to lose the ability to win more of them over as allies."

"That serious, huh?"

"Unfortunately, yes."

Stacy then turned to face Trish and Angelica with her arms crossed. "Heard that UT sprinter, Jason Black, just turned himself in weeks ago. Why didn't you tell me he was staying with y'all?"

Trish scrunched her lips up. Stacy chuckled.

"His case is going to put these crackers back on their heels. Probably shaking in their boots right now because they don't know how effective their precious Stand My Ground law is going to be in a case where both of the case participants are alive to testify before the jury. If Jason also alleges attempted murder, the jury is going to be hard pressed to decide on a ruling that satisfies the public."

"For sure," Trish said. Then, as she stood and walked to detach one of the bottled waters from the plastic wrapping on the kitchenette island, she continued, saying, "To hear him tell it, this Baker dude was the one who escalated the situation."

"Do you think you could get him to speak with me? Not to talk about his case, just talk generally about how black crime suspects are treated."

Trish peered over at Angelica, bidding her to offer a reply.

"He would like that," Angelica replied. "Especially with Malcolm Stillwell calling him out like he is. But what purpose will interviewing him serve?"

"It will give him an opportunity to respond to Stillwell's criticisms, let the reading and viewing publics know he's fighting back."

Trish took short sips from her now-opened water bottle while she stood over the kitchenette island. As a public relations/marketing major, she knew what Stacy had in mind. It was important that Jason defend himself in the court of public opinion. Having an article in *The Atlantic*, and the interview recorded for broadcast on YouTube, would serve this purpose, but she knew he would need much more than that. The general public also had to see his body language, facial expressions, the white in his eyes, during his responses to reporters' questions.

"He's staying at Sojourner Vista," Trish exclaimed, "at least until the trial is over. I'll check in with him, see if this is something he's willing to do."

"Thank you."

CHAPTER SEVENTEEN

A sense of relief consumed Jason as he sat alone on the back seat of the Suburban SUV. While Thelma had told him that he would only spend one night in a Knox County jail cell, the officials there ended up extending it to three, resulting from the fact that he had surrendered to the authorities on a Friday, and court is not in session on weekends. They had flown him in early enough to get him on the Friday docket, but the Knoxville clerk phoned Thelma while they were in transit to let her know a hearing on Jason's case had to wait until Monday. However, Jason knew it ran much deeper than a scheduling conflict. He had evaded law enforcement for close to two months, causing local precincts to spend thousands of dollars searching for him. They wanted to send Jason, and members of his ilk, a message, humiliate him even.

Most short termers receive cells by themselves, but not Jason. He was forced to share one with a black man named Demarcus James. Demarcus had been in confinement for a little over four days before Jason's placement in his jail cell. He had told Jason that "they" got him for assaulting his girlfriend in front of their three children. Demarcus admitted to hitting his girlfriend, but only after learning of her infidelity. She was knocking boots with a brother who he once considered a good friend.

"You him, aren't you?" Demarcus said as Jason spread his blanket over the bottom bunk mattress. "The brotha who stabbed that white man."

"Yeah. That's me."

Demarcus sat upright, swung his legs so they hung off the side of the bunk. "They 'bout serve your ass to the dogs, bro'"

Jason shrugged. Demarcus' calm demeanor revealed that his experience with the Tennessee judicial system had been long and extensive. What he said next solidified this revelation.

"You gonna be alright, though," Demarcus said as he climbed down to stand barefoot on the cold concrete floor. He then proceeded to pull his pants down below his knees to sit on the toilet. "You got the Marshall Group working for you. They win over ninety percent of their cases."

Demarcus farted and then his excrement could be heard going plop plop as it hit the water in the toilet bowl. It was going to be a long weekend, but Jason knew even then that Demarcus wouldn't be the only one using the cell's toilet. He held his breath briefly when his nose caught a whiff of Demarcus' intestinal stench.

"Glad to hear that," Jason replied as he sat on the lower bunk's edge. "But let's be clear: I'm no criminal."

"We know that, bruh. But too many of us are afraid to say it. I work for Waste Management. You know, the guy hanging off the back of the truck. When I was out and working, we would watch those manhunt stories they did on you in the break room with them crackers. We'd have debates up in there, the black and brown brothas telling them you were defending yourself. Sounded like that security guard had you down on your knees. They weren't hearing that. Kept calling you a thug. We know better, though. Ain't no world-class sprinter like you trying to be out there in these streets."

"No doubt."

Jason turned away as Demarcus wiped and pulled his pants up. He then looked up to stare at Demarcus' backside as he stood over the sink washing his hands. As he stood there, Jason fell back on the lower bunk to stare up at the top bunk's wiring.

"I guess what they say is true," Jason exclaimed.

"What you mean?" Demarcus replied while shaking his hands dry.

"We can work our asses off to be great at something, but when all is said and done, all our hard work is worthless. They automatically assume we're guilty because we're black. Niggers."

Demarcus sat on the floor, his back pressed against the back, cinder block wall, legs spread wide. "Maybe your case will change all that. You definitely not O. J. Simpkins, who everyone knew was guilty. But when he got off, black folk were happy, me included. He beat the system. You're going to beat it too, bruh. You just have to believe your lawyers know what they're doing. And you have the best that we black folk can get."

Jason considered Demarcus' words. But as he did so, he wondered why someone so wise could allow himself to become a caged bird. Jason had always been repulsed by men who hit women. Probably had something to do with him witnessing his maternal uncle, Willie Fortson, punching his girlfriend Olivia Wallace like she was a dude after Cynthia Black had driven Jeremiah and him to Richmond, Virginia to spend the summer with him, six months after Jerome Black's murder. And even though Uncle Willie was a bus driver with the Henrico County Public School System, Jason knew he was a good man. But once Jeremiah told their mother how Uncle Willie was treating Olivia, she drove all the way up from Wake Forest to pick them up, returning with them the same day to their Wake Forest home.

A week later, Uncle Willie showed up at their Wake Forest home to apologize to his sister. Jason was in the seventh grade, at Wake Forest Middle School. Uncle Willie also extended apologies to Jeremiah and him, but he also bore bad news. He was dying, of lung cancer, and there was nothing his medical team could do to stop it from spreading. Uncle Willie died within a month of letting them know. The fact that he grew the balls to apologize to his sister and her children was a reminder to Jason that bad, immature men are just more susceptible to making decisions that benefit themselves in the moment than appeasing the people around them. Demarcus was no different. This too would pass.

"We'll see." Jason sat upright before leaning over the side of his bed to glare down at Demarcus. "Yeah. We'll see."

Baker knocked on Bobby Ford's front door, nervously turning around to take multiple peeks at the group of teenaged boys that he saw chatting it up when he turned the corner onto Bobby's street. Even when he was a KPD officer, he knew Chilhowie Park was one of the safest areas in East Knoxville. Most of the residents there were white. But teenagers standing on street corners at noontime during the school day caused the wrinkles on his forehead to become more prominent. He knew they were up to no good, coming up with juvenile schemes on how they could make trouble in the neighborhood.

Prior to his retirement in 1985, when he was 46 years old, Bobby let it be known that he and his wife were moving into a smaller one-story, single-family home in Chilhowie Park. Bobby joked about his wife Mabeline's disappointment with this decision. She thought their future plans included a move to Destin, Florida, where their days would have been spent walking along and lying on the beach. But she relented when she accepted the fact that East Knoxville would always be their home because Bobby was too connected to the East Knoxville community, the children and adolescents living there. Consequently, she didn't balk when Bobby became the director of the Morningside Community Center within five years of his retirement.

The front door opened, and Baker smiled when he saw Bobby's youngest child, now a mature adult woman, standing there.

"Hey, April," Baker said. "It's been a while."

"It has," April replied gruffly. "But why now?"

"Because I need to speak with him. Need help making sense of it all."

April stepped back and to the side and then waved Baker in.

"He back there in the study, to your left," she said as Baker walked past her to enter the home.

"What's going on, Pops," Baker said from the archway leading into Bobby's study.

Bobby, who was sitting behind an oak desk in front of his desktop computer, looked up. As his eyes met Baker's, he leaned back in his ergonomic chair while placing his clasped hands on his stomach. Bobby's pursed lips let Baker know his being here was an unexpected surprise.

"Why you here?" Bobby asked.

"Because you once told me that I would always be your friend, my black father from a white mother. That I could always come to you for advice."

"But you done stepped in some deep doo-doo, Roscoe. What you did ain't right, and you know it. Keeping the peace has never been about terrorizing folk; it's about serving and protecting."

"Can I come in? Can I sit?"

"April done let you in." He pointed to the sitting area on the far side of the room. "Go on. Sit down."

Baker dropped to one of the antique chairs along the back wall as Bobby grabbed his walking stick and used it to limp over to where Baker was sitting. Baker noted how slowly Bobby moved and guesstimated that he had to be in his mid- to late 70s. Bobby sat on the matching antique love seat to Baker's left. Baker studied Bobby's dark face, admiring the wrinkles along his forehead and cheeks. He was no longer the giant of a man that he remembered from the 1980s and '90s.

"The woman was white, wasn't she?"

"She was."

"And you felt compelled to respond, to protect her honor. Right?"

"Right."

"Would you have done the same if the woman was Black?"

Baker shifted in his chair before leaning forward. "Yes. I believe I would."

"I heard the boy stabbed you. What prompted him to do that?"

"I don't know," Baker lied. "He just lunged at me, like he was on drugs or something. Never saw it coming."

Bobby noted the quickening of Baker's blinking, how his pupils bounced from him to the floor, other parts of the room.

"You lying. You pulled out your gun, told the boy to get on his knees while you pointed it at him. Didn't even give him a chance to deny the allegation. Am I right?"

Baker relented, saying, "Of course. You're always right. But I didn't know he had a weapon."

"You're a security guard, Roscoe. Not a police officer. You have no arrest authority. The best you can do is call it in, wait on actual police officers to arrive on the scene. Now, this boy's future is in jeopardy because of you. You just ruined his chances of competing in the Rio Games."

"So, you know him?"

"I do. He has visited the community center countless times, helping our kids with their homework during the school year, working our sports camp during the summer. That boy is one of the good ones. He's going places. So, my best advice to you: Drop the lawsuit."

Baker sat upright again. "Eunice thinks it's a little too late for that. And now that Malcolm Stillwell has chimed in, she feels we should allow him to use the trial to energize his base. You know me, Bobby. I've always been an Independent, someone who votes for candidates who are best positioned to put more money in my pockets."

"Sounds like Eunice has you on a leash, and she's the one dragging you where she wants you to be. That's not the Roscoe Baker I remember. Not the Roscoe Baker that so many of my kids remember. You used to have a heart for the community. What changed, son?"

Baker's gaze shifted to the books on Bobby's bookshelf as Bobby continued to stare at him. A number of the books were written by black, progressive authors, so he knew Bobby was not going to like what he was about to say.

"It's this new movement, this 1776 Patriot Movement. Been attending a few of the local chapter's meetings. They're saying all the right things, Bobby. Things that make me feel good about being conservative. They tell us that our conservatism should be considered a badge of honor, that we should not be ashamed of it."

"That's not conservatism, Roscoe, that's White Nationalism. They don't want you to think about all the black boys and girls that you tutored and coached with me back in the day. They don't want you thinking about how these black boys and girls, and their black parents, would feel if they were in the room with you, hearing all this talk about conservatism from a white perspective. Their meetings and rallies are nothing but Klan meetings in disguise if you ask me."

Bobby paused to collect his next thought. 'You ever wonder why I spent so much time coaching AAU basketball?"

"To prepare the next generation for the challenges of tomorrow."

Bobby chuckled at that as he gently tapped Baker's right knee with the handle of his walking stick.

"If you were paying attention, you saw that we weren't just coaching and tutoring black kids; we were coaching and tutoring all kids, no matter what color they were." Bobby cleared his throat. "You see, God doesn't see color, he sees hearts, the thing that motivates us to love others, to serve them. I loved you, Roscoe, like a son. Still do. Not just because we were colleagues, but because you're another human being who deserves to be seen, to be valued. Didn't matter if you're Republican or Democrat, Conservative or Progressive. Anyone who treats me with respect and doesn't make me feel as if I'm less than, is worthy of being my friend. My own kids, Michael and April, were taught that. The kids on our AAU teams were taught that. And that work continues today, at the Morningside Community Center."

Bobby stood and walked back over to his desk. He then reached into his drawer to pull out his copy of the New York Times special edition of *1619: The Year Black Folks Should Have Mattered.* He returned to the sitting area with it in hand.

"Have you read this?" he asked as he handed the folded newsprint to Baker. Baker flipped it open, allowing his eyes to survey the front cover, where the series title and a photo of chained black Africans were prominently displayed.

"No. I haven't."

"Well, you should. When you do, you will have a better appreciation for what we black Americans have been doing to get this nation to live up to its creed. Your 1776 Patriot Movement wants to erase us nonwhites from the history books. They don't want to accept the fact that we're all siblings struggling daily to get our relationships right. But what we're seeing out of them isn't new. Versions of it were around when Frederick Douglass asked why black Americans should celebrate the Fourth of July when they weren't even free during the country's founding in 1776. Freedom for black Americans didn't happen until 1863. Versions were around when Dr. King and other prominent civil rights leaders, both black and white, were marching on Washington in 1964 in anticipation of the civil rights act being signed into law by President Lyndon B. Johnson. Stillwell knows there is a segment of white Americans in this country that don't want black people and other racial/ethnic minorities to gain parity with them. They want to go through life thinking they are superior to us nonwhites. That, my friend, is why we can't make lasting progress on the racial front. And if Stillwell is elected to office, I fear the voices of these white nationalists, these white supremacists, will become even louder."

"Do you consider me a white nationalist, a white supremacists?"

"That's not how I viewed you, what, thirty years ago. But people change, for any number of reasons. I see that being married to Eunice has changed you, caused you to become a true conservative. But the Roscoe Baker I remember was more progressive. Why else would you help an older, black man like me coach a group of inner-city kids?"

Bobby grimaced. "I know you know why I retired; two years shy of my twentieth year."

Baker did know. Bobby had overheard a breakroom conversation between Oliver Franks, the KPD Human Resources Director, and KPD Chief George "Buddy" Hinshaw, one in which they freely joked about slowing down the recruitment of more minority officers. Bobby shared this information with Baker during the team's chartered bus ride to Bristol, Tennessee for the Arby's Basketball Classic. Baker was the only person he told; therefore, it didn't take a genius to figure out why Hinshaw would pressure Bobby to accept an offer to retire early with full benefits.

"Why did you do it, Roscoe?" Bobby asked. "You were like a second son to me. What I told you should have stayed between us."

Baker shifted uncomfortably in his seat. "I didn't think it would come down to that, them forcing you out. But when you wrote that op-ed piece about police officers needing to reside in the communities they serve, I kind of lost it. Didn't like that you were putting our business out there, making us feel guilty for not wanting to put our families in harm's way by moving to unsafe neighborhoods. But what pushed me over the edge were those comments you made at that conference. The National Organization for Black Law Enforcement, or NOBLE. Made everyone feel uneasy. You came right out and said it, in front of all those people, that white police chiefs don't want to recruit and hire more black officers."

"And that's why in the weeks that followed they accused me of falsifying my police reports, right? Said I violated my oath to offer honest and accurate accounts of my policing."

Baker stared into Bobby's eyes, seeking comfort where none could be found. Thereafter, he found himself blinking repeatedly in an attempt to suppress the bubbling tears. In the years following Bobby Ford's retirement, Baker had allowed himself to adopt the same shoot first, ask questions later mindset that had been adopted by many of his white brothers in blue. Sadly, the vast majority of the people these white officers shot were black. Now, as the tears flowed freely from his eyes, Baker acknowledged to himself that this mindset has always been rooted in racist attitudes and beliefs, which made him part of the problem rather than the solution.

Bobby grabbed the handle of his walking stick and stood up. "Let me get April," he said. "She will show you out."

Baker wiped his eyes with the front of his hands before standing himself. "I didn't mean to offend, Bobby. Wish there was something I could do to make things right."

"Haven't you done enough, muthafucka?" Bobby now glared at Baker under an angry brow. "My life, my reputation, was tarnished, because of your dumb ass." He gestured toward the archway. "Get the hell out my house. You're not welcome here anymore."

While standing on the front porch with April, Baker asked, "You mind me asking how Michael's doing? He still with the Hornets?"

"No. He been with the Wizards for the past two years. Doing the same thing he was doing over in Charlotte."

"Well, tell him Mr. Roscoe said hi the next time you speak with him. Rooted for him when he was playing with the Lakers. Sorry to hear about your mother. She was good people."

April drew her arms to her chest as she rocked back on her heels. Mabeline died over a year ago, from brain cancer, and even though Baker spent quality time with her when she was living, he didn't have the courtesy to pay his respects in person. In fact, none of Bobby Ford's white KPD colleagues showed up for Mabeline Ford's memorial and funeral services.

Both April and Michael had numerous conversations with their father about the things he had to endure as one of the KPD's first, black police officers. Bobby Ford recounted stories about finding nooses in his locker, and the words "Nigger Go Home!" written with permanent, black markers on the restroom stall walls. April had nothing but respect for her father, his commitment to serve and protect Knoxville residents, and even having the backs of his white KPD brothers during violent arrests. But he also shared that his white KPD brothers never seemed to reciprocate. This realization saddened him.

However, Bobby Ford thought Roscoe Baker was different. Baker was by his side as one of his assistant coaches when Michael's under 17 AAU basketball team made it to the 1987 national championship game that was played at the Disney Sports Complex in Orlando, Florida. Their Knoxville Bobcats lost to a team from Compton, California, but the experience seemed to strengthen their relationship.

"Daddy was wrong," April proclaimed as she peered down at Baker, who looked back at her from the bottom of the front porch stairs. "Should have known back then you weren't being real with us. Daddy allowed you into our space, but you never allowed him, us, into yours. Daddy had us calling you Uncle Roscoe. I know now why he did it. He wanted you to feel special in hopes that you would return the favor. But you never did. You never introduced us to your wife and kids."

Baker plunged his hands deeper into his pockets as he looked away while kicking a small pebble down the walkway.

"That's on my wife, not me. I wanted my kids to meet you all, but she wouldn't allow it."

"So, she's the racist in your family. Right?"

"I wouldn't say that. She' grew up in rural Alabama. Didn't have much contact with Blacks growing up. When she did, they were the ones still picking cotton on the plantations."

"So why you with her?"

"Because I love her. She's the mother of my kids."

"Well, I hope you do right by Jason Black. Release him so he can get back to living his life."

Baker pulled his hands from his pockets. He glanced at April one last time, and when he did, he saw Bobby standing behind her, inside the house, on the other side of the screen door.

Bobby shook his head as if he were responding to a question that only he could hear. Baker stared up at him, not knowing what to think, what to say.

Bobby pushed the screen door open for April, his gaze fixed on Baker as he walked away. But Bobby had heard the pain in his daughter's voice, her reminder that Baker never gave them the privilege to meet his wife, his children, and Baker sent flowers rather than grace them with his presence. While it was true Baker and he shared some fond memories, the fact still remained that Baker seemingly felt no obligation to relate to and with his family and him as human beings in search of authentic relationships. So, as Bobby Ford placed his right hand on the closed front door, he said a silent prayer, one in which he pleaded with God the Father to make Roscoe Baker do the right thing.

"You good, bro'." The driver's deep baritone voice snapped Jason out of his revelry. Jason turned from the window to the eyes staring back at him in the rear-view mirror.

Thelma had introduced the driver as Amos at the courthouse before Amos waved him into the Suburban SUV's back seat.

But Jason said very little to Amos as Amos steered the vehicle away from the courthouse and onto Interstate 40 North.

"Yeah. I'm good. Just ready for all this to be over."

"I feel you. But don't worry. Ms. St. James is one of the best lawyers in the Southeast. If she can't get you off, no one can."

"How long you been working for her?"

"Not working for her, working for the firm, the Marshall Law Group, MLG. Been with them for a little over two years now. Was living in Chicago with my ma. Barely had a pot to piss in. They pulled me off the streets when I was a teen, bruh. Got me believing I can be much more."

"By driving a car?" Jason blurted out.

Amos sighed deeply and then smiled out of the right corner of his mouth.

"Nah, man. That's not how it works. Driving you around is just one of the extra things they have us doing during our apprenticeships. Put a little extra spending money in our pockets. I'm studying Government and International Affairs at Carson Newman. Hoping to get admitted to law school on a full ride to Princeton next Fall."

Jason shifted in his seat, somewhat embarrassed for being so judgmental. It was demeaning, a clear signal to the listener that the speaker thought he was better than the listener.

"My bad, bro'. Back here making snap judgments like a know you. Tell me more about this apprenticeship program, though."

Amos began by telling Jason the origins of the Marshall Law Group, how it was formed by Morehouse's Kelvin Cochran, Harvard's ReShonda Gates and Columbia's Malcolm King three years after the January 24, 1993 death of former U.S. Supreme Court Justice Thurgood Marshall. Prior to being named to the U.S. Supreme Court on August 30, 1967, Marshall, who was the head of the NAACP Legal Defense and Educational Fund at the time, was the chief attorney in the *Brown vs. the Board of Educa-*

tion of Topeka, Kansas case. Amos reminded Jason that the 1954 landmark decision in this case is what made it possible for black children to attend the same public schools as white children, as the court at the time ruled that racial segregation of children in public schools is unconstitutional. Amos said the Marshall Law Group's aim is to honor Thurgood Marshall's legacy by fighting for the causes that made him a key figure in the fight for civil rights and social justice.

According to Amos, the Marshall Law Group apprenticeship program has been in existence since its 1996 incorporation. The goal of the program is to provide promising black high school and college students with the knowledge and experiences they need to enroll and succeed in law school and pass the bar. He explained that Justice Marshall applauded the efforts of Dr. Martin Luther King, Jr., Malcolm X, and their supporters, which included him, but he also knew that black Americans had to make the legal case for why their ancestors are owed reparations and their contemporaries equal protection under the law.

And American lawyer, professor and civil rights activist Derrick Bell had done just that, he explained. Amos noted that Professor Bell is credited as being the man behind Critical Race Theory. Working first for the U.S. Justice Department, then the NAACP Legal Defense Fund, where he supervised over 300 school desegregation cases in Mississippi, Professor Bell recognized that many of the decisions in landmark civil-rights cases were of limited practical impact. His analysis of these landmark decisions caused him to conclude that racism is so deeply rooted in the makeup of American society that it has been able to reassert itself after each successive wave of reform aimed at eliminating it. Bell believed racism is a permanent fixture in American society. Ultimately, though, Derrick Bell thought Critical Race Theory meant telling the truth, even in the face of criticism.

Cochran, Gates and King even sought Bell's counsel prior to operationalizing their efforts. They wanted to create a law firm that developed legal strategies for eradicating systemic racism, as well as creative public relation strategies for crafting truthful oral, literary and visual narratives about the plight of Blacks and other persons of color.

Amos stressed the importance of how Critical Race Theory is serving as the basis for all he and his fellow apprentices are learning at the Marshall Law Group's School for Social and Racial Justice. He said, "Their approach is sound because they're giving us the tools to expose the systems that perpetuate racism on Blacks, persons of color. It also exposes how these racist systems privilege Whites."

"But what does my case have to do with all that?" Jason asked. "I went on a jog, bruh. Was minding my own business."

"And that's why it matters. The other side – what we call the unenlightened – just see it as another opportunity to demean us. They call us lazy and thuggish. They don't believe we are deserving of civil rights, equal protections under the law. But we know the truth: That they enriched themselves off the free labor of our black ancestors, and their intent is to maintain a status quo that keeps us picking their cotton and shining their shoes."

"Damn." Jason then peered out the window, finally noticing that Knoxville's city landscape had now been replaced by foliage-covered hills and valleys. "Where we going?"

"Sevier County," Amos replied, "to the mountainside resort that has become MLG's base of operations. Sojourner Vista. A lot of history there."

Driving on the winding road leading up the side of the mountain was a feat in itself. Sevier County was home to Molly Peyton, the white country music star who is a staunch supporter of both the Civil Rights Movement of the 1950s and '60s, as well as the current Black Folk Matter movement. It was also the last place you would think black people would want to be. But here he was, a black man, in transit to the black-owned and operated Sojourner Vista Mountain Resort and Conference Center situated among the foothills of the Chimney Top Mountains.

As they drew closer to their destination, Jason's body tensed. The Confederate flags perched high on poles attached to the dilapidated homes of their impoverished white occupants didn't go unnoticed.

"That's how they roll over here in Upper East Tennessee," Amos said. "But at the end of the day, the only color that matters is green. White folks can't get enough of Sojourner Vista."

However, Amos was singing a different tune as they got closer to the resort's front gate. A long line of protesters, all white, stood alongside the paved road, behind barricades erected by Sevier County Police Department officers, holding signs that read, "NIGGERS GO HOME!" and "White Race Is The Superior Race". Mixed in with signs like these were even more signs that read, "Stillwell 2016". The icing on the white supremacist cake was the Confederate flags meticulously sprinkled in for dramatic effect. The angry expressions on the protesters' pale faces let you know that they were performing for the local and national news reporters that stood nearby with their notepads, microphones and cameras at the ready. Police officers responded quickly when one or more of the protesters tried to brush past the barricades.

"Here every year," Amos announced. "All's good most of the time, but shit hits the fan the second week in November. You know how white people do when too many nigga's get together."

Jason pursed his lips. "They lose their damn minds."

But moments later, after they rolled past the yawning front gate, Jason could see why even white folks were willing to spend their hard-earned money at Sojourner Vista. The place was beautiful, as a large statue of black abolitionist Sojourner Truth standing on the jagged edge of a mountaintop loomed large as the roundabout's centerpiece. Jason also found himself becoming enraptured by the wooden structure that was the main building. While he knew the building was reinforced with steel beams and concrete, the designers went out of their way to give it the outer appearance of an oversized log cabin that seemed to just out of the mountainside.

Leaning forward and straining to look higher on the structure's roof, he spotted two, black men with assault rifles hanging from straps around their necks. "Who are those bad asses?"

Amos tilted his head to his right. "The Sojourner Vista Tactical Group. Vista Guard for short. They are on post twenty-four seven, for if and when shit goes sideways. Pulled from every military branch. All Black military force. They don't play."

The passenger side door swung open. "Welcome to Sojourner Vista, Mr. Black," a young, attractive and petite black female greeted. She was dressed in a black vest and miniskirt, white shirt and bowtie. She waved Jason to the main building's entrance, where Kelvin Cochran and Reshonda Gates stood waiting.

"Jason," Mr. Cochran said, extending his arms to him. He embraced and released Jason. He then introduced him to Ms. Gates.

"How was the drive up?" Ms. Gates asked as they stood a few feet away from the concierge desk.

"Very scenic," Jason replied.

Mr. Cochran followed with, "I hope our uninvited guests didn't startle you."

"No," Jason replied, "they didn't.   Heard they're here every year."

"Yes, they are," Mr. Cochran replied.

"But we're wearing them down," Ms. Gates shot back.

Ms. Gates then turned on her heels to follow Mr. Cochran's lead into the spacious lobby. Jason marveled at the oversized painting of enslaved blacks picking cotton, with musical notes drifting over them under the hot sun.

"First time?" Mr. Cochran interjected.

"Yeah. Can't afford anything like this. I'm a broke college student."

"Damn shame," Mr. Cochran said. "Even college athletes should be able to make money off their likenesses. A college like Tennessee raking in all that dough, and all their student-athletes have to show for it is a college degree. Corruption in plain sight if you ask me."

The threesome stopped at the check-in desk, where an attractive black female stood behind it, a biracial male in front.

"We know you had a long day," Ms. Gates said, "so we're going to let you get on up to your room, relax. But just so you know, Thelma and her team will arrive in the morning. The plan is to meet down here on Tuesday, in the conference room over there, around nine to start developing our legal strategy for next month's trial." She then lovingly patted the biracial male on his shoulder, as the black female standing behind the check-in desk handed Jason his room key. "Calvin here will show you to your room."

Mr. Cochran added, "You being here now is a good thing, Jason. Our Racial Justice Conference commences in two days, bright and early on Monday morning. We hold it annually, over five days, as a way of reflecting on where we have come as a people and what challenges we must still overcome. Since you're our special guest, the sessions are free to you. You good with that."

Jason didn't know how to respond. They had selected Sojourner Vista because of its proximity to Knoxville, the Knox County courthouse. It was only coincidental that he happened to be lodged here during the Marshall Law Group's annual Racial Justice conference.

"Yeah," Jason replied. "Sounds great."

Mr. Cochran went on to explain that the conference would be attended by black legal scholars and practitioners, law enforcement officers and college students. Some of the brightest black minds from the for-profit and not-for-profit sectors would be facilitating interactive workshops. He urged Jason to attend the session *Black Student-Athletes: The Case for Getting Paid to Play*.

"Like I alluded to earlier," Mr. Cochran said, "We must stop allowing these colleges and universities to take advantage of you, our black college athletes. They enrich themselves and their institutions off your blood, sweat and tears. And over eighty percent of you are black. Just imagine the type of power, influence and control members of the Black Diaspora could amass if you all are ever able to get paid for your performances on the court, the field of play."

Jason held his mother Cynthia tightly in the foyer to the standalone cabin that seemed to extend from the mountainside above the main resort below. Calvin placed Jason's luggage in one of the two bedrooms with the king-sized beds. Jason matched his mother's embrace, even as he breathed in the fruity fragrances emanating from her hair.

Cynthia lifted her head to peer into Jason's eyes. They then stood there staring at each other, each noting the changes that come when one hasn't seen the other in a while. There were others in the room, including White and Rev, his two best friends from the Tennessee track and field team, and their elderly Wake Forest tenant Ms. Jacobs.

"I'm whole again," Cynthia announced, as she released Jason to get a better look at him, holding onto his hands.

Jason smiled upon hearing this sentiment before silently mouthing, "So am I." The toilet flush from the bathroom and the whoosh of the bathroom door opening caused Jason to look up and away from his mother. His eyes were greeted by the sight of Jeremiah hurriedly wiping the front and backs of his wet hands on his jeans.

"Hey, little bro'," Jeremiah said, standing in place with his arms spread wide to let Jason know he wanted some of the love that he was giving their mother. Jason obliged, rushing over to Jeremiah to engulf him in his arms, lift him off the carpeted floor. Afterwards, he leaned over to kiss a seated Ms. Jacobs on the cheek. She reached for his hand and squeezed it, a smile on her wrinkled face.

"When did you get in," Jason asked Jeremiah."

"Last night," Jeremiah replied. "Told my C. O. I had to get home to deal with a family emergency."

"That's what's up. Glad you're here."

Jason eventually got around to sharing heartfelt embraces with White and Rev. White told Jason that a number of their teammates wanted to join them, but a member of the resort's security team limited them to two visitors from the university. Upon hearing this, Jason surmised that Coach Highsmith hand selected White and Rev because of his close relationship with them. But he still thought it would have been great if more of his teammates could have been present.

Jason, Jeremiah, White and Rev sat on the plush furniture in the standalone cabin's spacious common area. The wall-mounted television was on, but only for background noise. Jason had already spent hours sharing his experiences with all of his visitors. But it was now well past 10 p.m. Cynthia and Ms. Jacobs had already excused themselves to the adjoining bedroom that they would be sharing during their stay at Sojourner Vista, allowing the four men to talk further amongst themselves.

"This is a great setup," White said. "With all the attention your case is getting, your being here makes it harder for the media to know where you're at."

"And even if they did," Rev interjected, "they would need to have special access just to set foot on the grounds. Those armed guards on the rooftops ain't playing. And there's a stone wall surrounding the joint."

"Ms. St. James told me when we first got here that it's been this way for a while," Jason replied. "Said the owners are always receiving threats from white supremacist that they're going to blow it up, burn it all down. The threats started coming in on the regular after Malcolm Stillwell announced his presidential run. Doesn't help that he got in front of the camera a few weeks ago and told reporters that Mr. Cochran and his partners rejected his offer to purchase the place. No doubt that he was intentionally making the place a target."

"So why bring you here?" White asked. "Seems like the hate for this place will get much worse once the white supremacists learn they have you holed up here."

"I think that's the point," Jason replied. "I'm slowly learning that this Marshall Law Group has a longstanding tradition of fighting fire with fire, or countering lies with inconvenient truths. When I was chatting with Ms. St. James the other day, she reminded me that this is what Dr. King and all the other civil rights advocates were doing back in the day, marching through the streets, sitting at Woolworth counters, so the media could report on how those racist, white mobs reacted to what they were doing." Jason swallowed hard. "But enough about that. How you all been. Y'all gearing up for indoor, right?"

"Yeah, man," Rev replied. "But before we go there, I got to let you know that everybody was down after we learned what was going on with you. Coach Highsmith gave us about three days off just to process the news. But we all think he was fighting with the trustee board during that time. He told us during a team meeting about them suspending you without giving you a chance to share your side of the story."

Jason shrugged. "I know. That was some foul shit. But can you blame them? They didn't know where I was. But it's all good."

"You working out?" White asked.

"Nah, man. Been a nervous wreak. Sleeping late most days and going to bed early. But I'm feeling better now, now that I turned myself in."

Jeremiah returned from the kitchen holding the tops of three bottled iced teas in his left hand, a single one in his right. He placed the three on the coffee table, and as he sat in a plush chair across from Jason, he watched as Jason, White and Rev each grabbed one for themselves.

Jeremiah sipped tea from the uncapped bottle. "You're the third fastest man on the planet, Jase. That's big, bro'. But losers are the only ones that feel sorry for themselves, and I know you're not a loser. The least you can do is start jogging through these mountains, do some hill work, lift weights."

"I plan on getting back to it after the trial is over, after this mess has been resolved."

Jeremiah continued, saying, "So, I guess you're a loser now. Huh?"

"No. I'm not. I just can't think straight right now not knowing what my future looks like."

"Your brother's right, Jay, man," White said. "You have to start acting like none of this shit ever happened. If you don't, it's going to be harder for you to get back to where you left off last season."

"If you don't," Rev proclaimed, "that Jamaican, Nigel Grimes, and his Jamaican teammates are going to make our American sprinters look bad. We all watched that race in Oslo, when he ran that season-ending nine point seven zero, remember?"

"Yeah. I remember. Been watching it over and over on YouTube. But like I told you then, I was more impressed by his two teammates, Jacob Reed and Benjie Stallworth, running low nine nines in the same race. It was tight all the way to the finish line. They looked good."

Jeremiah licked his lips. "So, what do you think they're doing right now in preparation for the Jamaican trials, the Rio Games?"

White, sensing Jason's hesitation, chuckled as he feigned sheepishness while raising his hand. "Oh. Oh. I know." His hand returned to the armrest. "They're working their asses off in hopes that they can dethrone the king, Mitch Newman, and his sidekick, Jason Black. Remember what you told me our first day of practice in August. You told me to believe. I believe you're capable of running Newmanequese times. I believe the Jamaicans can do the same. But not like this, in the condition you're in right now. You have to get your competitive drive back, bro'."

White stood up first, stretching his arms wide and then allowing them to flop back down to his sides. Rev followed suit.

"We out," White announced. "Gotta get back to campus. Rest up before tomorrow's early morning practice."

"We'll roll back over this way on next weekend," Rev chimed.

Jason stood and fist-pounded his teammates near the front door.

"Hey," Jason said as they stood at the opened doorway. "I need a favor."

"Sure," White replied. "What do you need?"

"You know how we used to talk politics after practice on the indoor basketball court at Stokely with Allen Hopkins, Chuck Webster and a few of the other basketball and football players?"

"Yeah," both White and Rev replied in unison.

Jason continued, saying, "Allen is the first brother I ever heard say anything about black athletes using their influence to bring about social change. What he was saying is so on point."

"Yeah," Rev replied. "Said we should be using our influence to draw attention to issues like unarmed, black men getting shot in the streets by white police officers. Had a lot to say about voter suppression too."

"Right. I've had nothing but time to think about these things, while I was down in Atlanta, time spent in the Knox County Jail. I believe it's going to be us, black athletes, leading the next phase of the civil rights movement. We're the ones with the most influence."

"But we're also the ones with the most to lose," Rev said. "These white owners in the NFL and NBA aren't going to put up with black athletes who are always drawing attention to controversial issues. If anything, they're going to cut them from the team, blacklist them. Sure, they'll come out like they did and say in the heat of the moment that they support Black Folk Matter, but once our feet come off the pedal, they ignore our concerns. They just want their athletes to shut up and dribble, score touchdowns."

"I guess you're right. But if you see Allen, give him my new number. Got something I'd like to run by him."

White nodded and then turned to exit through the front door. Rev trailed behind him.

Jason returned to the living room. Jeremiah sat on the sofa using the remote to flick through the channel lineup. He stopped flicking when he heard the voice of Bob Kessler calling the UT versus Florida home football game. The replay on the big screen television showed Chuck Webster bursting through a crowd of defenders to score the first touchdown on the Vols opening drive.

"I see where your head is at," Jeremiah said after Jason sat on the sofa to the left of him. "Got me thinking back to how you used to dress up like Spider-Man and Superman as a child, wanting to be the hero. But the questions you have to ask yourself are, who am I trying to save and how will I do it?" He paused, giving Jason time to fully absorb his words. "You also have to determine who the villains are and what you as the hero need to do to take them down."

"But that's the thing. The villain that needs to be taken down is not a person, it's a system, it's White Supremacy. And we black people have allowed them to control narratives that we should be telling ourselves. Seems like the white supremacists are telling white people that we're against them, their whiteness, but we're not. We're against white people who think they're better, more supreme, than us blacks and other persons of color."

"Definitely not Little Jase from the hood anymore."

"Nah, bruh. I'm not. I'm trying to become someone who pushes all of us to become much more."

"He's right, you know," Jeremiah said, leaning on the kitchen island to his left as Jason stood in front of him with his arms crossed.

Jason had just gotten off the phone with Allen Hopkins. During the call Jason shared with Hopkins his thoughts about forming a coalition, one comprised of black and brown athletes, that could draw attention to their issues, their concerns. Hopkins told Jason that he didn't need any controversy in his life right now, as he was projected to be the number one pick in the 2016 NBA Draft after his final season as a Tennessee Vol hoopster. "I can't control what white folk think or do," Hopkins had told Jason over the phone, "but I can control how I'm going to get paid. Check back with me after I get signed and a few of those NBA checks have been deposited into my bank account. May have more options then."

Jeremiah continued, "You also need to tend to the things you have control over. All this other stuff – this trial of the century – is going to take care of itself. But if you want to give Mitch Newman a run for his money next year, in Rio, you have to work harder than ever, because he's not going to go down without a fight. And those Jamaicans. They're coming for you all, with one goal in mind: To bring glory and honor to Jamaica. Those brothers want to show you cocky Americans, and the world, that there is greatness in black Jamaicans' DNA."

Jason stood tall, pulling his crossed arms tighter, his chest and shoulders square with Jeremiah's. "Why should I care about any of that, bro'? Bring it, out of loyalty for my country? Why? My country doesn't give a shit about me. If it did, the bastards would have dismissed the charges, say no harm, no foul. I had just as much of a right to defend myself as that white man did. And the university. Hell, I can't even get my degree on time now because of the suspension. So, as far as I'm concerned, I don't owe my country a damn thing."

"That may or may not be true, Jase. But you owe yourself everything. The more you focus on what they're not doing, and what the University of Tennessee did to you, the further you drift from what you want to do with your life. I'm going to be real with you, though, little brother: This bullshit that you're going through right now is going to end, and I have no doubt that you're going to be exonerated. The question you must answer is are you positioning yourself for the opportunities that are still there?"

Jeremiah lightly thumped Jason on his chest with a balled-up fist. "Track and field has been good to you, little bro', allowed a poor boy from Wake Forest, North Carolina to see the world. You done been to Paris, Switzerland, Doha, Barcelona, Oslo and Amsterdam, more places than I could ever hope to see. I want to be in that Olympic stadium next year, with Moma, to see you compete, but getting to Rio has to start now, not next week, not next month. You have to qualify, and trials are in May. Come on, man. Get your shit together."

Jason leaned back on the kitchen island behind him as he watched Jeremiah peel away and disappear into one of the other adjoining bedrooms. He's right, Jason thought. I have to be ready. But he then thought about seeing Roscoe Baker in a courtroom for the first time since their physical altercation three months prior. Would he have the will to look the man in the eyes, or would he look down and away the whole time because he was convinced that the white man was in the right, and he, the black man, was in the wrong. What he would do was to be determined. But judgment day was coming, and all he could do was hope that Thelma St. James was cut out for the shit storm that was about to rain down on them.

Not many people were in the chamber when Jason and Thelma entered the courtroom. Upon entry, Jason immediately spotted Roscoe Baker and his attorney, Mason Chase, sitting to the right of the judge's stand in the foreground. It was a preliminary hearing, so there were only a few people seated on the benches to the left and right of the center aisle.

Thelma led Jason down the center aisle and was the first to push past the swinging door on the three-foot, wooden barrier that separated the spectators from the judge and the warring legal teams. As he walked behind her, Jason couldn't help but admire how firm Thelma's buttocks looked under her purple skirt. He was dressed to the nines as well, wearing the black suit, white button-down shirt, and purple tie that her boss Kelvin Cochran had hand delivered to his hotel room the night before. When he talked to Mr. Newman on the phone, Mr. Cochran told him that he needed to make a good first impression from jump. He added that purple is the color of royalty.

The black bailiff standing in front of the judge's bench discreetly greeted both Thelma and Jason with a hand gesture that Jason didn't recognize as they moved past the barrier to take seats behind a table to their left, his right.

Jason could hear his heart pounding in his chest as he sat there, less than fifteen feet from the man who once stood over him holding a pistol to his head to whisper, "There's going to be once less nigger in the world tonight." When he shared this nugget with Thelma 48-hours earlier, Thelma told him this was an important detail, but they would take their time weaving Baker's racist words into their legal narrative. Both she and Jerome knew any talk of Roscoe Baker being racist would cause the white members of the selected jury to immediately take sides before testimony could be provided. Consequently, she knew they had to walk softly at first, because in Knoxville, Tennessee, the racial politics were real.

"All rise!" the black bailiff ordered when the door behind the judge's bench opened, and Judge Sinclair Stevens, a portly, middle-aged white man, emerged from his chambers. Jason and Baker stood, along with their attorneys. Judge Stevens then ascended two stairs to walk around the oversized leather chair to sit. He peered down at both parties from his high position on the bench. He then opened the file on the desk in front of him, fumbling with the documents inside.

"You may be seated," Judge Stevens said. Members of each party reclaimed their seats.

Judge Stevens continued, "I understand that a counter suit has been filed. Is that correct, Ms. St. James."

Thelma stood up. "Yes," she replied. "That is correct."

"And your affidavit states that the Stand Your Ground law should apply to your client only, and not Mr. Baker."

"Yes, your Honor."

"On what grounds? You do realize Mr. Baker was the only person injured during this altercation, right?"

"I do, your Honor. But it is also true Mr. Baker threatened my client, Mr. Jason Wayne Black, by holding a gun up to his head while he was on his knees. I submit that Mr. Black reacted the way he did out of self-preservation. In short, he fought back because his life was threatened."

Judge Stevens shifted his sights to Mason Chase. "And what do you have to say about Ms. St. James' motion, Mr. Chase?"

"I say it has no merit here," Chase replied. "My client, Mr. Roscoe Baker, was injured by Mr. Black while executing his duties as a law enforcement officer."

Thelma directed a side-eyed expression at Chase. "You mean security guard, right?"

Chase ignored Thelma's interruption.

Thelma continued, saying, "And my client was only jogging through the neighborhood, not causing any harm."

Judge Stevens leaned back in his chair, causing it to squeak under his weight. He then shifted his weight to the front of the chair to lean onto the bench.

"If I allow this new motion," Judge Stevens said, "the question to be considered is which defendant was within his right to stand his ground. We must also determine if Mr. Baker has immunity from prosecution because he was a police officer who retired to become a security guard. This law states that an individual or entity cannot be held liable for a violation of the law, in order to facilitate societal aims that outweigh the value of imposing liability in such cases. If this immunity applies, Ms. St. James, your motion will be denied. How would you like to proceed?"

Thelma replied, "I would like to address the immunity question first."

"On what basis?"

"On the basis that the immunity from prosecution law only applies to service men and women, as well as law enforcement officers. Mr. Baker is a security guard, not a police officer. Therefore, he is not protected by this law."

Judge Stevens peered over at Baker, who was dressed in a grey suit that he had purchased off the rack. He then trained his eyes on Mason Chase. "Ms. St. James is correct, Mr. Chase. Your client no longer has blanket immunity from prosecution. Her affidavit against your client is valid and deserves a hearing before this court."

"Thank you, your Honor," Thelma exclaimed.

"Let's start with you," Judge Stevens said, pointing to Jason. "How do you plead?"

Jason stood. "Not guilty, Your Honor" he replied.

"And you?" Judge Stevens asked, pointing at Baker.

Baker stood and replied, "Not guilty, Your Honor."

"Thank you both for submitting your pleas. Jury selection for this case will be held next week, on Tuesday, October 13th, at which time the date for the trial will be set. Any questions before we adjourn."

"No questions from us, your Honor," Chase replied.

"None from us, your honor," Thelma said.

"If that the case, this preliminary hearing is adjourned."

As soon as they exited the Knoxville City-County Building, Jason spotted Mason Chase standing behind a rostrum with Roscoe Baker by his side. Thelma motioned for him to stop, so they could listen to what Mr. Chase was saying. Thelma knew it would not be much because the whole purpose of that day's hearing was to enter pleas. But the rumblings that she had heard about Mr. Chase let her know he didn't mince words when speaking into live mics.

Garrett Meyers, Thelma's young assistant, leaned in to whisper in Thelma's ear. "Who's that standing up there with him?"

Thelma studied the elderly, white man dressed in a tailored suit standing behind Chase, to his right.

"Did you take his picture?" Thelma asked.

"Yeah," Garrett replied.

Jason leaned in from Thelma's other side, saying, "Looks like they're going all out for this guy. He must have some high-profile connections."

Thelma turned her lip up at his remark. She wanted to tell him that they had connections as well, but she knew Baker's whiteness entitled him to the best lawyers in the country. Many of these lawyers were white, educated at Ivy League institutions like Harvard, Princeton and Yale. But she knew that coming in. She didn't blink then, and she wasn't about to blink now.

Jason pointed and said, "Who's that brother standing up there with them?"

Thelma's gaze shifted to the tall, light-skinned man standing to the right of the elderly, white man. "That's Bryce Cameron. He's a partner with MMC." Cameron acknowledged Thelma's presence with a subtle head nod. "Don't pay him no mind, though. He one of their house negroes. Done forgot where he came from."

Mason Chase stepped forward to speak.

"During today's preliminary hearing," he began, "my client, Mr. Roscoe Lee Baker, pled not guilty to the charges levied against him by Mr. Jason Wayne Black. The charges against Mr. Baker are frivolous and will be proven to hold no merit in these proceedings." He paused to look up from his notes to survey responses to his previous statement. "Jason Black is no different than these other thugs testing the patience of our Men in Blue. They terrorize our city, making patriotic citizens feel unsafe in their homes, neighborhoods, communities." Slight pause as he peered down at his notes. "This team," he continued, motioning to Cameron and the elderly, white man to his right, others to his left, "will not allow this criminality to stand. Our hope is the public will stand with us."

And with that, Mason Chase, Cameron, the elderly, white man and the other members of Team Baker walked off stage toward the parking garage. Once they were out of sight, Thelma bounced onto the stage with Jason and Garrett in tow.

"Good afternoon," Thelma greeted. "My name is Thelma St. James with the Thurgood Marshall Law Group. I'm here representing Olympic hopeful Jason Black. Like Roscoe Baker, my client, Jason Black, has pled not guilty to the charges levied against him. He pled not guilty to the charge of assault and battery because he did nothing wrong. If anything, he was jogging while black, and the last time I checked, that's not a crime."

Jason smiled, his hands clasped together in front of him out of nervousness, as he felt all eyes turn to him. But then he saw her, the white lady, Sandra Talbot, who he had joked during the latter stages of his evening jog. The intense look on her face was somewhat unsettling to Jason at first, but then he watched as she brushed past the people in front of her to stand near the edge of the makeshift stage.

"I'm sorry," Sandra silently mouthed to Jason, tears glistening on her pale cheeks, around her bloodshot eyes.

Thelma looked to her right as soon as Sandra mouthed these words. She stepped away from the microphone to turn to Jason. "Is that her?" she whispered.

"Yeah," Jason whispered back. "That's her."

"I guess I did it out of fear," Sandra told Jason, Thelma and Jerome once they were settled around a table in one of the St. James & Associates conference rooms. "My car was broken into the week before you ran by me. With that hood over your head, I just thought you looked suspicious. Never in my wildest dreams did I think it would escalate to this."

"Has anyone from Mr. Baker's team approached you?"

"Yes. Wanted me to be their star witness, but I told them no."

"Why'd you do that?" Thelma blurted.

Sandra replied, "Because I'm like Jason, ma'am. Ran middle distance at Carson Newman. The night I found out it was him, I cried all night. I've seen him run. You're fast. Ashamed that something I did got you implicated in all this mess."

"What do you do here at UT?" Thelma asked.

"I'm an associate professor in the Psychology department."

Thelma and Jerome eyed each other.

"Look, I know what black folks call impulsive, white bitches like me. Karens, right? Wasn't my intent to stir the pot. Shit just went sideways on me; probably because I was still mad about someone breaking into my car. Hell, I voted for Dupont. Love my black brothers and sisters. Came here hoping I could work with you all, make things right."

Jason leaned back in his chair with a contemplative expression on his face. Thelma's knee bumped up against his under the table.

"Give us some time," Thelma said. She laid her pen on the legal pad and pushed both to Sandra. "Write down your mailing address and telephone number, and we'll reach out to you in a few days with our answer."

Sandra did as she was told.

Dr. Benjamin Whitaker sat on the leather sofa in the UT Tower lobby, waiting patiently for the female, front desk attendant to tell him that members of the Education, Research and Service Committee would see him now. As he sat there, several students that he had taught or was teaching waved at him, some stopping to have brief conversations with him about his most recent classroom lecture. But when he was allowed to sit there alone, he questioned his rationale for going to bat for this Jason Black kid, why he went through all the trouble to submit the online form that allowed him to have an audience with the ERS Committee, and, if necessary, the full 12-member Trustee Board.

Jason had already missed the deadline for submitting the final draft of his paper, and during the next three weeks, students would be presenting their full projects to the class. After that, each student's submitted work would be graded, and the Fall Semester would be over.

Like most Knoxvillians, Dr. Whitaker had consumed every article and news report that local news outlets had published or produced about the incident. And in each one, they portrayed Jason as the perpetrator, Roscoe Baker as the victim. But something didn't seem right about the reporting.

Jason had only been in his class for a little over a month before the incident, and during that limited amount of time, he became fond of the young man. He wasn't that impressed by Jason's athletic exploits, even though they were commendable. He was most impressed by how Jason framed historical facts and political events. While he concluded that Jason's leanings were clearly progressive, he also sensed that Jason wasn't shy about publicly criticizing Democratic Party leaders for failing to produce results for black Americans and other Americans of color. "My politics are all about outcomes," he once heard Jason say during a classroom debate with his peers. "Outcomes that lift all boats not just a select few."

The statement ruffled the feathers of many of his conservative-minded classmates, who considered abortion and same-sex marriage as two issues worth fighting against. But Jason boldly proclaimed that the American electorate should not allow white men to make decisions about women's bodies or tell American citizens who they can or cannot love. Dr. Whitaker observed that a majority of the class agreed with Jason, to the chagrin of the conservative-minded students in the room. And truth be told, he felt himself being pulled into Jason's orbit as well, largely because of Jason's charisma, his ability to use compelling real-life stories to highlight his arguments. The ease with which this occurred surprised Dr. Whitaker because he prided himself in being a staunch, conservative Republican.

"The committee will see you now." It was the female, front desk attendant bidding him to enter the conference room behind her, to her left.

The Trustee Board's Education, Research and Service Committee was comprised of seven members, which included a student trustee and faculty representative for votes, and the Commissioner of Agriculture and Chair of the Board for Ex Officio voting. Dr. Whitaker recognized the student trustee. Her name was Madison Chase, daughter of Mason Chase, Malcolm Stillwell's self-proclaimed fixer. She had taken Dr. Whitaker's political philosophy class last Spring. Madison and the other six committee members would decide if Dr. Whitaker could petition the full board to reinstate Jason Black, or they could take a vote and present his recommendation to the full board themselves.

"So, let's get right to it," Committee Chair Paulina Clemons said from the head of the large oak table once Dr. Whitaker was seated across from her. She was flanked by three colleagues on her right, three on her left. "What more do we need to know about your student, Jason Black? As a point of reference, he was suspended for a student code violation."

Dr. Whitaker's eyes skipped over the faces of the six committee members before coming to rest on Ms. Clemons.

"In America," Dr. Whitaker began, "a person is innocent until proven guilty. Jason Black has not even had his day in court, and you all voted to suspend him. Why? The question about him having a right to defend himself against unreasonable detainment hasn't even been settled."

"But he has been indicted, for stabbing a man," Ms. Clemons asserted. "The man he stabbed had to be hospitalized. We cannot let what he did stand."

"And I'm not here to defend what he did. I just feel the board's decision was a hasty one. He should have been able to present his side of the story before the decision was made."

The tightening of Madison Chase's jaw gave Dr. Whitaker the sense that she agreed with portions of what he was saying. But with her being the daughter of a man who represented someone who had a high probability of becoming the Republican Party's presidential nominee, he knew she was susceptible to falling in line with conservative Republican shenanigans. He knew that she was nominated and voted in as the President of the UT Student Government Association off of her father's reputation within legal circles, and his proximity to Stillwell. Dr. Whitaker just hoped Madison would be the one committee member who was the most empathetic to how hard Jason had worked to graduate a semester earlier than members of his cohort.

Dr. Whitaker had a difficult time reading the others. They just stared back at him, a mix of contorted and blank facial expressions.

Dr. Whitaker continued, saying, "I have been a professor on both the Knoxville and the Chattanooga campuses the past nine, almost ten, years. In that time, I have gotten acquainted with a number of students, some who have successfully run for political office themselves, or secured high-profile positions within local, state and federal governmental agencies. Jason is an enigma. He possesses charisma, charm, and an uncanny ability to present coherent arguments. All gifts that we want to see in our emerging leaders. I don't know what his future holds. But he has great potential, to do great things. This incident should not cause a hold to be placed on his education. This semester is his last. He has worked too hard to not be awarded his degree now. Would set a dangerous precedence, bring undue attention to the university."

"How so?" Ms. Clemons asked.

"Just learned that a protest is scheduled for the day after tomorrow, on the Humanities Building Plaza." Dr. Whitaker shifted in his chair before resting his forearm on the table's edge. Unbeknownst to the committee, Dr. Whitaker's dummy Facebook account served as the catalyst for getting students to organize around this issue. "Over five hundred students have already said on Facebook that they're going to be there, all to demand Jason's reinstatement. They have threatened to boycott their classes if their demand is not met."

"Doesn't matter," Morris Chambers, a black man, blurted out from Ms. Clemons' right. "This board is not going to be intimidated by a bunch of protestors. We have to do what's best for the university."

"That's just it," Dr. Whitaker continued. "What you're doing to Jason is not serving the university's best interests. Many of these students feel if the board has the power to suspend Jason without probable cause, then the same thing could happen to them. I'm certain many of you, and others on the full board, do not want this blemish on their resume. You all are volunteers, not paid employees. My hope is you can reach a compromise with Jason and whomever is representing him. Reinstating Jason will prevent the campus from being overrun by protestors, our classes from being empty next week."

"As SGA President," Madison offered, "I can attest to the student body's sentiments around this issue. I have been approached by several of them. All of them feel the board's reaction is premature, politically motivated even."

A look of disgust possessed Boris Chambers' face, causing Madison to sit up straight in her chair. Chambers was one of Mason Chase's closest friends, so Madison knew he would be complaining about her to her father.

Ms. Clemons glanced at the colleagues to her right then left. The nodding of a few heads suggested they viewed Dr. Whitaker's points as valid. "We will consider your recommendation; let you know within the next twenty-four hours if there's a need for you to state your case before the full board."

"That's all I'm asking for." Dr. Whitaker stood. "Thank you for your consideration."

CHAPTER EIGHTEEN

Jason walked along the trail dressed in the light jacket and hiking boots that had been purchased for him prior to his arrival. Down in the valley, the morning dew caused fog to form over the foliage, which was transitioning from green to a mix of browns and yellows. He had only been walking along the trail for ten minutes, and he could still see the resort's rustic lodges behind him, looming large on the mountainside above.

Thelma had sensed that Jason felt some kind of way after his release. Therefore, she encouraged him to take a hike on the resort grounds, which stretched for five miles beyond the resort's 10-foot stone border wall. But she kicked herself for not warning him that there was a good chance he could spend some time behind bars if they did not arrive in time to appear before the Magistrate. They had arrived at the courthouse well before the cut-off time of 3 p.m., but the magistrate judge, a Republican named Dean Matthews, was unable to hear Jason's case, citing a family emergency at the 11th hour. Thelma knew the motherfucker was lying, because everyone, at least the ones in Upper East Tennessee, knew he had only recently been separated from his wife, and his children couldn't stand his ass because they learned he was pulled over for speeding a month ago with a scantily clad female who wasn't their mother sitting next to him in the passenger's seat.

Jason spotted the rooftop to the three-story cabin that Thelma had told him about on a high landing to his right, around the bend. Thelma had told him that he would come up on it before he reached the eastern border wall. She had said it was home to the Sojourner Vista family's matriarch, Mama Joyce

Truth Washington, who, in 2015, and at the age of 94, was the oldest living descendant of Sojourner Truth.

Mama Joyce was born and raised in Tulsa, Oklahoma, in the Greenwood District, in what was affectionately known as Black Wall Street. She was six years old in 1921 when the white mob burned the black-owned businesses and residences that lined the district's streets to the ground. Several hours before the smoke had cleared, Geoffrey and Pauline Truth had abandoned their seven-bedroom, single-family home to seek safe haven in Upper East Tennessee, with her and her older siblings - 10-year-old brother Jacob and eight-year-old sister Lynette - in tow. They were hopeful that the grass would be much greener in the southern states to the northeast of them. They ended up settling in Pigeon Forge, Tennessee, in the foothills of the Great Smokey Mountains.

Pauline Truth died in 1967. Geoffrey Truth would follow her in death three years later, in 1970, from a broken heart. Prior to Geoffrey Truth's death, Mama Joyce worked beside W. E. B. Dubois as a civil rights attorney with the National Association for the Advancement of Colored People, or NAACP. But after her father died, she convinced her husband Ronald Washington to move their family, which also included five-year-old son Enoch and two-year-old daughter Chelsea, into Geoffrey and Pauline Truth's old residence. Prior to moving back to Tennessee, they had been living in Durham, North Carolina.

When they had arrived in Pigeon Forge in 1921, Mama Joyce had considered the wooden frontier paradise, for Jacob, Lynette and she spent countless hours frolicking among the overgrown trees and squatting down often to pull craw daddies from the streams. They would frequently come across log cabins and shacks with the Rebel flags of the old Confederacy hanging from flag poles, and when they did, they heeded their parents' warning to immediately walk the other way. But even then, the young Mama Joyce had a problem with that, walking away, resulting from the fact that their white Rebel flag-furling neighbors still had the gall and audacity to burn crosses in their front lawn.

However, the young Mama Joyce had commended her parents for not allowing these intimidation tactics to force them to abandon another home. Because in time, the Rebel flags of the old Confederacy were replaced with the Stars and Stripes of the United States, which allowed the Truth family to unfurl one of their own. She was also grateful that her family's presence in these foothills drew more black families to the area. But more than anything, both the young and old Mama Joyce were grateful that the white people that resided there became more accepting of them, their black neighbors, because they had been presented with opportunities in their schools and neighborhoods to know them as people and not as colors.

"Welcome," an older, black woman greeted Jason from the porch as Jason stood in the grass at the bottom of the tall, composite lumber stairs leading to the cabin's entrance.

"Hello," Jason replied, slowly ascending the stairs.

"You must be Jason."

"I am. And you must be Mrs. Chelsea."

"I am. Sounds like Thelma has briefed you well."

Jason extended his hand. "She has." Mrs. Chelsea placed her small hand into Jason's larger one, shaking and then releasing it. "She encouraged me to come over here and spend some time with your mother, Mama Joyce."

"She's back there." Mrs. Chelsea pointed to her left, toward the outside corner of the home. Jason looked in the direction she was pointing, expecting to see Mama Joyce. As Mrs. Chelsea led him there, Jason marveled at the composite lumber deck that extended well beyond the outside corner, to the side and back of the rustic single-family home. As he looked out to his right, he had an unobstructed view of the vast valley below. And when he shifted his gaze back to what was in front of him, he saw the elderly Mama Joyce seated in one of the two rocking chairs positioned behind a coffee table made of the same composite lumber, giving occupants an even better view of the valley below. Her legs were covered with a wool blanket, and the King James version of the Holy Bible rested, unopened, in her lap.

Jason smiled when his eyes met Mama Joyce's. Mama Joyce greeted his smile with one of her own.

"Mama, we have a visitor," Mrs. Chelsea announced.

Mama Joyce blurted, "He's even better looking in person than he is on T. V."

Jason chuckled. Mrs. Chelsea exploded with cacophonous laughter.

Mrs. Chelsea patted Jason on his left shoulder. "Beatrice and I are in the kitchen preparing breakfast." She bid Jason to sit in the rocking chair adjacent to the one Mama Joyce was sitting in. "Go on over there and sit a spell." Then, as she walked away, "He don't need to hear your life story, Mama."

Mama Joyce chuckled at that.

"I hear you done got yourself in a pickle," Mama Joyce proclaimed.

"Yes, ma'am," Jason sheepishly replied.

"I've been listening to what they been saying about you on the T. V. They trying to convict you before giving you an opportunity to be heard. How you feeling about that?"

"Scared. A nightmare that will never end. Really grateful to the Newmans, though, for taking me in. Also glad Ms. St. James and the Marshall Law Group agreed to represent me."

"That's what we do." Mama Joyce lifted the bible from her lap and gestured for Jason to take it from her and place it on the coffee table. He did. She then continued, saying, "What you're going through is much bigger than you, or me even. We - black people I mean - have always been trying to counter their lies with our truth. But I've been watching, listening. This fight, this fight for diversity, equity and inclusion, is taking a turn for the worse. We're still pressing our black leaders to fight more vigorously to level the playing field. But white folk pushing back, saying we black people are not taking enough personal responsibility for our own collective growth and development."

"I just want my life back. Get back to my studies, training for next year's summer Olympic games."

"Being in the public eye carries weight. Being a black public figure carries even more weight. Every move you make is scrutinized by the media, and anyone with a stake in this game of racial politics. No, we didn't get a chance to hear Trayvon's version of what happened because that security card ended his life, thinking he was a threat for carrying a bag of Skittles and a can of iced tea. But we will get a chance to hear from you. What you say will either push our agenda forward or allow people like Malcolm Stillwell to bamboozle us into believing their ancestors' crimes against black people and other persons of color don't matter."

"How did you all do it? Win all those legal battles, I mean?"

Mama Joyce made a bridge with her hands and drew it close to her face, her quizzical eyes studying Jason. "Chile', I wish I had something to do with that, but I didn't," she said as her hands returned to her lap. "I was one of Thurgood's secretaries - there were three of us, you know. But I was also one of his biggest cheerleaders before, during and after they got that victory against the Topeka school board. The prosecution's lawyers did everything they could to say the field was level, and it was black people's responsibility, not white people's, to build opportunity and sustain success for ourselves. But Thurgood argued that we did that, in Wilmington, Tulsa and Rosewood, and they burned what we had built down in 1898, 1921 and 1923 because they were envious of our success, our collective prosperity. They wanted us to return to their plantations, tend to their children, their fields, freely contribute our labor to their financial well-being. But we said, 'Never again.'"

"This white lady, Sandra Talbot, she apologized to me, for calling the police. Said she has been a long-time fan of UT Athletics, what I have been doing on the track. Said she's willing to testify to that during the upcoming trial."

"I heard," Mama Joyce replied, scrunching her lips.

Jason leaned forward in his chair, allowing his elbows to rest on his thighs while clasping his fingers together. "From Thelma?"

"Yes, chile'. She tells me everything."

"Do you think we can trust her? This Talbot lady, I mean?"

Mama Joyce tilted her head upright as she pondered Jason's question. "In order to trust someone, you must be willing to place your life, your fortunes, in that person's hands. Like I told Thelma, this woman, this Sandra Talbot, is having regrets about causing all this mess. But what is done is done. But can she be trusted? Probably. Her apology comes across as sincere. But will her testimony make a difference. Probably not."

Jason looked up to see Mrs. Chelsea walking toward them with a tray topped with two tall glasses of orange juice, a bowl of oatmeal, and a plate containing scrambled eggs, three slices of bacon and two buttermilk biscuits. Mama Joyce said, "Thank you, dear," as her daughter placed the tray on the coffee table. He then saw another person, Mrs. Chelsea's 43-year-old son Roderick, walking toward them with tray tables dangling from his left and right arms. He handed the one in his right arm to Jason and set up the other one to the right of Mama Joyce's rocking chair. "Thank you," Mama Joyce said, gently grabbing, squeezing and releasing Roderick's hand as she smiled up at him. He smiled back at her, leaning over to kiss her on the cheek, before walking away.

"Eat up," Mrs. Chelsea demanded, "'fore it gets cold."

Mrs. Chelsea then moved her mother's tray table into position and placed the bowl of oatmeal on it. She tried to do the same with the orange juice, but Mama Joyce gestured with her hand for her to hand it to her. She did, and Mama Joyce took a sip, even as she peered over at Jason as he chomped down on a piece of bacon.

Mama Joyce pulled the tray table closer so she could use her spoon to scoop oatmeal from her bowl. Jason continued to make quick work of his own meal across from her.

"You're the next, bright, shining light, chile'," Mama Joyce continued while chewing, swallowing. "They're going to exploit your situation, turn it into a statement about how criminal black people are. If you did something bad way back then, we're going to hear about it, just because it was bad." Mama Joyce gently placed her spoon on the tray. "I told Thelma this, and now I'm telling you. Racism is their invention. Created to keep us black people on the lowest rungs of the social and economic ladder. Your situation allows them to appeal to the fears and resentments that white people have about black people, other persons of color. Make us the perpetrators, people that are always out to take things from them. Truth is the only thing we ever wanted to take back from them was what they stole from us - our life, our liberty, our happiness – our freedom."

Jason used both hands to place the tray with his empty plate and glass on it on the coffee table. "How do I move past this then?" he asked. "I'm now questioning if what I have to say about what happened will matter. From where I was sitting - kneeling really - he was about to end me."

"But he didn't. Now, he will have to justify what he did in a court of law."

Mama Joyce swatted at the fly swirling around her head, and then continued, saying, "Big Mama – Sojourner Truth – would have been proud of the things we black people have accomplished. Many of us received our forty acres and a mule and so much more. But she would have also recognized the threats to our movement, especially after Martin's death in '68. They murdered him, thinking if they cut off the head, the rest of the body would die. They thought the same with Malcolm. Problem is Martin and Malcolm were not the heads of anything; they were just the most vocal." Mama Joyce paused briefly to look out at a pack of birds soaring above the fog in the valley below. "All of us have been called to be leaders, chile', in our own special ways. How you make this moment part of our movement is up to you."

Jason would go on to spend another hour with Mama Joyce and her family. Even when Mama Joyce went back inside to lay down, he spoke extensively on the back patio with Mrs. Chelsea and her 39-year-old daughter Patience, a practicing attorney from Chicago who had come to Sevierville early to attend the following week's Social and Racial Justice Conference. Patience shared with Jason that she has been attending Marshall Law Group events in cities all across the world since high school. She said her attendance at these events has been a blessing because the facilitators go out of their way to help them analyze current events in a way that exposes new threats to the black civil rights movement.

Mrs. Chelsea added that the conference planners always give Mama Joyce and about six other elders an opportunity to speak. "They call their session *Lessons from Old School*," Mrs. Chelsea explained. "It's one you don't want to miss."

Jason chuckled to himself. *Lessons from Old School.* He immediately thought about the life lessons Jeremiah tried to impart to him on and off the track, and the ones his mother taught him throughout his childhood. He recalled how Jeremiah once told him that life is nothing but a race – a marathon, not a sprint. He had said obstacles will get in our way, but the objective is to overcome them, reach the finish line unscathed. Jason accepted the fact that he was in a race, running a marathon, not a sprint, but he asked himself what lessons could be learned from this experience. He was joking with the white lady; he wasn't trying to rob her. In the final analysis, Jason acknowledged that there are a different set of rules for people who look like him, and that some white people, because of their white supremacist views, feel they are the arbitrators of these rules.

"Thank you all for your hospitality," Jason exclaimed, "and the words of encouragement."

Mrs. Chelsea smiled at him while Patience peered over at him with her hands behind her back.

"Thank you for coming by," Mrs. Chelsea replied.

Jason then turned on his heels to round the bend to his left to walk down the row of stairs leading to the dirt trail that would lead him away from the residence. But as he did so, he saw a casually dressed and grinning Thelma emerging from the brush.

"I come bearing good news," she exclaimed. "Just got the official word from the UT Trustee Board. They just reinstated you, by a seven to five margin."

"Sweet," Jason replied, smiling, as Thelma patted him on his left shoulder. "Thank you."

"Don't thank me. Thank Dr. Whitaker. Just got off the phone with him."

Jason could feel his eyes beginning to swell. He tried to hold the tears at bay but failed miserably. He covered his drenched face with his hands. As he did so, Thelma pulled him close, allowing him to sob on her shoulder.

Mrs. Chelsea and Patience peered down at the two from the top of the porch stairs. As Jason sobbed on Thelma's shoulder, Mama Joyce sidled up next to them with the support of her wooden cane.   Jason looked up to see her reaction to Thelma's news. Using the back of his hand to wipe his face dry, he watched as Mama Joyce shifted her wooden cane from her right hand to her left and extended her wrinkled right hand to give him a thumbs up. After that, she turned to begin her slow stroll back into the residence with Mrs. Chelsea and Patience walking lockstep with her to her left and right.

Later that same day, around 3 p.m., Amos came to Jason's room to see if he wanted to travel with them to Pigeon Forge to get a bite to eat. Jason was reluctant to do so because he thought his presence would draw too much undue attention to the group. Amos provided assurances that four members of the Sojourner Vista Tactical Group would accompany them. He also told Jason that no one turns down an invitation to eat at the world-famous (and black-owned and operated) Uncle Clive's Barbecue.

Several of Jason's teammates, including White, had told him about Uncle Clive's, saying both their pork and beef ribs were to die for. But the restaurant was also known for its mac and cheese, baked beans and corn bread. The mac and cheese supposedly had the right mix of cheeses, and the baked beans the right amount of brown sugar, mustard and barbecue sauce. Jason had added a visit to the Uncle Clive's to his to-do list when he first arrived on the UT campus, but, unfortunately, his busy schedule prevented him from ever making the 45-minute drive down I-40 East to Pigeon Forge. The faster he ran, the more demand he received from meet organizers to compete in sprint races.

After finishing second to Mitch Newman at the national championship meet, he received an invitation to compete over the summer break in the 100-meter dash at the Bislett Games in Oslo, Norway. Mitch was a late scratch, which was disappointing to the meet organizers, but the race still featured Jason and two of the world's other top sprinters, Jamaica's Nigel Grimes and the U.S.'s Kobe Vincent. Jason was only able to finish third in this race, as Grimes won with a time of 9.70, two hundredths of a second slower than Mitch's 9.68 world record. And Vincent just missed Jason's personal best by three hundredths of a second at 9.80. Jason still ran a respectable 9.84, but he knew even then that the long collegiate indoor and outdoor seasons had taken a toll on him.

"Believe it or not," Amos explained when their group of four were seated around a round table with six chairs, "there are a number of black restaurants opening up 'round here. A lot of black folks live in the area as well. I think it has a lot to do with being able to look up and see Sojourner Vista from the valley, knowing the joint is black-owned and operated."

Jason peered over at the other people seated around the table, Claudia Banks and Reginald Overton, as their nodding heads enshrined their agreement. Amos explained from the driver's seat before they had hopped into the back seat of the company-owned SUV, that Claudia and Reginald were also in the MLG Apprenticeship Program, but for different reasons.

Claudia was a third-year Criminal Justice major at the University of Virginia in Charlottesville and was doing a summer internship with the Sojourner Vista Tactical Group, or the Vista Guard. Reginald was also a third-year student, majoring in Pre-Law at Washington, DC's Howard University. Claudia knew she would have to secure employment with a local police department or federal law enforcement agency in order to become a full-time SVTG staff member. Reginald, however, was on pace to become a civil rights attorney with the Marshall Law Group or some other reputable law firm. All he had to do was pass the bar examination.

"I'm shocked that it took me this long to discover Sojourner Vista, the Marshall Law Group," Jason offered.

"All of us were," Claudia countered. "Ms. Reshonda reached out to me. Said they were trying to attract more black females to the SVTG. Invited me here for the summer. So far, I'm impressed by what I've been able to learn."

"What have you learned?" Jason asked.

"That the tactical group was formed by two DC police officers – Melvin Watkins and Henry Jacobs – and a civil rights attorney - Wallace Roberson – in 1995 in response to the stop and frisk policies up in New York that had been leading to the unlawful arrests, detainments and deaths of innocent, unarmed Blacks. But it mostly had a lot to do with how J. Edgar Hoover and the FBI unlawfully infiltrated and disrupted the legitimate work of the Black Panther Party back in the sixties and seventies. They wanted to create an organization that allowed them to investigate old and new crimes against black people, as well as provide reliable security and protection for black people, their private and public interests."

"How did it get connected to MLG?" Jason asked.

"Through an invite from the Founding Trio. Cochran, for one, thought it would be the perfect partnership. Before they became known as the Sojourner Vista Tactical Group, they called themselves Beltway Investigations, Security and Protection, or Beltway ISP, and they relied on private attorneys, many of them white, to prosecute and defend their black clients. Their partnership with MLG changed the game for them. Now they could transfer their dispositioned investigations – both old and new – to MLG's predominately black prosecutorial and defense teams. With everything being in house, there was less of a chance of their efforts being influenced by white prejudice and discrimination."

"What made them change their name?"

"Does she really have to spell it out for you, dude?" Amos interjected, smiling.

Claudia chuckled.

"It's fine," Claudia replied. "The resort had been around long before Beltway was formed. And its founders participated in the Racial and Social Justice conferences, and the forums, workshops and town halls they hold at Howard, Morehouse and Spelman, oftentimes serving as presenters and panelists. They also had a sit-down with MLG's matriarch, Mama Joyce Truth Washington. After chatting with Mama Joyce and hearing from Mr. Cochran that the resort was in desperate need of round-the-clock protection, they decided to bring their operations under the Sojourner Vista umbrella. Their primary aim has been to keep the resort's patrons safe, its perimeter secure. But they still offer their investigation, security and protection services to outside clients."

"Y'all need to stop with all this heavy shit. Thought we came here to take our minds off work. What you been up to Big A. You still rocking the mic in East Knoxville, at Club Deja Vue?"

"For sure," Amos replied. "Hoping to chat with Mr. Newman next week during the conference. Give him my demo."

"You didn't tell me you were into music," Jason quipped.

"You didn't ask."

Reginald continued, asking, "Why you so focused on Tribe, dude? Don't you think Jay-Q's Roc-A-Bye Records would be a better fit?"

"Nah, bro'. Don't want no part of that gangsta' rap shit. Not about to end up like Tupaq. That brutha got caught up. Didn't know when to shut the hell up. Great artist and all. His love letter to his mother is still at the top of my list. He s the main reason I spit verse that educates people 'bout the struggle, inspires the movement."

"You consider 'Paq the greatest?" Claudia asked.

"Nah," Amos replied. "Jay-Q hands down. Like the positive things Q's doing outside the studio, through his Roc-A-Bye Foundation. The brother done sent over one hundred black and brown kids to college. He's also buying up property in cities like Chicago, New York, Atlanta and LA, just so he can make more single-family homes, apartments and condos available to working class, black families. Damn shame what these white city planners are doing to make it more expensive for black and brown people to live in the inner city. They're the ones that abandoned these neighborhoods. Now they're doing a lot of underhanded things to get them back."

"I thought we were talking about dude's side hustle," Jason said, leaning back in his chair.

Amos blew past Jason's comment, saying, "We are, bro'. You just have to give me a minute to get to the best parts." He then took a deep breath in before expelling it. "I admire both Jay-Q and even Tupaq for their artistry, but what Jay-Q has been able to do when he is not spitting verse is what inspired me to get into the rap game. Greatest rags to riches story ever told. Street hustler to business entrepreneur. I want to do the same, just differently."

"But why?" Jason exclaimed. "I thought all rappers wanted to do is collect them Benjamins."

"They are. At least the ones that are under contract with mainstream labels like Sony, Atlantic and Columbia. Tribe is different. Just read an online press release that said they're seeking more rappers like me. Had a link to a website that allowed us to upload up to three audio files. They have three of my joints, but Mr. Newman agreed to meet with me because he knows me. His daughter Trish and I graduated high school together."

"You're going to be a big, fucking deal," Claudia proclaimed.

"Agreed," Reginald cosigned. "We both done seen you put in that work. You're the real, fucking deal, bro'. Remind me of that rapper Uncommon."

"But don't forget about us little people after you make it big," Claudia added. "Remember, we knew you when you didn't have a pot to piss in."

Amos sheepishly grinned back at her.

Jason brought his right arm to rest on the table's edge. As he did so, he marveled at the ease with which these three friends related to each other. That caused images of his time with his own friends to filter through his mind. The stretching on the Tom Black Track infield with White, Rev and others. Members of the group cracking Yo' Mama jokes in the Presidential Court Complex cafeteria. But just as he was about to ask Amos another question about the significance of socially conscious rap, a bearded, gray-haired black man adorned in an apron seemingly popped out of nowhere to greet them. A young, petite black female holding an iPad trailed behind him.

"Uncle Clive," Amos said as he stood to accept the bearded, gray-haired black man's embrace, clasping his right hand with his own and pulling him close.

"What's going on, Big A?" Uncle Clive exclaimed while falling away and releasing Amos' hand. "Been awhile. Thought you had left the area, resumed your studies down at Morehouse."

"No, sir," Amos replied. "Taking my final two classes online this semester. Allowed me to come back up this way to work at the resort and participate in Dr. Gates' Bar Exam Intensive." Amos then waved his hand at Jason. "We decided to roll this way to get my friend here out the house." The tight expression on Uncle Clive's face let Jason know that Uncle Clive recognized him as "that black kid that stabbed that white man." Jason stood to shake Uncle Clive's hand and then sat back down. "Don't want him going stir crazy up at the Vista. Trying to give him a sense of normalcy."

"Understood. Just know you're welcome here, Jason, isn't it?"

"Yes, sir."

"We're rooting for you, young blood. Keep your head up."

Amos then gestured to Claudia and Reginald. "You already know these two. They're the ones keeping this joint in business."

Uncle Clive chuckled. "True. But y'all could have waited. You do know we're catering the luncheon next week, on Wednesday."

"Of course, we know," Claudia chimed in. "But me and Reggie have you penciled in for, what, every other week? Them ribs of yours are addictive."

"I'll have to get that on camera, for our YouTube channel," Uncle Clive guffawed. He then turned to the waitress that had been trailing him. "This here is our new girl, Jessica. Her first day on the job. She'll be taking your orders."

After Uncle Clive walked away to give the other patrons the same attention that he gave them, and after Jessica took their orders, the group resumed their conversation about Amos' rap aspirations. When their food arrived, Reginald used a napkin to wipe barbecue sauce from his hands and mouth before pulling his vibrating cell phone from the back pocket of his slacks. His eyes widened when they flashed across the tiny screen. Another mass shooting, this time at a Fort Worth, Texas movie theater. Multiple gunmen brandishing assault rifles were believed to have been embedded among the moviegoers during a showing of the 1991 cult film classic *Boyz in the Hood*, killing seven teenage males, four teenage females, all black. The article noted that the shooting was believed to be gang related.

"Ain't no way it was gang related," Claudia asserted. "Not in Fort Worth, Texas. That gang shit only happens in places like LA, Chicago and New York."

"Why you think that?" Jason asked. "Even the place I grew in, Wake Forest, has Bloods and Crips beefing."

"I get that," Claudia replied. "But those are wannabe Bloods, wannabe Crips. The key word here is embedded. When have Bloods and Crips been known to be at the same place at the same time?" She gestured with wide eyes as she awaited a response. "Never! These shootings, especially the ones attributed to black gangbangers, are getting more suspicious every day."

"No doubt," Amos said. "Feels like a setup to me."

"Setup?" Jason said. "By who, to who?"

"Us," Reginald replied. "You, me, black people." He placed his phone face down on the table. "Read an article the other day that talked about these rubber masks that look like the real faces of real people, black people. Read that they even feel like real skin to the touch. Wouldn't be surprised to learn that a lot of these shootings were done by white dudes wearing masks."

"Could explain why so many of the cases go unsolved," Claudia said. "Hard to arrest white shooters when eyewitnesses say the shooters are black."

"So, you believe shit like this isn't coincidental, it's coordinated," Jason asked. "A coordinated effort to make everyone think black people are a danger to themselves, menaces to society."

"Exactly," Claudia replied. "These white lawmakers are always popping up on the news channels, telling us black people that black-on-black crime is the greatest threat to the 'American

Way of Life'. They do that to make it easier to criminalize black bodies."

The more Jason listened to Amos, Claudia and Reginald, the more he acknowledged how Kelvin Cochran was ushering in a new era of civil rights advocacy for black Americans. His brief exchange with these three adherents was teaching him that the Marshall Law Group was more than a law firm, and its founding father was interested in more than just law. Kelvin Cochran wanted to change the game, develop strategies that helped more black people become victors instead of victims.

Jason thought Cochran's formation of the Sojourner Vista brand of mountain resorts was brilliant. Their existence in places like Denver, Colorado, Mt. Snow, Vermont, and Sevierville, Tennessee enabled black owners to tap into the multi-billion-dollar travel and leisure industry. And by tapping into this industry, these owners were able to make more jobs available to black and brown citizens. Moreover, his partnership with the former Beltway Investigations, Security and Protection firm presented Cochran's group with a vehicle they could use to obtain recompense for past crimes against humanity and provide more immediate responses to criminal and civil matters involving black defendants.

He had only spoken briefly with Mr. Cochran during the flight up from Atlanta, mostly about the affidavit that Roscoe Baker's defense team had submitted to Knoxville's Criminal Court. But the passion that Jason heard in Amos, Claudia and Reginald's voices made it apparently clear that Mr. Cochran was building a legacy that outlasted him. Mr. Cochran's vision for black Americans transcended the focus on marches led by Dr. Martin Luther King, Jr. and the fiery speeches delivered by Malcolm X.

"What brought you to Knoxville, to UT, Jason," Reginald asked. "What's your major?"

"Heard a lot of good things about their Business Administration program with a focus on global affairs, global commerce and trade. That's my major. Minoring in Political Science."

"Impressive," Claudia quipped. "You ever travel abroad?"

"Once, the summer after my second year. In Paris, at Sorbonne University. Felt out of place at first because my French wasn't where it needed to be. But the more I was forced to understand and speak it, the better I became."

"You speak it fluently now," Amos asked.

"Nah, bro' But I speak it well enough to know if you're talking shit about me."

Chuckles reverberated around the table.

Claudia said, "I'm a big fan of study abroad programs. I did six months in Madrid the second semester of my freshman year, and again, in Japan, the second semester of my junior year. But it was the paid internship I did in London with Interpol that sealed the deal with me. Didn't have to learn a new language, but what I did learn was invaluable. Learned so much about how law enforcement agencies across the globe are working together to fight international crime."

"Do they murder black people in London at the same rate they're murdering us here in the U. S.?" Amos asked.

"Not quite," Claudia replied. "But the black murder rate over there is still high. Remember, they're the ones who invaded parts of Africa, made the enslavement of black people a thing."

Jason scratched the right side of his face. "You all ever wonder why they're so quick to intimidate us, shoot us dead in the streets, then give other Whites a pass? I wonder about that shit all the time. Think they do it to keep us off balance, prevent us from getting together to create our own exit strategies, our own solutions. It's like they want the uneducated among us to rely on them, keep accepting jobs that pay pennies on the dollar."

"It's not just the uneducated, dude," Claudia said. "Even educated, black people are having a difficult time securing jobs, specifically management positions."

"That's why I'm so focused on my poetry, my rap," Amos exclaimed. "Definitely feeling the attorney thing and all, but I also need to know if I have what it takes to have my name up there in lights with Jay-Q and Paq, dude. If people buy my songs, I'll be like, 'Let's go.' Ain't nothing wrong with being my own boss, being an entrepreneur."

Jason nodded his approval. But as he did so, he wondered what would happen if more black workers became aware of their own ability to generate wealth. What would be necessary to bring something like this to fruition.

Jason believed many of these black workers are beholden to the white owners of multi-billion-dollar corporations because they're content with being paid livable wages. They dare not say anything controversial about their supervisors or their companies out of fear of losing their jobs. And they look beyond the fact that most of the profit earned by these corporations goes directly into the pockets of white business owners and predominately white corporate shareholders, who, if they choose, don't ever have to set foot in their corporate offices.

Almost immediately, Jason remembered an article he read before his altercation with Roscoe Baker, how some Walmart employees in cities across the nation receive public assistance. However, the Walmart Director and CEO gives himself an annual salary increase every year because of the company's record profits. He had long thought Walmart employees being on public assistance while the owners and executives receive salary increases was an oxymoron. But what made it even worse is these owners and executives were also receiving additional stock option payments if and when the company did well.

"I agree with what Claudia said earlier," Jason proclaimed. "They been calling us lazy since we stopped working for free. Sounds like Mr. Cochran is trying to shut that kind of talk down."

"He is," Reginald replied. "But MLG is focused on the Rule of Law, not American capitalism, how it chooses winners and losers. They're focused on unlawful black deaths; black people being discriminated against in the workforce. But more needs to be done to seat more black people at board room tables where consequential decisions are being made. These white executives don't want that kind of smoke, though. Why? Because having black executives seated at these tables means they will have to invest in diversity, equity and inclusion programs."

"Sounds like we should create our own table," Jason continued, "one that allows us black people to make consequential decisions about our own stuff."

"That's never going to happen," Claudia said. "Too many of us too busy stepping on each other. Crabs in a barrel. And when black people do own their own businesses, other black people don't support them. Rather support the white-owned ones because they think their products, their services, are better."

Amos interjected, "That's why I like what Jay-Q is doing with Roc-A-Bye. He's the founder, owner and CEO, free to sign his own artists. Cornelius Newman is doing the same at Tribe."

"But that's the thing, Amos," Jason replied. "It has to be more than a hand full of people owning things..."

"...and it can't just be in sports and entertainment," Claudia interrupted.

"Right," Jason continued.

"But here's the thing," Amos said, "These brothers are also into beverage and fashion brands. Jay-Q is always rocking his Jay-Q Brand leisurewear, the shoes and sweat suits. And look at what Bronson James, the most dominant player in the NBA, is doing up in Cleveland with his charter school Momentum Academy. A lot of fam doing exciting things. We're just so fragmented. Too many of us are always out to enrich ourselves and not others."

Jason reared back in his chair, pondering all that had been said. He thought back to his *The Politics of Race* presentation, the research that showed how racism causes people with good intentions to take sides, all to advantage themselves and people they share the same skin color with.

But then he had an epiphany.

What if more black people worked together to generate the kind of collective wealth that can be used to uplift the poorest among them? What if black people pooled their knowledge and resources to reconstruct black labor.

The following Monday, Jason woke up to the brilliance of the sun rising on the eastern horizon. He was tempted to grab his cell phone off the nightstand to capture the perfect photograph. But instead, he just sat up and took it all in through his room's bay window. It was early Fall. The leaves on the trees below were changing, a hodgepodge of browns, yellows and reds.

Moments later, he was in the conference mix, dressed in a suit that he found hanging in his guest room closet, with a bunch of other properly sized clothes. A sea of mostly black professionals, both male and female, sat on sofas and in chairs, or around the edges, exchanging business cards or just re-igniting old acquaintances. But Jason was also surprised to see several white professionals in the crowd, as well as Hispanic, Asian and Native Americans. But Jason still felt like a fish out of water, at least before he saw Trish and Angelica sitting on a sofa in the right-hand corner of the room.

"Funny seeing you two here," Jason said once he was within earshot. Angelica was the first to stand, smiling. Trish followed.

"I've been attending this conference since high school, son," Trish exclaimed, leaning in to hug him. "First time for Angelica. So, don't think we just here to see your trifling ass."

Jason chuckled at that. He then leaned in to accept a hug from Angelica.

"How you holding out?" Angelica asked, noticeably taking her time to release him. "Heard they set your trial for the middle of January."

"Yeah," Jason replied. "Guess they can't wait to lock my black ass up again. Ain't stressing, though. Didn't do nothing wrong."

Trish studied the expression on Jason's face. The sternness that she saw there told her that he was at a minimum worried about his fate.

"We're here for the Black Student-Athletes session," Trish said. "I was selected to be on the panel. My father definitely had something to do with that."

"That's great," Jason replied. "Look forward to hearing what you have to say."

"My brother Mitch is here too," Trish added. She peered over to her right. Jason followed her gaze. "There he is over there. Couldn't discuss student-athletes getting paid without the world's fastest man being present."

Mitch fixed his gaze on Trish before directing it onto Jason. The change in his facial expression let both Trish and Jason know that recognition had set in.

"Should have known they were lodging you here," Mitch said, extending his hand to Jason. Jason gripped Mitch's hand, shaking it vigorously. Jason hadn't drawn any pleasure from losing to Mitch at the 2015 nationals, but he respected what he did that day. He knew he had to work a lot harder if he wanted to beat him moving forward.

"Nice place," Jason replied. "Wish I could be here under better circumstances."

Trish interjected, pointing to the buffet tables lining the lobby's left-hand wall. "We're going over there to get something to eat, give you two time to catch up. I believe the session is in the Harriet Tubman Room, Mitch. See you there, at eight forty-five."

"Cool," Mitch replied. "See you there."

Mitch then shifted his attention back to Jason, who he noticed was busy admiring Trish and Angelica's skirted backsides as they walked away.

"Been awhile, Jason," Mitch interrupted. "Besides the obvious, how you been?"

Before Jason could reply, an attractive, Hispanic waitress walked past with a tray of unclaimed Mimosas. Both Jason and Mitch each swiped one from the extended tray.

"Better now. Your father did me a solid by allowing me to stay with him, your family. Don't know how I will ever repay him."

"He wouldn't allow it if you asked. I know he told you that. If he went through all this trouble, that means he believes you and not the other guy." Mitch paused briefly to look Jason over. "You still working out?"

"Not since all this went down. Been a nervous wreck."

"You still looking fit, though."

"Active metabolism."

"You do know everyone in this joint knows you're innocent, right?"

"How you know that?"

"Because they're not star struck, trying to ask you fifty million questions. They know you'll have plenty of time to do that during your trial."

Jason shifted his weight to his right leg. "You think they should pay us? That is what ya'll are talking about this morning, right?"

"Yeah."

"Damn shame that this wasn't up to debate three years ago, when I was a freshman," Jason replied. "Probably wouldn't have done me any good, though. The big bucks would go to the star football and basketball players. One-hundred meter world record holders."

"You are probably right. But don't underestimate yourself, Jason. You posted a 9.77 in our last race. To tell the truth, you beat me out the blocks. Had me working twice as hard to catch up. You know how many brothers wish they could run that fast?"

"But you ran faster."

Mitch smiled, but it didn't come from a deep sense of pride, gratitude. If anything, he felt foolish for even mustering enough gall to bring it up. At that moment, he had a much clearer view of the skeleton in his closet.

"Better not go down that road right now. Gotta get to the plenary in the ballroom. You down for meeting up in the fitness and wellness center tonight, after all this is over for the day? Put a few miles in on the treadmill, lift a little weight?"

"Sure."

"Cool," Mitch said, peeling away. "See you in a few." He then stopped in his tracks, turned, and added, "Don't be asking us any dumb-ass questions."

Jason chuckled.

"Dude, bye."

The conference's plenary speaker was Michael Eric Tyson, a black Harvard Professor and noted author. The ballroom was packed, and a few of the attendees had to stand along the walls just to be present when Dr. Tyson delivered his remarks. Jason spotted Mitch sitting with Trish and Angelica to his right, near the stage. Jason was tempted to join them but opted to remain standing in the back of the room to avoid unwelcome scrutiny. While most of the people knew he was innocent until proved guilty, he knew there were a few who may have thought his attack on Roscoe Baker was unjustified.

Standing alongside the side wall, a sense of comfort washed over him. This comfort was derived from seeing so many individuals from different racial/ethnic groups in one room. Mr. Cochran had explained to him a day earlier that those members of the Marshall Law Group's Racial Justice Coalition, and their invited guests, came to Sojourner Vista every two years to learn and strategize. He said this learning and strategizing would seem hollow without the participation of their white allies.

That last sentiment stuck with Jason, even as he surveyed the audience's rumblings. His roommate was a white boy from Henderson, North Carolina. He considered Greg White one of the coolest white dudes on the Tennessee campus. He acknowledged White didn't have much experience with black people. Not a lot of them living in a hick town like Henderson. But none of that mattered. All that mattered was White had a genuine desire to befriend people not color. And when his black teammates became unhinged after seeing another unarmed killing of a black person by rouge police officers, White was slow to speak, quick to listen. Jason surmised that the conference's white attendees were at Sojourner Vista to do the same. However, the nodding of their heads as they listened to the black professionals at their tables let Jason know they were prepared to do much more.

Kelvin Cochran stepped onto the stage to stand behind the rostrum, on which the Sojourner Vista logo was prominently displayed. Two hills with the rising sun in the foreground between them.

"Good morning, all," he began. "My name is Kelvin Cochran, and, as many of you already know, I am one of the Thurgood Marshall Law Group's three principals, the others being Reshonda Gates and Malcolm King. Welcome to the 2015 Social and Racial Justice Conference, where every October we once again commit ourselves to bringing about the kind of institutional changes that work for everyone, regardless of their race or ethnicity.

"Today's plenary address will be delivered by Dr. Michael Eric Tyson, a Georgetown University sociology professor, a New York Times contributing opinion writer, and a contributing editor of The Atlantic, and of ESPN's The Unbothered website.

"I don't want to steal any of this brother's thunder, but I will say this: Dr. Tyson was right when he wrote in his book *Uncivilized: The Fight to Gain Sanity in an Insane America* that there are unenlightened leaders on both sides of the political spectrum who are hell-bent on winning elections by reversing all gains that we Blacks made during the Civil Rights Movement of the 1950s and '60s. Their calculus falsely asserts that their chances of winning elections is better when they rail against the Black Folk Matter Movement and legal constructs like Critical Race Theory. I even heard through the grapevine that in upcoming elections, conservative Republican candidates plan on using Critical Race Theory as a wedge issue to inflame white voters' fears, resentments. In other words, they're going to tell white folks that CRT is being taught in our primary and secondary schools." Slight pause, then, "Everyone in this room knows that's a damn lie." Laughter. "CRT is only being taught in graduate schools. Law schools to be exact. But what is most disturbing is this effort is being publicly endorsed by black conservatives like Wesley Allen and Krystal Owens. Read the other day, in the Wall Street Journal, that Randall Cobb, the distinguished black linguistics professor at Columbia University, issued a statement about book retailers like Barnes & Noble only hyping victimization books by black authors." Mr. Cochran paused again to allow that last statement to sink in. "I know we aim to be nonpartisan and apolitical at these Sojourner Vista gatherings, but black conservatives giving white conservatives permission to rail against works and efforts that promote racial diversity, equity and inclusion is just deplorable."

Many in the crowd shouted, "Amen" and "Preach, brother, preach," as Mr. Cochran swiped to the next page on his iPad. Dr. Tyson stood behind him, to his left, smiling, clutching the leather binder that contained his speaking notes.

"But enough of me dropping knowledge from my soapbox. Ladies and gentlemen, please join me in welcoming Dr. Michael Eric Tyson to the stage."

Mr. Cochran and Dr. Tyson embraced and released each other before Mr. Cochran exited stage right. Dr. Tyson then stepped to the podium, adjusting the microphone to his liking.

"Good morning, brothers, sisters, allies," Dr. Tyson greeted. He searched the audience for Mr. Cochran, who was reclaiming his seat at a table next to Dr. Gates, Mr. King and five others about ten feet to the left of the stage. Spotting a seated Mr. Cochran, and smiling down at him, he quipped, "Yes, you did steal some of my thunder, brother, but that's alright when it's done by one of my brothers from another mother."

Laughter from several of the conference attendees.

"But I'm here to add another log to my good brother's fire," he continued, "because there is so much more to say about unenlightened, conservative Republican's divide and conquer strategy." Dr. Tyson grunted to clear his throat, and then continued, saying, "The first thing we must ask ourselves is why. Why are white, Republican conservatives – who take great pride in being the party of Abraham Lincoln, the American President who signed the Emancipation Proclamation that freed enslaved black Americans – railing against efforts, books even, that promote racial diversity, equity, and inclusion? I'll tell you why. Because Black America has become a force to be reckoned with in local, state and federal elections. They know that over ninety percent of us vote for the Democratic Party. But they also fear the changing demographics – that come 2030, white Americans are going to be a racial majority minority – and the emerging enlightenment among Blacks and Whites and every race in between that is sweeping across America. The racial reckoning that has been long overdue is here. It is now up to us to ensure that the U. S. government comes through for its citizens of color."

Jason joined in with the audience to applaud Dr. Tyson's last statement. It all made sense to Jason now, why Republican presidential nominee Malcolm Stillwell referred to him as "the type of thug that needed to be taken off the streets." The more these conservative Republicans commented about court cases that pit Blacks against Whites and railed against solutions espoused by critical race theorists and anti-racists, the more they were able to mobilize their voters for the political fights ahead. And their disparaging remarks about Blacks carried more sway when they were uttered by the de facto leader of the Republican Party, Malcolm Stillwell.

Jason hadn't read Dr. Tyson's *Uncivilized* book, but he did manage to watch and listen to him during his appearances on MSNBC's Rachel Madison Show. During these appearances, Dr. Tyson explained how, in the coming years, the Republican Party would use racist dog whistles rather than their ideals to mobilize and expand their base. Jason once heard Dr. Tyson tell

Madison that unenlightened, white people want to hold onto the notion that they are superior to everyone else, even though reality shows they only gained power, influence and control by oppressing and terrorizing Blacks and other persons of color. He said the enlightened white people, allies to the "Rainbow Coalition", shun this notion, preferring instead to work with black people and their allies to demand that this nation live up to its creed, that all men (and women) are created equal.

But Dr. Tyson also noted on the Rachel Madison Show that any discussions about racism, specifically white racism, makes white people feel uncomfortable, as it should. He once told Madison that the talking heads on Fox News would publicly exploit white discomfort with race by telling lies about how white parents' white children are made to feel uncomfortable when receiving lessons about black enslavement and oppression, and the Civil Rights Movement. He further predicted that these types of remarks would promote white solidarity and cause public and private sector employers to make life difficult for employees of color who complained about being discriminated against in the workplace. In short, he said, unenlightened white, Republican conservatives want to cast white people as victims of reverse racism, persons of color as perpetrators of this same racism, to free members of their race from the white guilt that is derived from their white ancestors' legacy of legalized prejudice, racism and discrimination.

Jason had sat in his apartment shaking his head at the idea that white people could ever be freed from their ancestors' crimes against humanity, their ongoing efforts to keep the country's black, brown, yellow and red citizens in their place. That's why it felt so good to see Hispanic, Asian and Native attendees sitting around linen-covered tables to hear Dr. Tyson's remarks. This multi-racial coalition of socially conscious professionals knew what was up: white conservative Republicans were making an appeal to the white populace only, making false claims about white people being forced to give something up to the "woke" (wary, really) liberals.

"I told myself that I wasn't going to do this," Dr. Tyson continued, "but I must, because it's a hot topic. By now, everyone has heard that University of Tennessee sprinter Jason Black turned himself in, and the trial is set for January 2016." Dr. Tyson extended his arm toward Jason at the back of the room. "Jason is here with us today."

All eyes turned to the back of the room, where Jason stood nervously with his arms crossed.

"Join me up here on the stage, son," Dr. Tyson coerced.

Jason didn't like being called out like this, but he knew there had to be some method to this man's madness. As he made his way to the stage, he received thunderous applause. This was indeed a friendly crowd.

Dr. Tyson continued as Jason stood beside him on the stage, his left hand gently touching the curve in Jason's back. "First off, I want to apologize to this brother for calling him out like this." Jason nodded to let Dr. Tyson know his apology was duly noted. "I just think it's important to deal with the elephant in the room. This brother is being vilified by the Republican presidential nominee, and others on the right, for jogging while black. They have labeled him a thug, and Fox News commentators have even slipped up and used the n-word when talking about him. That's a hot mess because nothing they're saying about him is true. Jason Black is an upstanding member of the community, and come 2016, he will undoubtedly be representing the United States at the Rio Summer Olympic Games. So, what I would like to do now is pray for this brother."

And with that, members of the audience closed their eyes, some of them extending their hands and arms toward the stage. Dr. Tyson started off by praying for Jason's family, that they may find comfort during this difficult time. Reverberations of "well" and "Amen!" bellowed from the audience. He then prayed about the jury selection process, how its members needed to reflect the communities' racial/ethnic makeup. He ended his prayer by asking God to ensure that true justice prevails through Jason's exoneration.

After his prayer, Dr. Tyson embraced Jason near the center of the stage. "Everything is going to be alright, son," he whispered into Jason's ear. "Just keep the faith."

"Thank you," Jason whispered back. Then, after being released, he descended the stairs to walk back to where he had been standing earlier. As he stepped off the bottom stair, his eyes caught sight of a bespectacled, white female seated on the front row, in an aisle seat, uncrossing and then crossing her legs.

For a brief second, Jason stood mesmerized by the cherry panties blinking back at him from under her form-fitting miniskirt. He then directed his gaze at her made-up face. She gave him a thumbs up, causing Jason to make a mental note to himself that he needed to get her room number and digits as the conference goers exited the ballroom.

But even during the lewd thoughts that followed, the conference attendees applauded, and as they remained standing, many of them patted Jason on his back as he passed, some of them allowing their extended hands to lay longingly on him. Jason cherished their well wishes, for he knew the world outside of Sojourner Vista would not be so kind.

Later that day, after the last session of the day, Jason followed through with his commitment to meet Mitch in the resort's fitness and wellness center. Mitch said a lot of things as they jogged three miles on the treadmill, mostly prying for information about what he had seen his sister doing on campus. Jason let it be known that he only saw Trish during practices and dinners at the university's Presidential Court Complex. He told Mitch that a number of the guys on the team tried to push up on her when she first got there, but backed off as soon as they found out she was Tommy Rollins' girl. He admitted to Mitch that he was smitten with Trish as well, but her pretty face and fit body intimidated him. "I usually don't have any problems stepping up to the ladies," he bragged. Mitch then told him that he met Tommy once, a few months after his record-setting race, during the Fourth of July holiday. He confessed that he's still trying to figure the dude out.

Mitch hit the stop button on his treadmill, causing the belt to come to a screeching halt. Jason followed suit, snatching his already wet hand towel from the bar under the treadmill controls. The treadmills faced the plate glass windows, and if it had been day, they would have had a perfect view of the foliage in the valley below. But because it was night, they could only see the row of lamps dotting the outdoor walkway a few feet down the hill in front of them.

"You're still in pretty good shape, bro'," Mitch exclaimed. "What'd you have it on? Seven point five? Eight?"

"Seven. That's only an eight-minute mile."

"But you kept it there for thirty minutes, dude. That's amazing for someone who hasn't been working out. What was my mother feeding you?"

Jason bent at the waist to stretch the back of his hamstrings. "Same thing she was feeding you, I guess. You just got more of it. Guess I should be blaming her for you running these fast times."

Both men chuckled at that, continuing as an unassuming, gray-haired, black woman dressed in Nike tights, sports bra and running shoes entered the room. She nodded and smiled at Jason and Mitch as she walked over to the treadmills. Jason and Mitch nodded back at her.

But then a noticeably somber expression appeared on Mitch's face. "Really looking forward to running with you next year in Rio, dude. Like I told you that day, if not for you, I would have never run that fast. You beat me out of the blocks and led the field through the first seventy."

"And then your ass shifted to another gear. Thought I had you, but you passed me like I was standing still."

Mitch reached into his gym bag to retrieve his weight-lifting gloves with the Florida Gator logo on them. He slowly slipped them onto his hands just as Jason stood upright again.

"You about to make me turn what we do here into a competition, dude," Jason said while taking a swat at Mitch's gloved hands. "And you're doing it knowing I don't have any Tennessee gear up in this joint."

"That's what you get for running from a crime scene. Always be prepared to rep your school, dude."

Jason nodded at that as he dropped to the floor to stretch other parts of his body. Soon, Mitch was seated on the floor directly across from him, cycling through a series of his own stretching exercises. A few beats of silence passed as Jason wrestled with what he wanted to say next. Mitch beat him to the punch.

"If we play our cards right, we can sweep."

"I know we can. Kobe Vincent may have finished third in our race, but he is down there in Austin working with Coach Eldridge Fortson. Fortson was a beast when he was running for Trinidad and Tobago. I'm sure he'll have ole' boy ready for trials."

"Hey, man, you mind if I run something by you.".

"Sure. What is it?"

"Nothing about track. About something I was talking to Ms. St. James about yesterday. We were talking about the work that the Marshall Law Group does on behalf of me and others. She kept telling me MLG exists to provide legal representation to black victims of prejudice, bias and discrimination. Told her how much I appreciate what they're doing for me. But I also asked her if there is something more we – black people I mean - should be doing."

"You and I are on the same page on that one. When Smith and Carlos did the Black Power salute in Mexico City, in 1968, I wondered why the other black athletes didn't come out in droves to rally around them. Robert F. Kennedy and Dr. King had been shot, and people were burning cities down. Today, cops are shooting black men, black women, dead in the streets, with impunity, bro'. They're incarcerating us at record levels. But I have a theory, about why other black athletes didn't do what was necessary at the time, why they don't rally around brothers, and sisters, even today, to take stances against White Supremacy. They're too damn selfish. More concerned about the money they're making than the black people out here suffering.

"These white owners in the NFL pumping their heads with nonsense, that their shit don't stink. But when it's all said and done, and their careers are over, they still get called niggers. My pops told me that. Niggers who will get invited to the white man's picnic, receive complimentary tickets for life to big games like the Super Bowl, sitting up in heated press boxes snatching hors d'oeuvres from trays. These are the perks of being perceived as powerful and influential. But I keep asking myself how they remain this way when so many of us are suffering through it all?"

Jason nodded. "About two years ago, I read William C. Roker's book *40 Million Dollar Fools*. Great book. Tells the history of black athletes navigating the racist efforts to limit their participation in sports. Goes all the way back to the 1700s. But just talking and writing about the problem isn't going to change anything. All talking and writing does is raise awareness about the issue. We're still enslaved mentally, some of us physically. Hell, look at us. We're considered two of the fastest men on the planet, you the fastest. Are we willing to sacrifice our careers to advance the black agenda, shine brighter lights on social inequities, the wrongful treatment of our black brothers and sisters. Hell no. Would hit us too hard in our pocketbooks."

"Why should we, have to sacrifice anything, I mean? Why can't we maintain our power, our influence, our control while still serving black interests? See, that's how they keep us enslaved. By making us think that without them we're nothing, that we would be powerless and voiceless. That's why we have to clap back at them in different ways, focus their attention on our black prowess in sports, entertainment and the arts. Identify and affirm the leaders of this new Black Folk Matter Movement, the NAACP, National Urban League, and the Marshall Law Group. Let them know we appreciate their activism in the streets and in the court rooms. I'm convinced, when white people see us, every hour, every day, they find themselves grappling with their mistreatment of us. And when they do that, again, every hour, every day, some of them will display more empathy toward us."

"I agree." It was the gray-haired, black woman dressed in Nike tights, sports bra and running shoes. Mitch immediately recognized her as Dr. Reshonda Gates, a member of MLG's founding trio, and one of Cornelius Newman's closest confidantes. Mitch wasted little time jokingly rushing over to her, leaning in to give her a hug.

"What's going on, Auntie Re-Re?" Mitch exclaimed as he held her close. Drawing back, he inspected her, his left hand loosely clasping her right. "Coming up in here looking all incog-negro. You looking good, though. Fit."

"Stop it, boy," Dr. Gates blushed. "I'm still Aunt Re-Re. Just forty pounds lighter." Her gaze then fell on Jason, who stood a few feet away from them, nervously rocking side to side as the two of them talked. "Interesting conversation," Dr. Gates continued. "Sounds like you have a lot on your mind, Jason. What drew you to Roker's book?"

"Ran across it my sophomore year, right before I decided to declare Sports Management as my major. Always had an interest in the intersectionality between sports, history and politics. And as a black athlete, I was intrigued by the book's title. Wondered how Roker could call black athletes who are getting paid fools. Didn't make sense to me at the time."

"But here's the thing," Dr. Gates said, "it's not just black athletes. It's all of us. Black people I mean. We still harbor the slave mindset. That's why so many of us still can't get ahead. Always going out of our way to please Massa. But that thing you said about focusing their attention on black prowess, in sports, entertainment and the arts. I like it. Display black prowess not black power."

"You should know all about that," Mitch said. "With all the success you're having with your company, *Strut*."

A confused expression flashed across Jason's face. He knew *Strut* to be a fashion brand that catered mostly to mature adult women, forty and older.

"That's because we place purpose over profit, Mitchell," Dr. Gates replied. "I consider us a for-purpose organization, its employees, social entrepreneurs. We're in the business of making peoples' lives better."

"You need to tell him what all that means, Auntie. Like you did for me when I spent that summer interning with *Strut*."

Dr. Gates walked over to the wall-mounted mat rack to retrieve three mats, one for each of them. Both Jason and Mitch accepted their mats from Dr. Gates, and then allowed them to fall to the composite floor before sitting on them.

"A lot of the work we do here at MLG is considered social entrepreneurship. We're equipping the next generation of black lawyers with the skills to build upon the gains of the civil rights movement of the fifties and sixties. But that focus doesn't prevent us from representing clients who have been wrongfully accused of crimes. Our cadre of attorneys have all passed the bar exam, and they do their due diligence when representing plaintiffs and defendants. With *Strut*, all we're doing is offering weekly job training classes and donating new and refurbished business suits that our female participants, as well as those in homeless shelters, can wear to job interviews. About ninety-five percent of our job training participants successfully secure gainful employment within four weeks of their graduation."

"That's awesome," Jason exclaimed. "Question, though. Why focus on jobs, employment?"

"Because if you don't work, you don't eat. And many of the women in our program haven't eaten right for months, years. How can they when they have toddlers standing to their left and right, infants on their hips? The problem is worse for black and brown women. While there are plenty of black men remaining loyal to their children's mothers, black and brown women are the ones caring for the children following a separation, divorce. That's why we also operate childcare centers for our job training participants. All we require is they pay us ten percent of their bi-weekly earnings."

"Ninety-five percent," Jason emphasized. "What kind of jobs are we talking about?"

Mitch interjected, saying, "Most of them are working as office assistants, secretaries, with small and large companies mostly. But *Strut* also offers childcare to participants who want to upgrade their resumes by securing degrees from two- and four-year colleges. They also offer trade school and college scholarships."

All of this was blowing Jason's mind. As a child, both Jerome and Cynthia stressed the importance of education, consistently telling Jason and Jeremiah that it should be viewed as the great equalizer. They told them that when slavery was an institution, the white masters didn't allow enslaved Blacks to learn how to read, write, and to think critically. They said these white masters attempted to keep books out of enslaved Blacks hands because they didn't want them knowing about the Constitution and the Declaration of Independence. They also did not want them to know that they too were men, women, humans, who had been endowed with inalienable rights to life, liberty and the pursuit of happiness.

Dr. Gates continued, saying, "The more I do this work, with MLG and *Strut*, the more I realize nothing can be done to unrig American capitalism. They have too much of a lead. And even when some of us catch up to them, even surpass many of them in the wealth department, they still have the power to make the wealthiest among us subservient. Just look at John Roberts, the black founder and former owner of Black Entertainment Television. Roberts built a media empire that was supposed to be for and by us black people. But when Viacom came calling, offering Roberts and his partners three billion dollars, he sold it to him. Now the company that was supposed to be for us by us is under White Rule, not Black."

"I read about that," Jason replied. "Thought it was a bad decision on Roberts' part, mainly because I knew the programming would change. BET's staple is Hip-Hop and R & B, and I knew none of that would go away. But their black news. Man! It's almost as if they're afraid to talk about what's really going on in the hood, presenting uplifting black stories, the kind that don't make white people feel, well, uncomfortable."

"Those uplifting stories need to be heard, but we also need to hear the ones that make it necessary for black people to chant 'Black folk matter.' This country has a white supremacy problem, Jason, Mitch. We black people are the only group that has never been afraid to call it out. But they're pushing back, demonizing progressive organizations that fight for more diversity, equity and inclusion in educational and corporate settings. They're even denying the existence of White Supremacy and White Privilege."

"So, we can't win for losing, right?" Mitch said.

"No," Dr. Gates replied. "I'm not saying that. We can win, but it has to be a personal victory, for the Black Diaspora. I firmly believe if more of us black people stay in our lane, commit to educational and vocational excellence, tighter familial relationships, we won't have to compete with white people. We just choose to challenge ourselves, both individually and collectively, to be better as parents, learners, workers and leaders."

"I've been feeling like many of us are sitting back," Jason said, "waiting on a Dr. Martin Luther King, Jr or Malcolm X to step into the fold to lead us to the Promised Land. Feel we sit because we don't want to be subjected to white America's criticism, their ridicule, their crocodile tears about how uncomfortable we're making them feel. But the black brothers and sisters in Greenwood, Rosewood, Knoxville and Wilmington were developing and maintaining thriving black communities that asked white people for nothing. And what'd they do to them, their communities? They shot them dead in the streets - much like they're doing now - and they burned their communities to the ground."

"That just means we have to stop being so accepting of what happened," Dr. Gates replied. "People died. Black people died, many of them relatives. From gunshot wounds or from being hung by their necks from trees. All because the white people around them were envious of what they had accomplished, their progress, their excellence. But don't think I don't recognize the progress we're still making, in sport, entertainment, the arts, and education. But is it enough? No, it's not. We have to be about the ancestors' business, Jason, Mitch."

"It's almost as if we have to create something new," Mitch said, "something that requires them to see us, but does it in a way that allows them to join us if that's something they want to do. Doesn't mean we're going to go out of our way to make them feel comfortable. They would be in our space, not the other way around. We would be allowing them to learn more about our hopes, dreams, aspirations, share and experience our pain and our joy. But they would ultimately help us advance the black agenda."

"Exactly," Dr. Gates exclaimed. "Activism is necessary because people like Malcolm Stillwell are appealing to white fears and resentments about black people and other persons of color. Why else would they say out loud that Critical Race Theory is being taught to students in public K-12 schools. That's why MLG has been creating a network of intelligent and compassionate black folk who are not afraid to lay it all on the line to collaborate on projects that increase our power, influence and control over our bodies, our collective destiny.

Mitch said, "Whatever is created must be global, to repatriate members of the Black Diaspora to the African continent. Because we descend from Africa, we undoubtedly have kinfolk there. That means every black person on the planet should do an Alex Haley, discover their African roots, reconnect with African relatives. When we do these two things - discover and reconnect – seems like we will reclaim the narrative about who we were as a black people before the Trans-Atlantic Slave

Trade. By discovering and reconnecting, we could also more fully support black Africans' efforts to develop the continent, preserve their resources."

"Exactly," Dr. Gates exclaimed, smiling. She then stood. "I have to scoot. Sitting on another panel at ten." Then, as she walked toward the exit door, she continued, saying, "Your heads are in the right place. Go where your hearts lead you. Something good could come of it."

After that, Dr. Gates exited the room, leaving Jason and Mitch alone to make sense of her parting words.

"Let's put something together, a business plan," Mitch finally exclaimed. "Share it with my dad. His company isn't called Tribe Records for nothing. He's all about all this, advancing the black agenda. That's why he has signed so many socially conscious rappers. He uses them to inject hope into hearts and minds. Question, though. What would we call this new thing, this new organization?"

"BLACK," Jason replied. "Because we need to be about the business of building a legacy of activism, community and kinship."

"Love it. But where do we start?"

"With us. We're the U.S.'s best hopes for bringing home medals next year in Rio. And if Kobe Vincent is still running the kind of times he was running last year, we could sweep."

"So, you thinking what I'm thinking, right?"

"Hell, yeah. All eyes will be on us during the medal ceremony. I say don't just raise black-gloved fists like Carlos and Smith. We should raise them while also taking a knee."

"For sure. But how do we sustain the momentum?"

"By getting buy-in from other black athletes, specifically the ones in the NBA, the NFL. We have to start thinking like the black entrepreneurs of the early nineteen hundreds. We have to create something that allows black owned and operated businesses to develop and thrive, bro'. Establish a bank for us, by us. That way we have a place to pool our money, our resources. Capitalism is all about exploiting the labor force. White people been exploiting black labor for financial gain since 1619, bro'. But if enough of us can come together, we can take this control back, become the kind of capitalists that give as much to the black community as we take. We can show black people how to generate and manage their wealth."

"I like it. I know my pops will too. But before we go all in, let's run it by a few of my NBA and NFL friends."

"Who you thinking?"

"Well, I know Bronson James with the Lakers would love it. Brother just built a school for underprivileged kids in his old Cleveland neighborhood. He also runs a media production company called Springfield Films. Brother does more off the court than on it. We get him, he'll get others. But we specifically want to invite Damian Littlejohn with the Trailblazers and Carson Anthony with the Knicks."

"You have any connects in the NFL?"

"No doubt. Met up with them in LA back in July, during the ESPYs. Have pretty good relationships with the Ravens' Jackson Lemar and the Broncos' Rustin Wilson. Talked to them extensively about a whole bunch of nothing during one of the after parties. There's also Colin Capshaw, the former quarterback with the 49ers. He still hasn't secured another NFL quarterback job after being released from the team for those kneeling protests, but that hasn't stopped him from making fiery speeches about the ongoing need for criminal justice reform."

"Yeah. I admire that brother. He sacrificed everything to shine a brighter light on black causes."

Mitch stood. "Swing by my room tonight, between ten and eleven. Let's do a Zoom call with these brothers, see if this is something they would be willing to support financially."

"Bet."

Mitch continued, saying, "Even if all six of these brothers get on board, we still have to do our part. We have to be ready, for the most important race of our lives. The Jamaicans are coming for us, dude. Probably take a nine seven to get on the podium. Hopefully, Kobe will be right there with us for an American sweep. If we do that, I have no doubt about us taking the relay. You gonna to be ready for that?"

"Yeah. I'll be ready. Just have to get this legal bear off my back."

Mitch smiled as he extended his hand toward Jason. "No doubt," Mitch replied. With their hands clasped tightly together, Mitch now had extra motivation to say no to the Yellow Jacket vitamin. Mitch pulled Jason up from his chair, drew him close and then released him. He watched as Jason bent over to touch his toes before standing upright again. "Now, let's go on over to this bench so I can see if your strength matches your endurance."

But even as he generated enough nerve to utter these words, Mitch could feel his heart sink a little. He wondered now more than ever how his body would react from not having traces of the Yellow Jacket vitamin flowing through his veins.

Later that same day, Jason looked up from his front row seat, with Mitch, Angelica and Trish seated to his left, to see Mrs. Chelsea pushing Mama Joyce up the ramp and onto the ballroom stage, near the center. He then watched as Mama Joyce stood, allowing Mrs. Chelsea to pull the wheelchair from under her. A bent-over Mama Joyce then shuffled about three feet to her right, with her wooden cane in hand, to sit on one of the two purple love seats with extra cushion. The four younger members of the panel, which included Dr. Tyson, Mr. Cochran and Maryland Congresswoman Pauletta Charles, claimed seats on the matching sofas to the left and right of the two centered chairs.   When the five panelists were seated, two black sound technicians distributed handheld microphones.

Jason smiled when he saw Thelma walk onto the stage. She had been chosen to moderate this discussion, *Lessons from Old School.* Before sitting, she looked out into the audience, a toothy smile on her caramel-colored face. As she took a slight bow toward the audience, Jason sensed that she was just as excited as the assembled audience members to hear what the panelists had to say.

"Welcome, everyone," Thelma greeted, holding her hand-held microphone inches from her mouth as she walked toward the front edge of the stage. She held a brown binder in her other hand. "We have a lot to cover, so please take your seats." She lowered the microphone, seemingly to clear her throat. "My name is Thelma St. James, and I am the moderator for this session, which we affectionately call *Lessons from Old School.* Some of the individuals assembled on this stage do not consider themselves old, but Mama Joyce, the woman in the middle, wears her age like a badge of honor. How old are you, Mama J?"

Mama Joyce drew her microphone to her mouth. "I'll be ninety-four next month."

Jason and the other audience members stood on their feet to applaud Mama Joyce. As they applauded, Thelma used the allotted time to claim the seat next to her. When the applause ended, and the audience members were seated again, Thelma proceeded with her line of questioning.

"This first question is for Mama Joyce," Thelma said while looking down at the sheet of questions in her opened binder. "America's first, black president, Nelson Dupont, is stepping down after two successful terms in office. How will he be remembered?"

Mama Joyce pondered the question. "That's a good one," she began, "but the real question should be how did President Dupont's presidency change the populace's thinking about race relations, our creation of a more perfect union. We all know it wasn't easy for him. Yes, he and the Democrats passed the Affordable Care Act during his first four-year term, when they controlled the presidency and both houses of Congress, but when the Democrats experienced major defeats during the 2010 midterms, elected Republicans did everything they could to prevent it from being enacted in their states. They cast it as the government once again giving away free money to poor Blacks and other persons of color, which even appealed to poor Whites who benefited most from the legislation. Again, they are the majority. But what it really showed is how white politicos have used our electoral system to condition white people to do their bidding. It's not coincidental that so many white people - white voters really - so easily turned against President Dupont during the 2010 Midterm Elections. Targeting white fears and resentments has worked well for the GOP."

Jason turned to his left to see Mitch's response to Mama Joyce's answer. Mitch's buttocks rested on the front edge of his chair as he listened intently with his arms crossed. When he saw Jason peering over at him, he nodded to let Jason know he too was tracking what Mama Joyce was saying. But Jason wondered if others in the room agreed with Mama Joyce, that the Grand Ole' Party had learned valuable lessons from the 2008 defeats that allowed the Democratic Party to control the Presidency, the Senate and House of Representatives. In 2008, Dupont's message to the electorate was "Yes we can!" and the Democratic Party did. But a closer examination revealed that Republicans were slowly taking control of state governerships and legislatures. This state control put them in positions to gerrymander the hell out of their states, place more control in the hands of white voters who were moving from urban centers to reside in the new housing developments in the suburbs. At the same time, their Republican acolytes in city halls all across the country were imposing taxes that made living in urban centers less affordable for the hordes of black people who had been living there for generations. The GOP was intent on turning over the urban fruit cart so they could woo white people back to these urban centers.

"My next question is for Representative Charles," Thelma continued. "You represent Maryland's second congressional district, one that includes Baltimore City. Republicans have been criticizing you for not doing enough to change the complexion of the urban neighborhoods you represent. They cite statistics that show high incarceration rates, high death rates, poor schooling, and your inability to secure corporate investment. Why are they giving you such a hard time when the same can be said about many of the rural neighborhoods that many of them represent?"

Representative Charles repositioned herself in her chair, opting to sit up to cross her legs at the knees. "That's what they do," she said. "They distort the truth so it fits their negative narrative about black and brown citizens. We have high incarceration of black and brown people because the police officers there have been conditioned to believe more crimes are being committed by black and brown people. We have high death rates because hospitals are being closed in urban communities and being opened in rural ones. Urban schools are poor by design because city planners want to move more of the population to the suburbs so they can have an electoral advantage during elections. When you add all this up, it seems as if corporate investors have a legitimate excuse for not investing in urban cities like Baltimore. But real people, real Americans, live in our urban centers. They deserve better."

"And what do you have to say to your critics?"

"That this game of racial politics must end. That it's not a game. People's lives are at stake. We must stop making it more difficult for people to keep roofs over their heads, clothes on their children's backs. We have to create more jobs that pay people more livable wages. We have to close the socioeconomic gap between black people and white people because it makes black people easy targets for manipulation, false narratives about their willingness to work."

"I'd like to add to Representative Charles' response," Mama Joyce interjected. She then proceeded to talk about Tulsa, Oklahoma's Greenwood District, or Black Wall Street. How a white mob burned it all down based on the lie that Dick Rowland, who worked in the downtown area shining shoes, sexually assaulted a white female elevator operator. "Tulsa's Black Wall Street would still be here today if the white people there were more accepting of black progress. But they weren't, and they still aren't, mostly because many of them thought we were taking things from them. But we weren't. We just knew that in order for Greenwood to survive, to thrive, we had to keep more of our money in Greenwood. We need to do more of that now, in Baltimore, Chicago, Atlanta and Los Angeles. More of the power must remain in the hands of the black people living in these places. But I fear these neo-conservatives in state houses and Congress are taking this power away from us. That's unacceptable. Goes against everything this country stands for."

"But how do we counteract this kind of thievery, Mama Joyce?" Thelma asked. "Seems like these neo-conservatives have the momentum right now."

"If I knew the answer to that question, chile', I wouldn't be here right now; I'd be living out my final days on some Caribbean Island, reading romance novels on the beach. But you're right; they do have the momentum. They have been amassing it for some time now. It mostly comes at us in waves, every four years, during presidential elections. President Dupont won in 2008 because more white people thought voting for a black man would be right for the country, get it to a place where white people could finally right the wrongs of their ancestors, gain the admiration and respect of their black neighbors. But the whole time President Dupont was in office, these white neo-conservatives demanded that he show proof that he was born in the United States, and not France, the country of his father's birth. When he made his birth certificate public, we learned that he was indeed an American citizen, the bi-racial child of a white American mother from Hawaii."

Jason could feel himself moving to the front edge of his chair. He was a 14-year-old, high school freshman when Nelson Dupont became the United States' first, black president, so at the time, he was too young to participate in the 2008 presidential election. But he had been sitting in the living room with his mother, brother Jeremiah and Ms. Jacobs that November as the results came in. When the words President-Elect Nelson Dupont appeared on the screen, his mother, brother and Ms. Jacobs leaped to their feet to dance in jubilation. The United States of America had elected its first black president.

But this brief exchange between Thelma, Mama Joyce and Congresswoman Charles was causing Jason to think differently about what black people in general had to do to improve their fortunes in the United States and around the world. When he was conducting research for the first term paper that he wrote for one of his Political Science classes as a Business major minoring in Political Science, he already had suspicions that the allure of integration had caused preceding generations of black Americans to lose their way. The paper dealt with how white-owned companies wooed black consumers for profit while failing to offer black people jobs that paid livable wages and invest in their predominately black schools and communities. He suggested in the paper that white-owned companies' failure to make these offerings and investments came from their unspoken desire to keep black people dependent on them. But Mama Joyce's reminder about what happened to Tulsa's Greenwood District served as Jason's wake-up call. He now realized, more than ever, that contemporary members of the Black Diaspora had to do more to take their power back by building upon the legacy of activism, community and kinship.

Jason got out of his seat and walked to the back of the room. A microphone had been set up in the center aisle for audience members who had questions for the panelists. Jason was third in line. After Thelma buttoned everything up with a summary of her takeaways, she invited audience members to step to the microphone to pose their questions.

"My question is for Mama Joyce," Jason began. Mama Joyce smiled down at him, causing Jason to smile back at her. "I personally believe the murders of Dr. King and Malcolm X left us black people searching in the dark for a leader, a charismatic black man, or woman, who can serve as our mouthpiece, share our grievances with the world. I, like so many others, applaud the young leaders in the streets and on the Internet chanting, 'Black folk matter,' but they have become an easy target for conservative, white Republicans who are going out of their way to cast BFM as a hate group. So, my question to you is, do you think all this marching in the streets is passe? Shouldn't we focus more on ourselves, do more to promote black uplift, black excellence?"

Mama Joyce cleared her throat. "Black uplift? Black excellence? Over marching in the streets? I believe we need all three. Black people don't march in the streets just to be seen; we march to be heard. But we must do it peacefully, not like we have seen being done in cities like Chicago, Seattle and Los Angeles. When our people destroy property and attack police officers, they're giving conservative, white Republicans the gift that keeps on giving. They now feel they have proof that we all are bred to be criminals because a small contingent of us are committing criminal acts. And they would be right. If you commit a criminal act, you are a criminal. But you want to know if we should focus more on ourselves. Do more to promote black uplift, black excellence. Of course. But in order for that to happen, a group of us must come together to initiate campaigns that get more of us to consolidate and collaborate.

"That's what Dr. King did. Malcolm as well. Sure, they were the most outspoken, the ones people were listening to. But they also had other black people, and their white allies, supporting what they said, developing strategies together in secret. They identified moral pressure points and then established timetables for when they would exploit them for collective gain. Dr. King, especially, recognized the power of images of black folk being beaten being transmitted across the nation and globe by the major television networks."

Jason shuffled his feet before leaning toward the microphone once more. "I have a follow-up, if that's okay." With a wave of her hand, Thelma bid him to proceed. "Cell phones and the Internet are allowing the images you're talking about to be transmitted much faster now, and to more people. I do think seeing these images causes some white people to work with black people to solve the racism problem, but there are others who refuse to acknowledge the problem even after seeing these images. This latter group doesn't believe in the concept of White Privilege. So, my question to you is, how do we black people get our fair share of this privilege?"

"Consolidation," Mama Joyce replied.

"And collaboration," Thelma added.

Jason pressed his hands together, bowed, and then returned to his seat.

"Glad you decided to come," Trish exclaimed as she sat across from Mitch on the Mosaic Lounge's outdoor patio. Mitch was still dressed in his suit but without the tie. Trish had showered and changed into jeans and a blouse.

"Me too," Mitch replied. "How you been?"

"Good. You?"

"No complaints."

Trish then reached to her right, taking Mitch's hand into her own. "I've missed you, big brother," she said as they exchanged side glances at each other while holding hands. "And I'm sorry. Sorry for just thinking about myself."

"Still think I should have done more. The mothafuka drugged and raped you."

"But I realize now that we wouldn't be here, in this place talking, if you had done anything more."

Mitch turned to face Trish head on, taking both of her hands into his own. "Guess you're right. Just know, I'm sorry, for not seeing the warning signs, letting you know he was no good. Hell, I'm sorry for not being there for you."

"That's old news, big bro'. Let's move on."

Mitch released her hands and sat up straight. "How you liking Tennessee? They treating you good?"

"They are. Killer workouts in practice, but I'm adapting. Looks like things are going well for you over in California. Nine point six eight. World's Fastest Man. The coaches at Team Elite must know what they're doing."

The frown on Mitch's face didn't go unnoticed.

"Did I say something wrong?" Trish asked.

"Nah," Mitch said with a shrug of his shoulders. "Just thinking about our practices. It's hot as a mug out there."

Trish chuckled. "That shouldn't surprise you. All that time we spent vacationing with our parents in San Diego, on Coronado Island."

"Vacationing is a lot different than repeatedly running four-hundred-meter sprints on a blazing, hot track."

"You thinking about going back down to Gainesville, aren't you? Train with Coach Tyson?"

"Yeah. But it would mean being in a long-distance relationship with my girl Yasmin. She just started her MFA program at UCLA. She needs me. I need her."

"Sounds like you're staying in LA then, right?"

"Nah. She knows I'm about winning gold next year. And that I'm only a phone call away."

"What did you think about that last session?"

"Mama Joyce didn't skip a beat. She still dropping knowledge after all these years."

"I guess Daddy knew what he was doing, allowing us to join him up here. Who would have thought that this place would mean so much to so many people?"

"Your boy Jason seemed to be moved by what the panelists were saying. Did you or Angelica get a chance to speak with him?"

"I didn't, but Angelica is with him now. I'm sure she'll let me know what's percolating in his mind."

Mitch placed his arms and elbows on the iron-cast table. "Sounds like ole' girl is digging him."

"She is."

"How are things with you and Tommy?"

"We're still together..."

"...but."

"There's no but."

"Oh. Just thought I sensed one coming."

"The season just ended. He and a few of his Atlanta Braves teammates flew out to Vegas for the week. When he returns, he plans on flying up to Knoxville, stay with me a few weeks in my apartment."

"Is he the one?"

"Don't know. I hope so. He's been good to me. But I have to take care of me first. Get my degree. Get my own record deal. Didn't allow Daddy to pamper me with his millions. Not about to start taking handouts from Tommy."

"You running indoors?"

"Yeah. Going to focus on the four and the eight. But I've been doing some hurdling as well. Coach Sinclair thinks I could be a pretty good four-hundred intermediate hurdler."

Mitch's body rocked with laughter. "I told you that would happen once they got a closer look at you. How you feel about that?"

"I feel good. And I agree. Doing the high hurdles during indoor for speed. When outdoor starts, I'll have to spend more time learning how to switch up my lead leg for the longer race."

"Watch out world. Here she comes."

"No doubt."

"How you feel about them calling you out like that?" Angelica asked. She and Jason stood along the Mosaic Lounge's back patio railing peering out at the darkness, down into the valley below.

"Was only a matter of time before it happened," Jason replied. "Just glad it happened around good people."

"Did you know Sojourner Vista was black owned and operated?"

"I didn't know anything about it. Not surprised, though. Most black owners go out of their way to hide the fact that their companies are black-owned and operated."

"That's true."

"Andre thinking about going to Howard."

"Oh, really. I thought your little brother wanted to be a Tar Heel."

"I did too. But he changed his mind after those cops roughed him up. He hasn't been the same since. Daddy told him HBCU degrees aren't worth the paper they're printed on. Said he needed to go to an Ivy League, or an elite school like UNC or NC State."

"I used to think the same way, but seeing all of this, all this black excellence, is causing me to have second thoughts. Being around our people isn't all that bad. It's refreshing and energizing. He ready for indoor?"

"He is. He called me the other day to tell me he clocked a four eight nine over the first three hurdles."

"That's fast. I know he's on Coach Highsmith's radar. If he runs faster than the thirteen nine he ran last year at the state meet, Coach will probably show up at y'all's crib to beg him to bring his talents to Rocky Top."

Angelica smirked at that. She then turned completely around to face Jason. "I been missing you," she shyly announced. "Miss seeing you on campus, in the cafeteria I mean. White and Don been missing you too. Had no idea not having you there would affect me like it did, but it has. Wish things could return to normal."

"So we can resume what we had started?"

Angelica peered up at Jason before abruptly looking away.

"Look. I like you, a lot, but I'm not looking to get into a steady relationship right now. This mess with this security guard has gotten me off my game. I'm all about bringing home Rio gold next year."

"Does that mean last Spring didn't matter, that it never happened?"

"Oh, it matters. It happened. Just know this has nothing to do with you, and everything to do with me. Just feel bringing home Rio gold next year is the assignment."

"I met that man you were talking about," Angelica said, "Patrick Ahern, Chair of the Democratic National Convention. Found out Trish knows him from the time she spent with her family up here. Looks like this place is a utopia, a safe place, for Black professionals, Black intellectuals, to congregate."

"And that's a good thing. Black spaces like this are hard to come by. After all our people went through during the Antebellum and Jim Crow eras, it's way past time for us to have our own."

"You're one of them black nationalists, aren't you?"

"No. Why you think that?"

"Because of what you did last year when that security guard Jimerson shot Jaylen Martin down in Florida. The only thing the boy had in his hands was a can of Arizona Iced Tea and Skittles. But you were the main one, among a handful of other Tennessee athletes, to join on-campus demonstrations calling for Jimerson's immediate arrest. Why'd you have the guts to do that when so many others didn't?"

"Because of what happened to my father, I guess. He died when I was four, a victim of senseless gun violence. Police never told us who pulled the trigger, but we found out a few weeks after the shooting that a gang of white boys in black face were caught doing drive-by shootings in predominately black and brown neighborhoods in Raleigh. Part of me wants to believe one of them gunned my old man down. Don't want to believe he was murdered by another black person."

"So, you draw motivation from your father's memory, right?"

"Right. I guess. There are times I feel he's whispering things in my ear, making things real, plain, for me. Lately, well since I've been here at Sojourner Vista, I've been thinking about race, white supremacy really, and what we as a people must do now to overcome it. Even had a conversation with Mitch about it this morning."

"Well, what are y'all going to do about it?"

Jason chuckled as he allowed more of his weight to rest on the patio rail.

"Mitch and I are exploring our options. But I'll let you know as soon as we know."

Jason looked at the time on his watch.

"Gotta roll, girl. Told Mitch I'd meet him in his room between seven and eight."

Angelica placed her right hand on Jason's shoulder and then proceeded to squeeze the top of his left forearm with her left hand. "Thank you for taking the time to let me know your thoughts about us. It means a lot. See you on the other side. That is if you're okay with that."

Jason covered Angelica's right hand with his right hand. "For sure." He then leaned in and kissed Angelica on her right cheek before walking away and reentering the Mosaic Lounge.

"BLACK," Bronson James exclaimed from his on-screen square. Jason and Mitch were sitting in chairs in Mitch's guest suite staring at Mitch's laptop computer on top of the wooden desk. The five athletes on Mitch's laptop computer screen nodded their heads in agreement. "I like it. Building a Legacy of Activism, Community and Kinship."

Damian Littlejohn interjected, saying, "I have a question, though. What will you be asking us to do? Kneel during the national anthem like Colin here..."

"...or raise black-gloved fists like Tommie Smith and John Carlos?" Jackson Lemar completed the sentence for him.

"If we have to do any of that, I'm out," Rustin Wilson said. "The reality is these white owners - and I'm speaking specifically about the ones in the NFL - just want us to play ball. They not down with all this Black Folk Matter shit."

"And we get that," Jason replied. "But we wouldn't lead with our truest intention, which Bronson just noted is building a legacy of activism, community and kinship. It will probably have more to do with what we heard Mama Joyce say earlier today. She said black people must take the lead in reconstructing black labor."

"Damn," Colin said. "That's dope. Also makes a lot of sense when you consider the disparities. Black people are the last to secure jobs that pay livable wages. If we focus on doing just what this Mama Joyce said, we will make them look like fools whenever they say black people are lazy."

"And they'll start to understand that when black people do well, everyone does well," Jason replied.

"Mitch chimed in. "I need you brothers to understand we're going to need a major infusion of cash. With black players being major forces in the NBA and NFL - what, over seventy percent majority in both - we were hoping you could conduct an informal poll to see how many of them would be willing to support this effort."

"I have no problem with that," Carmelo Anthem said.

"Me neither," Damian Littlejohn added. "I just need to see a detailed business plan." Bronson James, Colin Capshaw, Jackson Lemar and Rustin Wilson all either said "For sure!" or "No doubt!" in unison. "But here's a thought: What if we put Jason here in a position to be the founder, president, CEO. Use his last name so we can freely display the word Black on any signage we produce. Having BLACK with the words building a legacy of activism, community and kinship would freak white folk out. At least the unenlightened, conservative ones. But with its name being derived from the founder, president and CEO, they wouldn't have a problem with it."

Mitch burst out laughing, even rocking backwards and forward in his chair. Jason heaved with laughter as he transitioned to sitting up a little straighter in his chair. Mitch then looked over at Jason, which caused Jason to instinctively look back at him. Jason nodded to let Mitch know that he had no problem with Bronson's proposal. It made perfect sense to him.

But then Jason noticed that Rustin didn't seem as amused by what had just been said. He sat there with a stoic expression on his face.

"You brothers aren't dealing in reality," Rustin asserted. "We're going to be hard pressed to get our teammates, the black ones even, on board with this proposal. You all know that the only thing that matters to them, us, is the team. You also know that members of teams are conditioned to follow the lead of their coaches. Been engrained in us since our days playing pee wee ball. Coaches have the power, influence and control over our minds, brothers. Most of these coaches are white, and they do what the white owners tell them to do."

Bronson said, "Excellent point, Russ. But we have to change the way we think. Winning games, championships, is what we do, and head coaches and assistant coaches draw up the plans to make that happen. Something more drastic on the civil rights front has to be done, though. Something that lets them know we support diversity, equity and inclusion in our schools, communities and workplaces. We're the ones in the driver's seats, not them. If we can get buy-in from at least fifty percent of the black players in our leagues, they would be powerless to stop us. If we don't play, no one gets paid."

"We also need to hear what the ladies in the WNBA think about all this," Damian said. "I have no doubts about them supporting us, especially since they started that Say Her Name campaign following the Sandra Bland hanging death in Texas. Our black sisters don't get the credit they deserve brothers. It's always the men being seen speaking into microphones or being interviewed on TV. But they have always been the ones working behind the scenes to set things in motion."

"You're right," Mitch replied, "and we will, get them involved. But, for now, we just wanted to focus this initial conversation on the NBA, the NFL."

"Who should we approach?" Jason asked. "Not just in the WNBA but in women's sports in general?"

"If it were me," Damian replied, "I would start with the Wilson sisters. Serenity and Velma have been dominating tennis for over a decade now. They also have been very outspoken about Sandra Bland's unlawful arrest and suspicious death."

"And Candice Barker," Carmelo interjected, "is the face of their league now. If you get her to believe in what we're doing, she will bring others to the table."

"What do you want us to tell them?" Bronson asked.

Jason took a few seconds to think long and hard about Bronson James' question. He then replied, "Tell them that a group of black athletes have started a discussion about what we can do to build...build upon the gains... of the civil rights movement of the 1950s and '60s. Tell them one idea is to develop strategies around activism, community and kinship. That we want to focus on rethinking the way we look at black labor today for the jobs of tomorrow. Position black people to generate, maintain and transfer wealth."

Mitch added, "That we believe building community and establishing kinship should be, and will be, foundational to what we're trying to do. Mama Joyce was a child when that white mob massacred all those black people in Greenwood. We must create more Greenwoods here in the United States but also in other parts of the world. And when it comes to kinship, we must follow Alex Haley's lead. Every Black person in America should be able to reconnect with black people, their black families really, in Africa, discover their African roots. We have to create better systems for accurately uncovering our African ancestry, something white people made more difficult for us to do."

"Double damn," Colin said. "Has anything like this ever been done before, proposed?"

Jason leaned closer to the computer screen. "Elements of what we're proposing aren't new. Just think of Marcus Garvey with the Pan Africa Movement or W.E.B. Dubois and his writings about the Talented Tenth. But the difference here is us, black athletes, pooling our time, talent, treasure and testimony for the advancement of the Black Diaspora worldwide. The white supremacists are going to push back. You can count on that. But that's when we come out and expose them, their thoughts about being better than everyone else. We need to let white people know the problem is white supremacy and white supremacists, not white people. I have no doubt we'll gain more white allies when we frame it like that."

Moments later, Jason and Mitch offered the black athletes well wishes during their respective NFL and NBA seasons. All six of them returned the favor by wishing Jason and Mitch well in their preparation for the 2016 Rio Summer Olympic Games. Bronson and Colin, specifically, told Jason that everyone knows he didn't do anything wrong, adding they know he will be exonerated during his upcoming trial.

Mitch fought hard not to show any emotion. He knew having financial backing from professional black athletes for their black social and economic empowerment project could potentially be the straw that breaks white supremacy's back.

Mitch pressed a few keys on his laptop computer to end the Zoom call and then shifted in his chair to square up with Jason.

Jason pursed his lips, bracing himself for what Mitch was about to say. But Mitch opted to say nothing. Instead, he extended his arm and balled up fist to Jason. Jason stood, rocked forward, gently pounded Mitch's balled up fist with his own, and then rocked backwards to reclaim his seat.

CHAPTER NINETEEN

Roscoe Baker emerged from the back of the limo feeling like a million bucks. That's what happens when your wife gets you fitted with a tailored suit and you're meeting with the Grand Ole' Party's presidential nominee. Eunice exited the limo and followed close behind, her purse dangling from her bent elbow while dressed to the nines as well. Malcolm Stillwell's people had reached out to Eunice to schedule a private meeting at Stillwell Towers, located in New York City's Midtown Manhattan. The fact that Stillwell wanted to meet with him was flattering. But the conversations he had with Eunice prior to their boarding Stillwell's private jet at Knoxville's McGhee-Tyson Airport were reminders that the results of his upcoming trial would have repercussions for him, for sure, but also for the Confederate States of America and its 1776 Patriot Movement as a whole.

Stillwell's 1776 Patriot Group, which was a political action committee funded by dummy corporations operated by CSA citizens, was close to securing complete control of the Republican Party. If their "Great White Hope" secured the United States presidency, they would be able to appoint even more of their people to the Stillwell administration and take complete control of executive, judicial and legislative branches on the local, state and federal levels through the appointment of Stillwell loyalists. Again, Eunice didn't consider herself a racist – she always got along with "the Blacks" that worked with her at the freight company – but much like her father, CSA elder Broderick Turnbull, she also felt they were ill-equipped to sit with Whites at tables where consequential decisions were being made.

Like so many unenlightened white people in the modern age, she feared the racial reckoning that was sure to come from black Americans and other non-white Americans. Her white ancestors had committed some of the most heinous crimes against their fellow human beings of color. And she and her contemporaries, whether they wanted to admit it or not, benefited from their commission. But Eunice firmly believed, like other citizens in the Confederate States of America, that you had to crush a few grapes to get grape juice.

If asked, Eunice would probably tell you that even the 12 men comprising the CSA's Inner Circle did not consider themselves racists. They believed that the country, the world, needed the kind of leadership that only white Anglo-Saxon Protestant males could provide. And Eunice was alright with that. The GOP was alright with it as well. Of the fifty-two Senate seats won by Republicans in 2014 midterm elections, only four were occupied by women, albeit all white. This lack of racial and gender diversity is something progressive Democrats were quick to take issue with – been making this predictable move since the Richard Nixon administration - but most conservative Republicans didn't care. Conservative Republicans only cared about the almighty dollar. If their calls for less government regulation resulted in receiving monetary benefits from their corporate donors, and re-election of career Republican politicians that could do them a solid, they could care less about diversifying their House and Senate memberships.

Stillwell Tower has fifty-eight floors, with Malcolm Stillwell's Stillwell Organization operating on floors fifty-seven and fifty-eight. Stillwell also maintained a condominium there, and many members of his family resided there as well. The plot of land that Stillwell Towers stands is where the department-store chain Bonwit Teller was formerly located.

The elevator door slid open, and a uniformed elevator operator, a middle-aged, white male, adorned with a black top hat and matching black suit, greeted them with a head nod and "Welcome to Stillwell Tower."

"Thank you, sir," Baker replied upon entry.

"Thank you," Eunice repeated as she entered to stand to Baker's right.

Moments later, the elevator doors opened, and they stepped into Malcolm Stillwell's spacious, corner office. Plate-glass windows extended from the left to the right, giving onlookers a clear view of New York City's hustle and bustle below, as well as Fifth Avenue's towering buildings. They spotted Mason Chase sitting in the center of the room on a U-shaped sofa, writing notes on a legal pad. Malcolm Stillwell stood a few feet away from him peering out the window holding a short glass of bourbon in his right hand. He turned and Chase looked up as they entered the room.

"The man of the hour has arrived," Stillwell greeted, walking toward the couple with a toothy smile on his face. "Welcome to New York City, my friend." He extended his arm and hand toward the sitting area. "Please. Take a seat."

After exchanging a few more pleasantries, the group got down to business.

"Your case could potentially be the straw that breaks the camel's back," Chase said. "Our strategy all along has been to get the white race from under this guilt. We know what our ancestors did. The way our ancestors secured power, influence and control. But history always reminds us that there are winners and losers. And while we will never admit it, we, their contemporaries, inherited a slew of privileges from our ancestors being on the winning side."

Stillwell shifted in the recliner, directly across from Roscoe Baker. Even as he took a sip from his short glass, his eyes remained fixed on Baker.

"How do you feel about your case serving this higher purpose," Stillwell asked Baker.

Baker paused briefly before answering. "Like I've always felt, I guess," he replied. "Most of the people – and by that, I mean white people – know that our freedom and liberties are at risk of being taken away if the Blacks get their way. I'm willing to do what I need to do to preserve The Way."

Eunice interjected, "This Jason Black. He's represented by Thelma St. James. Isn't she the one who almost foiled our last attempt to take down one of their black icons?"

Eunice was referring to the Xavier Charles Trial, in which Charles was declared guilty by a mostly white jury because Thelma asserted throughout her defense that there was not enough evidence to connect him to his wife's murder. If not for the CSA loyalists on the jury, she would have received a not guilty verdict for her efforts.

"She is," Chase replied. Then, "I see your father is keeping you updated on our covert operations, huh?"

"He is. Not saying I agree with the group's methods, but who am I to judge men who obviously know what they're doing?"

Chase stopped writing and looked up. "Sounds like you don't agree with these methods. I can hear the sarcasm in your voice."

"No. I don't."

"What would you have us do, then?" Stillwell asked. "These methods were determined to be effective when the nineteen female operatives, all white, came forward to accuse black actor and comedian Hugh Crosby of drugging and raping them. Before that, he was viewed as the ultimate father figure for America's children following the success of his sitcom The Hugh Crosby Show." Stillwell flared his hands in exasperation at this notion. "We couldn't have that. A black man can never be viewed as a father figure to white children. Our methods were also effective in the T. J. Simpkins case."

"The former NFL running back who was convicted of murdering his wife and lover?" Baker asked.

"Yes," Chase responded. "We got word of his wife's extramarital affair, so we hired one of our operatives to take his wife and lover out, knowing full well that Simpkins would be implicated. When we take down their icons, we take the fight out of them."

"They – the Blacks – are creatures of habit," Stillwell added, "always looking for some charismatic figure to lead them. When our CSA operative assassinated King, we knew that was a major blow to their movement. But we also knew others would try to follow his lead, either as part of their Civil Rights Movement or as public figures in government, entertainment and industry. But we have contingencies for their infringements on white freedoms, white liberty."

"And that's what brings us here today," Chase said. "To sync your court testimony with Mr. Stillwell's public statements on the victimization of white patriots. Our messaging must appeal to the fears and resentments of our white brothers and sisters. They must believe that the Blacks are trying to take something from them. Again, their freedom, their liberty." He pointed at Stillwell, and added, "And with Mr. Stillwell amplifying what you say on the stand, we can almost guarantee Mr. Stillwell will be elected the forty-fifth president of these United States."

Baker looked over at his wife. He didn't think he would have to take the stand. Eunice just shrugged her shoulders and pursed her lips because it wasn't her call to make. Malcolm Chase was the shot caller on this one.

"This plan to take the fight out of them was hatched decades before I was born," Stillwell said. "People much smarter than us knew this racial reckoning would come, and they instituted counter measures, to make sure the white race could fend off any and all threats to our power, influence, control - our privilege. Make the true victims the perpetrators. Make it toxic for them to speak out against racism. In other words, their aim was to cast them as racists just for accusing white people of being racist. That's why we counter their chants of 'Black Folk Matter' with chants of our own – 'All Lives Matter' and 'Blue Lives Matter'. By doing that, white 1776 patriots everywhere rally around...rally around whiteness."

"What do you want me to say," Baker stuttered.

Chase smiled,

"Your truth, but through a 1776 Patriot – a Confederate States of America - lens."

Chase winked at Eunice, who sat across from him with a stern expression on her face, her hands in her lap. Then, he proceeded to provide Roscoe and Eunice Baker, and Malcolm Stillwell, the details of their master plan.

Moments after Baker and Eunice's departure, Roderick Stern emerged from an adjacent room, dressed in a black, two-piece suit. Stern had been the CSA's Director of Covert Operations since 2004, after serving as a Confederate militiaman the previous seven years. He also happened to be the man who fired the shot that ended Jerome Black's life.

"Did you catch all that?" Chase asked as Stern approached.

"I did." Stern claimed the chair that centered him between Stillwell and Chase. "Fortunate it is the husband of the daughter of a member of our inner circle at the center of this story."

"Indeed," Stillwell replied. Chase nodded in agreement.

Chase continued, "Not good enough, I fear. We need to take the porch monkey out, not allow him to testify. My team fought too hard to get those Stand My Ground bills passed by Republican-controlled legislatures. If he successfully uses it in his defense, in Tennessee, and wins, it will impact our efforts to reestablish White Rule in Confederate states. That black bitch has already signaled that she will use it."

"Our intelligence team just confirmed that they have him holed up at that resort of theirs, Sojourner Vista," Stern said. "Four of our operatives are in attendance. Just awaiting the kill order."

Chase opened his mouth to speak, but Stillwell shushed him. He glared over at Chase. "Tell me again why you think it's so important for us not to allow him to speak."

"Too risky," Chase replied. "If they're successful, the tables would be turned against our fellow patriots. Our white brothers and sisters would become victims at the hands of gun-toting niggers claiming they were defending themselves, their property. Not something we want."

"But won't taking him out at this late stage raise suspicion?"

"Probably. But, again, that's a risk I'm willing to take if it prevents him from telling the jury his side of the story." Chase tossed his legal pad onto the coffee table. "The judge has already announced that cameras will be allowed in the courtroom. MSNBC and CNN will undoubtedly have around-the-clock coverage, and it will be the lead story on the major networks at six and six thirty."

Stern remained silent in his chair, awaiting Malcolm Stillwell's response with an emotionless expression on his face. The awkward silence caused Chase to squirm once in his chair.

"Were they able to get all four past their security checks and into their suites?" Stillwell asked, shifting his gaze from Chase to Stern.

"They were," Stern replied. "All I have to do is give the order, and they know what to do when it's time to let our paramilitary troops in." Stern then asked, "Do you want our CSA operatives to continue with the 1776 protests outside their gates?"

"Yes." Stillwell swallowed hard. "They will want to know what I have to say about the 'Seize on Sojourner Vista.' I will denounce it, of course. Send heartfelt prayers to the grieving families. Our people just have to make it appear we're occupying their...their cook-out."

"Understood, sir," Stern replied.

Chase added, "Time to let these uppity apes know we're still their masters."

"My father must have faith in you and your story," Mitch exclaimed from the other side of the table. "That's when he fights the hardest."

He and Jason were seated at a table in the mountain resort's Mosaic Lounge. Light instrumental music played in the background. It was day three of the Sojourner Vista justice conference, and the two had agreed earlier in the day to meet for dinner for a much lengthier conversation.

"Maybe so," Jason replied. "And I'm grateful. Never been in trouble like this before. Looking forward to putting it behind me." He shifted in his seat. "How have things been with you, bro'? Training with Franklin Moses out there in Cali and all?"

"It's been good. Can't beat the warm weather, running into celebrities."

"You think he could help me go sub-nine point eight oh?"

Mitch lied. "Only if you're willing to put in the work. But don't give up on your coaches at Tennessee, bruh. Coach Highsmith is one of the most respected coaches in the sprint game. Because of him, you're one of the five fastest men in the world."

"But it's still not enough to beat your black ass." Jason abruptly changed the subject. "You been attending these conferences long?"

"My father used to bring us up here when we were kids. Mainly to support Mr. Cochran, black business. Probably been up here maybe two, three times. Love being up here, though. Breathing in all this fresh, country air. Came up here for a week before my senior year of high school. During the pre-season, to train. Mug had me running hills and shit. It was worth it, though. I rushed for over two thousand yards that year."

Mitch leaned forward. "I saw you running on the treadmill this morning. Good to see you slowly getting back into the grind. I know this court crap is weighing you down mentally, but I hope you intensify your training. It'll help relieve the stress. It's the end of October. The indoor season kicks off in January, and outdoor trials are in May."

Jason studied the lines in Mitch's brow. Mitch's sincerity was positioned well, but Jason was used to overcoming obstacles in an orderly fashion. In his heart and mind, he knew he couldn't move forward until this trial was placed in his rear-view mirror.

"I get that," Jason said. "But I'm not there yet. I do plan on getting there, though. When? I wish I knew. But with this Stillwell dude saying all these crazy things about me, my family, I know my life will never be the same. Wish he would just keep his mouth shut."

"I hear you, bro'. But that's what these 1776 Republicans do. They're opportunists, pouncing on any news event that will get them front-page coverage. Stillwell is no different. The news media talks more about what he says about the case than the case itself."

Jason nodded at that. But as soon as he does so, both he and Mitch look up to see a bearded, white man standing over them.

"Mind if I join you?" Malcolm King said. King was a respected member of the Marshall Law Group's founding Trio.

"Most definitely, sir," Mitch replied, once recognition set in. Mr. King claimed the seat next to Mitch and across from Jason.

"You fellas enjoying the conference?"

"We are," Mitch replied. "Was on Monday's student-athlete panel."

"I was there. Really enjoyed your take on why student-athletes should get paid. I'd like to talk with you more about that before the conference ends. Many of the points you raised coincide with my theories about why reparations should be paid to the descendants of enslaved black Americans."

"I'd like that," Mitch replied, smiling.

Mr. King turned his attention to Jason. "And how are you doing, Jason?"

"I'm doing well. Sir. Really learning a lot here."

"Glad the Law Group brought you here, to Sojourner Vista. I know it's not home, but your family and you get a chance to relax together as you weather through this trial. Have you been taking advantage of the amenities?"

"I have. Visited the fitness center again this morning. Hopped on the treadmill, lifted a little weight."

Mitch interjected, "You sore, aren't you?"

"...than a mothafuka."

Mr. King continued, "I'm here for obvious reasons, Jason. I'm assisting Thelma with the case review, but it's hard to do when I know so little about you. Would you mind sitting down with me sometime tomorrow?"

"For sure," Jason replied. Then, "I have a question. What compelled you all to purchase this property? Isn't this where all the racist, white people live?"

Mr. King studied the quizzical expressions on both Jason and Mitch's faces. "Plenty of them scattered throughout these hills and valleys. But they're not all racists, and they're not all white." He cleared his throat and continued, saying. "The area that we're in right now played a major role in the Civil Rights Movement. About fifty miles north of us – in New Market, Tennessee – is the Highlander Research and Education Center. Reshonda, Kelvin and I attend training there at least once a year. The site was also the host location for the Southern Negro Leadership Conference's strategic planning sessions. Dr. King was a frequent lecturer there."

Jason and Mitch exchanged knowing glances. There was an elephant seated next to and in front of them. To let this moment pass would be unwise. Therefore, Jason asked, "What drew you to the movement? Most of the white people I know want us to just forget the past and move on."

Mr. King nodded. "I'm not like most white people. I was adopted by two amazing, black parents as a six-month-old infant, back in 1951. They provided me with the love and support that every child needs. When I reached a certain age, around thirteen, fourteen, years, I guess, I started noticing differences between how I was treated in school and how my black classmates were treated.

"Still remember how white people would react when they saw me out in public with my parents. They were noticeably repulsed by the sight of us, by the sight of me being with two caring, black adults. When I reflect on moments like these, I realize I didn't choose the movement, the movement chose me, at a very early age."

"Is that what caused you to choose a legal career?" Mitch asked.

"Oh, most definitely. But Thurgood Marshall being appointed to the Supreme Court in 1967 is what sealed it. I was sixteen when this happened. I still recall how my parents reacted when the great Walter Cronkite of CBS News announced that Lyndon B. Johnson made this historical appointment. I had already been reading about his work with the NAACP's Legal Defense Fund. And when Dr. Bell started talking about the intersectionality between race, law and history, I realized there was so much I didn't understand about how white segregationists crafted policies that guaranteed certain advantages, privileges, for Whites only. However, with Justice Marshall on the court, I knew even then that these schemes would be exposed. If not by Marshall, by young lawyers like ReShonda, Kelvin and me, who were all about the Rule of Law and American democracy."

"Why is this Stillwell dude so concerned about my trial?" Jason asked. "He doesn't even know me."

"It's not about him knowing you, Jason. It's about him expanding the Republican base by appealing to white fears and resentments. Nixon employed it, as did Reagan."

A brief silence hovered over the threesome, as Jason and Mitch glared at Malcolm King, bidding him to say more. He continued, saying, "It all started in 1964, at the Republican National Convention in San Francisco, California. Arizona Senator Barry Goldwater, a staunch conservative, had just been nominated as the Republican Party's presidential nominee. The conservative movement was in its infancy back then, but they rallied around Goldwater because he was opposed to the Civil Rights Act of 1964, as well as the Civil Rights Movement."

Mr. King swallowed hard. Jason and Mitch waited patiently for him to tell them more.

"These feelings didn't change, even after the convention goers received word about murders being committed in Mississippi and other parts of the South, to preserve White Rule, the Southern way of life. During his nomination speech, Goldwater told the convention that he was a proponent of smaller government.

He continued by saying his government would not have laws that interfered with states' rights or conducted a war on poverty. But the straw that drove the black electorate to the Democratic Party was what he said about them. Goldwater said his administration would oversee a government that doesn't give handouts to Blacks."

"Damn," Mitch blurted out. "He said that out loud?"

"Yes, he did," Mr. King replied.

Jason interjected, "I remember reading about that in my Political Science classes. About one-third of the black electorate still voted Republican, right?"

"Right. But now over ninety percent of the black electorate votes for Democratic candidates. Total sea change, but one that was, and is, welcomed. If not for the Democratic Party, we wouldn't have the Civil Rights Act, which offers protection of citizenship and voting rights."

"They called it the Southern Strategy, right?" Jason implored. Mitch allowed his arm to fall from the table to his lap.

"They did. It is a strategy that was used successfully by Nixon and Reagan in later years. But it caused that remaining third of black Republicans to exit their party. Of course, the party's leadership didn't care. They just wanted to fan white fears and resentments so more white people would vote Republican on Election Day."

"So now I'm part of their Southern Strategy, huh?" Jason said.

"Most definitely," Mr. King replied. "But for different reasons. Today's 1776 Conservative Patriot Movement has initiated a campaign to free white people from any guilt they may have about the legacy of slavery and Jim Crow. They have already initiated a campaign to spread dispersions about Critical Race Theory. Their plan is to use these CRT dispersions to undermine what public primary and secondary school students are being taught in their history classes about white racism, prejudice and discrimination. They claim teaching about white racism, prejudice and discrimination makes white children feel uncomfortable. And believe it or not, they're even trying to make it harder for black employees to say they were discriminated against by white people in the workplace. They dream of a day when white people will have more ammunition to dispute these claims."

"Does it make them feel uncomfortable?" Jason asked.

"No!" Mr. King blurted back. "It's all an effort to recast white people as victims, black people as perpetrators. Again, these white conservatives are appealing to white people's need to be free of any guilt they may be feeling from the legacy of slavery and Jim Crow. These unenlightened, 1776 conservatives are trying to tap into what they believe is the white electorates deepest desire, and they're succeeding. White guilt is what causes white people to be sympathetic to black pain and suffering. In their minds, it's a sign of progressive thought, which leads to 1776 conservative Republican defeats at the ballot box."

"So," Jason said, leaning back, "if Baker's side wins, it will be a victory for the Conservative Movement. Right?"

"Yes. That's how they will perceive it."

"Why, though?" Mitch interjected. "Based on what you told me, J, you were the one defending yourself, not him."

"But they will find some way to say Roscoe Baker was executing his duties as a law enforcement officer. And I have no doubt they will use the immunity clause that is afforded to law enforcement officers, as well as the new Stand My Ground legislation. Mark my word. The battle we're raging now is more symbolic than substantive. Even on the micro level, they're going to do everything they can to make you the perpetrator, Roscoe Baker the victim."

"Race shouldn't have anything to do with it," Jason exclaimed. "Am I more of a criminal just because I'm black? Hell no! But I've been thinking. We black Americans seem to be more complacent, more willing to give white Americans a pass for maintaining polices and legislation that ensures that we never have a connection with the motherland, Africa." Jason waved his hands in front of him. "I love what the Marshall Law Group is doing here, on the legal front, but the research I did last year, in one of my Political Science classes, suggest that black Americans could make more gains if we focused on building a legacy of activism and community, as well as our kinship with black Africans."

Mitch smiled at Jason. But then he looked up and to his right. The bespectacled, white female that winked at him in the ballroom stood at the bar talking to one of the black, male bartenders. Jason raised his hand, silently requesting that they press pause on their conversation. He then got up from his seat and walked over to her.

"I was wondering when I would see you again," Jason greeted during his approach. The bespectacled, white female turned and smiled, feigning lack of recognition. The Mosaic Lounge was packed, as attendees sat on stools at the bar and circular and rectangular tables sprinkled throughout the spacious room.

"Just making my rounds," the bespectacled, white female replied. "How are you doing this fine evening."

"Better, now that you graced us with your presence." Jason motioned to the stool next to hers and said, "Mind if I join you?"

"Not at all."

Jason claimed the stool, turning it oh so slightly so he wouldn't have to strain to sneak glimpses at her toned legs, and breasts that seemed to be fighting to be free of her low-cut blouse. The bespectacled, white female smiled when she caught him admiring her cleavage. Jason looked away momentarily upon realizing he had been caught in the act, but when he peered into her eyes, he could tell that she welcomed these types of stares from potential suitors.

"What can I get you, bruh?" the black bartender asked Jason from behind the bar.

"Whatever the lady is having," Jason replied. The black bartender nodded and then walked to the other side of the bartender's station to prepare his drink. Jason then shifted his attention back to the bespectacled, white female.

"What's your name?"

"Gabrielle," the bespectacled, white female replied. "But most people just call me Gabby."

"I'm going to assume you're a paralegal or a practicing attorney since you came all this way to attend this conference."

"I am. Civil rights attorney, up in Boston. With Bain Legal. Been there for a little over a year now, but this is my first time at one of these Sojourner Vista gatherings."

"Mine too. Really learning a lot."

The black bartender returned, placing the couple's drinks on the counter in front of them. Gabby was the first to take a sip of her martini. Jason could feel growth in his loins as her glossed lips sucked the liquid through the tiny straw.

Gabby scooted her stool closer to Jason and leaned in. She then whispered into his ear. "You want me, don't you?"

"For sure," Jason replied softly.

"You want to plunge that big, black cock of yours into my wet, white pussy, don't you?"

"No doubt."

Gabby then leaned forward to reach between Jason's legs with her right hand, gently squeezing his erection over his slacks.

"Looks like Little J wants to come out and play."

Jason chuckled as he pushed her hand over and away. Gabby grinned at him, but then pulled her extra card key from her purse. She then flipped Jason's suit jacket open and slipped the extra card key into his inside pocket.

"I'm in room one, two, two seven," she whispered. "Don't worry. It will be dripping wet by the time you get there."

"And Little J will come ready to play."

Gabby stood, pressed her fingers to her lips to blow Jason a kiss, and then turned on her heels to accentuate the sway in her hips on her way toward the exit door. However, as she exited, Jason spotted Trish and Angelica sitting at a table, peering over at him with disgusted expressions on their faces.

"Really, J," Angelica exclaimed as Jason approached their table. As Jason stood over them, he could sense their pain. They had watched him, in real time, violate one of Black America's long-held rules – that black men and women should develop loving relationships with other black men and women – and it was obvious they didn't want him venturing any further down this slippery slope.

Trish reached up and pulled him down to the empty chair on her left.

"Why are you here?" she asked. "Shouldn't you be up in your room?"

"Mitch invited me down, to chat about old times," Jason replied. "Then Mr. King showed up."

Angelica interjected with a hint of sarcasm in her voice, "So now you're about to go up to that white woman's room and get down with her, right?

"Something like that." Jason's brow tightened. "Why you all up in my business. We brothers have needs too."

"That's the problem," Trish snapped back. "You 'brothers' always thinking with the head between your legs and not the one on your shoulders. Why are you settling for that when you have all us fine sisters up in here?"

"Because I can. And because I'm horny as hell."

"Don't let them talk you down, J," Mitch joked as he approached to stand over their table. "I'd hit it too if I was single."

Trish replied, "You are single, Negro."

Mitch held up his opened left hand for all to see then made a clamping motion with his fingers. "Not your story to tell, lil' sis." He then leaned over to kiss the top of her head. As he pulled back, he added, "Early flight back to Cali." Then, walking away, he added, "See you down in Atlanta in December for Christmas?"

"I'll be there," Trish replied.

"We'll talk more then. Okay?"

Trish feigned a smile. "Okay. Love you."

Mitch pointed back at her to say, "Love you too." He then shifted his attention to Jason, pumping his arms once, twice, to let him know the time to get back on the track is now. Jason's body rocked from a muffled chuckle as he watched him exit the restaurant and veer right.

Jason stood. "I guess I better get too so I can put in this work."

"Sit down," Angelica sternly ordered.

"We ain't done with you yet," Trish added, matching Angelica's sternness. Once Jason was seated, she continued, saying, "So, what were you all talking about with Mr. King?"

"He was just giving us a history lesson about this place, this area really. Said it played a very significant role in getting more people on board with the black civil rights movement. First time hearing about the Highlander Center."

"Yeah," Trish replied. "Mitch, Rayvyn and I learned about it when we participated in the special training they had for kids. All of these gains that black Americans have made can be traced back to the hard discussions that a multi-racial coalition of activists made there. These conferences are nothing more than a continuation of what they started at the Highlander Center."

Angelica's stare caused Jason to shift uncomfortably in his chair.

"I was telling them about the research I did on a paper I wrote last year. Was writing about the global impact of the Trans-Atlantic Slave Trade, Reconstruction and Jim Crow for one of my Political Science classes. Connected the dots. Showed how unenlightened whites went out of their way to sever our connection to Africa. If the Marshall Law Group is not doing anything to repair this connection, what's it doing?"

"Plenty," Angelica chimed in. "Based on what I heard earlier today, they're representing black families who have lost loved ones to police brutality, or who have been wrongfully convicted of crimes. With advances in DNA evidence, they are getting wrongfully convicted Blacks out of jail, even the ones who have served lengthy sentences, like ten, fifteen, years or more."

"They're primed to win the legal battles," Trish interjected.

"But is that enough?" Jason blurted back. "Is that enough to restore our dignity, maintain a sense of culture and community within the Black Diaspora? I don't think so. Seems like we have to do more to restore that sense of black solidarity."

"You should talk to Mr. Cochran," Trish encouraged. "My father consults with him all the time, even though they're around the same age. Mr. Cochran is half the reason why Daddy decided to call his company Tribe Records. He wanted to make his black performers feel like they were members of one African tribe. If you talk with them, though, you have to come correct."

"For sure. But I'm still trying to make sense of it all. Never knew all of this was going on behind the scenes. By black people, for black people. Now that I know, I feel like I want to help them do more."

"Well, knocking boots with that white chic ain't gonna be one of your best moves," Angelica snapped back. She extended her hand toward Jason. "Hand it over."

"What are you going to do with it?" Jason asked.

"I'm going to take it up to her room, give it back to her," Angelica replied. "Her room, 1227, is right down the hallway from ours. Need to send her a message. Let her know you're taken."

This last statement caused Trish to push away from the table to stand. She knew where this was going, and she wanted no part in it.

"I'm going to bed," she exclaimed. "Whatever y'all plan on doing, don't bring it to the room. Can't have someone thinking I'm at Sojourner Vista cheating on my man."

As she said this, Angelica's eyes remained fixated on Jason. Jason peered up at Trish before allowing his eyes to fall back on Angelica.

"Is that an invitation?" Jason asked after Trish had walked away.

Angelica replied, "Maybe. It all depends on you, whether you're into bitch-ass hoes or a strong, independent, voluptuous black woman like me."

Jason pursed his lips. "Language. You plan on kissing me with those dirty lips of yours."

Angelica replied, "Baby, if you allow it, I plan on kissing you all over with these dirty lips of mine."

Jason's right hand then reached into his suit jacket's inner pocket to pull out his card key. "I'm cabin 026," he announced. He then sucked in on his lips and proceeded to slide his tongue along the crevice, from right to left, as he handed it to Angelica.

Angelica accepted it, the contact with his hand eliciting a subtle but noticeable shudder. "See you in fifteen?"

"Not if I see you first," Angelica joked.

When Gabby entered guest suite 1227, which was directly across the hall from 1229, the attention of her three 1776 Patriot colleagues, two white males and one white female, dressed in suits and skirt, turned to her.

"Are we good?" Gabby asked.

"We're good," the white male standing in the spare bedroom doorway exclaimed as the other white male and female stood. "They will enter from the back, right-side patio, up the stairs, and into the main lobby. Once there, they have been instructed to beat as many of them down as they can."

"Is our man in place to take eyes off their entry?" Gabby asked.

The other white male replied, "Cameras going black at ten o'clock sharp. Be that way for about fifteen, twenty, minutes. Should give them more than enough time to get up to the lobby. Once they're in position, our operatives outside will storm the front gate."

"Did you establish contact with the mark?" the only other white female in the room asked.

"I did." Gabby replied, trying her best to stymie a smirk. The two of them exchanged a knowing glance. "Almost wish I could have a little fun with him before y'all take him away."

"We have our orders, Gabrielle," the standing white male exclaimed. "Before this day ends, that nigger Jason Black is going to be hanging from a tree by his neck."

CHAPTER TWENTY

bout 30 members of the Confederate States of America's 1776 Militia milled around in various sections of the alcove, awaiting orders from their leader Benjamin "Benjie" Stoops. Their upright stances, with AR-15 assault rifles hanging from straps around their necks and shoulders, let you know that they were bubbling with anticipation. Yes, they would have to scale the 15-foot stone wall surrounding the Sojourner Vista Resort and Conference Center, but this would not be a problem, resulting from the fact that they had spent six months training for this moment.

They all wore black, military fatigues. Coupled with the cover of night under a half-moon, they knew they would be somewhat invisible to Sojourner Vista's equally equipped and skilled security team, the Vista Guard. They also knew that the Vista Guard was always in a perpetual state of high alertness because of the 1776 protesters perpetual parade outside their front gate. But they were banking that this same Vista Guard would think its leaders were dumb enough to view the 1776 protesters as their greatest threat.

Benjie and another man, his second in command, Vincent Thomas, stood high on the hill closest to the resort's stone wall. Benjie held night-seeing binoculars up to eyes, using them to scan the resort's oversized patio that was wrapped around the resort's outside seating area. As he shifted from left to right, he felt envious of the mostly black conference attendees, as they accepted glasses of wine from waiters and stood in line to load prepared appetizers onto porcelain plates. But he was looking for Gabby, or a member of her four-person infiltration team. His left hand fell to his side with the binoculars as his right hand with his watch on it came up. Nine fifty-five. They now had less than five minutes before their months of training would be put to the test.

Stoops turned toward his men, holding up five fingers to let them know how much time they had to get ready. The sound of rifles cocking briefly filled the air as they all coalesced at the bottom of the hill. Then, peering over and up at where they knew the log-cabin-style structure was, they saw a small flicker of light coming from the right edge of the oversized patio.

"Let's go," Stoops said, pushing through bushes and vines to step into the clearing that offered direct advancement on the resort's southern border. Thomas and the 30 other members of the 1776 Militia followed close behind in a single-file line.

The Vista guardsman sat in the control room, surveying the twenty surveillance monitors on the wall in front of him. Under his bulletproof vest, he wore a black long-sleeve shirt with the Sojourner Vista logo patch sown onto it. On one of the monitors, all he could see was snow, which meant the camera that covered the resort's southern border was malfunctioning. And his efforts, and those of the male colleague sitting to his left, weren't enough to get it working again.

The Vista guardsman pressed the walkie-talkie device clamped to the right-side of his vest. "Unit One," he said into the device. "We have a malfunctioning, ground-level camera in Sector D. Need you to go down there and check it out."

A crackling sound followed by, "Roger that."

The responding Vista guardsman walked under and past the composite awning to stand in the courtyard. The soft lighting from the lanterns allowed anyone wanting to enjoy what the courtyard had to offer visibility. Light jazz music could be heard playing in the background, as the indecipherable conversations of conference attendees on the wrap-around patio above him filled the night. As he walked down the brick walkway toward the ground-level camera, his eyes scanned everything that was in front of him, from right to left. He spotted a black couple on his left facing him, cuddled up on an outdoor love seat. The black man acknowledged the Vista guardsman with a head nod. The black woman just smiled at him and then slid her tongue across her painted lips. The Vista guardsman gave them a nod of his own, his wandering eyes taking a brief moment to take a sip of the black woman's assets, which were covered by nothing more than a spaghetti-strap dress.

At the front gate, repetitive chants from the protesters. "You will not replace us. You will not replace us."

Seconds later, the window to the front gate guard station imploded, causing the two Vista guardsmen inside to cower and shield themselves from their rolling chairs as broken glass rained down on them. When they arose again, they were met by the sight of a baseball bat-wielding protester dressed in military fatigues climbing through the shattered window and swinging downward with it, onto the skull of the Vista guardsman closest to him.

"Breach," the other Vista guardsman shouted into his walkie-talkie as he backed away from the attacker. "Front gate." He then snatched his side arm from his right hip and pointed it at the attacker, even as the attacker continued to pummel his colleague over and over again with the bat. He fired one shot into the attacker's right shoulder. The blast sent the attacker reeling backwards, but his quick recovery indicated that his bulletproof vest did what it was designed to do. The Vista guardsman fired again, this time at the attacker's head. The protester's head exploded, coating the guard station walls with blood, flesh and bone.

Mitch exited the elevator to step into the long hallway leading to his guest room. He held his cell phone to his ear.

"I just told him."

Yasmin's silence caused Mitch to walk a little slower.

"I still think what they don't know won't hurt them," Yasmin replied.

"Milk it for all it's worth, right?"

"Hell, yeah," Yasmin blurted back. "Make what you can and get out. They do it all the time. Lie and cheat. Why should things be different for us?"

Mitch's mind immediately thought back to those days when he and Yasmin would have thought-provoking discussions about white privilege and entitlement. He knew Yasmin had a tremendous amount of disdain for white people, resulting from her childhood experiences in the West Indies. Willie Lynch had brought his theories about how best to turn African captives into slaves to the Virgin Islands, and this legacy robbed her ancestors and their contemporaries of opportunities to control the land.

Yasmin once told Mitch the story of her great grandmother Annie Mae Mendoza, how her white Portuguese owner would take sexual liberties with her and the other female workers whenever he saw fit. Annie Mae became pregnant with Alejandro Ortiz's child, Yasmin's grandmother Olivia Mendoza, and decades later, Olivia Ortiz gave birth to her mother Claudia Ortiz.

Yasmin continued, "You took a pill that makes you run faster. So what? I just think you're within your rights to what they been doing for centuries."

Mitch pursed his lips as the elevator doors opened. He stepped into the hallway, onto a carpet adorned with the tiled silhouette of abolitionist Sojourner Truth. He sensed someone approaching him from the other side of the hallway. When he looked up, he saw a masked man dressed in black military fatigues walking toward him brandishing a long-gun rifle, with a silencer attached to its nozzle.

Mitch immediately turned on his heels to run to the back stairwell. The masked man aimed his rifle's barrel at Mitch's backside. He then pumped a single bullet into Mitch's lower back. The bullet's impact sent Mitch's body flying further down the hallway before slamming to the floor.

The masked man lowered his weapon as he walked closer to Mitch. He took special care in checking his left and right flanks for guests opening their doors, thinking they heard something. The pool of blood under Mitch's pelvic region swelled. The rise in his stomach and chest indicated that he was still alive, but the lack of movement in his lower extremities suggested paralysis.

A male voice resounded over the resort's intercom system. "Attention, guests. The perimeter has been breached. We ask that you return to your guest rooms and shelter in place."

The masked man stood over Mitch, a smirk on his face. But the shuffling of feet and clicks of another set of assault rifles being readied and aimed caused him to assume a defensive stance as he raised his weapon. Standing directly in front of him were two members of the Vista Guard.

"Drop your weapon," the guard to the masked man's right ordered, "and back away."

Still lying limp on the floor, Mitch watched as the masked man bent down, seemingly to place his firearm on the floor. But that was all a ruse. From his bent-over position, he fired a barrage of bullets at the Vista guardsmen. The Vista guardsmen dropped to the floor before the masked man could get his first shots off. The Vista guardsmen then fired shots of their own at the masked man from the floor, not relenting until the masked man lay on his back, bloodied, dead.

The Vista guardsman on the right brushed past Mitch to snatch the masked man's assault rifle from around his neck.

"You alright, son," the other one asked from a kneeling position beside Mitch.

"I can't feel my legs," Mitch strained to reply.

Jason emerged from the Mosaic Lounge to chants of "You will not replace us." A crowd of all-white 1776 protesters forced their way into the spacious and furnished lobby. The unarmed members of the Sojourner Vista security team, dressed in black suit jackets, slacks and white button-down shirts, were overwhelmed by the sheer number of protesters that flowed past them. A few of the 1776 protesters held their cell phones high above their heads to livestream their occupation of the black-owned establishment. A number of others held up signs that read "Blue Lives Matter" and "Just Say No To CRT". With the size of the protesting mob swelling, Jason watched as the resort's mostly black guests hastily retreated to the confines of their guest rooms.

As Jason and the other Mosaic Lounge patrons backed away from the white protestors, about seven rifle-toting members of the Vista Guard trotted past them to form a line in front of them. The all-black regiment of Vista guards stood tall, regal even, as several of the protesters got in their faces and taunted them. A white male protester with a "Nigger Go Home" sign got in the face of a Vista guardsman near the center of the line and stared him down. Seeing that the Vista guardsman was unmoved or unnerved by his antics, he sucked in the snot from his nose and spit it onto the Vista guardsman's face. The Vista guardsman kept his composure, not flinching, blinking even. His colleagues on his left and right kept their composures as well.

Jason spotted Kelvin Cochran exiting a back room to enter the lobby with a bullhorn in his hand. Cochran brought the bullhorn to his mouth, and said, "Please remove yourselves from the premises. You are not welcome here."

"Fuck you, nigger," Jason heard someone shout out from the protesting crowd.

"Take your asses back to Africa," said someone else. "You're not welcome here either."

Jason immediately thought about Angelica, her going up to the white woman's room. He had been told that the resort was surrounded by a 15-foot wall, and several layers of surveillance and protection, but he now found himself beating himself up for allowing her to leave the lounge by herself. However, he found himself pausing briefly to see how Kelvin Cochran and his Vista Guard were going to clear the trespassers from the lobby.

Jason watched Cochran shrug, noticeably upset that his Vista Guard had allowed them to get past the front gate. Cochran motioned to the Vista Guard leader, Sgt. Frank Ross. Sgt. Ross then gave a hand signal that caused each of the Vista guardsmen to take a single, but big, step forward. When they did, most of the 1776 protesters turned back toward the front atrium. However, there was a hand full who tried to leap past them, only to be caught in midair by the Vista guardsman closest to them and carried back toward the front atrium in the Vista guardsmen's continuing advance. Jason watched all of this from the back hallway, near the elevator and stairwell.

Jason was impressed by the Vista guardsmen's professionalism, admiring them for how efficiently they were clearing the room without having to beat any of the protesters into submission or fire a single shot. But then the ratatattat of a machine gun rang out, causing everyone that remained in the lobby to scurry for cover or drop to the floor. Three gunmen strode through the retreating mob of protesters firing indiscriminately at the Vista guardsmen. The Vista guardsmen that were able fired back at them immediately, with shots to each of their heads, taking all three of the armed attackers down.

Angelica stood in the second-floor hallway, knocking on the door to room 1227. She held Gabby's card key in her right hand.

The door to room 1227 swung open, revealing a bespectacled Gabby, dressed in nothing but her cherry-colored bra and panties. Her eyes widened when she caught sight of Angelica, and her arm instinctively crossed her chest to hide her nipples, clearly seen through the sheer fabric of her bra.

"Not who I was expecting," she exclaimed, smirking. The door on the other side of the hallway – room 1229 – clicked and swung open. Angelica turned to see a burly, white man dressed in suit and tie step forward. "But I guess you will have to do."

The burly, white man grabbed Angelica from behind – making sure to cover her mouth as she struggled to break free – and pushed her into Gabby's room. Once they were inside, Gabby took great care to grab the door to ensure it closed somewhat silently behind them.

Malcolm Stillwell sat upright on his bed peering across the bedroom to watch live footage of injured Sojourner Vista guests being wheeled to ambulances on gurneys, or being tended curbside, or on the resort roundabout, by first responding paramedics and police officers. His forty-something-year-old wife Danella, brushing her teeth in the adjoining bathroom, peeked out repeatedly to see what was being shown on the wall-mounted television. She returned to the confines of the bathroom as images from Sojourner Vista were replaced by the Fox News talking heads sitting in their New York studio.

Stillwell heard his cell phone ringing on the nightstand to his left. Answering it, the voice of Mason Chase asked, "Did you catch all that?"

"I did," Stillwell replied. "But did they get the boy?"

"I'm afraid not, sir. But they did get a girl, a friend of his, we believe. How would you like us to proceed."

Silence, as Stillwell weighed the pros and cons of holding the girl hostage.

"Get rid of her," he replied. "Do to her what we had planned for the boy."

"Understood, sir."

Thelma St. James watched sullenly as a female paramedic tended to the cut on the left side of Kelvin Cochran's head. When the shots rang out, Mr. Cochran had tripped and hit his head on the edge of the concierge's desk. Trish had rejoined Jason, both of them recognizing how fortunate they were to be under the Vista Guard's protection.

"This is reminiscent of what happened in Tulsa," Trish whispered to no one in particular, "in the Greenwood District."

"Could have been," Thelma replied. "Just glad they didn't get a chance to burn it all down."

"But why?" Jason asked. "Why would they attack us like this? Were they trying to get at me?"

Thelma replied. "We're in the South, in Tennessee, the seat of the Confederacy. Too many of us in one place. Stresses them out."

Jason pondered what Thelma was saying. It then dawned on him that when he finally appears in court on the assault and battery charges, he may not receive a fair trial because of juror prejudice and bias.

"What's going to be interesting," Thelma continued, "is what Stillwell has to say about what happened here. Anytime guns

"Gabby," Jason blurted out while standing back on his feet and walking over to them. "Or Gabriel. Didn't get her last name."

King replied, "What you have given us is enough." He then nodded at Sgt. Ross. Sgt. Ross walked away, and Jason watched as he detached the communication device attached to the right side of his bulletproof vest to speak into it. The other Vista guardsman remained by King's side, hands resting easy near the trigger and barrel of his assault rifle.

"Who would do this?" Trish exclaimed, crossing her arms.

"People who don't agree with what we're doing up here," King replied.

Trish then looked over to see Jason, his back to them, watching the two EMS workers descending the ladder with Angelica's lifeless body and placing it on the gurney. She walked over to him, first touching his right arm, near the elbow. Jason turned slightly as she sidled up to his right flank, draping her left arm around his waist.

"Stop beating yourself up," she consoled. "You had no way of knowing what that bitch's intentions were." Trish breathed in deeply, her body heaving during both the inhale and exhale.

Jason draped both arms around Trish's shoulders and neck and just held her there for a few seconds before leading her in a dance that had them repeatedly rocking from side to side, one foot to the other. They then turned, watching the EMS workers as they carried the gurney with Angelica's blanket-covered body over the grassy field to eject the gurney's wheels once they reached the concrete walkway. After they disappeared behind the resort's southern border wall, Jason and Trish held each other tight, then even tighter when the full weight of what had just happened moved from being surreal to real.

CHAPTER TWENTY-ONE

oscoe Baker experienced a momentary wince on the living room love seat as the images of red, yellow, black and white bodies being wheeled from the fire-damaged Sojourner Vista resort covered the television screen on the other side of the living room. Two days had passed since the deadly assault on Sojourner Vista, and as he sat there, he felt repulsed by what was being shown on screens all across America, if not the world. All of this for one man, he thought. All of this to project fear and hopelessness into the hearts and minds of the descendants of enslaved Africans.

Baker was starting to have doubts about the appropriateness of these actions. Their star witness, Sandra Talbot, the white woman who told the police that she was being harassed by a black man, had opted to side with Jason Black's team, not his. In a written deposition, she suggested that her call to the police was a mistake, an overreaction. She went on to write that if she had known the person playing with her was University of Tennessee sprinter Jason Black, she would have never called the police on him.

Eunice emerged from the back room holding a black suit in her right hand, a navy blue one in her left. The upcoming hearing was now about six weeks away, on a Thursday. "Which one?" she asked.

Baker thought long and hard before saying, "The navy blue one."

Eunice hung the navy-blue suit on the hallway closet doorknob and then walked over to sit to the left of her husband on the love seat. "They really hit them hard, didn't they?" Eunice asked.

"They did," Baker replied. "But is all of this necessary? Isn't it enough to get a guilty verdict against him in court?'

"Not when one of our own is running for the highest office in the land." She paused as they both listened to the field reporter provide an update on Mitch Newman, the son of Tribe Records Founder and CEO Cornelius Newman and the current 100-meter dash world record holder at 9.68, how he is currently being treated in Knoxville, at the UT Medical Center, for injuries suffered during the series of explosions. The field reporter added that recent reports from the hospital staff suggest that Newman is experiencing loss of motion in his lower extremities.

"Malcolm Stillwell is our White Knight, dear," Eunice continued. "With him in office, and Republicans taking control of the House and Senate, our 1776 movement can enact legislation that preserves White Rule for the next twenty, thirty, years."

Baker's eyes darted to his wife then back to the television monitor. "I get it. But why do people have to die, get maimed, for us to preserve this White Rule?"

"Because it's all about the messaging that follows. The Blacks will come out and call it an act of terrorism. But we have already conditioned the white American public to associate terrorism with Muslims, especially after 9-11, when those Saudis hijacked those planes and flew them into the World Trade Center towers."

"But all we're doing is telling more lies to cover up the previous ones. Everyone knows most acts of domestic terrorism are being carried out by White Nationalist groups, not Muslims, Black Nationalists, or groups like Black Folk Matter. All I see Black Folk Matter protestors doing is leading mostly peaceful protests in the big cities. Yeah, some of them lose their minds by looting and burning down buildings. But, for the most part, most of their members are just marching through our streets, chanting."

Eunice stood to hover in the space between the television monitor and her husband. "We have less than two months to go before your trial begins. Are you prepared for the line of questioning that that black bitch is going to throw at you?"

"I am," Baker replied. He then made a gesture with his hand at the television monitor. "But I'm disturbed by all of this property damage, all this violence, Eunice. It's not necessary."

Eunice reared back as she crossed her arms on her chest. "Yet you pulled your firearm on the boy. Were you trying to intimidate him, or were you prepared to end his life?"

Baker raked his right hand across the right side of his face, wiping at the sweat coalescing there. "You know I was only trying to scare him, make him think twice about doing what he did."

"I'm sure you will share these sentiments when your ass is seated on the stand. But for now, you need to stop showing so much empathy for them. Their complaints, their grievances, should mean nothing to you. There's no better time for us white Americans to break free of this guilt that just keeps gnawing at us. All we have to do is play our part in this long-term effort to take back the narrative. Push them back. Make them think that their inability to get ahead, their lack of progress, is because of them not taking personal responsibility for their own lives." Eunice uncrossed her arms and then walked over to grab both the black and navy-blue suits. "You told Mr. Stillwell and Mr. Chase that you're in," she continued. "What I need to know is are you? Are you all in?"

Baker wiped his face once more with his right hand, even as he grabbed the television remote with his left. "I am."

Eunice smiled at that then walked away.

The deadly assault on Sojourner Vista brought an abrupt end to the Marshall Law Group's Social and Racial Justice Conference. Half of the resort had been blown to smithereens while the other half was in shambles due to the 1776 protesters ransacking the place. Consequently, Jason and his family were relocated to the Hilton Hotel in Downtown Knoxville. Truth be told, this was a better location for them. The courthouse where Jason's hearing would take place was right down the street. And their being at the Hilton rather than Sojourner Vista also put Jason in closer proximity to the UT Medical Center, where Mitch was being treated.

Jason stepped up into the backseat of the Suburban SUV, the satchel bag containing his notepad and laptop computer bouncing against his hip during the ascent. "What's good, bro'?" Amos solemnly greeted as he peered back at Jason through the front rearview mirror. Amos took notice of the redness in Jason's eyes. Jason took notice of the two other Suburban SUVs in front and behind them. He could clearly see two armed, plainclothes members of the Vista Guard seated in the passenger and driver's seats of the Suburban behind them.

Jason slammed the right, rear passenger side door and then looked up to see Amos' eyes peering back at him in the front rearview mirror.

"This shit is tough, man," Jason exclaimed. He made a circular motion in front of his face with his hands. "Guess you can tell your boy ain't sleeping well."

Amos followed the lead SUV, steering his own away from the hotel roundabout, as the one in the rear trailed them. "I feel you. Just know it's not just you. It has taken a toll on all of us."

"I keep thinking I'm the cause, of all this."

"You shouldn't, and you're not. Those crackers been protesting against the S & R conference since 2007, when President-Elect Dupont was our keynote speaker. They only show up for high-profile events featuring notable speakers. Like what happened in DC a few weeks ago, when their so-called 1776 Patriots threw rocks and glass bottles at attendees at that Indivisible assembly on the steps of the Lincoln Memorial. I believe Hillary Rosen Clifton was scheduled to speak then. It's all a game to them, bro', in their ongoing campaign to own the libs."

"That's foul."

"For sure. But that's all they got. Conservative Republicans, I mean. Ms. Reshonda seems to think their burn-it-to-the-ground strategy stems from their reading the writing on the wall, that in thirty years, white Americans are going to be the majority minority, second to Hispanic Americans. That's why Republican legislators in both the House and Senate never offer practical solutions to the immigration problem at our Southern border and are against efforts to create a pathway to citizenship for immigrants who have been living here for most of their lives. She told us conservative Republicans fear immigrants who become American citizens, especially the ones from Mexico, will vote against them, not for them."

"She's right," Jason said. "But I've been noticing some things about the Mexicans coming to this country, how some of them are always voting against their own best interests. I see Republicans go on Fox News on the regular talking about quote unquote illegal aliens from Mexico smuggling drugs into the country. Say they even have ties to that gang, MS-16, and the Mexican Cartel."

"You know it's not the new ones," Amos replied. "It's the ones who gain citizenship who have been bamboozled by white conservatives to forget where they came from, where their parents, grandparents and great grandparents came from. They're the ones supporting conservatism and Republicans. But they see what every citizen of color sees: That the Republican Party is appealing to white fears and resentments, thinking this is their only path to securing and holding onto power. But to bolster victories in local, state and federal elections, these same white conservatives make the pale-skinned Mexican immigrants believe they're targets of this appeal by allowing them to check the white box on the national census. Divide and conquer, bro. Divide and conquer."

Amos peered back at Jason through the front rear mirror. He waited for Jason to stare back at him through the front rear mirror before returning his gaze to the road. He could tell Jason felt like the weight of the world was on his shoulders, and he wished he could do more to convince him that it was not. But then they arrived at their destination, the UT Medical Center. Amos backed the Suburban into a space in the crowded outdoor parking lot. The operators of the Vista guardsmen-driven SUVs did the same on their left and right.

Walking toward the hospital entrance, with three of the plainclothes Vista guardsmen walking in lockstep with them on their left, right and rear flanks, Jason and Amos found themselves stepping through an assembly of reporters and television crews from stations like cable networks CNN, MSNBC and Fox News, as well as the local and national affiliates of ABC, CBS and NBC. Jason made eye contact with a white Fox News cameraman standing behind a taped barrier to his left.

"Hey," the cameraman exclaimed. "That's Jason Black."

His female reporter colleague jabbed a microphone at Jason as he passed. The Vista guardsman on Jason's right gently pushed the microphone aside. "Mr. Black is not taking any questions right now." Seconds later, the entourage walked hastily though the hospital's sliding glass doors.

When Jason and Amos exited the elevator and entered the 6th floor lobby, they spotted Trish and Mr. Newman seated beside each other in a sitting area to the side. Trish's head rested on her father's shoulder as her father sat upright to support her. Mr. Newman's personal bodyguards had already positioned themselves in the four corners of the room. The three Vista guardsmen that had escorted Jason and Amos to the fourth floor fanned out to occupy the unoccupied spaces. Mr. Newman shifted his gaze from the magazine that he was reading, trying to feign a smile. But his smile quickly devolved into a frown, which didn't go unnoticed by Jason as his entourage stepped off the elevator. Trish removed her head from her father's shoulder to sit up straight.

"How's he doing?" Jason asked.

"They finished operating on him about three hours ago," Mr. Newman replied. "Had to remove a bullet lodged in his lower back, two inches from his spine."

Amos interjected, "I heard what he said when the paramedics were wheeling him through the lobby. Kept saying he couldn't feel his legs. Are the doctors able to do anything about that."

"All we can do is pray on that one, Amos," Trish replied, "but they're hopeful that the paralysis is temporary, that he'll make a full recovery." She wiped at the wetness coalescing on her pecan-brown face.

"They're thinking his body needs several months to heal," Mr. Newman added. "His rehab will start immediately."

Jason could sense their sadness, their pain. His own heartstrings were being tugged as well. Yes, he and Mitch were competitors when they stepped on the track, but when off it, they were, at the very least, close acquaintances. And now that he had spent so much time with the Newmans in Atlanta, reluctantly wearing Mitch's old Florida Gator gear during his time there, it was becoming increasingly apparent that they were becoming fast friends. And the more he thought about his own ideas about white racism and race relations, the more he felt they were destined to do something much greater together, and it had nothing to do with their exploits on the track.

"You think this is all your fault, don't you?" Mr. Newman asked from the other side of the sitting area. Trish stared at Jason in anticipation of his response.

"I do," Jason replied. "If I hadn't been there, none of this would have happened."

"You, we, can't control what they do," Trish interrupted. "Their problem has never been with you; it has always been with us, all of us, black people. They can't stand seeing too many of us getting together. When we do, they think we're plotting against them. But our getting together at Sojourner Vista has never been about them. If anything, it has always been about finding a better way forward for all of us, them included."

"Mitch is going to be fine," Mr. Newman boldly proclaimed. "Just won't be lining up against you in Rio."

"That means you have to go over there and represent," Trish proclaimed. "Bring home the gold."

On the other side of the room, the three of them heard the local news anchor on the television say Malcolm Stillwell's name. Mr. Newman's gaze bounced from Jason to the television. Malcolm Stillwell was on screen, standing behind a podium with a Stillwell 2016 placard on it, delivering another one of his fiery speeches. Mr. Newman, Trish and Jason got out of their seats to draw closer to the television.

"The Siege on Sojourner Vista is both a travesty and tragedy," Stillwell began. "A lot of innocent people – on both sides, mind you – were either hurt or lost their lives. That's unacceptable. That's not what this country, these United States of America, is about. We're a melting pot, founded in 1776, and when I am elected president, it will be my personal mission to ensure that all Americans – the red, the yellow, the black and the white – have equal opportunities to pursue life, liberty and happiness without fear of being treated differently because of their race or ethnicity."

Jason crossed his arms, bracing himself for the but.

Stillwell didn't disappoint. "But don't organizations like the Marshall Law Group invite trouble when they hold these Black Supremacy rallies? In courtrooms all across America, their attorneys have been lambasting white people for their use of the n-word, or their perceived discrimination against black people in their places of employment. I have reviewed their stances in some of these cases. They're not trying to make America great again; they're trying to burn it all down, to remake this country into something the founding fathers never envisioned."

Jason found himself peering down at his feet, skimming his right foot once, then twice, across the tile floor. He could feel Mr. Newman and Trish looking over at him out of the corners of their eyes.

Stillwell continued, saying, "The one court case that I have my eye on involves the man they are protecting. Jason Black. They claim he's a good man. I have no way of knowing that. But what I do know is he assaulted Mr. Roscoe Baker, a twenty-year-plus veteran of the Knoxville Police Department. Mr. Baker was only doing his job, protecting the interests of the good people in the Fort Sanders neighborhood. But after Jason Black stabbed him, he was on the run while doctors fought tooth and nail to save Roscoe Baker's life. The fact that Mr. Baker is still living is a testament to these doctors' expertise, but it also reinforces the need for us to develop more protections for our law enforcement officers. The reports that I've been receiving reveal that Roscoe Baker encountered a suspect, a thug, that made him fear for his life. Jason Black was that thug. We the people must remain vigilant in our efforts to expel him, and others like him, from our communities."

Jason shrugged. The Republican Party's presidential candidate had, once again, blatantly signaled to his white conservative base that he would use the *Baker v. Black* trial to garner the support and publicity he needed to win both the GOP nomination and United States presidency. Having such a large target on his back was cringeworthy yet expected because of all the innocent black men and women that had proceeded him in death, all victims of police brutality. The disdain in Stillwell's retorts let Jason know that Stillwell resented the fact that he was still alive to tell his side of the story. Jason's living was another threat to the white conservative-backed Standing My Ground defense that allowed so many white American citizens to shoot black American citizens dead in the streets with impunity if they too feared for their lives.

Jason turned on his heels to walk over to a window overlooking lanes of cars rolling down Papermill Drive. Cornelius Newman joined him at the window.

"You can't let him get to you," Mr. Newman said.

"But he's coming after me, hard," Jason replied. "I didn't ask for any of this."

"But you're receiving it. Now, you have to do what my wife always says, 'Turn lemons into lemonade.'" Mr. Newman leaned against the wall to the left of the window. "Before everything went sideways, Mitch and I were talking. He told me about your ideas, how innovative and revolutionary they are. Said you had this insane acronym for BLACK – Building a Legacy, of Activism, Community and Kinship."

Jason's hand wiped away the crust forming in the corners of his mouth.

"I like where your mind is at, but probably too bold in this racially and politically polarized environment. These days, we black people have to hide our true intentions by doing things that don't make white people feel so uncomfortable."

"Any thoughts on how we do that?"

"Yes. I have plenty. Been thinking about it a lot actually. The two of you should establish a company, one that reimagines, or reconstructs, how we all think about black labor. Put black people in positions to become better employees, better entrepreneurs, better money managers. Lord knows they did a number on us. Making our ancestors pick cotton for free. Hell, even now, they want us to believe we're not hard workers, that we'd rather receive government handouts than livable wages."

"But there is so much more that needs to be done. We have to bring people together to fight against the policies and practices that are holding us back. And because we're descendants of African kings and queens, we have to find better ways to connect with our brothers and sisters, uncles and aunts, in Africa."

"More reason for Mitch and you to offer something that allows black people as a whole to work together to determine what needs to be done."

"What about the black athletes, the ones in the NFL, the NBA? You think they'll get on board as investors, donors?"

"Only if you do something bold, something that can become emblematic of black people's frustrations, our fears, while also being mindful of our hopes, dreams, aspirations. The tactics that Stillwell and these out-of-touch and tone-deaf white conservatives are using against you are baseless, rooted in lies and more lies. The two of you must counter their falsehoods with inconvenient truths about the struggle, what black people have done, and continue to do, to be viewed as their equals."

"No doubt."

Jason then looked up to see two black men stepping off the elevator. It was Franklin Moses and Jacob Wilson. Jason watched as Mr. Newman's demeanor became more tepid.

But it was Trish who was the first to walk over to the two men, vigorously shaking each one's extended hand. Mr. Newman remained in the background with Jason, seemingly studying them. Trish brought them to where Jason and Mr. Newman were standing.

"Definitely know who this is," Coach Moses said as he tightly gripped Jason's hand. As he stared intently into Jason's eyes, Coach Moses continued, saying, "Really pushed our boy at nationals." The praise from the highly respected coach evoked a smirk from Jason as he receded into the background to allow a similar greeting to occur with Mr. Newman.

Mr. Newman's hands went into his pockets as his eyes skipped from the smirking Jason to Trish before coming to rest on the two coaches. Jason noted the sudden tightness in Mr. Newman's jaw.

Coach Moses greeted Mr. Newman with an extended hand, but when Mr. Newman's hands remained in his pockets, he played it off by patting Mr. Newman's left shoulder with his right hand. Coach Wilson's head dropped as he plunged his own hands into his pockets.

"Got on the first flight out of LAX when we got the word," Coach Moses said. "How's he doing?"

Mr. Newman's eyes locked onto Coach Moses' eyes for maybe two or three ticks before he turned his back to him to stare out the hospital's plate-glass window. "I know, Franklin," he muttered in a low voice. "He told me everything."

Coach Moses turned to his right to exchange a knowing glance with Coach Wilson. A rise in Coach Wilson's brow clearly communicated his discomfort.

"Leave," Mr. Newman continued. "Cheats have no place here."

Coach Moses started to step forward, seemingly to explain himself, but Coach Wilson held him at bay, near his elbow. "We'll holla' at you later then, Cornelius," Coach Wilson exclaimed while leading Coach Moses back to the elevator. "Just know we're praying for him, though. He's a good kid."

"What was that all about?" Trish said, joining her father at the window as the elevator engulfed the two. Jason was there as well, anxiously awaiting Mr. Newman's response, his arms crossed, a perplexed expression on his face.

Mr. Newman glanced over at Jason and then peered down at Trish. "Not my story to tell," he said. He then used his right hand to cover his face and massage his temple as Trish settled in beside him, the side of her head near his armpit.

Trish locked eyes with Jason. She had heard it too.

But before anything else could be said, Henry Sadler, the doctor that had performed the emergency procedure to remove the bullet from Mitch's back, rounded the corner, iPad hanging loosely in his hand.

"He's awake," Dr. Sadler announced.

Jason watched from the far wall as Mrs. Newman doted over her son from his bedside. She had arrived with Rayvyn about fifteen minutes after Mr. Newman, Trish and he had entered Mitch's recovery room. The only light in the room came from a tabletop lamp in the room's corner.

Mitch was still feeling the effects of the sedatives coursing through his veins. He lay on his back, his eyes barely open, arms to his sides above the covers. Mr. Newman stood behind his wife to the right of the bed, gently massaging her shoulders, while Trish and Rayvyn stood to the left. But every now and then, the slight tilt of Mitch's head toward him let Jason know that Mitch was looking past his family members to study him. This head tilting did not go unnoticed by Jason. When it became too much for him to bear, Jason retreated to the hallway.

While standing in the hallway, where two impeccably dressed members of the Vista Guard stood on either side, Jason couldn't shake the fact that he had just learned that Mitch was a fraud. It now dawned on him that absent Nigel Grimes' 9.70 at the Bislett Games in June, his time of 9.77 at nationals would have been the new 100-meter world record. It all made sense to him. Even after Mitch had run his 9.68, he thought something had gone wrong with the timer, or the wind had been above the allowable. He never doubted the legitimacy of Mitch's sprint races because they had raced two times before, at the Sea Ray Relays in Knoxville during the start of the 2015 outdoor season and at the Southeastern Conference Championships at LSU's Bernie Moore Track Stadium. At both meets, Jason crossed the finish line second with times of 10.01 and 10.07.

Jason felt a woman's petite hand grazing his back. He turned to see Trish standing there. He stopped his pacing to lean back against the wall, his buttocks resting on the chair rail.

"I'm sure he was going to tell us at some point." Trish said, her hands clenched tightly in front of her. Must have got to my pops first."

"It's all good," Jason replied as he wiped at the tears coalescing in his eyes. "I can't get over what they did to Angelica, why they hate us so much. Why do they fight so hard to make our lives miserable?"

"Because they can. But that shouldn't stop us from being proud of the skin we're in. How we have overcome their racism, their bigotry. We just have to keep our eye on the prize, Jay. As long as we continue to do that, they'll never win, they'll never defeat us."

"I'm tired, Trish. Feel like someone just punched me in the gut, knocked the breath out of me. What they did to her was intended for me."

"I feel you. But I truly believe she is looking down on us right now, wondering what we're going to do to make her death matter. I know what I'm going to do. I'm going to do whatever it takes to ensure that piece of shit Stillwell never becomes President. If it wasn't for him, none of this would have happened. Angelica would still be here."

"Makes me want to strangle the first white person I see," Jason said with his hands lifted high in front of him, as if he were choking the life out of an invisible person. Seeing this, one of the Vista guardsmen took a few paces in their direction and then stopped. "But I recognize there are too many white people out there standing with us, fighting the good fight. I see them on television marching in the streets, boldly chanting alongside their black brothers and sisters, 'Black folk matter!' The racist bastards aren't hearing us, though."

"One of the most important lessons I learned in one of my classes, the creative writing one, is great writers do a good job of showing not telling. We black people just have to keep showing them who we are and stop telling them who we are."

"But even when we do that, they turn a blind eye to what we're doing, what we have accomplished. And when they think we have accomplished too much, start accumulating more than they have, they either steal what we have from us or burn what we own to the ground."

"We're still standing, though, Jay. And as long as we're still standing, we're still fighting. For what's right. For life, for liberty, for happiness."

Jason nodded his approval. But after Trish patted him on the shoulder and then returned to Mitch's room, leaving him standing alone in the hallway, he could feel his heart beating faster in his chest.

Now that he knew Mitch's dirty, little secret, would he share it with USA Track and Field? The answer to this question was obvious. No. He would leave it to Mitch to share this information with USATF and the world. The brother couldn't even feel his legs. There was no way he would be lining up against him in

Rio. And sharing it would be equivalent to beating a man when he is down. Besides, his chances of winning a medal had improved drastically. However, he craved more than a gold, silver or bronze medal. If Mitch's 9.68 remained the standard when it was time for him to line up against the world's best sprinters in August of 2016, he wanted to be the one to break it. He had no choice. A healthy Nigel Grimes would force his hand.

When Mitch saw Jason reentering his recovery room, he asked his family if he could speak with Jason alone. Once the room was clear, an awkward silence occupied the space between the two world-class sprinters. Soon, Jason found himself sitting on one of the two chairs to the left of Mitch's bed. Mitch fumbled to lay hands on the remote that he had been using to raise himself to a more upright position, and when he held it in his hands, he used it to do so.

"Heard my pops let the cat out the bag," Mitch exclaimed, his voice raspy.

"He did," Jason replied, crossing his legs.

"I know what I did was wrong, bro'. And I've owned it, prepared to take the shit to my grave." His upraised arms gestured at his immobile legs. "Have to come to grips that I may never walk again, that this is my penance for cheating."

Jason didn't offer an immediate reply. He just allowed more awkward silence to do his bidding.

Mitch continued, "After I graduated last December, before outdoor, Pops encouraged me to go out there, to Cali, to train with Coach Moses. Loved it out there, bro'. Still do. But after I set the record, I started feeling uneasy. Felt like I had to tell more lies to cover up the first one. But it hit me the hardest at the awards ceremony when they honored me with the Sullivan. Pops wasn't there. Ma, Trish and Rayvyn were. That's when I knew he knew."

"Got my grade back on that paper I told you about, the *Politics of Race* one," Jason said. "Did the class presentation using Zoom."

"That's great, bro'. What'd you get for the class?"

"An A minus. My professor, Dr. Whitaker, had jokes, though. Said he would have given me an A if I hadn't brought so much drama to his class. He's the whitest dude I've ever met. But he became one of my biggest advocates. Found out from Ms. St. James that he was the one who petitioned the Trustee Board to reinstate me."

"What does that mean? They gonna give you your degree?"

"Yeah, man. Just can't attend the ceremony. Have to watch it on YouTube, listen for the university president to say my name. Not what I expected when I came here. Hell, I wanted to be able to hold that piece of paper high in the air and point it at my family as they cheered for me in the upper decks, bro'. But it's all good. Could have been much worse."

"That's great, Jay."

Mitch then thought back to his own graduation ceremony, in Gainesville, at the University of Florida. Cornelius Newman had been in a better mood, mostly because, again, it occurred before he started training with Coach Moses' Elite Track and Field Club and his world record-setting performance at the NCAA Outdoor Track and Field Championships in Eugene, Oregon. And when his father embraced him, his burly frame engulfing him well past the time most men would feel uncomfortable, Mitch knew he was addicted to the kind of love only his father could provide.

"I ain't gonna tell it," Jason said. "That's on you, bro'. But don't believe I'm not going to do what it takes to break it."

"I wouldn't expect anything less." Mitch used both hands to push his body further up the mattress. "Angelica. Where the two of you tight?"

Jason shifted uncomfortably. The last image he saw, of her hanging by her neck from a tree, possessed his mind.

"I'm sorry, bro'. If it's too soon, just let me know. Trish told me what happened."

"Nah, bro'. It's not. And, yeah, we were tight, at least that's what she wanted."

"What she wanted. You didn't want the same?"

"I did and I didn't. That night, I was horny as hell and was just looking for a booty call. Especially after she coaxed me into giving her that white woman's card key."

"Trish said it was a setup. That you were their intended target."

"Apparently so. Now know that it was this bitch Gabby's job to lure me to her room."

"It is shit like this that makes me hate them even more. The white supremacists, I mean."

"Right there with you, bro'. And you're right. All white people aren't bad, just the racist ones. But we have to ask ourselves, what's the cure to all this hate for us, all this violence toward us?"

Mitch peered over to his left, at the hand-written cards and notes, the bouquet of flowers and Get Well Soon balloons. "They have made it their mission to keep us in our place. If this is how they want to play it, seems to me we have to fight their fire with our water. The only cure for white supremacy is black excellence."

Jason stood to hover near Mitch's bedside with his hands in his pockets. "When you get out this joint, we going to puts some meat on them bones."

"BLACK Global?"

"Yeah, bruh. If we do it right, and recruit others to support our efforts, we could be singing a different tune within the next five, ten, years."

"You sure you can walk and chew gum at the same time?" Mitch asked, a somewhat subdued grin on his face. "We still licking our wounds from what they did to us up at Sojourner Vista, and with this Stillwell dude mouthing off, all eyes are going to be on you, on your trial."

"Like you said, we have to fight their fire with our water. I feel more motivated to speak up, to speak my truth. And since Stillwell is using the press to focus all this attention on me, I have to find a way to show him and the world that our brand of black excellence isn't about doing better and being better than white people, or any other racial/ethnic group. It's time to show them black excellence is about black people stepping into the best versions of themselves while simultaneously showing the ones who will listen how to build a legacy of activism, community and kinship. Gotta make his ass blink."

Mitch extended his hand; Jason encased it with his own.

"Talk to Trish," Mitch exclaimed, still holding and squeezing Jason's hand. Then, as he released it, he continued, saying, "Public Relations, Publicity, is her jam. Pops had her working on X-Man's publicity campaign. I'm sure she can create one around black excellence. Pops will bankroll it. Also talk with Ms. St. James. She'll make sure you're not held in contempt for the things you say and do outside the courtroom. You just have to start stacking up some victories, dude. Win each day, every argument in the court of public opinion."

Jason stared down at Mitch as he basked in the glow of his radiating support.

"And the race of all races come August?" Jason offered.

"Yeah, man! You have to go out there and show them mofos what it means to be made in America."

"Give them a dose of this black American excellence."

"Say you right."

CHAPTER TWENTY-TWO

The six pallbearers came to a stop under the oversized canopy and then laid the shiny, wooden coffin containing Angelica's body onto the iron supports. Angelica's adoptive father, mother and 17-year-old brother Andre stood a few feet away from them, under the canopy, wiping their drenched faces with handkerchiefs, the back of their hands. Jason stood just outside the canopy, with Trish, White, and Rev, as well as Coach Highsmith, her staff and several of Jason's other UT track and field teammates. Mitch wanted to be there, but he was still being treated at the UT Medical Center. Amos, Claudia and Reginald stood among a mingling hodge-podge of family, friends and close acquaintances of all racial/ethnic hues as the pallbearers stepped from under the canopy to join them on the canopy's edge.

The Marshall Law Group's Founding Trio were also present, along with Thelma and Cornelius Newman and his family. Several plain-clothes members of the Vista Guard stood guard, far removed from the assembly, taking positions on the cemetery's rolling hills and winding roads to ensure that the perimeter remained secure. Their bulging suit jackets indicated that they were armed with company-issued Glocks, ready to take out any motherfucker that tried to disrupt the proceedings.

Jason had never met Angelica's adoptive parents in person, but their first in-person meeting two hours earlier, at the memorial service that was held at Angelica's childhood church, Asheville's Abiding Faith Baptist Church, was memorable. Claudia Sinclair, Angelica's adoptive mother, actually managed to flash a toothy smile at him as he stood in the line of well-wishers to shake family members' hands, offer his condolences. When it was his time to bend over to offer these condolences, Mrs. Sinclair stood up and hugged him. Of course, this caught Jason by surprise, but he eventually put two and two together. He undoubtedly had been a frequent topic of her conversations with Angelica.

And Angelica didn't just talk about him with her adoptive mother. William Sinclair, Angelica's adoptive father, also stood to accept Jason's handshake and uttered condolences. Mr. Sinclair grabbed Jason's extended right hand and then pulled him close to hug him for what seemed like an eternity. As Mr. Sinclair held him, Jason spotted a still seated Andre, from over Mr. Sinclair's shoulder, glaring up at him from the pew. The fire in his teary eyes did not go unnoticed.

Jason almost got the sense that Mr. Sinclair's actions were calculated, a show for the row of congregants in the spacious Abiding Faith sanctuary. But such thoughts dissipated when he realized that Mr. Sinclair probably had been hopeful that he would one day be able to refer to Jason as his son-in-law. During his brief courtship with Angelica, Angelica had introduced him to her parents during one of her Google Duo video chats with them. The first words out of Mr. Sinclair's mouth were questions about what Jason wanted to do after graduation. Jason had responded kindly, saying he wanted to move to New York City and secure employment with either the McKinsey or Bain consulting firms, all to gain real-life business consulting experience. After working at these places for two, three, years, he told

Mr. Sinclair that he wanted to start his own company, one catering to the technology, media and telecommunications sectors.

Abiding Faith's Senior Pastor, the Reverend Dr. J. Anthony Sparks, loosely gripped the cordless microphone as he stood under the canopy near the head of the coffin. Angelica's adoptive father, mother and brother sat in folding chairs to his right.

"Thank you all for coming here today," Reverend Sparks began. "I knew Angelica when she first came to reside with Brother William and Sister Claudia, when she was twelve years old. Most of you know her story, how she was removed from an abusive home and placed with them. This placement was intended to be temporary, not permanent. But it became permanent because of all the things they had to go through with Angelica.

"You see, Angelica was, let's say, a firecracker. When she was first placed with the Sinclairs, she made it clear that she didn't want to be in their home. William and Claudia gave me permission to share that she ran away from their home at least a half a dozen times during that first year. And when she was finally able to will herself to remain in the home, she would have heated arguments with Claudia, with William, telling them both how much she hated them, that they couldn't tell her what to do. She was also doing very poorly in school. But God...God intervened. He showed up for this family because they were obedient...obedient to his word. They showed Angelica through their righteous words and deeds that their love for her was becoming real and unconditional. Before long, the bitterness that prevented Angelica from loving them disappeared, being replaced with gratitude, an appreciation for the kind of life only her new parents could provide her.

"Today, we celebrate the life of Angelica Monique Sinclair. Her ability to love again after experiencing so much adversity as a child. She has left us now, gone to be with the Lord. My prayer is we will not fret about the way she died. No, my prayer is we will remember how she lived, how she loved, and how she persevered. More importantly, I pray that we will begin to look past skin color to love our neighbors as ourselves. For the struggle isn't about overcoming prejudice, discrimination and racism. The struggle is about all of us becoming more selfless and less selfish, putting the needs of others above our own."

Putting the needs of others above our own.

Jason could feel the tension swelling in his chest and arms. Even through Carmelita Newman had given him his own bible, stressing the importance of relying on God to get him through, he questioned why her God would allow this tragedy to happen to someone who had done nothing wrong.

"Don't think I blame you," Andre said after the gravesite service had ended. He had gotten Jason's attention before Jason could climb into the backseat of the Amos-helmed SUV.

Rather than talk within earshot of Amos and the others, Andre asked that they cross the winding street lined with cars to talk briefly on the hillside. Once there, Andre continued, saying, "I've been reading all the articles they been writing about you. Been watching the news as well. I know how they are, how they are always trying to provoke us. Happened to me. I was driving, and the muthafuckin' cops pulled me over. Told me to get out the car. I did, and they slammed me against it before patting me down. My friends, all of them white, kept telling them from the car that I hadn't done anything, but the cops kept asking me if I had any drugs on me. Told them I don't do that shit. We had just left Burger King, and before that we were at the game. But the cop that was patting me down waved a bag that had about five or six joints in it. He lied, told the judge that he pulled it from my back pocket."

"I remember," Jason replied. "Angelica told me all about it. They made your parents pay a fine, made you do community service, right?"

"Yeah, man. Hated every minute of it, but the whole experience taught me a valuable lesson."

"And what was that?"

"That you can't trust white people. There were four of us in the car – me and my boy Hank – he's white - and two white girls, Natalie and Karen. But I was the only one they told to get out the car, the only one they patted down."

"Don't think like that. All white people aren't bad. There are some trustworthy ones out there. But I feel you. When this kind of shit happens, you want your friends to do more, say more."

"Yeah. 'cause when they didn't fight harder for me, get out the car even, I asked why. But now I know. It's because of their privilege, of being white. They don't just come out and say they have it; you just know it's there, an unspoken agreement between them that if they just let things play out, nothing bad will happen to them. And that's what they did. Let things play out with those cops."

Jason could feel the mood becoming more intense, so he went out of his way to lighten it. "And that's why you're going to Howard next year, right?"

"Yeah, man. Already signed the letter of intent."

"I've been checking you out, bro'. Think you'll go faster than thirteen nine this year?"

"No doubt. I'm trying to go thirteen five."

"Coach Highsmith could really use you at Tennessee. Some of the greatest names in hurdling got their start there."

"He reached out, but I told him not interested. The shit that went down with those racist cops changed me. Made me want to use my talents to draw more attention to Howard, historically black colleges and universities. They don't get the attention they deserve. After I get my bachelor's, plan on attending law school there. We have been full citizens since 1868 and have had the right to vote in free and fair elections since 1870. I just want to do my part to protect people, black people mostly, from being wrongfully charged and convicted of crimes."

"And you will."

Jason then leaned over and tightly embraced Andre, the same way Andre's father had embraced him. As he held onto Andre, he spoke into the teenager's ear, saying, "Angelica is looking down on us now, bro'. Probably applauding everything we do. Don't plan on letting her memory die without a fight."

The man and the boy who would one day become a man released and dapped each other up. They then walked down the hill together at first and then deviated in different directions the closer they got to the bottom of the hill. As they walked to their parked cars, you could tell from their confident gaits that they felt more hopeful about the future. More than anything, though, they seemed to be more committed to showing the world that they are, or will continue to be, the embodiment of black excellence.

"Your own daughter voted in committee for his reinstatement," Malcolm Stillwell exclaimed as he stood in front of the plate glass window from the ivory tower of his Manhattan office, peering down at the activity below. It was midafternoon, and he unflinchingly took sips from the short glass of bourbon in his right hand.

"Nothing I can do about that, Malcolm," Mason Chase's voice boomed from the loudspeaker on Stillwell's desk. "She has always been a loose cannon. Always bucking me, any advice I give her. Too much of her mother in her. I'll sit her down. Remind her about the stakes, why it is so important for her to walk the party line."

"That won't be necessary. You told me yourself that she despises me. Won't be surprised if she votes for Crocked Hillary in November. Just don't let her get in front of any cameras anytime soon. Besides, she wasn't the only one to have a change of heart."

"I honestly didn't see that coming. With the amount of money the CSA has been doling out to that darky Morris' private business affairs, I would have thought his loyalty would have remained rock solid. Saw it coming with Clemons. Remember, she was a Democrat before she became a Republican. Looks like she's reverting back to her old ways because a woman is the Democratic Party's presidential nominee. You want to stop their loyalty payments and add some misery to their lives.'

"Let them be. I will call them personally, let them know they're dead to me, dead to the CSA."

"Got it. Just know I'll be standing back and standing by if something more needs to be done."

Jason sat in a chair, his mother Cynthia on his left, Ms. Jacobs on his right. Jeremiah stood directly behind Jason, every now and then smacking the back of Jason's head in passing to keep him from getting down about having to watch his own college commencement ceremony on the projection screen at the front of the Downtown Hilton's spacious banquet halls. But that was the agreement that Thelma had brokered for him. He could complete all remaining assignments for Dr. Whitaker's *Political Philosophy* class, affording him the opportunity to receive his bachelor's degree in business administration, but he could not set foot on the University of Tennessee campus, even though it was within walking distance of the hotel.

After Thelma told him that the full Trustee Board had voted 7-5 for his reinstatement, Jason felt as if a weight had been lifted off his shoulders. Yes, he still had to contend with the attempted murder charges being levied at him by Roscoe Baker, and the thought of being locked up was, at the time, still overwhelming. But none of that seemed to matter now. He looked forward to being the first of Jerome and Cynthia Black's children to earn a college degree.

Cynthia had gone out of her way to make things special for him. In the weeks leading up to this special day, she mailed invitations that bid family and friends to join them at the Downtown Hilton. Two days before, she decorated Jason's guestroom with streamers, balloons and "Congratulations, Graduate" banners. Jeremiah did his part as well, as he worked with Amos and Reginald to arrange for Uncle Clive's catering staff to cater the event.

When graduation day arrived, family and friends from places like Rancho Cucamonga, California, Kansas City, Missouri and Jacksonville, Florida filed into the banquet hall bearing wrapped gifts and cards. For many of them, the event served as a reunion of sorts, as he watched his uncles, aunts and cousins from both his father and mother's sides greeting each other with warm hugs and heartfelt kisses. Jason felt blessed. His family, his friends, had thought enough of him to come all this way to celebrate his achievement, knowing that he wasn't permitted to accept his degree in person.

Decorated tables and chairs were sprinkled throughout the banquet hall, so everyone in attendance could clearly see the graduation ceremony being projected onto the screen from seated vantage points. As the UT President delivered his remarks, Jason was mesmerized by shots of seated cap and gown-clad students on the gymnasium floor, proud family, friends and acquaintances in the stadium's upper decks. Jason glanced over at his mother. She smiled back at him and then kissed him on the cheek. "You did it," she announced. "You're about to become a college graduate."

Jason felt Jeremiah's hands on his left and right shoulders. "This is it," he said, squeezing then patting Jason's shoulders once before falling away. "Dad would be proud."

"What y'all doing up in here?"

Jason looked up to see Mitch being pushed in a wheelchair by his father through the banquet hall door. Trish followed, with her mother and sister Rayvn in tow.

"Mitch," Jason exclaimed rising from his chair to jokingly wade past seated and standing kinfolk and friends to dap him up. "I thought they weren't releasing you until tomorrow."

Trish said, "The doctor granted him an early release, for good behavior."

Mrs. Newman draped her arm across Mitch's head and shoulders. She then kissed him on the top of his head. "Don't joke with my baby like that. You know how sensitive he is."

Mitch grunted and gestured to his father that he had it. He then used the joystick on the wheelchair's right armrest to propel himself forward. As he rolled through the assembly, he nodded at the people he didn't know, accepted hugs and kisses from the few that he did. Jason peered up at the projection screen and noted that the college president and faculty members were already reading the names in alphabetical order. They were nearing the end of the A's, so Jason knew they would be calling his name soon.

As Jason sat back down beside Cynthia, she reached over to clutch his hand. "This is it."

Jason tightened his grip around his mother's hand. He felt Jeremiah's hands return to his shoulders and remain there.

On the projection screen, Jason, his family, friends and acquaintances watched as members of the UT Class of 2015 stood in line to the left of the stage to ascend a set of stairs and walk across it to accept facsimiles of their degrees from the UT President and his aides. Upon being handed these facsimiles, each graduate would stop in the middle of the stage to face forward with the UT President, allowing the team of photographers to memorialize their achievements with their cameras. After their photos were taken, the conferred graduates would walk down the stairs to the right of the stage. Jason chuckled as he watched several of them throw their arms up to garner more applause. Others hollered at the top of their lungs. One even flipped head over heels in front of the university faculty before skipping to the opposite side of the stage.

"Jason Marcus Black."

Jason heard the UT President say his name. This utterance caused the family and friends closest to him to shout, "Yeah, boiiii!!" and "That's what I'm talking about!" while patting him on his back, shoulders and chest. Thunderous applause reverberated throughout the banquet hall. When the patting subsided even as the applause continued, Cynthia draped her arm across Jason's broad shoulders and then pulled him close. She then kissed him on his cheek before allowing him to sob on her shoulder.

It was official.

Jason Black was a college graduate.

END OF BOOK ONE

BLACK
Novel Series

BOOK ONE
The Bear on Our Backs

BOOK TWO
The Skin That We're In

BOOK THREE
The Fruit of Our Labor

About the Author

J. A. Faulkerson is a Northern Virginia-based Author, Poet and Screenwriter. His stories pay homage to the Black leaders of the Civil Rights Movement of the 1950s and '60s, individuals he calls compassionate neighbors because they were, and continue to be, led by the unconditional love and neighborly compassion in their hearts. He also has a heart for youth, evidenced by his years of service as a TRIO Upward Bound and YMCA Youth director. Through his written and spoken words, he admonishes adolescents and young adults to balance their lives on the Four Pillars of Prosperity (i.e., nurturing, learning, working and leading). A graduate of Dobyns-Bennett High School (Kingsport, Tennessee) and the University of Tennessee (Knoxville, Tennessee), J. A. has been happily married to his wife for over 32 years and is the proud father to his 21-year-old son.